PenWorks

Publishers

Dance of the Mantis

Wally Wiggins

ACKNOWLEDGEMENTS

During the ten years it has taken me to finalize Dance of the Mantis, there have been many who have contributed substance and structure to make it a more interesting book.

If the reader is entertained by the story, it will be due in measure to the encouragement, support, and professional critiques of Michael Pastore, Katie Williams, Susan Shefter, Leah Cook, Beth Evans, and David Brownstone.

I am especially indebted to my friend and legal assistant, Evelyn Houston, who has shared with me the joys and agonies of making the transition from a rough manuscript to a completed novel.

Dance of the Mantis
A PenWorks Publishers Book

All rights reserved
Copyright ©2005 by Wally Wiggins
Cover Photography and Book Design by Mark Costa
Edited by Beth H. Evans

For information address:
    PenWorks Publishers
    144 Ridgecrest Road
    Ithaca, New York 14850
    www.PenWorksPublishers.com

ISBN 0-9768575-0-2

10 9 8 7 6 5 4 3 2 1

For my best friends,

Kaethe, Marcus, Scott and Jonni

PROLOGUE
July 25, 2003

Frank Dunn had difficulty inserting his key into the lock. As soon as he entered the apartment, he went directly to the bar and poured himself his fourth double Scotch of the day. He spilled half of it when he sat down on the couch and reached for the television's remote control. The phone rang.

"Hello," he answered.

"Darling —"

"Where are you?"

"I'm sorry, honey,"

"Where the hell have you been?"

"I got tied up in traffic but I'll be over by nine-thirty at the latest, I promise."

"I'll leave the door unlocked for you."

"Yes, Love."

He hung up the phone, took off his shirt and trousers, and stumbled toward the bedroom.

The next morning Sy Sherman, the superintendent of the Manhattan-East condominium complex, rang the bell twice and waited before unlocking the door. He'd promised Mrs. Dunn he'd have the master bedroom repainted while she was visiting her parents in Dallas. After entering the apartment, he hesitated when he noticed light from the bedroom spilling into the hallway.

"Hello! Anybody home?" No one answered. He stuck his head in the bedroom door and saw the blood and torn flesh, smelled the stink of the shit that had drained from the body when the sphincter muscle died. There was dried blood everywhere.

CHAPTER ONE

The superintendent's 911 call was transferred to Pat Turner, a forty-one-year-old investigator in the homicide division of the New York City Police Department. Her burnished red hair, green eyes and freckles would have qualified her to lead a St. Patrick's Day parade, anywhere.

When she and her rookie assistant Ken Wolcott arrived at the scene of the homicide, the coroner and several members of the Forensic Investigating Unit were already there waiting for her: Jim Downing, the photographer, and his helper; Bob Oski, the fingerprint man; and Dave Marano, blood and bodily fluids. An officer was standing guard at the door, across which a yellow security tape was stretched. Pat approached him and asked that he fill her in. He told her that the super had come in early in the morning to look at one of the bedrooms the owner wanted repainted. He discovered the victim and immediately called 911.

"I was told to come over here right away and secure the area," he said, "which I done as soon as the guy showed me which apartment it was. I started the log and took a statement from him. I sent him downstairs to his apartment to wait for you."

"What'd he tell you?"

"The victim's name is Frank Dunn. He and his wife and thirteen-year-old daughter have lived here for the past five years. The wife's name is...," he checked his notepad, "Helen, Helen Dunn. She left yesterday to visit her parents in Texas. She told the super that the victim would be spending the night at his club, so he could start the paint job any time he wanted. He didn't know where the kid was."

Before opening the door Pat checked it for any sign of forcible entry. There was none. On a gesture from her, Downing immediately began to photograph the plush carpet in the entrance foyer for footprints. It was a little known fact that more crimes were solved with footprints than with fingerprints. Before the day was over, Downing would take more than three-hundred photos.

After removing their shoes and donning paper booties, Pat and the rest of the team moved cautiously into the apartment. Downing took multiple shots of the victim from every conceivable angle before allowing anyone else to enter the bedroom. As the photographer at a homicide, he'd have to prepare a log called a General 34 to document the when, where, and how of every picture taken at the scene of the crime, as well as the make of the camera, lens and film used. The photos would be developed as soon as possible so that they could be studied while the area was still secured. Crime scene photographs invariably revealed considerable evidence that had been overlooked by the investigators in their initial walk-through.

The victim was wearing only his socks and undershorts. There were five bullets lodged in his body: two in the chest, one in the neck, which had severed the carotid artery, one above his right eye, and one that had shattered his lower jaw. Based on the color of the dried blood, the patina of his skin, the rigidity of the body, the glaze of his eyes, and the color of his lips, the coroner guessed he'd been dead about twelve hours. The medical examiner would later confirm the coroner's opinion, establishing the time of death sometime between 8:00 PM on the 25th and 3:00 AM on the 26th.

By all rights there should be a sixth bullet, Pat thought, given that the gun carries six bullets in the chamber. It wouldn't make sense for the murderer to pump five into the victim but leave the last one sitting in the chamber.

"Except for the fact that there doesn't appear to be a forcible entry, it could be a botched burglary," she said to no one in particular.

"I doubt it," Marano, the blood expert, responded. "Look at this." He waved his hand to indicate the blood spattered across the wall. "The blood stain pattern tells me it was the person firing the pistol who was on the bed when the shots were fired."

"Maybe he had a female partner and they were taking a

break between jobs," somebody quipped.

Ignoring the banter, Pat began a mental list of questions that would require answering. Why were ladies' magazines strewn all over the bedroom floor? Why was the victim in his underwear, while his shirt and trousers were tossed about the living room? Why was an upturned booze glass lying in the corner of the bedroom?

Each member of the team got busy with his specific duties. Along with countless other evidence-gathering tasks, they encased the victim's hands in brown paper bags to preserve any evidence found beneath his fingernails.

After the ambulance left, taking the body to the hospital for autopsy, Pat glanced at her watch and dismissed the team. She told them all to prepare their reports and meet her back at the station house by 8 p.m. sharp.

When everyone had gone she walked cautiously through the three-bedroom penthouse again, making sure she hadn't overlooked anything that might be crucial in her search for the person who had blasted Frank Dunn.

———

All the members of her team were seated around the battle-scarred table in the conference room, coffee mugs in hand, when Pat arrived. She glanced at the memo she'd received from the coroner. Frank Dunn: age 43, height 6'2", weight 227 lbs., hair brown/gray, eyes brown.

"Okay, Ken, why don't you fill us in first," she said.

Wolcott flipped through several pages of his notebook. "I've made a rough sketch of the premises, which includes a living room, dining room, kitchen, three bedrooms, a man's den, and a sort of studio, which I assume is used by the lady or the daughter. I've noted the precise location of a pair of trousers and a shirt in the living room, which appear to belong to the victim, unless the murderer hightailed it out of there without his pants." Ken, a typically serious-minded young man, enjoyed the chuckles his remark produced. "You all saw the victim's shoes, and his wallet lying open by the couch — which Bob tells me has no fingerprints on it. There's no money in the wallet. According to the super, the last time he saw the victim alive was late yesterday afternoon just before the guy drove his wife out to the airport. The super also said that when he arrived this morning, the door was locked."

"How many doormen have they got?" Marano asked.

"Four. I told the guy on duty today that we'll need their schedules and that I will be taking statements from all of them later. By the way, Pat, Frank Dunn was a big-shot attorney in a downtown law firm."

CHAPTER TWO

When she was eight years old, Pat's mother died on the operating table during a routine appendectomy. Her father, Pete Turner, had been a patrolman with the Brooklyn P.D. for twenty-nine years, and had been seven months away from retirement, when he caught two teenaged punks breaking into a liquor store on Flatbush Avenue in Brooklyn. They shot him in the face and he died on the way to the hospital. No one who knew Pat was surprised when, after high school, she enrolled in the City College of New York, where she majored in criminal justice.

Upon graduation, she became a rookie cop with the NYPD, and after basic training she was assigned to the Division of Forensics under Victor Moretti, one of the most respected technicians in the system. Moretti had known Pete Turner well and gladly became Pat's mentor and champion. By the time Pat arrived on the scene, Moretti had lost enthusiasm for the job over the years, and Pat's appointment as his assistant was the best thing to happen to him in a very long time. They became inseparable friends, meeting for breakfast every morning at a little Greek restaurant around the corner from their office building, and sharing the box lunch Moretti made for them every day. Their workday didn't end until one or the other said, "Miller time," at which point they'd close up shop and walk six blocks to Muldoon's Pub, where the bartender would automatically draw two Miller draughts and carry them to the table next to the video game machine. After their first beer, Moretti and Pat would play three games of "Sleuth," never more, never less. The loser paid for the beers. If Pat had a date, they'd have just the one beer and split. If she were free, they'd have a second beer and decide where to eat dinner. Somewhere along the line, Pat decided Vic was gay. She never asked. He never told.

She was thirty-eight years old when she was promoted to the rank of detective in the homicide division of one of the toughest cities in the world. She credited Victor Moretti with preparing her for the job. A single woman in a traditionally masculine profession, Pat smiled and ignored the men's sexist remarks until, eventually, they realized they were wasting their time.

At noon on a humid day in July, after twelve years on the force, Pat found Moretti slumped over his desk, dead of a massive coronary occlusion at age fifty-seven. She was granted a thirty-day leave of absence and rented the cabin she'd stayed in once with Vic on a small lake in New Hampshire.

When she returned to her duties, she took on a bruising schedule. Her workday began at eight o'clock in the morning, and she rarely made it back to her apartment before nine at night. She wasn't just working through her grief; the loss of Vic had reawakened her outrage at the murder of her father and she became even more obsessed with avenging justice for other victims. She would do everything in her power to find and convict anyone guilty of murder, and to that end she made sure she was assigned to every homicide committed in her precinct. By Saturday, July 26, 2003, the day Frank Dunn's body was discovered, she was the Senior Investigative Officer in the precinct.

———

After a few restless hours of sleep Saturday night, she had an early breakfast and returned to the Dunn apartment. She sat at Frank Dunn's antique roll-top desk and called her office on her cell phone. She learned that they'd located the wife, Helen, at her parents' home near Dallas, Texas, and had notified her of her husband's death. The daughter was out of town on vacation with friends and would return later that night. Mrs. Dunn was flying back to New York immediately.

While she was still seated, staring absently at the antique roll-top desk, Pat noticed a compartment she'd missed the first time around. Opening it she found a sophisticated taping device that automatically recorded all telephone calls made to and from the Dunn residence. Removing the tape carefully, she tucked it into her briefcase.

Back in her office she slid the tape into the player. The last message recorded a conversation between the victim and an unknown female.

"Bingo," she said aloud.

———

On Monday morning there was a voice mail message from Bob Watson, the fingerprint expert, asking her to stop by the lab.

"I think we've got our first break in the Dunn case," he said when she pushed into his office moments later. "At least it's worth pursuing."

"Lay it on me."

Watson told her that he'd lifted four sets of prints from a waist-high marble-top table just inside the front door of the Dunn apartment. He'd been able to identify the victim's prints because Frank Dunn had possessed a pistol permit and his prints were on file. Watson believed that two of the unidentified prints were female and belonged to Mrs. Dunn or the child, because they were evident throughout the apartment, but that the fourth set belonged to a young kid who had recently been released from Elmira Correctional where he'd done time for burglary. Watson picked up a computer printout and handed it to her: Joseph Pesci, age 18; father: Luigi Pesci, whereabouts unknown; mother: Angela Pesci. Home address: 29 West Market Street, New York City.

Pat let the air hiss slowly through her teeth. "You're right, it's a break. Say this punk kid gets into the Dunn apartment, we'll figure out how later, since there's no evidence of a break-in, but he's in there. When he hears Dunn coming home, he hides in the bedroom. Dunn starts to get undressed and goes into the bedroom where the kid is crouched beside the bed. Dunn flips on the light and sees him. The kid panics, maybe he's on drugs, and pow, it's all over. Then the kid ransacks the place, grabs the money out of Dunn's wallet and takes off."

"So case closed?"

Pat grinned and dialed her assistant, Ken Wolcott. "Get me everything you can on a kid named Joey Pesci, recently released from Elmira. And prepare an affidavit in support of a search warrant for wherever he's hanging out."

Wolcott called back within the hour to say that Pesci's probation officer reported that the kid had failed to show up for his regular meeting the previous week.

"So technically he's in violation of probation and we can pick him up for questioning. And something else that might be important. The doorman on duty the night Dunn was killed remembers that a lady by the name of McDonald or McGee or McSomething came to visit Dunn. The guy can't remember when, exactly, and he doesn't remember ever seeing her before, but he'd only started working there a month or so before Dunn died. Oh, and he thinks the woman said she was a lawyer. I'll follow up on that lead and keep you posted."

When she returned to her desk, she got a call from Jason Whitman in ballistics saying he might have something interesting for her. Pat had asked him to run a computer search on .38 caliber pistols registered in the five boroughs.

"An interesting name popped up."

"So give, Sherlock."

"Frank Dunn."

"Frank Dunn what"

"Owns a .38. Have we got a suicide here, Sergeant?"

"Oh, there's a scenario for you, Jason. Dunn takes off his clothes and shoots himself five times with his own gun. You wouldn't happen to know what he did with the gun and the bullet casings after he killed himself, would you?"

"Hey, that's your department. I just work here in my little laboratory peering through my microscopes. But I'm sure you'll figure it all out, right, Sarge?"

"Yeah, right."

———

All the way in to the office the next morning Pat's thoughts turned to how lovely it would be at the cabin in New Hampshire. The city was going to be a scorcher. Nobody's making you do this, you know, she reminded herself, and then she had to laugh. Nothing and no one could drag her away from the Dunn case.

Ken Wolcott was already in the office when Pat arrived.

"I got it," he said, waving the Pesci search warrant in the air.

"Beautiful. Let's go."

———

When Pat nodded, Ken knocked several times on the door where Joey Pesci and his mother were supposed to be living. Finally they heard movement and muffled conversation inside.

"Who is it?" a woman demanded from behind the door.

"Detective Ken Wolcott, New York City Police."

"What do you want?"

"We need to speak with Joey Pesci."

"He ain't here. What do you want him for?"

Pat stepped closer to the door and said, "Mrs. Pesci, I'm Sergeant Turner. If you'll open the door we can explain the situation to you."

"I can hear you okay. Tell me what you want."

"We need to talk to you about Joey."

"I got nothin' to say. Joey ain't here."

There was whispered conversation behind the door. Pat and Ken put their pistols in the ready position. The door suddenly swung open wide, and a young man wearing only a pair of cutoffs said, "I'm Joey Pesci. What's your problem?"

Pat said, "We've got a couple of things to talk about, Joey."

"Like what?"

"Like the reason you didn't show up for your appointment with your parole officer last week. Like what you were doing in Frank Dunn's apartment a week or so ago."

"I don't know no Frank Dunn."

"We know better than that," Ken said. "This is a search warrant, Joey. We're going to have a look around."

Pat pushed the door open with her foot, her pistol still at the ready, and went into the apartment. On top of the dresser in the bedroom were a handful of change, cigarettes, a cigarette lighter, a switchblade knife, and several lottery tickets. Ken, right behind her, picked up a set of keys and dropped them in a plastic bag. When he saw the gold cigarette lighter, he put on a pair of rubber gloves and smiled. He slid the lighter carefully into another small clear bag and handed it to Pat. She stared at the initials engraved on the lighter: FMD.

She looked up at Joey and said, "Where did you get this?"

"A kid give it to me."

"What kid?"

"What is this shit? What are you guys all worked up about? The hundred bucks that jerk claims I stole from him?"

"What jerk is that, Joey?"

"I was on my way back to the pizza place when some guy mugged me and ripped me off."

"What pizza place was that?"

"Forget it!" Joey snapped.

"Before you say anything more, Joey, I want to make sure you understand that you have the right to remain silent and that anything you say may be used against you in a court of law. You are entitled to an attorney. If you can't afford one, the court will appoint an attorney to represent you."

"I don't need no attorney. I didn't do nothin'."

"We're taking you in with us," Pat said.

"On what grounds?"

"Parole violation, and suspicion of murder."

"Murder! You're crazy!" Joey cried. "Damn right, I want a lawyer."

CHAPTER THREE
July 26, 2003

The old man awakened from a rough night's sleep under the 59th Street Bridge. For a while he lay staring up at the wavering shadows on the underbelly of the bridge caused by the sun reflecting off the East River. His head throbbed, as usual, from too much cheap wine and too little food. He got up painfully, and as he was walking down to the water's edge to relieve himself, he spied a pistol a few feet from the shoreline. He couldn't believe his good fortune. Within an hour he'd sold the pistol and bought a gallon of Manischewitz. The pistol changed hands three more times that day before it reached Shadrack.

Shadrack didn't have a last name. He'd been a crack baby, and by the time he was eight, he'd been on his own, living by his wits. At age fifteen, he made his first kill in a gang skirmish. Now he was the nineteen-year-old leader of his own gang, the Bendigos.

AP - August 4, 2003. Last night in the Peter Stuyvesant section of Brooklyn, New York, a youth gang skirmish between the "Bendigos" and the "Blackjacks" erupted into a full-scale gun battle by the time the police arrived. When order was finally restored, there were five dead and three on the critical list in Bellevue Hospital, where scores of others with serious injuries are being treated. Among the dead was Patrolman Jaime Hernandez, killed in a point-blank duel with Shadrack, the nineteen-year-old leader of the Bendigos, who was also killed in the fray. Details of the event, which has been dubbed the "Shadrack Massacre," may be found on page 10A.

———

On the morning after the Shadrack shootout, Pat received a message to call ballistics ASAP.

"What's up, Jason?"

"I think we've found the murder weapon in the Dunn case."

"You've got to be kidding! Where, what, when, how?"

"Two days ago, but we just made the match-up about an hour ago."

"Between what and what?" Pat demanded.

"Between the bullets that killed the police officer in that Shadrack slaughter and the bullets that killed Frank Dunn."

Pat sucked in her breath. "You're sure?"

"I've been checking the bullets they took out of Frank Dunn against every .38 caliber weapon we've confiscated in the city, and it looks like maybe we've hit pay dirt."

"I'll be right down. Don't go away." She dialed Ken's extension and told him to meet her in the lab.

They arrived at Watson's door in a dead heat. Jason waved them in and shut the door behind them.

"Mind if I show your assistant here some of the tricks of my trade?"

"Suits me."

Ken took a seat beside Jason next to the microscopes.

"There's no way we can make a comparison between the imperfections inside the barrel of a pistol and the impressions they make on a bullet unless we have possession of the suspect weapon. So when the Shadrack weapon came in, we fired a series of test bullets from it into what we call a bullet trap, that box over there filled with cotton waste. Then we took the bullets retrieved from Dunn's body, which we call the control bullets, and the test bullets we fired from Shadrack's pistol, and we put them under this device called a binocular comparison microscope." Jason swiveled to face the microscopes, and Ken did the same.

The device was actually two separate microscopes mounted side by side, allowing the technician to put the control bullet on one side and the test bullet on the other. The first bullet was rotated to locate its most significant striations and then fixed in place. The second bullet was then rotated to search for a corresponding area with the same characteristics. Once they got a match, they rotated both bullets simultaneously to determine whether there were similar characteristics on other portions of them.

Watson reached behind him and grabbed an 8" x 10" glossy. "What I've got here are photo enlargements of the significant surfaces of the test bullets fired from the Shadrack pistol. We compared them with the bullets taken from Dunn's body, and I'm telling you flat out, there isn't one single difference between them."

Pat moved up to the microscopes and had her own look. One more piece of the puzzle seemed to have fallen into place.

"Have you had a chance to check out the registered owner of that pistol?" Pat asked. "I doubt Shadrack had a permit."

"I'm afraid that's a problem. The serial number has been filed off and there's no way to tell where the weapon came from before Shadrack got his hands on it."

"It doesn't really matter, I suppose," Pat said. "He had possession of it, and with his record he's a pretty good candidate to be the perp." But how the devil had he gotten into the apartment in the first place? she wondered. She couldn't see either Frank Dunn or Mrs. Dunn or the daughter willingly opening the door for the likes of Shadrack.

She turned to Ken. "Take the list of all of the registered owners of this same model Smith & Wesson .38 pistol and check them against reports of lost or stolen weapons."

"That's going to take a million years, Sarge! There's got to be..."

"I can tell you one name I'd check out, if I were you," Watson said.

"Say who?" Pat demanded

"Frank Dunn owned a Smith & Wesson .38 that nobody could locate. Might not be a bad place for Ken to start."

I should have thought of that, Pat cursed herself.

CHAPTER FOUR

Helen Dunn was a bright, attractive woman. She'd been a student in the School of Veterinary Medicine at Cornell University when she married Frank Dunn upon his graduation from law school. She'd continued her education at NYU when Frank joined his father's law firm in Manhattan. But on the birth of their only child, Jennifer, Helen discovered that she liked being a mother more than anything else and gave up the idea of becoming a career woman, settling comfortably into the role of wife and homemaker.

After Jennifer was born, Helen and Frank drifted apart emotionally. Her sexual relationships prior to marriage had been limited to a few unrewarding adventures in college. She assumed that with the attentions of a loving husband she'd experience those joys of sex claimed in the popular literature of the day, but she didn't. When, after five years of marriage, Frank seemed to lose interest in her sexually, she had mixed feelings. She didn't know if she was the problem or if Frank was an incompetent lover. But, although she regretted failing Frank in that area of their life, she personally didn't consider their reduced love life much of a loss. She felt secure in Frank's adoration of Jennifer, and believed that the child's very existence cemented their bond.

Jennifer became the love of Helen's life, and a source of great happiness, for about twelve years. But as adolescence set in, they couldn't seem to get through a day without a blow-up, usually ending with Jennifer retreating to her room in tears. Frank invariably made matters worse by taking Jennifer's side, whatever the controversy, and Helen despaired of resolving the breach between herself and her daughter. Having read scores of parenting guidebooks and having sought professional counseling, she ultimately accepted the proposition that puberty is not a terminal disease, and took solace in the advice, "This too shall pass."

Her one-time hobby of breeding her golden retriever had developed into a full-time business over the years. Before Jennifer's metamorphosis from angel to devil, Helen had purchased a kennel on Long Island near LaGuardia Airport, where she bred and boarded dogs. It was a perfect match for her academic background, her maternal instincts, and her engaging personality.

As the years passed, with streaks of gray sneaking almost imperceptibly into her ash blond hair, she coped with Jennifer's teenage myopia and was generally content with her life, with one exception: whenever Frank drank too much, which was becoming more and more frequent, any small disagreement could quickly escalate into a raging argument that not uncommonly ended in physical violence. At first, Frank's abusiveness was minor, but in recent months it had begun to turn more severe. Helen considered the idea of divorce but decided to suffer the consequences of staying married in order to keep the family together, at least until Jennifer went to college. She realized it was a demeaning price to pay, but she considered the alternatives to be worse.

———

When Helen was notified of Frank's death, she immediately flew back to New York. She was contacted by Pat Turner shortly after her arrival and agreed to meet with her as soon as she'd completed Frank's funeral arrangements.

When they met, twenty-four hours later, Pat learned that Frank had taken Helen to the airport around 5:30 PM on the day he was killed. Helen said she hadn't noticed anything unusual about her husband on the day she left to visit her parents and, in fact, except for the traffic problem, he seemed quite lighthearted. He knew the painters were coming in the morning, and told her he intended to have dinner at his club and go to bed early because he had a Saturday morning golf date out on the Island at the Westbury Country Club.

Pat did not discuss the contents of the tape that revealed that her husband did indeed intend to go to bed early, but probably not alone.

Ken was waiting for her when she returned to the office. He handed her a sheaf of sworn statements he'd obtained from the doormen, and sat down at the desk across from her.

"I've got something for you, too," she said. "It looks as if Mr. Dunn was playing footsie with a lady Friday night, shortly before he got canceled out. I want you to track down the women in his life — besides his wife and daughter, that is. Check with his office staff, his favorite bartender, his barber. Check his telephone bill, his credit card accounts. The works. Then I want you to tape a phone call with every one of them. Keep each of them on the line long enough to get a good voiceprint to compare with another taped telephone conversation I've got. And I need to have them say a few particular words." She flipped through her notebook. "*Promise, fault,* and *nine-thirty.* On Sunday, I went back to take another look around the Dunn apartment," she explained, "and found a telephone recording device. At the end of the tape, a lady calls Dunn around nine o'clock on Friday night, the night he was killed."

She pulled a typewritten transcript of the taped conversation out of the file and slid it across the desk to Ken.

When he finished reading he said, "Hey, wait a minute. Remember I told you one of the doormen said that a lady by the name of McDonald, or McGee, or something like that came to see the Dunns around the time Dunn was shot? I went back to see the doorman again yesterday and he finally recalled the lady's name. McBride. And she's a lawyer. I haven't had a chance to follow up on that yet because the computer's down."

"The computer's down? Why didn't you just look in the damn phone book?" Pat shook her head as she rifled through the yellow pages. "Here she is, in bold print. Margaux McBride, under the law firm heading of Dunn & Dunn." She slid the book across the desk to Ken.

"Sorry, Pat, I —"

"Never mind, I don't want to hear it. You've known since yesterday that a lady lawyer by the name of McBride came to the Dunn apartment at the time Dunn was killed and you haven't found time to open up a damn phone book?"

"I —"

Pat interrupted him. "Forget it. Sit down and listen. I'm going to tape a conversation with her and get a voice-print to match against the voice of the lady talking to Dunn on the phone. If it turns out that she's the one who was talking to him just before he was shot, then you're going to investigate her down to the color of her... long underwear." Pat turned on the tape recorder on her desk and dialed the number of the Dunn law office.

"Dunn and Dunn."

"May I speak with Attorney McBride, please?"

"Just a moment."

When McBride came on the line, Pat introduced herself and explained that she was involved in investigating the murder of Frank Dunn. She said she had a few questions she'd like to ask. As soon as she and McBride disconnected, Pat delivered the recording to the forensic lab and told them to call her when they had completed their voice analysis. Within an hour the lab called back and advised her they had a match, beyond a reasonable doubt.

Pat opened her notebook, flipped to the page headed *Suspects*, and entered the name *Margaux McBride*. Okay, she said to herself, who are these people? And what's the relationship between Frank Dunn and Margaux McBride?

CHAPTER FIVE

Maggie Doyle was the product of a college fraternity party coupling between a strikingly attractive "townie" and Brandon University's scholarly senior class president. When Maggie was two years old, her mother was thrown from the jump seat of a 1967 Harley Davidson traveling over eighty miles an hour on the New Jersey Turnpike. She and the driver were killed instantly. Maggie was turned over to Ruthann Doyle, her thirty-six-year-old grandmother, a waitress at a local roadhouse who resented both the financial burden and the time-consuming responsibility of caring for the child. Ruthann was looking for a man who'd be willing to share more than her bed from time to time; someone who would pay half the rent and the groceries. A kid wouldn't exactly increase her odds.

When Maggie was four, Ruthann's temporary live-in boyfriend took the child on his lap and sexually abused her. Maggie screamed in pain, wriggled out of his grasp, and ran away. The boyfriend washed the blood from his fingers and forgot about the incident. Maggie never did.

By sixteen she was moody, bright, beautiful, and out of control. She experimented with every vice the mean streets of Bayonne, New Jersey had to offer, including drugs, booze, and, occasionally selling her body if the price was right or the spirit moved her.

The summer before Maggie's senior year in high school, one of her girlfriends contracted AIDS and her boyfriend of the month almost died from an overdose of ecstasy. The realization that she herself had escaped the same fates only by chance forced her to take a hard look at the direction her life was taking. She knew she was smarter than the kids she hung out with and that she got above average grades without much effort, but she'd come to the conclusion that brains alone weren't going to save her from following in her mother's and her grandmother's footsteps. There were plenty of really smart girls on the streets.

———

Chauncey Halsey-Jones taught English at Bayonne North High School. Slight, bespectacled and balding, he was a Bohemian graduate of the '60s. His passion was theater, and although he had failed as a professional, he had found his niche as a high school drama coach. When he noticed Maggie in his Senior Lit course, he thought she might be perfect for the lead in *Sabrina*, the play he had chosen for his Christmas production. She was drop-dead gorgeous, and he hoped she might have some talent as well. At the end of class he called her to his desk and asked her to meet him in his office after her last class.

"Yeah, sure I can act," Maggie told him later that day. "I act every day. I act like I like English Lit, don't I?"

Halsey-Jones gave Maggie the part and never regretted it. Based on her class attendance he worried that she might cause problems by missing rehearsals, but she never did. She always had her lines memorized, and worked harder than anyone else in the cast. At the afterglow party following the highly acclaimed production, Halsey-Jones dropped down on the couch beside her and asked what she was planning to do with her life.

"Go to Hollywood and become rich and famous," she grinned.

"I would never tell you that's impossible, Maggie, but I wouldn't count on it." He studied her for a moment. "Maybe I have a better idea."

"Like what?"

"Like going to college. Maintaining your interest in theater and at the same time gaining some skills that you can fall back on if you don't make it."

"Skills like what?"

"Maybe teaching; maybe the law, or marketing, or politics. There are lots of professions in which projecting an image, the way you do on the stage, can be a tremendous asset."

"Where would I ever get the money to go to college? Besides, if I go to college I only want to go to Harvard."

Halsey-Jones laughed. "Why's that?"

"It's the best."

"Are you willing to compromise?"

"You mean like going to a community college?" She shrugged. "I can't even afford that."

"No, I have something different in mind, if you're willing to work your butt off next semester."

He watched her eyes widen with what looked like excitement, then narrow again. It was like watching her switch roles before his eyes.

"I'd do anything for you if you could help me go to college, and I mean anything," she purred.

Halsey-Jones got up from the couch. "All you need to do is get no less than a B-plus average next semester and..."

"And what?"

"Play the part of Eliza Doolittle in our spring musical?"

"Deal," she said, holding out her hand. He took it and couldn't help holding it longer than he should have.

———

Chauncey Halsey-Jones had written fifty percent of his classmate John Newcomb's senior theme paper. It was of such high quality that John was accepted in graduate school, obtained a Ph.D, and was teaching English at a small college near Cleveland. Chauncey called Newcomb. It was their first contact in about five years, and they exchanged information about their wives and children before Chauncey got down to business.

"I need a favor, John."

"As long as it's not money, I'm your man."

"It involves a student of mine. I want to get her into college, and she'll also need a job to pay for her room and board. I was hoping you might be able to help me get her admitted to Greenstone this fall, if it's still as good as you claim."

"It's better, honestly. How bad are her marks?"

"Disgusting early on, but pretty good now, especially in this last semester. She played the lead in a couple of things I directed, and I've sort of taken her under my wing. She's a great kid. She came up the hard way. Her parents died when she was two, and she needs someone to believe in her. I really think she can go somewhere. I was hoping maybe you could take over for me after she graduates."

John agreed to take the baton from his old friend. As chairman of the admissions committee, he was willing to take Chauncey's word that Maggie Doyle was right for Greenstone.

"As for the job, I'm sure we can find something, but what about tuition? I'm afraid we have only limited scholarship funds available."

"I think we've got the first year covered okay. I helped her get a small scholarship and a student loan, and apparently some family friend loaned her enough to make up the difference."

"She'll have to send me her transcript and a two-page biographical sketch. Also, I'll have to interview her myself so that I can explain why I'm recommending her after we closed out admissions for the fall term."

"Just tell me when you want to see her. You won't be disappointed, John."

———

"Maggie? It's Mr. Jones."

"Oh, hi. What's happening?"

"If you can get past a personal interview with my friend John Newcomb, you'll be a freshman at Greenstone College in September, that's all."

"Oh wow! Where's that?"

"It's a fine small college outside Cleveland."

"Where's Cleveland?"

"In Ohio, Eliza."

"Where's Ohio, Henry Higgins?"

———

When Maggie was escorted into Professor Newcomb's office, he couldn't believe his eyes. He'd been expecting a male version of his scholarly college roommate, someone flat-chested with stringy long brown hair and horn-rimmed glasses. But the young woman who stood before him with an open friendly smile, hair cascading to her shoulders in waves of ebony curls, and penetrating, mischievous dark eyes, was extremely attractive.

He swept a stack of papers off the only other chair in his tiny office to allow her to be seated. "Welcome to Greenstone, Miss Doyle."

Maggie delivered the speech she'd rehearsed with Halsey-Jones, speaking slowly and meticulously. "I'm very grateful for everything you have done to make it possible for me to attend Greenstone College, Dr. Newcomb ..." She fumbled her next words, sighed and said, "My problem is that this interview is so important to me, I'm afraid I'll make a mistake and you'll send me back to Bayonne."

"My goodness, you mustn't be frightened, certainly not of me. We're very pleased to have you join our Greenstone family, Miss Doyle."

———

When she auditioned for a part in the college's production of *Twelfth Night*, Maggie discovered that the competition was fierce and her high school successes were meaningless. She realized she was outclassed in every way and was humiliated when, after her reading, one of the seniors remarked that he'd never before heard Shakespeare spoken with a Noo Joisey accent.

By the middle of the spring semester she'd gained a B average, won a small part in *Oklahoma* — and lost her accent.

That summer she took a job as a waitress in Smokey's bar on the waterfront in Bayonne. Her first night on duty she met Dan McBride, a young naval officer who was on leave and visiting his brother.

At eight a.m. the following morning Maggie's phone rang.

"May I please speak with Maggie Doyle?"

"That's me. Who's this?"

"It's Dan...Dan McBride."

"Dan?" Maggie's heart was pounding as hard as her head.

"We met in Smokey's bar last night. Remember?"

"Oh, Danny, of course I remember, but how come you're calling me at eight o'clock in the morning?"

"I couldn't get you out of my mind and I wanted to be first in line to invite you to dinner tonight."

"I'm working tonight, but maybe tomorrow."

On their first date, they talked non stop until four o'clock in the morning.

"So when can I see you tomorrow?" he asked.

"I'm sorry, Danny, but I'm committed tomorrow. Maybe we could get together Sunday if you want to."

"You don't understand, Maggie. I have two weeks left on my furlough and then...I'm not supposed to say anything, but then I'm headed overseas. It's plenty hot where I'm going, and I don't just mean the temperature." He shrugged his shoulders. "Who knows?"

Six days after they met, Danny asked her to marry him, and on the night before he was due to return to the Bethesda Naval Base in Maryland, a justice of the peace pronounced Margaret Doyle and Daniel McBride husband and wife.

Maggie decided the name Maggie was inappropriate for the wife of a naval officer and began to introduce herself as Margaux McBride.

With Danny's encouragement she was accepted as a student at the University of Maryland for the 1990 fall term.

————

Iraq invaded Kuwait on August 2, 1990, and shortly thereafter Danny's team flew off in the direction of Saudi Arabia.

On January 18, 1991, Margaux McBride received notice that her husband had been killed in action in Kuwait. She dressed in black and shed some genuine tears, and when she received Danny's' military service life insurance proceeds in the amount of $50,000, she put it in the bank. She graduated in the top 10 percent of her class at the University of Maryland in 1993 and was accepted at Blackstone Law School.

————

Walden Danaher taught constitutional law at Blackstone. He knocked on the dean's door and entered without waiting for permission. As the oldest member of the faculty Danaher dispensed with most social amenities that interfered with his immediate objectives.

"Come in," Dean Meisner said sarcastically after Professor Danaher eased his massive body into the chair across from the dean's desk.

"Got a problem I want to run by you, Skip. Do you have a minute?" Without waiting for an answer, Danaher continued. "You know Margaux McBride, of course."

"Who doesn't? What's she up to now?"

"Well, either I have to give her an A+ on her final or ask that she be dismissed from the school."

"How come?"

"I'm certain she cheated on my final exam, but I can't prove a damn thing."

"Great beginning," the dean scoffed.

"As you know, she failed my course in her first year, but we let her stay on with the understanding that she couldn't graduate unless she took it again and passed it."

"I remember." The dean got up and poured himself a cup of coffee from the pot he kept brewing at all times. "Want one?"

"Sure. This isn't easy you know. I really like Margaux."

"What's not to like?"

"Her morality, that's what!" Professor Danaher replied emphatically.

The elderly scholar sat slumped in his chair, shoulders sagging, staring at the words emblazoned on the front of the coffee mug he held in his hands: *The law is an ass.*

Danaher blew air through his pursed lips. "The problem is that when these kids graduate year after year, they're equipped to handle corporate mergers but they don't have a clue as to what's right and what's wrong. A few months after graduation they go racing down to New York City and immediately start picking up a weekly pay check that's fifty percent higher than mine."

"I dare say that's true to some extent," the dean replied. "But they don't come to us for character building. They come to gain knowledge of the law ... how to use it and, regrettably in some cases, how to abuse it. And by the time they've completed four years of college and three years of law school, many of them need that high-paying job to pay off their school loans. But I don't suppose this colloquy is helping you with the McBride dilemma." The dean blew on his cup to cool the steaming coffee.

"You're right on all counts, Skip, but let me give you the ungarnished facts. I promise to submerge my own bias."

"Ungarnished? Is that a word, Walden?"

"If it wasn't, it is now. It means to describe without garnishment."

"I'll buy that. Okay, give me your ungarnished version of the facts."

Professor Danaher took a sip of the coffee. Removing his eyeglasses, he polished them with the end of his necktie, carefully returned them to his face, closed his eyes, and leaned back in the chair, and began.

"Margaux had put off taking my course until her last semester here. All the kids in the class worked hard enough at it to get by. Except Margaux! Jesus Christ, Skip, one day I caught her doing her nails and reading *Vogue* magazine while we were discussing Brown v. Board of Education. Last month I had her in my office and read the riot act to her. I told her that unless she got an A on her final exam to offset her poor work throughout the term, I was going to have to fail her and she wouldn't be able to graduate. Do you know what she said? She asked if I'd like to come up to her apartment, where she'd cook me a fabulous dinner and we could discuss the problem over a bottle of wine — which she suggested I bring along, preferably a Merlot."

The dean tried unsuccessfully to stifle his laughter, but once he started he couldn't stop. Professor Danaher's face turned crimson and then even he allowed a small chuckle to escape his lips.

"How was the food, Walden?"

"I should have known you wouldn't be any help." Professor Danaher started to get up but he was having trouble easing his great bulk out of the chair.

"Sit down, sit down, Walden. You must admit there's an element of humor in this. Tell me how she did on the final."

"I already told you. The paper she handed in deserves an A+! I have never given an A+ on a final in my life. And it's not copied from any other paper. I've scrutinized them all and I watched her like a hawk throughout the entire exam."

"So how do you think she did it?"

"She stole the exam. It's the only answer."

"Aw, c'mon Walden, you must be joking."

"I'm not, damn it. There is no other plausible explanation."

"How could she have managed that, for God's sake?"

"The transom in my office. She must have climbed through the damned transom the night before the final and found the exam in my desk."

"The transom? You mean that little window?" The dean pointed at the narrow horizontal window above his office door. "That's ridiculous, Walden. There's no way Margaux could have squeezed her chest through that tiny window."

"Actually, I thought of that," Walden said, feeling his face flush. "I think she got a step ladder or an accomplice and a bicycle tire."

"A bicycle tire?"

"I found a bicycle tire in the trash can outside the building yesterday and that was the missing link. She must have climbed on someone's shoulders or got a stepladder, opened the transom, stuck her head and arms through, and lowered the bicycle tire down inside the door. Then she pulled it up tight around the inside door knob, twisted the knob with the tire and opened the door." Walden leaned back in his chair, smiling triumphantly.

"I'm sorry, Walden. Your theory is ingenious, but it doesn't have the ring of beyond a reasonable doubt to me. How about this simple theory: She took your warning seriously, studied like crazy, and got lucky. She's no dumbbell, you know."

"Impossible! I want your permission to call the police and have them check the transom for fingerprints."

"Forget it, Walden. Give her the A+ and if you're right about her, she'll flunk the bar exam and that will end it."

Three months later the dean chuckled when he read in the *New York Times* that Margaux was among the 51 percent in the state who passed the exam. The following week, at Margaux's request, and with only a slight hesitation, he gave her a letter of recommendation to accompany her application for a job interview with Frank Dunn, a graduate of Blackstone Law School, and the junior partner in the Manhattan law firm of Dunn & Dunn.

———

Before interviewing Margaux McBride, Pat decided she should know as much as she could about the victim, Frank Dunn. She went on the Internet and got a profile from the Dunn & Dunn law firm website.

Frank Dunn took over the leadership of Dunn & Dunn upon the death of his father, Michael Dunn, a highly respected member of the Manhattan bar. He attended Syracuse University, obtained his law degree from Blackstone Law School, and was admitted to practice in New York in 1985. He specializes in corporate and securities law, mergers and acquisitions, trusts and estates.

She checked several other sources of information available to her, but nothing of interest turned up.

What I really want to know about him, she mused, is what motivated someone to pump five slugs into him at close range. What kind of a man was Frank Dunn?

CHAPTER SIX
June 1996

Frank Dunn had joined his father's law firm when he graduated from Blackstone Law School in 1985. He'd played football at Syracuse University and continued to work out at his club. His classmates at the university considered him to be a regular guy. He could hold his own in a bar room; he was generous but not ostentatious with his money. In terms of romantic interests, he played the field vigorously until he met his wife to be, Helen Ransom. Frank proudly paraded his young bride through the social circles of Manhattan, and they made an extraordinarily handsome couple. Helen's shoulder-length ash-blonde hair, bright hazel eyes, her ready smile, and her "body to die for," as her classmates jealously noted, contrasted with Frank's solid frame and his soft brown eyes and dark hair.

Shortly after their first anniversary Helen enthusiastically announced that she was giving up her dedication to the care and feeding of animals and would concentrate upon the care and feeding of their first child. Initially, Frank was as excited about becoming a parent as his wife, but it proved to be a difficult pregnancy for Helen. At the start, he was sympathetic to her discomfort, but when she lost all interest in continuing to share the conjugal bed with him, his disappointment was followed by frustration. At first he directed his anger toward himself, deciding he was being insensitive, unreasonable and selfish, but after the exhilaration that accompanied the birth of his daughter began to diminish and Helen became totally preoccupied with the care of their child, with little time or energy left over for Frank, he reverted to his self-centered persona. Without revealing his dilemma, he asked his colleagues in an offhand way about their experiences with firstborn babies, and was appalled to learn that after their six-week postpartum checkup, those wives had been eager to resume sexual activity.

Frank was furious. Jennifer was three and a half months old, for chrissake, and Helen still had excuses. Were his colleagues bullshitting him, or was Helen giving him the business? He had some rights dammit — she was his wife!

He started to revisit his old bachelor haunts, telling himself he was just touring some old scenery; just window-shopping. One night he drank too much and met a newly divorced, young professional woman who had her own reasons to prove that she was still attractive to a handsome, successful man.

Frank slipped into bed in the guest room in his home at 4:17 AM The next day he was consumed with guilt and vowed he would never fall from grace again, but ten days later, when he approached Helen and she gently but firmly turned him down because she was exhausted, he called his new friend. She was ready, willing, and able. Although Helen eventually succumbed to Frank's demands, by the time she did he had embarked upon an irreversible course of extramarital affairs. His sexual appetite increased with the number and variety of his bedmates, and he was finding considerably more satisfaction from the adrenaline rush of adultery than from sex with Helen.

But he never wavered in his devotion to his daughter. He vowed never to leave Helen until Jennifer was grown.

His professional life, on the other hand, was going well. Although his legal skills were not outstanding, he was popular with the wheeling-and-dealing New York investment banking firms, which were expert at manipulating the truth, themselves. The young, hard-driving executives of such companies were very impressed with Frank's creativity in negotiating hostile takeovers, and his father Michael Dunn was amazed to discover that by 1990, Frank's clients were bringing in fees that equaled his own.

In the 80's and 90's, the demand for aggressive, bright young lawyers willing to work 80 hours or more every week had reached into every law school in the country. Even the less prestigious law schools were sending their top graduates to metropolitan law firms, which were paying up to $100,000 a year as starting salaries.

Frank studied the applications on his desk. They'd been reviewed by one of his associates who had graded them, putting the most promising on top. He needed at least two new lawyers to handle the increased caseload and had chosen a young man from Syracuse and a young woman from Cornell without bothering to study the remaining résumés. As he was about to throw the rejects in the out-basket, his eye caught the application on the bottom of the pile. It was the only one that had a photograph attached, and it portrayed an extremely attractive young woman. He retrieved the résumé and studied it. Margaux McBride. Born June 23, 1972, in upstate New York. And she was a graduate of his old alma mater. He was impressed with the fact that her transcript indicated that she'd received an A+ in constitutional law, taught by Professor Walden Danaher. Frank had been required to take Danaher's course twice and finally managed to pass it with a D that both he and Professor Danaher recognized as a gift.

Margaux had answered the question, "Why I would like to work for Dunn & Dunn," as follows: "I have studied the history of the Dunn & Dunn law firm and noted that shortly after Frank Dunn became a partner in the firm, it expanded from six attorneys to seventeen attorneys and gained a reputation as one of the fastest-growing small law firms in New York City. I want to work for a winner. I believe Dunn & Dunn is a winner and that I can help to keep it that way. P.S. I also like the high salary being offered."

Frank smiled and added Margaux McBride to the list of applicants he intended to interview.

CHAPTER SEVEN

"Ms. McBride is here for her appointment, Mr. Dunn," the receptionist announced when Margaux presented her appointment card.

Frank had forgotten who Ms. McBride was until she entered his office, but he would never forget her again. Every young woman lawyer he had ever interviewed had worn a traditional dark blue suit and conservative white blouse. Margaux was wearing a red blazer and miniskirt with a bold black-and-white print blouse with two large buttons. When she sat down in the chair opposite his desk, the top button popped open, but she seemed not to notice. It remained that way during the entire interview. Frank tried not to stare at the partially exposed mounds of soft cream-colored flesh, but every time Margaux leaned forward to emphasize a point, he could not ignore the fully erect bright red nubbins. He didn't remember ever being totally aroused so quickly before in his life. He tried desperately to pay attention to what the young woman was saying and to carry on an intelligent discussion with her, but he'd been lost from the moment she sat down. Without having learned anything about her ability to do the job he needed, he heard himself say, "When can you start?"

—

Within five years, Margaux became the highest-paid associate attorney in the firm, a fact that was carefully hidden from the other associates who were her seniors. Her ability to get what she wanted, when she wanted it, quickly became legendary. One of her male colleagues commented that negotiating a business transaction with Margaux was like dancing with a praying mantis. "One minute you're laughing together and she's looking directly at you with those enormous, sensual dark eyes, and the next minute you realize you're standing in a pool of your own blood. You don't even feel it when she bites off your head and consumes it."

Alma Haverstock, who had been Frank's father's secretary and law office manager since before Frank was born, was equally sanguine. She attributed Margaux's meteoric rise in the firm to her extraordinary good looks, her keen mind, and her willingness to share her bed with Frank Dunn.

———

When Maggie Doyle was a sophomore in high school, Carl Stassi was a ruggedly handsome twenty-six-year-old Bayonne hood. On a Friday afternoon in May, he swaggered down Bayonne's 53rd Street feeling the money in his pocket. Twenty-five big ones, he laughed to himself, just for smackin' a couple of welshers around a little bit. And Arty said there was lots more where that come from.

He slipped into Gino's bar on 53rd Street and Avenue E, where the hardwood floors were worn uneven by the work boots of two generations of laborers. For old-timers and cool guys, Gino's was an institution. There was a long bar against one wall, and ceiling fans that hadn't worked for twenty years.

It was two in the afternoon. Carl ordered a Dewars on the rocks and glanced around the room. A few regulars were nursing some cheap wine. Dago Red, he called it. He was hoping somebody important would come in so he could flash his roll of bills. Then he saw her at the far end of the bar. He motioned to the bartender.

"Who's the broad?" he whispered.

"Maggie Doyle. A real looker, hey? But she's too young for you, Carl."

"How old is she?"

"Her I.D. says she's twenty-one," the bartender snickered.

"That's good enough for me," Carl said, and they both laughed. "Anyway, I figure any skirt what's wearing a 36B bra is old enough. What's she drinking?"

"Screwdriver."

"Send one down on me."

"Sure thing."

When the bartender delivered the drink, Maggie smiled and held up her glass in salute to Carl. An hour later they left the bar together. For the next two years Maggie made herself available to Carl PRN, like a prescription drug to be taken on an as-needed basis whenever she needed money or he wanted sex. They were both comfortable with the arrangement.

It was Carl who shelled out the money for her first year in college.

She saw him when she came home at the end of her freshman year, but by that time she'd entered a different world. She tried to separate herself from him, but he was persistent, and she'd had a hard time avoiding him until Danny McBride came along and rescued her from Bayonne.

Six months after she'd begun working for Frank Dunn in Manhattan, she went home to Bayonne. She stopped in at Gino's, where she ran into Carl and made the mistake of agreeing to have dinner with him. For old time's sake, as he put it. By then he'd moved up in the New Jersey underworld and had become accustomed to having things his own way. He refused to accept Margaux's unwillingness to renew their relationship. The more she rejected him, the more desirable she became.

———

One Sunday Frank took Margaux to the Meadowlands to watch a pro football game. As they were leaving the stadium after the game, Margaux asked if they could drive to Bayonne and have a drink at her favorite bar.

"I'm sorry, but I really should head back to the city. I told Jennifer I'd take her to a movie tonight."

"So, let's hurry," Margaux teased, pulling Frank with her as she started to skip toward the car. Frank checked the time. It was 6:55. He knew it would take at least a half-hour to get out of the parking lot.

"We'll do it another time, I promise."

"I don't want to do it another time. I want to do it now. It's only ten miles from here."

"I know, honey, but it'll be bumper to bumper all the way. We won't get there until 8:00 or 8:30, and by the time we have a drink and get back to the city, you know...and it's a school night and..."

Margaux began to sulk, responding to Frank in monosyllables. Finally they stopped talking altogether. Margaux sat slumped against the passenger door as far from Frank as possible as they inched their way through the massive parking lot. When they reached the point where they had to turn north on the Garden State Parkway toward the Lincoln tunnel and Manhattan, or turn south on the New Jersey Turnpike toward Bayonne, Frank hesitated and at the last moment turned the car south to Bayonne.

Margaux hugged Frank closely as she led him into Gino's crowded bar, where 80 percent of the patrons were male, the talk was 100 percent football, and all eyes were turned to the big TV screen where highlights of the game were being replayed. Margaux squeezed between two men hunched over the bar to order drinks. An old-timer, recognizing her, gave up his precious stool to her. She kissed him full on the lips. He turned scarlet and laughed at the envious wise-ass remarks of his buddies.

Frank was standing close beside Margaux when a large man shoved himself between them.

"Hey, hey, Maggie, where the hell you been?" He put his arm around her shoulders and, taking the martini glass out of her hand, yelled at the bartender. "Charlie! Bring a bottle of Dom Perignon for the lady."

"You know we ain't got any of that shit here, Carl," the bartender said.

"You better find some in a hurry, Charlie, or when I get through with you they'll be callin' you Charlene," Carl Stassi snarled. Charlie immediately opened the cash drawer, took out one hundred and fifty dollars and gave it to the kid helping him behind the bar. "Get your ass over to the Marriott on the Boulevard and buy a bottle of Dom Perignon champagne – fast," he whispered to the kid. "It's on its way, Carl."

"Excuse me, sir." Frank tried to ease his way back in next to Margaux. Carl shoved his elbow hard into Frank's stomach, knocking the wind out of him. "Is this creep botherin' you, Maggie?"

Margaux looked over her shoulder and saw Frank gasping for breath. She slid down off the stool and went over to him.

"Let's get out of here," she whispered.

When she turned back to the bar to get her purse, Carl grabbed her arm.

"Your friend ain't got no manners, does he, babe? You're back in Bayonne, kiddo. Park Avenue is on the other side of the river. Can your friend swim across the river? I mean, if I accidentally dropped him in the river, do you think he might sink? Who is that pussy, anyway?"

Margaux pulled away from Carl, took Frank's arm and hurried him out of the bar.

Carl turned to one of his cronies. "Find out who that asshole is," he commanded, slipping him a one hundred dollar bill and the keys to his car.

A black Mercerdes sedan with New Jersey license plates followed discreetly behind Frank's car until he parked it in the underground parking area beneath his apartment complex.

CHAPTER EIGHT
November 2002

Lying beside Margaux McBride in her Third Avenue apartment, Frank was thinking about the fact that the king-sized bed he'd paid for was all out of proportion to the tiny bedroom. This was the third time in a week they had ended up in her bedroom. Glancing at his watch, he said, "Christ, I've got to go," and gathered up his clothes strewn about the room.

"It's only 9:30," Margaux sulked. "I don't want you to leave now." She studied him as he buttoned up his monogrammed shirt, put on his suit with the Madison Avenue label, and slipped on his Bally cordovans.

"I don't want to go either, but you know I have to." He shrugged apologetically, then turned to tie his tie in front of the antique full-length mirror he'd given her on Valentine's Day.

"No, damn it, I don't know you have to."

"Helen's holding dinner for me."

"We can't keep old Helen waiting, now, can we? Why don't we just make her disappear, like into thin air? I really hate her."

"Margaux, you know I –"

"Yeah, yeah. But if she's the nag you keep telling me, why don't you move out?"

"Ah, come on," he said, reaching down and pulling her up beside him.

He held her close and stroked her long dark hair, and they began to kiss again. She teased him with her tongue and tried to coax him back down on the bed. When he resisted, she pushed him out of the way. He stared at her firm bare buttocks as she marched into the bathroom, slamming the door. He went over and turned the handle. It was locked.

"I'm sorry, okay?" he said. Her only response was to turn on the shower. He envisioned her slender nude body, her head thrown back, the tangled mass of jet black hair falling to her shoulders, her eyes closed and her long slim legs spread apart; he imagined the rivulets of water cascading down over her perky breasts, flat belly and sleek hips; the water crystals sparkling on the fringe of a nest of tight pubic curls.

He leaned against the doorjamb.

"Hey look, Margaux, maybe I can stay a little longer. Open the door, okay?"

She turned off the shower, reached for the plush towel and began to rub herself down in the steamy bathroom.

"Margaux?"

"Yes, Frank?"

"I said maybe I can stay a little longer. Open the door, please."

"Will you take me to dinner, Frank?"

"I can't tonight but..."

"Good-bye, Frank. I'll see you in the office Monday morning." She turned the shower back on.

"Bitch." He turned away, hurried down three flights of stairs, and hailed a cab.

———

After wrapping herself in a huge Turkish towel, Margaux settled on the couch with her bare feet up on the coffee table to do her toenails. The phone rang. As she picked up the receiver she flicked on the TV by pressing the remote button with her big toe.

"Hello."

"Maggie?"

"You must have the wrong number."

"Hey, Maggie, you can't fool me. It's Carl."

"What the hell do you want, Carl? Did your wife kick you out of the house again?"

"I want to see you, babe."

"No Carl, I'm no longer a Bayonne teenager at your beck and call. I told you it's over, it's all over. "

"For you maybe, but not for me. How about what I did for you?"

"Not for me, Carl, you did it for yourself."

She shifted the phone between her chin and shoulder and lit a cigarette, inhaling deeply and letting the smoke drift slowly out of her nose and mouth.

"I really need you, babe."

"You don't need me, you need a shrink."

"Aw, c'mon, Maggie, you used to tell me I was the greatest."

"You were great in the sack when I was seventeen and didn't know any better."

"What do you want from me for chrissake?"

"I want you should have a brain, but you've got styrofoam between your ears. I paid my dues and now I want you to get out of —"

"Don't say it, babe, just let me come over. You'll see, it'll be like old times."

"Look, Carl, it was a mistake. So now let's just forget it, okay?"

"I can't forget it, Babe. Don't you understand I'm hooked? Like an addict. I'm hooked and you gotta let me come see you."

"Listen, Carl, let's get one thing straight. I don't gotta do anything. Go talk to your consigliere if you have a problem. I'm going to hang up and I don't want you to call me again. Understand?"

"Hey, hey, just slow down here. What about the money, hey? What about the goddamn money? The ten grand I give you for that college shit."

"You told me it was a gift. Remember?"

"Gift my ass. You said you'd pay it back with interest."

"Even if I said that, which I absolutely deny, it's unenforceable because the statute of limitations has run out, and besides, I was underage—to say nothing about the statutory rape aspect of it. You have a very poor memory, Carl. Besides, when I asked if I owed you anything, your exact words were, 'Forget it kid, you already give me $10,000 worth of head.' I wrote it down in my diary, just the way you said it."

"That was a joke for chrissake."

"No, Carl. You're the joke. That stunt you pulled at Gino's was the last straw. Now, I'm going to hang up. I'm expecting a call."

"From that hotshot lawyer you're working for, right? I think I'll stop by his fancy penthouse some night and give him the straight shit on you. I know where he lives, you know. How would you like me to do that?"

"What would your parole officer think about that? I'm warning you, Carl, if I get one more phone call from you, I'm going straight to your P.O. and have you charged with harassment. If they cancel your parole, you've got eight years left to spend inside – am I right? Good-bye, Carl."

"Maggie, don't hang up. Our problem is that goddamn shyster lawyer. I can solve that problem real easy, you know. All I have to do is give the word and he's –" The dial tone buzzed in his ear. He immediately redialed her number and got a busy signal.

"Bitch!" he hissed as he slammed down the receiver.

———

When the taxi dropped Frank off at his apartment house, he realized he'd left his cell phone at Margaux's place. He dialed her number from the pay phone on the corner across from his apartment house. The line was busy. He waited a few minutes and tried again. This time there was no answer. Frank slammed the receiver on the hook and waited for the return of his quarter. The machine swallowed up his coin. "Shit!" He pounded on the side of the telephone box, and then walked slowly back to the lobby of his apartment house.

Frank nodded to the doorman, crossed the marble tile lobby floor, entered the elevator, and fumbled with his key until it finally eased into the slot marked penthouse. When he entered the apartment, he heard Helen in the kitchen. Without a word, he went directly to the refrigerator and began to fill a tumbler with ice.

"Dinner's ready. In fact, the roast is overdone."

"I'm going to have a drink first. Go ahead and eat. Where's Jennifer?"

"She's over at Suzy's. Studying for an exam."

"She's always over at Suzy's. What's the matter with her own home?"

"Maybe if her father came home for dinner on time once in a while she'd stay around."

"What's that supposed to mean?"

Helen watched him filling his glass with scotch. She started to say something and then changed her mind. She put a small portion of food on her plate and took it into the living room and set up a snack table in front of the blank television screen. Frank followed behind her, his ice clinking in his glass.

"What's bugging you?" he demanded.

"I made a really nice dinner and now it's spoiled. You promised to be home by nine o'clock, and..."

"And, and, and! It's always the same! All you ever do is bitch. Every night it's the same."

Frank stared out the window facing Central Park. Neither of them spoke for many minutes. Finally, Helen broke the silence.

"When I was waiting for you to come home, I happened to look out the window and saw you get out of the cab and go in the phone booth."

"Is that a crime, for chrissake?"

"Of course not. You can call whomever you wish from a public phone, even though you have three phones here at home. Which woman were you calling? I can't keep track of them all."

"You're pissing me off with your snotty mouth, Helen."

"I'm right on the mark, aren't I, Frank?"

"Goddamn you, Helen!" Frank grabbed her arm. As she tried to pull away from him, he struck her. She began to sob, more from humiliation than from the blow. Frank put on his coat and left the apartment.

Sometimes the only way to make a woman understand is to put an end to the discussion, he decided.

CHAPTER NINE

At 10:00 AM Helen sat sipping coffee at her dressing table. The large bedroom was lavishly decorated with zebra-striped silk drapes, drawn back to reveal a floor-to-ceiling view of the East River. Her antique chaise, easy chair, and boudoir bench were covered in white silk. Chagall clowns hung on each side of the mirror.

She began applying her makeup. She had become expert at covering up skin discoloration. Finally the face reflected in her gilt-framed mirror was nearly without blemish except for the purple bruise beneath her left eye. When she finished disguising that, the flaw was nearly undetectable.

She had a lunch date with her best friend, Kate Connors. After a final glance in the mirror, she pulled her fur coat out of the hall closet, stepped out into the hallway, and pushed the button for the elevator that serviced their apartment exclusively.

"Can I get you a cab, Mrs. Dunn?" the doorman asked when she entered the lobby.

"No thank you, Charles. It's such a beautiful day. We don't get too many of these in November."

"It's still mighty cold out there," he cautioned.

"I don't mind. I'll enjoy the walk."

She stepped out into the sunshine and headed toward Fifth Avenue. She loved the variety of lifestyles that made Manhattan such an exciting city. As she strolled down the avenue, she gazed in the windows of the exquisite shops along the way, stopping for a moment to enjoy a sidewalk trio playing reggae. The lilting rhythms made her want to hop on a plane and head to the Caribbean. When the song was over, the small impromptu audience applauded appreciatively, and Helen dropped a $5 bill into the open guitar case placed strategically in front of the performers. Her encounter with the street musicians had lightened her mood, and she continued down the avenue until she reached *Trattoria*, her favorite meeting place. When she entered the restaurant, the owner met her.

"Bon giorno, signora," he said, smiling.

"Hello, Antonio. Today I think I would like that table over there." She pointed to the rear of the dining room where less light might prevent Kate from detecting her bruises.

"Whatever you wish, signora." He led her back to the darkened corner. "May I open a nice bottle of Mazzi Amarone to keep you company until your friend comes?"

"That sounds lovely, Antonio. Thank you." She settled back in the booth to await Kate's arrival. They'd been college roommates and had remained best friends ever since. Helen had often joked that her decision to marry Frank and take up residence on the east side of Manhattan was 70 percent love for Frank and 30 percent desire to be near her best friend. Now after almost fifteen years of marriage, she thought the percentages might be reversed. She smiled the moment Kate's silhouette appeared in the doorway of the tiny restaurant.

"Hi, hon. What are we doing back here next to the men's room?" Kate wrinkled her nose as she slid into the booth opposite Helen.

"I just felt in the mood to snuggle in the corner."

Antonio poured a glass of wine for Kate. She took a sip and looked at Helen warily. "Well, you look as gorgeous as ever, but..." She stared intently at her friend, took another sip of wine, and said, "Okay, love, which door did you run into this time?"

Only Kate would have been able to discern the slight swelling under Helen's left eye and known it for what it was.

"I'll tell you something, Helen. If I were married to him and he hit me just once, I'd –"

"Well, I suppose having had two husbands and searching for a third qualifies you to give me that advice," Helen replied.

"None of them ever beat up on me, none of them hit me so hard I lost half the sight in one eye!"

"Can we change the subject, please?"

"Look, Helen. When you don't catch the brass ring on the first ride, get on another horse."

"That's just not my style, Kate. It's okay for you. It's just not okay for me."

"So, what brought about this little altercation?"

Helen hesitated before answering. She didn't want to discuss it, even with her dearest friend.

"Well, it always starts with his drinking," she said. "He never touches me when he's sober, you know."

"That's the other problem," Kate said.

"I mean, it was an accident. He never abuses me unless he's had too much to drink." There was a long silence between them, and finally Kate said, "Accidentally punched you in the eye."

"No, no. He didn't mean to hurt me. This morning he was terribly upset by what he'd done."

"He was probably upset because he had a hangover. But it's your life. How's my favorite thirteen-year-old?"

"She's doing fine. The only problem is that Frank spoils her rotten. He thinks she can do no wrong, so I'm the only one trying to keep her within bounds. Of course, she hates me for it. Whenever she and I have an argument, she runs to her father, who lets her do whatever she wants.

"Sometimes I feel like I'm the hired maid working for the king and the princess. I hate burdening you with all this, Kate, but I don't know what I'd do if I didn't have your shoulder to cry on. I'm just afraid I'm in a no-win situation where I'm losing my husband *and* my daughter."

Kate started to speak, but Helen interrupted her. "Now it's your turn," she said. "I want to know everything that's going on in your wild, exotic life." Kate seemed equally happy to change the subject and began to describe in graphic detail her affair with the surgeon who had removed her appendix.

"Why do I have this feeling that you're just trying to bait me and that there isn't a word of truth in what you say?" Helen asked.

"Because I shock your puritanical Episcopalian sensibilities, and you are subconsciously jealous of all the fun I'm having. Shall I tell you more about Morton?"

"Morton?" Helen said, covering her smile with her napkin.

"Well, I'm not going to tell you everything, because if I did, you'd dump that creep you're married to and steal Morton from me. He is truly everything a woman could ever want in a man. He makes great money. He's got a neat condo on the East River next to the hospital and a cottage right on the beach in Barbados. He's a wonderful cook and spends most of his time in the operating room. I know I'm right this time."

"Can he carry on a conversation?"

"If you must know, darling, we haven't reached that stage in our relationship."

When lunch was over and the last bit of gossip had been exchanged, Kate eased out of the booth. "Gotta run, dear. I'm meeting Morton at his apartment for a quickie between a gall bladder removal and a thoracotomy."

"You're too much," Helen laughed.

"I love you too, sweet." Kate blew a kiss and was gone.

By the time Helen left the restaurant, it had started to snow. She turned up the collar of her coat as big, fat, lazy flakes quickly covered her shoulders. Ambling home, she couldn't free her mind from Kate's comments about Frank and her own acknowledgment of the deterioration of their marriage. She was certain he was involved with another woman again. But if they divorced, Frank would never consent to giving her sole custody, and she was terrified that she'd lose Jen if it ended up in a court battle. She would just have to do whatever was necessary to keep the family together until Jennifer was older.

Now, as she continued her walk home, Kate's words echoed through her mind. "When you don't catch the brass ring on the first ride. Get on another horse." But I can't do that, Kate, I just can't. You don't understand. Jennifer needs me...or maybe I need her...or maybe we need each other.

The question is, do I need Frank?

CHAPTER TEN

On Monday morning, when Margaux came into Frank's office and flopped down in one of his leather chairs, he told her that he'd tried to call after he left her apartment, and then again several times on Saturday and Sunday.

Margaux smiled, but said nothing.

"Did you go away for the weekend?" he asked.

"Sort of, " she answered.

"Sort of? What the hell does that mean? I want to know where you went and who you —"

"Forget it, Frank. I'm not your wife, remember?" She sat erect, defiant, her eyes focused directly on his own.

He exploded, "I don't believe it! You're out whoring around all weekend and..."

"Don't yell at me, Frank, or I'll get up, walk out of this office, and out of your life."

"I'm not yelling at you, goddamn it!"

"Who are you yelling at then?"

"I'm yelling at you, that's who." Margaux started to leave the office. He blocked the door. She smiled and said, "Do you really want to know how I spent the weekend?"

"Damn right, I do!"

Margaux walked slowly back and sat down in his high-back leather chair.

"Okay," she began, picking up Frank's sterling silver letter opener from his desk and teasing it between her fingers. "Shortly after you left, Carl called. He wanted to take me to Vegas. I turned him down. He got nasty, so I took the phone off the hook for a half-hour. As soon as I put it back on, Ron called and invited me to spend the weekend skiing at Mount Snow in Vermont. I accepted his invitation. We flew up in his private plane on Saturday morning. That's it."

"I want to hear it all," he said, turning his back on her.

She hesitated, and then said, "Okay. We skied all afternoon. We had dinner at a fabulous restaurant perched on top of Hogback Mountain, and then we went to bed and –"

"Shut up!" he hissed.

Margaux got up and walked slowly toward the door. Just before she left his office, she turned and said, "Let me give you a piece of advice, counselor. Never ask a question if you can't handle the answer."

———

The following morning Frank summoned Margaux into his office as soon as she arrived. When she entered, he leaned back in his chair and stared at her. She smiled and said, "Do you love me, Frank?"

He started to speak but changed his mind. Turning in his chair, he sat looking out the window with his back to her. The only sound in the room was the ominous ticking of the grandfather clock that had stood in his father's office for many years. A police siren wailed down on the street twenty-three stories below them.

"Frank," she whispered. He turned back toward her.

She walked slowly toward him. He stood and opened his arms to her. They stood quietly, holding each other without speaking for a long time.

"Yes, Margaux, I love you very much. That's my problem," he whispered. "No matter what you do, I find excuses for it. I'm happy when we are together. I'm miserable when we're apart. How can I prove how much you mean to me?"

"It's very simple, Frank. Marry me."

Frank dropped his hands from her hips and turned away. "You know I can't do that, Margaux. Jennifer's only thirteen years old. I'll do anything else you want. All you have to do is ask. Anything. You know that."

She sat down in the big red leather chair across from his desk and smiled. "Okay, I want you to move me uptown into a decent apartment."

Frank eased back down in his chair and rearranged some papers on his desk. Looking back at Margaux he said, "It's not so easy to find an extra twenty-five or thirty thousand dollars a year for the kind of apartment you want."

"I guess I understand that," Margaux said pensively. "I'll tell you what. Why don't you find an excuse to get out of the house tonight and come by my place where we can relax and have a drink and see if we can't find a way to solve this problem? I do some of my most creative thinking while lying on my back looking up at the ceiling."

"Jesus," he said, shaking his head. "Just the thought of seeing you that way makes me —"

"Makes you what, darling?" Margaux whispered.

"I'll tell you tonight," he said, smiling. "I've got a dinner meeting with the guys from Merrill Lynch and I may not be able to get there until late, okay?"

"I'll be waiting."

———

After throwing the dishes in the washer that evening, she sat at the kitchen table with her pen and yellow legal pad. No matter how she moved the numbers around, a single undeniable fact remained. She needed an increase in annual income of at least $50,000 in order to live in the style she wished.

Frank called her from his meeting to say that it would be after midnight before he could get to her apartment. She could tell that he'd been drinking heavily. She hated his drinking.

When she picked up her pen and pad again, she concluded that there were only two options available to her. Either Frank came through with the money she needed or she'd find a new man, ready, willing, and able to do so. She could easily find someone with greater financial resources, but Frank was a known quantity, she could play him in her sleep, and he had only one serious fault. He could get stupid and nasty when he drank too much.

But she'd been handling stupid, nasty men since she was sixteen years old.

———

When Frank called again to tell her he was on his way, Margaux slipped on the sheer nightgown he liked best. It was one o'clock in the morning by the time he arrived, and he was drunk. He demanded that she make him a scotch.

"You've had enough scotch. I'll make coffee."

"I don't want any goddamn coffee, I want scotch."

"Why don't you go home and see if you can get your loving wife to sober you up? She must be used to it by now."

He went over to the liquor cabinet, which he kept stocked with his favorite drink. She grabbed at his arm when he pulled out the scotch, but he pushed her roughly aside and poured himself a full tumbler.

"Get me some ice, okay?"

Margaux walked slowly into the kitchen. Following her, Frank leaned against the kitchen doorjamb, watching intently as she removed the ice tray and dropped the cubes carefully into the drink he held out. He stirred the drink with two fingers, took a deep swallow, and wiped the dribble from his chin with the back of his hand. Margaux attempted to slip by him into the living room; he grabbed the top of her nightgown and ripped it off her shoulders. She turned to face him, allowing the torn silk to slide down her nude body. Smiling, she took a step towards him, cupping her bare breasts with her hands. She saw the animal hunger in his eyes. She laughed. When Frank clumsily reached out to caress her, she raked the side of his face with her long fingernails.

———

They didn't speak to each other for several days but, finally, Frank asked her to come to his office. "I guess I deserved what I got," he said, touching his cheek where the mark of her fingernails was still evident. "I'm sorry"

"I need more than an apology."

"What can I do to make it up to you?"

When she finished describing her needs and how he could fulfill them, he dropped back in his chair, stunned. "Jesus, Margaux, I can't do that. You're asking me to steal from a client who trusts me, for God's sake!"

"Don't go high and mighty on me, Frank. You've been stealing from your clients for years."

"The hell you say! I've never taken a dime from a client!"

Margaux burst out laughing. "Do you think for a moment that I'd have suggested this plan if I didn't have proof you've been ripping off your corporate clients for years?"

"What proof?" Frank demanded.

Margaux handed him a two-page memo.

"What's this?"

"Well, dear, the first column lists the dates and times you and I have spent together...intimately...during the past two years when we were supposed to be working. I was surprised, myself, when I added them all up in my diary. Would you believe we've spent an average of ten hours a week making love during office hours over the past two years? One-thousand and seventy-three hours to be exact, and that doesn't count nights and weekends. You see, Frank, all this time, I thought you were making a sacrifice for our time together, but I checked our office time records, yours and mine, and then I had the accounting office run off the billing records for those hours, and do you know what I discovered, Frank? You've been charging every hour that you and I've been together to fifteen different corporate clients. Look at the bottom line, Frank, it's pretty impressive."

Frank glanced at the memo warily. "Four hundred and twenty-nine thousand two hundred dollars," he mumbled. "That's impossible!"

"Just mathematics, love," Margaux said. "Two hundred fifty dollars an hour for your time and one hundred fifty dollars an hour for mine. That's four hundred dollars an hour for over one thousand hours...that's grand larceny, Frank, pure and simple. I must be the most expensive lay in the history of the world." She laughed.

"Perhaps I should go over my plan with you one more time, Frank. What do you think?"

He didn't respond. He just sat staring at her. Her silk blouse was low-cut but carefully designed to allow only a provocative glimpse of what lay beneath. The gold chain and diamond-encrusted heart he'd given her after their first night together was nestled at the base of her throat. She caressed her dark sculptured right eyebrow with her fingertips as she concentrated on the notes she'd made outlining her carefully constructed plot.

"I've already formed a Bermuda corporation called International Properties, Ltd. I will personally hold all of the company's stock in an assumed name. My company will borrow two hundred thousand dollars at 8.5 percent interest from the Shauffler Trust Fund, which you now control. I'll pay the interest on the loan, of course, and the money will never be missed. It's peanuts. Mrs. Shauffler's trust fund is now earning over two million dollars a year, and besides, there's no one but you to miss it. I realize you're only acting as an interim trustee until she appoints someone to succeed your father. But my whole plan is based on your being her trustee."

"There's no assurance whatsoever that she'll choose me. We've only met a few times since Dad passed away. I hardly know the lady."

"You must convince her. That's all there is to it."

"I'm telling you straight out, Margaux, no matter what she decides, I'm not going to take a penny from that trust fund that I'm not entitled to."

"Listen to me, Frank. As long as you are the trustee and the interest is being paid, the best auditors in the country would never pick up on it."

"You're not making any sense here, Margaux. At the end of two years, when the money's all gone, then what?"

"We'll just borrow more money from the trust. After all, my Bermuda company will have established an impeccable credit history by that time. Every interest payment will be paid to the trust on the first of the month, just like clockwork. Who wouldn't be willing to make another loan to a reliable company that's paying high interest rates, especially in these days, when prime is so low? We'll just keep rolling the note over until the old lady dies. Since Dunn & Dunn will represent her estate, you'll be able to bury the whole transaction in a footnote in the final accounting, which no one will ever read. And if anyone ever does ask you to explain why you invested in a Bermuda corporation that doesn't have any assets, all you need to say is that you were just following Mrs. Shauffler's instructions."

"Yes, but –"

"Please, lover, listen carefully to me." Margaux put her elbows on Frank's desk and cupped her chin in her hands, looking him straight in the eye. "I'm prepared to live in the shadow of the present Mrs. Frank Dunn until your daughter goes to college, as you've asked me to do. But you must remember that I will be thirty-one years old in June. The next five are the prime years of my life. You tell me I'm a beautiful woman with brains and a body that makes your thinning hair curl. I don't disagree. But you must understand that such a woman commands a price in New York, London, and Paris. I happen to love you, so our arrangement is particularly rewarding. But I got where I am the hard way and I'm entitled to the lifestyle I can command in the international marketplace. I'd rather be Mrs. Frank Dunn than Lady Littlefield or Madame Dubonnet, but if you can't meet my terms now, this little bird is going to fly away."

"But Margaux! Mrs. Shauffler trusts me. You're asking me not only to violate that trust but also to commit a felony. Yes, I love you. Yes, I hope to have you as my wife someday. But you must understand that there's a limit here. I mean, there is no way in hell I'm going to —"

Margaux stood up and started to walk out of the office. "Margaux, wait a minute," Frank said, reaching out to stop her from leaving. She turned back, her dark eyes flashing.

"You know, Frank, I've discovered something really interesting about you. When I'm on my back with my legs spread open, you're a man of tremendous courage. You tell me I am to die for. But when your passion is satisfied, your courage wilts like your cock." As she left Frank's office, she said over her shoulder, "Don't call me, I'll call you."

———

When Frank walked into his office the next morning at 9:35, there was a note in Margaux's unmistakable script propped against his telephone.

Dear Mr. Dunn

I hereby tender my resignation as an associate attorney with the firm of Dunn & Dunn.
I have no regrets.

Very truly yours,
Margaux McBride.

At 9:45, Margaux was summoned to Frank's office. By 10:30, Frank agreed that if Mrs. Shauffler appointed him as her permanent trustee, he would find the money to buy Margaux a condo uptown, one way or another.

CHAPTER ELEVEN

An elderly woman wearing a stylish mink coat walked cautiously up to the reception desk of the law offices of Dunn & Dunn, located in midtown Manhattan on the twenty-third floor of the Wickersham Building.

"I'm Katrina Shauffler," she said. "I have an appointment with Mr. Dunn at 9:30."

The receptionist assured Mrs. Shauffler that Mr. Dunn was eager to see her, and that as soon as he disconnected from his present phone call she would let him know she had arrived.

Katrina Shauffler relaxed in the comfortable antique chair and looked around the waiting room. It was quite changed from Michael Dunn's day. Oriental carpets covered the parquet mahogany floor, and the chairs and settees were upholstered in white and gold silk brocade. It had lost its homey feel.

Irving and Katrina Shauffler had been clients of Frank's father, Michael Dunn, for over fifty years, and Katrina was apprehensive about her first meeting with his son Frank. Waiting for him to arrive she spied a table lamp that she recognized. It had been in Michael Dunn's waiting room in his second-floor walk-up office on Flatbush Avenue in Brooklyn, when she first met him.

How long ago had that been? Oh, so very long ago, she sighed. That lamp must be a genuine antique by now, just like me.

Ordinarily, Frank's secretary would escort his clients back to his private office, but as soon as he learned that Mrs. Shauffler had arrived, he personally hurried out to the waiting room to greet her.

"Good morning, Mrs. Shauffler. I've been looking forward to

your visit." Frank Dunn grasped her hand between both of his.

"Good morning, Frank. I was just reminiscing about when I first met your father. It's amazing how much your voice sounds like his when he was your age."

Mrs. Shauffler stood up to be escorted back to Frank's office. When she was seated comfortably there, she said, "You know, Frank, your father was not only my lawyer, he was my financial advisor as well. When my husband died, I appointed Michael trustee of the Shauffler trust fund, and under his supervision the value of the trust fund has grown tenfold. But much more than that, your father was my friend and confidante. I trusted him implicitly in every way. "

"I know, Mrs. Shauffler. Dad spoke of you often and with great affection."

"Now that Michael's gone, I know I have to choose a new trustee and a new executor of my will, but I've kept putting it off. I just don't know how I can ever replace your father. He took care of everything for me."

Frank's heart was beating so loudly, he was certain Mrs. Shauffler could hear it across the room. He'd rehearsed this conversation in his mind a hundred times.

"I assumed that you might wish to discuss that with me, and I've thought about it quite a bit, Mrs. Shauffler. I thought perhaps —"

"Excuse me, Frank, before we begin, I wonder if I might have a cup of tea. Your father kept my special brand of tea here just for me," she stated proudly. "Ask Mrs. Haverstock about it. I'm sure she'll know."

"Exactly right," Frank smiled. He left the office and stepped quickly down to Mrs. Haverstock's cubicle.

Alma Haverstock had been Michael Dunn's personal secretary since graduating from high school over fifty years ago. Before his death, the senior Dunn had decreed that Alma would continue working for the firm on her own terms for as long as she wished. Although she was over seventy years old, she still came to the office three mornings each week and was beloved by all the staff. Not only did she know Mrs. Shauffler's brand of tea, she had all of the ingredients ready and waiting when Frank came to her office.

"Hello, Alma," Mrs. Shauffler said, as Mrs. Haverstock performed the ritual tea service. "It looks as if you are taking as good care of Frank as you did his father. Do you remember the first time Irving and I came to your old office in Brooklyn? It was up over a jewelry store, if I remember correctly."

"You are correct, Katrina. Abdulky's jewelry store on Flatbush Avenue. How are you?"

"Other than going blind and slowly falling to pieces, I'm just fine, thank you," she chuckled.

After Mrs. Haverstock had left, Frank said, "As I was saying, I've given the matter of your trust a great deal of thought —"

"Let me interrupt you again please, Frank. I am quite certain what I wish to do. Before I came here today, I had already decided to appoint the First National Bank as trustee, but the tea changed my mind."

"The tea?"

"Yes, the tea — and Alma, of course. Now I know I mustn't appoint the bank. I must appoint you. You must be my trustee, Frank."

"Well, I'm...I'm...very pleased, Mrs. Shauffler," Frank stammered. "But the tea?"

"No bank would understand about the tea. But you and Alma did. You're just like your father, and that's what I need so desperately. Someone I can trust completely. As I said, I can hardly see anymore. I read with a magnifying glass, one word at a time. I was dependent upon your father for everything. I didn't have to lift a finger. Of course, my needs are very modest. I own my brownstone, and my sister Sarah has been my only companion ever since Irving died. But I know very little about the administration of my financial affairs, and what's more, I don't want to know."

"I would consider it a privilege to take up where Dad left off."

"Oh, I'm sure that between you and Alma it will work out just fine." She hesitated and then continued. "I met your lovely wife and child at your father's funeral. Such a handsome family you have. Irving and I desperately wanted to have children, but we were not so fortunate.

"Well. I think I've had enough lawyering for today, Frank. I'll be back on Monday morning to sign the papers appointing you trustee, and then I want to discuss a few changes in my will."

Frank stood when she did and took her elbow to walk her across the room.

"Actually, Mrs. Shauffler, I have a young lawyer in my office I'd like you to meet on Monday. She'll work with you on the changes you wish to make in your will, but of course, I will personally review everything and supervise the signing of the will."

"That sounds perfect. I know how busy you are, and I'd be pleased to have your associate help me put my scattered thoughts into the proper form." Mrs. Shauffler's smile suggested total satisfaction with the way the meeting had gone. "Could you have someone call a taxi for me, and perhaps one of your secretaries could walk down to the lobby with me?"

"I'll call the cab right now and will personally see that you are safely on your way."

———

By four o'clock that afternoon, two hundred thousand dollars had been withdrawn from the Shauffler Trust Fund and deposited in the account of International Properties, Ltd., Margaux's Bermuda paper shell corporation.

CHAPTER TWELVE

"Good evening, Mr. Dunn."

"Hello, Gregory, how's it going?"

"Fine, thank you, sir. Go right on up. She told me she was expecting you."

The tall, handsomely uniformed doorman pressed the button under his desk unlocking the massive brass entranceway door to Margaux's new condominium complex overlooking the Hudson River. Frank hurried over to the bank of elevators. He stepped out on the seventh floor and walked quickly down the hall to 7C. Slipping the gold-plated key with his initials engraved on it into the lock, he entered Margaux's new condo.

She turned as he came into the living room, and Frank caught his breath at the sight of her. She was wearing a sleeveless black velvet gown with a gold choker and a slim gold chain around her waist. Her black hair was in carefully arranged disarray; the large single-diamond ring Frank had given her sparkled on the fourth finger of her left hand. As he walked across the deep-pile carpet, she smiled and raised her martini glass in salute.

He stood for a moment admiring her. Whatever it takes, he thought, whatever the cost, I'll never give her up. When she put down her drink and came into his arms, he buried his face in her luxurious hair and whispered, "I love you, Margaux, too much, too much."

"May it always be so," she said softly, and then led him into the dining room. The table was beautifully set with burning candles and a bottle of Chardonnay nestled in a silver wine bucket. Margaux went to the sideboard and poured a martini, dropped in an onion, and handed it to him.

"To us," he said, raising his glass.

"To us," she replied, touching her glass lightly against his. She continued looking into his eyes over the rim of her glass while Nat King Cole crooned, *"Are you warm, are you real, Mona Lisa, or are you a cold and lonely, lovely piece of art?"*

She disappeared into the kitchen and returned shortly with two plates of escargots and a basket of hot rolls. They began to eat in comfortable, intimate silence.

"The best part is dipping the roll in the hot butter and juice," he said, wiping his plate clean.

Margaux brought out a sizzling porterhouse steak for two, asparagus with hollandaise sauce and fresh mushroom caps. They finished up with apple pie ã la mode.

"You are absolutely amazing. It must have taken you hours to prepare all this," Frank said, admiringly.

"As long as you enjoyed it, it was worth all the time I spent." In fact, everything she'd served had been delivered to her apartment by Smith & Wolenski's Steak House, and all she'd had to do was slip the plates into the microwave.

Frank leaned contentedly back in his chair and said, "Not only is she a first-class lawyer and a spectacular lover, but she can cook as well. Wonders never cease. How come you never shared this talent with me before? Where did you learn to cook?"

"If I can read Williston on contracts, I can certainly read a cookbook."

After they stacked the dishes in the washer, Frank poured them each a brandy and they settled down on the overstuffed white leather sofa.

"I think I've never been happier in my life," he said, "I don't want it to end, ever." He reached over to caress her, but she pushed him gently away.

"Not now, not yet," she laughed. "You promised that tonight you'd go over the changes I have made in Katrina Shauffler's will."

"That can wait until tomorrow," he said, trying to prevent her from leaving the couch.

"You promised."

"Okay, I give up. Let's get it over with."

She handed him two documents, Mrs. Shauffler's fifty-six page will and a handwritten brief entitled *Master Plan.*

"First," she said, "Mrs. Shauffler is over eighty years old. Second, our new lifestyle, to which we have both become happily accustomed, thanks to Mrs. Shauffler's generosity, is costing every penny our wonderful arrangement has produced."

Frank winced at the reminder that he had already stolen two-hundred thousand dollars from Mrs. Shauffler's trust fund. But how sweet it is, he thought, as he looked around the lovely apartment. His eyes came to rest on the beautiful woman kneeling in front of him with her ripe young breasts exposed to his view. He became aroused and began to caress her. Margaux stopped him and said sweetly, "You have a choice, Frank. You can sit quietly and listen to what I have to say and when I am finished we can go into my bedroom and I will fuck your brains out, or you can sit here and play with yourself. What'll it be?" She stood up, her face flushed.

Margaux walked over to the floor-to-ceiling window and looked out at the sparkling city below her. Neither of them spoke for several minutes, and then she sat down across from him and picked up the handwritten memorandum she had prepared. "Mrs. Shauffler probably has less than a year to live."

Frank's interest in what Margaux was saying perked up at the thought of the fee he'd be entitled to as the executor of Mrs. Shauffler's estate. Five percent of twenty-five million dollars equaled...one million two hundred fifty thousand dollars.

"How do you know that?" he asked.

"When I was browsing through some of her personal documents while I was working on her will I saw a copy of her H & P report."

"What's that?"

"History and physical report. Before surgery, a physician must determine whether or not the patient is capable of undergoing the stress of surgery. In Mrs. Shauffler's case, it turns out that she's suffering from end-stage renal failure, hypertension, and gout, of all things. She also has a history of bronchitis, pneumonia, and s.o.b."

"Son-of-a-bitch?" Frank smirked.

"No, dummy; shortness of breath. The bottom line is that she was admitted to the hospital last month because she's had multiple hemodialysis access procedures and she was suffering from an arteriovenus fistula obstruction in her upper arm."

"Hold it. Where the hell did you learn all that medical stuff?"

"Just part of doing my homework, darling. The point is that statistically, someone in Mrs. Shauffler's condition can pop off any time. The U.S. Renal Data System Report of 2003, relating to the annual adjusted death rates for patients at risk with a medical condition like Mrs. Shauffler's, indicates that 13 percent die within one year and 50 percent die within five years."

"So she could live more than five years."

"Theoretically, but don't forget, Mrs. S. is eighty-four years old. Logic dictates that she'd be among the 13 percent to die within the year, and do you know what that means, Frank?"

"Sure, I'll earn a fee of over a million dollars as her executor," he laughed.

Margaux's demeanor changed like quick silver. Her voice became hard and edgy.

"Maybe that's what it means to you, but let me tell you what it means to us. The old lady has decided to end the trust and give the whole shebang outright to some stupid charities."

"What!"

"That's right, Frank. If it isn't already obvious to you, this means that on her death, your 'bonus baby,' Margaux McBride, won't be able to pay the mortgage on our little love nest. No more candlelight dinners, no king-size boudoir to go with the king-size bed and Margaux's king-size lover."

"Jesus, I didn't know she decided to terminate the trust."

"Well, she has, and I haven't been able to talk her out of it, although God knows I've tried." Margaux stood up and started to pace back and forth.

"Mrs. Shauffler has always kept her will in your office safe, right? So here's what happens. Tomorrow, I'll wait in the office until all the staff has gone home, and then I'll prepare a different page fifty-four of the will on your secretary's computer."

"What do you mean, *different?*"

"Instead of giving the proceeds outright to her favorite charities on her death as she intends, the will must provide that the charities don't get the principal of the trust fund until after *your* death, leaving the income from the trust to you during your lifetime perhaps as many as twenty-five glorious years, lived with your one and only love. The charities will eventually receive the principal of the trust fund, just as she wants, but not until after you die."

"You're crazy, absolutely mad."

"It's the only way, Frank. And it's so simple. Mrs. Shauffler has read every damn word in the copy of the will I gave her. I watched her move her magnifying glass along each line on every page. After having spent hours checking every comma, she isn't going to try to read the whole fifty-six page document again when you hand it to her to sign in your office. And, Frank," she sat down across from him, picked up her brandy snifter, took a sip of the golden liquid and looked him straight in the eyes, "with a yield of 8 percent, the income from the trust will be about two million dollars a year for the rest of your life!"

Frank started to speak, changed his mind, got up and ambled over to the Italian marble wet bar tucked in the corner of the living room. He scooped a handful of ice cubes out of the handsome polished brass bucket and threw them into a glass. Margaux came and stood beside him while he poured Chivas up to the brim and reached for the glass. She put her hand quickly over it.

"Patience, darling. When we finish our business here, you can have scotch and pussy, in that order, but not now, not yet."

He tried to push her hand away and pick up the glass. She put both hands on the glass and hissed, "Don't you dare!"

Frank could feel Margaux's hand trembling as she prevented him from raising the glass to his lips. He looked into her defiant flashing eyes and thought about the crime she was asking him to commit. He thought about Jennifer. He thought about what he might do with an income of two million dollars a year, and finally he thought about Margaux's bedroom and her promise of what they would do there. He put the glass down slowly, turned his back on her, and stood looking out at the river below. A large yacht was sailing past on its way down to the harbor. Several couples in evening clothes were dancing on the afterdeck. With two million a year he could own a boat like that. It could be himself and Margaux dancing under Manhattan's stars, maybe on their way to Bermuda, or the Caribbean.

Then he saw himself disgraced, sitting in prison.

Margaux intuitively recognized his turmoil. She stepped closer to him and laid her cool cheek against his. He turned to face her. She kissed him with an exploring tongue and held him so tightly to her body, he could scarcely breathe with the joy of it.

"Say you approve of my plan so that I'll be able to please you however and whenever you wish, forevermore," she whispered.

"What choice do I have?"

Margaux smiled and led him into her darkened bedroom. She lit a candle on each of the nightstands and turned on the stereo, filling the room with the beat of a primitive African drum. She swept a dozen silk pillows off the bed onto the floor beside a silver champagne bucket nestling an open bottle of Dom Perignon in a bed of ice.

As Frank started to quickly undress, she cried, "No! This is my show."

Frank shrugged his shoulders. "As long as I get to perform before the curtain goes down," he said, turning to embrace her.

"Don't touch me!"

"Hey, wait a minute, "

"Just be patient, darling." Reaching up, she loosened his tie. She began to slowly unbutton his shirt, and when the last button was unfastened, she drew her long fingernails across his chest with enough force to break the skin. A few drops of blood oozed from the scratch. She ran her tongue along the red welt until the droplets of blood disappeared. Pulling him down beside her onto the mound of pillows, Margaux slipped the straps of her gown from her shoulders, exposing her full breasts. When he reached up to caress them, she moved nimbly away. "Easy, darling, it's only a game."

"I don't think I like this fucking game."

"Your friend does. Look at him, Frank."

Frank stared down at himself, mesmerized at the sight of his throbbing organ. She swirled her tongue around its engorged magenta tip and cupped his aching testicles in both her hands.

"Jesus, Jesus," he cried, lying back on the pillows and closing his eyes. He felt her cool, soft breasts sliding up over his belly and chest. She brushed his lips with her taut nipples. When he opened his mouth, she immediately withdrew them.

"Not yet." She knelt over him, draping her long velvet skirt over his face like a shroud. She wore no underclothing. The fragrance of gardenias and cinnamon filled his head to bursting. Her triangle of black pubic curls caressed his cheek and came to rest on his lips. "Kiss me there, now," she commanded. He buried his face in her curls, thrusting his tongue deep into the soft petals of her sex, and then she slipped down his body and mounted him, riding him in a frenzy. As he arched his body to meet each of her demands, he became oblivious to everything but the need to consummate the act. When she reached her point of no return, she took a handful of ice from the silver bucket and crushed it between his legs. "NOW...NOW...NOW!"

Because of Mrs. Shauffler's sight impairment, which made it difficult for her to come to Margaux's office, Margaux offered to hold their conferences at Mrs. Shauffler's home. The Shauffler assets consisted of diverse stocks, bonds, mortgages, and real estate, about which Mrs. Shauffler had very little knowledge and very little interest, but she looked forward to her regular meetings with Margaux. They'd begun exchanging pieces of information about their lives, and their time together took on a social as well as a professional tone. Once, after Margaux left following a three-hour session, Katrina's sister, Sarah, said, "It's none of my business, I suppose, Katrina, but do you realize that it is costing you one hundred fifty dollars an hour to listen to Margaux's stories about how she grew up?"

"I enjoy chatting with her more than watching television, which I can't see anyway. So?"

"So nothing," Sarah replied sharply. "It's your money, and you should spend it as you wish. I only mention it because you've asked me to take care of all your personal accounts, and I just received a bill today from the law firm. They've charged you over two thousand dollars for the time Margaux has spent gabbing with you here, and more than three thousand dollars for the work she's supposed to have done for you at her office. And they have the nerve to charge you for her cab fare, besides."

"I can certainly afford it, and besides, I am quite taken by the child. She was an orphan, you know. Her mother was killed in a motorcycle accident when Margaux was only two, and she doesn't even know who her father is. Despite those handicaps, she graduated first in her class at law school. And look at this." Katrina handed Sarah an ornate birthday card inscribed, "To the mother I wish I'd had. Love, Margaux."

"Maybe I'm wrong, but I just don't trust her." Sarah shrugged her shoulders.

"Could it be you are just jealous of the time I spend with her?"

"Maybe," Sarah replied thoughtfully.

Katrina reached over and took Sarah's hand. "Oh, my dear Sarah. You must know I am only teasing you. I am so grateful to you for keeping track of all my bills and seeing that they get paid on time. It's just that I have so much money and so little time left. I don't really care what she's charging me. She has made the unpleasant task of redoing my will an interesting challenge; I've been motivated to think more carefully about how to leave my trust funds. Originally I was just going to continue the trust the way it is, but lately I've been thinking I should just give it outright to four of my favorite projects.

"And by the way, I've decided to give most of it to the Irving Shauffler School. I've enjoyed sitting on its board of directors, and it seems the right thing to do." Her face broke into a smile. "You should meet Lucas Alexander, Sarah, a new board member and a bit of a rogue, I think, but an absolutely charming one. He told me he'd been a trial lawyer for many years, but that he gave it up to teach law at Columbia. I asked him if he knew Margaux. He said he didn't, but when I told him she was very bright and very beautiful, he said he always thought that was an exciting but dangerous combination. Then I asked him if he thought I was a dangerous old lady."

"Katrina! You didn't!"

"Indeed I did, and he said he thought I was," Katrina laughed. "Of course, I know the reason I was selected to sit on the board is not because of my brains or my beauty. It's my money. But I enjoy the meetings very much, and Lucas is such a flirt. I'm telling you, Sarah, if I were forty years younger..."

"So now the truth comes out."

CHAPTER THIRTEEN

After everyone had left the office, on the evening before Mrs. Shauffler was scheduled to sign her will, Margaux lingered on, stating her need to catch up on paperwork. The document had been placed on the center of Alma's desk blotter, with red ribbons laced through the top waiting to be sealed with wax, once it was signed.

Margaux accessed the will in Alma's computer. When she began to type in the new page, overriding the termination of the trust and directing that Frank Dunn receive the income from it during his lifetime, another thought struck her like a sledgehammer.

What happens to Margaux if Frank gets killed in an accident before the old lady dies?

After several minutes of experimenting, she found that if she adjusted the margins, she could add a few more words and still easily fit everything on the page. She typed in the following: "In the event that Frank Dunn shall die before me, I give the income from my trust to Margaux McBride during her natural life."

She printed out the new page fifty-four, removed the ribbon and the old page, and substituted her new page. Reinserting the ribbon through the top of the will, she returned it to the exact place on Alma's desk where she'd found it.

Margaux had scheduled Mrs. Shauffler's will-signing ceremony for nine o'clock, the precise time when Alma arrived at work, so that Alma would not have time to review the will before it was presented for Mrs. Shauffler's signature. When Frank and his secretary, Miss Green, arrived, Margaux and Alma were already seated around the conference table. Frank placed the voluminous document in front of Mrs. Shauffler and began the legal liturgy.

"Do you swear that you have read this, your last will and testament, and that it accurately reflects your wishes?"

"I so swear," she replied solemnly.

"Please initial each page in the lower left hand corner and then sign your name at the end."

Katrina began the arduous task, with Frank turning the pages for her, allowing only the bottom portion of each page to be seen. When she reached the last few pages she hesitated, put down her pen and sighed audibly. Margaux's heart rate accelerated, and Frank stopped breathing. Mrs. Shauffler looked up at him, smiled and said, "Are you charging me by the page or by the pound for this will?" Everyone laughed appreciatively. She picked up the pen and continued initialing each page, finally signing her name at the end with a flourish. They all applauded.

"Would you like to have Alma and Miss Green act as your witnesses?" Frank asked dutifully.

"Yes, thank you. I'm so pleased to have this done and over with."

At Frank's direction Mrs. Shauffler pressed her signet ring into the warm, blood-red sealing wax, thereby signing and sealing her last will and testament. Frank brought out a bottle of sherry and glasses from an antique cabinet in the conference room. He poured wine into each glass and raised a toast to long life, and the dirty deed was done.

CHAPTER FOURTEEN

Once again Frank invited Margaux to accompany him on an extra-long weekend. This time, she accepted. Frank told Helen he had to go out of town on business for a few days, but promised he'd be back in time to celebrate their fifteenth wedding anniversary.

Helen had been secretly working for weeks on "Operation Seduction," the goal being to reinvent herself by the date of their anniversary. While Frank was away, from Friday to Tuesday, she would put the finishing touches on her plan and surprise him on his return.

As soon as he left, she let Jennifer in on her project, and sought her help in deciding how she might go about creating her new image. Surprisingly, Jennifer was enthusiastic about being involved, and together they spent hours searching through *Vogue* and *Elle* and dozens of other women's magazines, looking for the perfect hairstyle and color and the perfect outfit for the grand occasion.

They finally decided on a feather cut with just a few blonde highlights on the tips, and Helen chose the most exclusive salon in the city, arranging for the transformation to occur on the afternoon of their anniversary. The salon receptionist told her she'd be sitting in Kim Bassinger's favorite cubicle and that Julie Andrews might be there on the same day.

She went shopping and chose a red velvet dress with a plunging neckline, something more daring than anything she'd ever worn.

It was their fifteenth anniversary, after all.

Frank and Margaux were seated in the lounge of the Admirals Club at JFK when the departure of Flight 679 to Aruba was announced. As they left New York, the temperature was thirty-four degrees on a cold, blustery, end-of-March day. A few hours later they landed in bright sunshine, on the tiny Caribbean island located fourteen miles off the coast of Venezuela, and by mid-afternoon they were sitting on the terrace of their casita, nestled among a stand of stately palms beside a picture-postcard white sand beach. After a long silence, Frank looked over at her. Her eyes were closed, and her winter pallor had already begun to disappear. A few grains of sand sparkled on her cheeks like flecks of gold. Her long, tight black curls, still wet from the sea, framed her delicate features.

She opened one eye, looked up at him, and smiled. "I'm so happy," she said, "except..."

"Except what?"

"Except I want you to make love to me and I'm too lazy to get out of this chair," she laughed.

"Problem solved." Frank pulled her up from the lounge and led her in to their casita.

Just before they fell asleep, with arms and legs entangled and the smell of the sea and the tropics surrounding them, he whispered, "I will kill anyone who tries to take you from me."

She answered softly, "That won't be necessary, darling. Just make me Mrs. Dunn."

The fact that Frank and Helen would be celebrating their fifteenth wedding anniversary hours after he and Margaux returned from their Aruba tryst flashed briefly through his mind. But it disappeared in seconds, like the light of a firefly on a warm summer night.

When Helen arrived home from the salon, she found a message on the answering machine from Frank. "I just got back in town. I haven't forgotten our anniversary dinner, but I'll be spending the day down on Wall Street. Take a cab and I'll meet you at Le Cirque at eight o'clock."

"Wow! Mom, you look like a movie star!" Jennifer got up from the sofa when Helen emerged from her bedroom. "Dad won't even recognize you, you look so cool."

Helen arrived at the restaurant at 7:45. A few male heads turned as the maître d' led her to the table she and Frank reserved each year. Helen blushed happily when she realized that one of the men was staring at her partially exposed breasts. She knew she looked ten years younger. When she was seated, she ordered a vodka martini up, with a twist of lime, and settled back to anxiously await Frank's arrival. She had a second martini at 8:45. Frank finally arrived at 9:30 and slipped quickly into the chair opposite Helen.

"Sorry I'm late, I had an important business meeting and I couldn't get away." He looked closely at her and said, "What the hell have you done to your hair? And what's with the eye shadow and that dress? Jesus, Helen..."

She couldn't hold back the tears. The mascara ran down each cheek, and she feared she would throw up on the table.

CHAPTER FIFTEEN

Frank had asked his secretary, Carolyn Green, to track down his daughter.

"She's on the line, Mr. Dunn," she said.

He smiled and picked up the phone. "Hey, Pumpkin, where are you?"

"I'm at Suzy's. We're doing a social studies project. What do you know about Henry Ford?"

"He invented the airplane, right?"

"Dad, you are sooo corny. What are you calling me for? I'm really busy."

"Oh, nothing much, I just thought you and Suzy might like to fly up to Killington with me for the weekend. They're reporting eight inches of powder on hard pack."

"Oh my God! Do you mean it, for real? I mean, when? Hey Suze, you're not going to believe this!"

"I'll pick you guys up after school on Friday. We'll charter a small plane and be there in time for a night run."

"You is my man, Pops."

The four-passenger Cessna landed at the airport in Vermont, just as the sun dipped below the mountain. Frank helped the pilot unload their gear, and twenty minutes later they reached the cabin Frank had rented for the weekend. They decided to skip the night run in favor of going to bed early and getting up at dawn to beat the morning rush to the lift.

The girls had both graduated from the bunny slope the year before and were exhilarated, not only by the skiing adventure, but by the attention they were receiving from a group of freshman boys from the Putnam School. After the biting-cold gray days in the city, the cobalt blue skies and Disney-perfect snow scene transformed them into fantasy world princesses. At the end of the day, trudging up to the lodge for hot chocolate, Jennifer slipped her arm through Frank's and leaned her head against his shoulder. He responded by kissing the top of her glistening blond curls. Their eyes connected for a brief moment.

"I love you, Pops," she said, and then ran ahead to catch up with Suzy, who was only halfheartedly ignoring a couple of the Putnam School boys.

Both girls were tall and attractive in opposite ways. Jennifer was slim, blue-eyed, and graceful like the professional dancer she hoped to become. Suzy was dark haired, with wide black eyes and an athlete's body that had matured early. Neither of them chose to walk in the shadows, and they held their own among the beautiful people gathering at the lodge for the après-ski ritual. Frank's eyes misted as he watched his lovely daughter and her friend merge with the crowd of exuberant young skiers.

And then he saw her. She was squeezed in beside an incredibly handsome young man at a tiny table in the corner. Frank felt a razor-sharp, gut-wrenching spasm of jealousy. He hoped the guy was gay.

Margaux had spied him long before he saw her. She continued to chat amiably with the man she'd selected from among the several who'd offered to buy her a drink, and when she was certain Frank was headed her way, she laughed gaily and let her fingertips drift along the young man's shoulder. Frank grabbed an empty chair and brought it with him to their table.

"Sorry, this table is barely big enough for two," the young man said.

"Oh, hi, Frank. This is my friend Brett. He's an instructor at Aspen. He says he's here on a busman's holiday."

"What kind of bus does he drive?" Frank growled. "I've made dinner reservations for you and me and the girls for 7:30." He glanced at his watch. "I was hoping we might have a drink together before then."

"I have a ways to go on the one I've got," she said, holding up her almost-full drink. "And I've got to get changed and all. Why don't you spend some time with your girls, and I'll meet you at the restaurant?"

"As a matter of fact, I've spent the last twenty-four hours with the girls, and I must say I'm ready for some adult entertainment."

"There's a triple x-rated channel on TV, I could recommend," the other man suggested.

———

On their way to the restaurant, Frank said, "Guess what. While you two were flirting with those kids from Putnam, I ran into Margaux from my office. I invited her to join us for dinner. Apparently, her boyfriend pooped out on her for some reason, and she's sort of stranded up here. You know her, right, Jen?"

"Yeah, I met her a couple of times," Jennifer said without enthusiasm.

But by the time desserts were served, Margaux had completely captivated both girls. She knew as much about Leonardo DiCaprio as they did, and they were astounded by her knowledge of the music and musicians they idolized, though Frank didn't have a clue concerning the celebrities they were discussing. When the three ladies excused themselves to freshen up in the ladies lounge, he ordered a double scotch on the rocks and tried to sort the whole thing out.

Was it possible Jen could accept Margaux as a...as a what? Helen and Jen had never been able to carry on a conversation like the one he'd just heard between Margaux and the girls. All Jen and her mother ever did was argue. Maybe his take on the damage a divorce would cause his relationship with Jen was wrong, maybe...

His thoughts were interrupted by the return of his three "girls." He couldn't believe his eyes. They looked like sisters. Margaux had apparently shared her makeup kit and her expertise with the youngsters, who both now looked like young starlets. His amazement was so obvious that Suzy started to giggle, and soon the three females became hysterical with laughter.

The next day they all skied together, but Margaux spent most of the time with the girls. When it was time to leave, Jen asked Frank if there was any reason Margaux couldn't fly back with them, since there was an extra seat on the plane. Given that that had been his plan all along, Frank said, "Why not?"

On the way back to the cabin to pack up, Frank overheard a whispered conversation between Jen and Suzy.

"When I get old, I want to look just like Margaux," Suzy said.

"Fat chance, Suze," Jennifer replied.

———

Just before falling asleep in the car on the drive home from the airport, Jennifer put her arms briefly around Frank's neck. "It was fab, Pops, the best time we've had together...ever."

CHAPTER SIXTEEN

Following Helen's disastrous attempt to seduce her husband and hopefully to find new meaning in their marriage, she went into an emotional freefall. She didn't know where to turn. Ultimately, she accepted the fact that her marriage was not salvageable and that all she had to hold on to was her work at the kennel and her relationship with Jennifer. But that, too, seemed to revert to its old antagonisms after she and her father returned from their skiing holiday in Vermont. They appeared to be closer than ever, while Helen felt rejected by both of them.

On a Friday in early May Frank went on a fishing weekend with a group of men from his club — or at least that's what he said, though Helen suspected otherwise. But it didn't matter to her any longer.

Ordinarily, on a weekday, she'd leave the kennel in time to be home with Jennifer after school, but Jennifer was spending the night at Suzy's apartment. Helen therefore decided to give her employees the afternoon off and to close up the kennel herself. She was heading toward the front door to lock up when a man entered, leading a beautiful golden retriever. Helen was upset with him for coming in just before closing on a Friday night, but the sight of the beautiful animal softened her displeasure and she asked, "Hi, what can I do for you?"

"How about letting me leave my friend here for a few days?"

"That might be possible," Helen said. "Is this your first time with us?"

"Yes, but if things go well, it won't be our last." He looked at her and shrugged. "The truth of the matter is, yesterday the judge awarded my wife title to our home and all the furnishings. She allowed me to keep my six-year-old Chevy pickup and our dog, Regina." He'd told the cabbie the same thing. For whatever reason, he felt compelled to tell everyone who crossed his path.

Helen began to fill out the registration form. "Your name please?"

"My credit card says Chester Bartlett but everyone except my mother calls me Chet." He held out his hand.

"Helen Dunn." She took his hand. It was firm and felt nice to the touch. She studied him more closely as he reached down and petted the dog. He was wearing khaki trousers, a windbreaker and worn work boots. He had strong masculine features with close-cropped steel gray hair. She guessed that he was in his late forties.

"So what's the scoop on Regina?" The dog looked up when Helen spoke her name, as if she were expected to join in the conversation.

"I'm going away on business for about a week, and under my new living arrangements I don't have anyone to care for Regina while I'm gone. I don't imagine it's an unusual circumstance, but I was quite unprepared for it, actually."

"I think we can handle that. I'll put her in one of our deluxe corner suites with a spectacular view of a handsome Russian wolfhound."

"Sounds perfect. I'll be back to pick her up next Friday before 5:00. My plane gets into Kennedy at 4:05, so it shouldn't be a problem."

Chester Bartlett was staring at her, as if he wanted to say something.

"Is there a problem, Mr. Bartlett?"

"No, no, it's just..." He couldn't stop looking at her. "Actually, I was wondering if you might consider..." Whatever he meant to say, he got cold feet and mumbled something else incoherently.

"Excuse me?"

"I do believe I'm in a no-win situation here. If I tell you the truth...No, I can't do that...I think my best bet is to offer a small fib."

"Now, of course, I'll never know one way or the other, but I've lived all my life amidst a multitude of little white lies, so why don't you tell me a real whopper?"

"Perhaps I best save that until I see you next week. By that time I should have a little more courage.."

"Sounds intriguing. Don't forget to pick up Regina before 5:00."

"That's a date." Chet waved goodbye and hurried out of the office.

Helen felt a totally irrational heat in her abdomen. If she weren't married and the mother of a teenage daughter, she might be tempted to suggest that Chet pick her up as well as his dog, next Friday. She smiled and told herself to get a grip. She wasn't sure she still had a husband, but she did still have a daughter to protect.

Nonetheless, driving home her thoughts returned to Chester Bartlett.

Could Kate have been right? Was it time to move on? Of course, she really didn't know anything about this Chet guy, except that he...he what? Face it old girl, she laughed to herself. He turned you on a little, didn't he? Next Friday he'd be coming back to pick up his dog, and unless she'd totally misread him today, he might just ask her out for a drink. So would she say, "Mr. Bartlett, I have a husband and a thirteen-year-old daughter – but maybe just for fun? Maybe for just one drink"?

———

On Monday she changed her schedule so that she would not come in on Friday and would therefore avoid temptation, if, by chance, temptation was offered.

On Friday afternoon she sat at home trying not to think about Chet Bartlett. She glanced at her watch. It was 4:25 PM. If she left immediately, she might just make it to the kennel by 5:00. She grabbed her jacket and raced down to the parking garage for her car. When she arrived at the kennel a few minutes before 5:00, her manager was just closing up shop.

"Hi, Mrs. Dunn, what are you doing here?"

"I was out this way visiting a friend and thought I'd stop by and see how things are going." When she checked on the run where Regina had been placed, it was empty.

"Johnny, where's Regina, the golden retriever?"

"Mr. Bartlett came and got her a little while ago. He asked where you were and I told him you weren't coming in today. He said he wanted to leave Regina again next week, too, and pick her up the following Friday afternoon. Do you want me to hang around and help you close up tonight?"

"No, I'll take care of it. See you Monday." Helen quickly

turned away to hide her disappointment. She busied herself around the kennel for an hour and then headed home.

By mid-afternoon on the following Friday, she found herself constantly glancing at the clock and the front door. At 5:15 as she passed by Regina's pen to lock up, she said, "It looks like he'd abandoned both of us, Regina." By 5:45 she'd finished up everything she could think of that might delay her departure, and a few minutes later she left the kennel and headed for her car. It serves you right, she told herself as she slid behind the wheel.

As she started to drive out of the parking lot, a taxi turned into the driveway and blocked her passage. Chet Bartlett jumped out of the cab, threw a handful of bills at the driver and raced over to Helen's car waving his arms. She leaned on her horn and put the car in gear.

"No, no, no, don't leave, please don't leave."

She braked the car but left the engine running and rolled down her window. "The kennel closes at 5:00 on Friday, as you well know, Mr. Bartlett. You can pick up your dog tomorrow morning."

He bent his large frame down so that his face was on a level with hers. His face was so close to hers she could smell the fragrance of his aftershave lotion, and note a small scar on his chin. She found the wrinkles at the corners of his eyes reassuring and decided he needed a haircut.

"Please. It really isn't my fault. My plane was late and then when I got to the parking lot, my car wouldn't start because someone had stolen my battery. And then what happens? There's an accident on the parkway and we sat there without moving for over half an hour. I'm really sorry that I've kept you waiting."

The thought foolishly crossed Helen's mind that if he sang, he'd be a baritone. She turned off the ignition and got out of her car. He was as tall as Frank, but his shoulders sagged. He looked forlorn and apologetic, but she also noticed he was lean, with a flat belly and a firm butt in tight, faded jeans. Her disappointment quickly dissipated. In fact, she felt wonderful.

Unlocking the kennel door she asked, "Do you mind telling me how you're planning to pick up your dog if you don't have a car?"

"I didn't go through all this just to pick up my dog, for God's sake."

"So?"

"I was thinking that if you were here today I was going

to… that we might talk and get to know each other better and…you know…"

Take it slowly, Helen cautioned herself. But then, why should she? *Because I'm married, married, married.* The words reverberated in her mind like a Gregorian chant. "Come on, let's go talk to Regina in her royal suite and let her know that you are alive and well and haven't forgotten her. And then perhaps we can talk."

When the paperwork and payment were completed Chet said, "Despite what appears to be my scatter-brained personality, I wondered…would you have a drink with me?"

Helen smiled. "Maybe. But first you must understand that I'm a married woman with a teenage daughter at home and I can't have more than one drink."

"Deal."

"Where do you suggest we go for this drink?"

"Well, you're not going to believe this, but I swear to you it's true. I called an old buddy of mine who lives in Queens. I explained the problem to him and —"

"What problem?"

"The problem of where I might take you for a drink the next time I saw you…if you allowed me to do so," he stammered.

"Oh," she said softly.

"So, I asked my buddy if he knew a place I could take you. Incredibly enough, a couple of days ago he faxed me the list he'd compiled through careful research, along with a detailed bill for eight scotch and sodas. With tips he managed to spend over fifty dollars on this research, but I now possess an invaluable guide for the best and worst places to drink alcohol within ten miles of the Dunnrover Kennel."

"After all that, can you tell me where we're going?"

"It's called Matilda's."

"I don't believe it. That's my favorite bar. Okay, lead, follow or get out of the way," she said as she checked the door to make certain everything was secure.

"Ordinarily I'd consider that a challenge, but given the fact we're in your territory and I don't have my truck, ma'am, I'd be right honored to follow your lead."

Patting Regina's head and promising to return for her soon, they left the kennel.

Chet seemed to like Matilda's as much as she did, and without prompting, he ordered them two vodka gimlets, one of her favorite drinks. Their conversation was easy, spontaneous and exciting for her. She hadn't been in the company of an unattached man in a bar since she'd been married, a little over fifteen years ago.

But why was she doing this? she wondered. Because Frank hadn't looked at her with this kind of hunger in his eyes since before Jen was born, that's why. For that matter, Frank never seemed this anxious to please, or so sensitive, so...she must be crazy. This just wasn't right, she was a married woman and...she looked at her watch and discovered it was almost 8:00 PM.

"Oh God," she moaned, grabbing her purse and jumping up from the table. "Can you get a cab okay? I've got to go. My daughter's home waiting for me, and —"

"Sure, go ahead. I'll be fine. I'll pick up Regina, tomorrow."

"Bye. Thanks for the drink." She tossed him a smile as she raced out the door.

———

When she arrived back at the apartment, Jennifer was watching television.

"Hi, hon. Have you finished your homework already? You know the rule. No television until your homework's done."

"I'm hungry. Where have you been?"

"At the kennel. What about your homework?"

"Daddy agrees it's a dumb rule. He says I don't have to." Jennifer continued to stare at the large screen.

"Did you tell him you're failing algebra?"

"Get off my back, okay? Ask him if you don't believe me."

"I don't want to fight with you Jen I just want..."

"Yeah, I know, you just want what's best for me." She got up and sauntered down the hall to her bedroom, slamming the door behind her.

CHAPTER SEVENTEEN

When Chet called her at the kennel to arrange another Friday meeting for a drink and dinner, she refused. It was obvious to her where the relationship was headed and although the experience with him had been exhilarating, and the prospect of becoming intimate with him had been on her mind since they'd parted, she couldn't take the risk. It wasn't her marriage that was stopping her, she admitted to herself; it was Jennifer. She'd lost Frank, and she wasn't going to take the chance of losing Jennifer, too.

She told Chet that she'd thoroughly enjoyed their time together and if things were different she'd love to explore his offer of friendship, but that he needed to understand that she felt a tremendous responsibility for Jennifer's well-being, for her happiness. Chet pleaded with her to meet with him so they could discuss it face to face, but she knew that if she saw him again, she might not have the strength, or the will, to reject the relationship he offered.

As days turned into weeks, however, she continued thinking about him. She couldn't seem to bury the memory of their brief meeting. But she tried not to let her fantasies overrule her judgment. Nonetheless, one night when Frank had again failed to come home for dinner, she called Chet at home. She had no idea what she would say to him if he answered the phone, and she was both disappointed and relieved when she got his answering machine. She called back several times just to hear his voice on the machine.

A few days later when she arrived at the kennel, she discovered they were boarding Regina again. Chet was scheduled to pick her up on Friday afternoon. All through the week she agonized about what she should do. Her heart and her body were screaming to renew a relationship with Chet, while her mind and her sense of responsibility were demanding that she cancel him out of her life.

Friday morning, Jennifer announced she'd be going home with Suzy after school and that she was planning to spend the weekend with her. Helen would be alone until Frank came home... or didn't come home, as was often the case. At the last minute she decided to go to the kennel, meet Chet, and let the chips fall where they may. She grabbed her coat and raced down to the garage. When the car wouldn't start she realized she'd left the headlights on when she'd last parked it and that the battery was dead. She ran out to First Avenue to compete for a cab. Fortunately, one stopped on the corner to discharge a passenger, and Helen jumped into the back seat. "Dunnrover Kennel," she told the driver. "Next door to LaGuardia Airport."

He refused. He said it would take over an hour, maybe more, to get there, and then he would have to hang in line out there for another hour to get a fare back to the city.

"Please. I'll pay you double."

"I wouldn't go if you paid me triple or quadruple. I've been hustling since seven o'clock this morning and I'm headed home for dinner. If you was just going somewhere nearby I'd help you out, but LaGuardia? Forget it."

She got out of the cab and fought the urge to sit down on the curb and cry.

When she returned to the apartment, she was shocked to see Jennifer slouched down in front of the television set.

"How come you aren't at Suzy's?"

"Her grandmother died. They all went to Chicago," Jennifer said without looking up from the television screen. "What's for dinner?"

Helen's stomach clenched, realizing that if she'd met up with Chet and had not come home until late, Jennifer would have been left alone all evening with no dinner and no way to reach her mother or father.

"I don't know, I guess I don't much feel like cooking just for the two of us. How about a pizza?"

"Whatever."

Helen went to the phone and called the Neapolitan Pizza Parlor.

Joey Pesci had learned the key trick from a kid he met in the Elmira Correctional Facility. As soon as he was released he told his buddy Tango about it, and they decided to give it a try. Joey applied for a job as a delivery boy for the Neapolitan Pizza Parlor on 3rd Avenue, and within five minutes he was hired and given an order to deliver.

"Dunn, 299 East 72nd street, 8th floor," the manager said. "That's a regular customer, nice lady, good tipper."

Tango was waiting for him outside the shop.

When they arrived at the apartment house, the doorman called up to the Dunn apartment to check out the delivery. Jennifer confirmed it and the doorman took the boys over to the elevator and slipped his key in the penthouse slot.

On the way up, Joey said, "You carry the pizza and if there's a handbag on the table by the front door, like the kid at Elmira says there is, nine times out of ten, I'll grab the keys out of it." Joey handed the pizza box to Tango. "And remember, you gotta carry the box back into the kitchen, you gotta get the lady away from the doorway so I have time to look for them, understand?"

"Yeah, yeah," Tango answered. "You told me this shit a hundred times already."

The elevator door opened into a hallway that served only the Dunn penthouse. Joey slipped into the emergency exit stairwell.

"Here's your pizza, miss," Tango said, taking a few steps into the vestibule when Jennifer opened the door. When she reached out to accept the pizza box, Tango held it up and said, "It's really hot. I'll take it right into the kitchen for you. Which way?"

Leaving the front door ajar, Tango followed Jennifer down the hall toward the kitchen. Joey eased the door open, stepped inside, and quickly grabbed a set of keys out of the purse lying, as predicted, on the marble-top table in the foyer.

"Thank you, young man," Helen said as Tango carried the pizza over to the kitchen counter.

"My pleasure." Tango gave her his most engaging smile.

"How much do I owe you?"

"Twelve ninety-five."

Helen handed Tango sixteen dollars.

"Thank you very much, ma'am." Tango turned and began to walk slowly towards the front door. Jennifer was following him out, but when the telephone rang, she turned back to answer it.

As Tango traveled alone through the living room he spied a gold cigarette lighter on one of the end tables. He slipped it into his pocket and joined Joey in the hallway.

When the elevator door closed, Joey beamed. "I got 'em!" he said, flashing the keys for Tango to see.

"Right on, man!" Tango slapped him a high-five and flipped the lighter to him, as well.

CHAPTER EIGHTEEN

Mrs. Shauffler's medical condition began to worsen within a few months of signing her will. Her sister Sarah had taken over all of the household duties and was in touch with Frank on a regular basis with respect to Katrina's financial affairs. In early June, she notified Frank that Mrs. Shauffler was in intensive care, and that she'd asked that he call the physician who was treating her. Frank dialed the number she'd given him.

Dr. Braunstein took Frank's call and advised him that Katrina had had a massive heart attack. Her prognosis was not encouraging, and she wanted to see Frank as soon as possible.

When Frank entered her spacious private room, he was shocked at how frail and vulnerable she appeared.

"Frank?" she spoke, barely above a whisper.

"Yes, Mrs. Shauffler. Dr. Braunstein said you wanted to see me."

"I do. Please come closer. It's very difficult for me to speak." Frank took one of her withered hands in both of his.

"I just wanted you to assure me that everything will be taken care of for Sarah."

Frank squeezed her hand affectionately and said, "Of course, don't you worry about that. You know you can trust me to take care of everything."

"You and Margaux have been wonderful to me. And Frank, in the top drawer of the dresser over there, you'll find a little ring box wrapped in gold paper. Please give it to Margaux with my love." She closed her eyes. Frank placed her hand gently back on the bed.

When he left the hospital he was in turmoil. Initially, his only interest in Katrina had been as a wealthy client. The fee he received as trustee of the Irving Shauffler trust amounted to hundreds of thousands of dollars. But as they'd become better acquainted over the many hours the administration of the trust had required, his respect and affection for her had increased significantly. She was a genuinely kind and generous woman who derived immense pleasure from observing firsthand the positive impact of her charitable gifts, especially to the Shauffler School for disadvantaged adolescents.

What in God's name am I doing? he asked as he walked slowly back toward his office. He'd just made a commitment to that decent woman on her deathbed, for God's sake. He couldn't do this...this obscene thing Margaux was asking of him. He wouldn't do it!

He recalled the last time he'd visited his father in the same hospital where Mrs. Shauffler lay dying.

"Looks like you're going to have to uphold the good name of Dunn all by yourself, Frank," his father had said.

"I'll do my best, Pop, I promise."

"I know you will, son. I know you will."

The words kept racing through his mind, I promise...I know you will...I promise...I promise.

It was after seven o'clock by the time Frank let himself back into his deserted office. He called Margaux several times but she didn't answer. He left a message on her machine to call him at the office as soon as she could. He called again at eight o'clock but there was still no answer. He decided to leave a note that she would see first thing in the morning. It took him another hour to write the few words.

My Dearest,
I cannot approve the plan. It is impossible.
I beg you to understand.
Please meet me first thing in the morning
so we can put things back the way they should be.
        I love you...Frank

P.S. The gold box is a gift to you from Katrina.

He put the note in a heavy brown envelope, taped and stapled it closed, marked it Personal, and placed it on Margaux's desk along with the ring box.

———

By the time Frank returned to the office later in the morning, Margaux had cleared out. Every trace of her was gone. She'd left no message for him.

He went directly to the safe to retrieve Mrs. Shauffler's original will, so that he could change it back and carry out her wishes. The will was gone.

He dialed Margaux at home, only to discover that she had acquired a new, unlisted number. He drove to her apartment house.

"Good afternoon, Mr. Dunn."

"Hello, Gregory." The doorman stood imposingly in front of the entrance door. Frank waited for him to open it. He didn't offer to do so. There were a few moments of embarrassed silence.

"I'm here to see Margaux, Gregory," Frank said, taking a step forward.

"I'm sorry, sir, she left me instructions that she didn't want to be disturbed. She specifically mentioned your name, Mr. Dunn. I'm sorry."

"Sure, that's okay. Just buzz me through to her on the intercom."

The doorman shifted to the other foot and said, "She won't take no calls either, Mr. Dunn. She specifically told me that if you —"

"Fuck her!" Frank hissed. He marched out of the foyer more determined than ever to make things right for Mrs. Shauffler, but he realized that he must retrieve her will from Margaux and correct it before Katrina died. If anyone ever discovered that he'd participated in altering the will, he'd be disbarred and criminally prosecuted. A will that is prepared by an attorney who ends up being the beneficiary of millions of dollars is highly suspect on its face, and any one of the charities would have legal standing to challenge the will. But if he acted quickly, while Mrs. Shauffler was still mentally competent, she could make a new will, even though Frank would have to explain why a new one was necessary and, in doing so, be required to admit his participation in the fraud against her. He knew Mrs. Shauffler was a forgiving lady, but under the circumstances she'd be crazy to trust him to prepare a new will. "I really want to do the right thing," he said aloud, "but..."

He did nothing. A week passed with no word from Margaux, and then he received a call from a lawyer he detested.

"Hello, Louis, what's up?" Frank said.

"Not much, Frank. I just want to ask you about a young lawyer who's looking for a job. She gave me your name as a reference. Her name's Margaux McBride. "

Frank's stomach plummeted. "Is she there?"

"Yeah, she's out in the waiting room."

"May I talk to her, please?" Frank could feel his heart thumping in his chest.

"Eleanor, tell Miss McBride to pick up on line four in the conference room."

"Hello."

Frank sucked in his breath at the sound of her voice. "Margaux, it's Frank."

"Hello, Mr. Dunn. Did you give me a good recommendation?"

"Margaux, what the hell are you —"

"I think I'd best hang up, Mr. Dunn."

"No, no, Margaux, I'm sorry. You know how I hate Louis and I've been trying desperately to reach you —"

"Mr. Cardamone seems like a very nice man. He has offered me a lot more money than you were paying me, and I just want you to tell him how highly you regard my legal skills."

"I want you back, Margaux."

"I'm afraid that's impossible."

"No, it's not. All we need to do is sit down together and work it out."

"There's nothing to work out, Mr. Dunn. As you know, I have certain financial obligations and —"

"But, Margaux —"

"Goodbye, Mr. Dunn."

"No, please, Margaux, I miss you terribly...I love you and..."

"I'm sorry, Mr. Dunn, Mr. Cardamone is waiting for me. I understand you have to do what you have to do...but...so do I."

"Listen to me, Margaux. I —"

"Shall I put Mr. Cardamone back on the line?"

"No, Margaux, wait...please...I give up."

"What does that mean, exactly, Mr. Dunn?"

"Bring back the will, Margaux. We'll leave it the way it is. I want us to be together, the way we were. That's all that matters to me."

"I'll come to your office tomorrow. Perhaps we can talk about it."

"Look, Margaux, I want to see you right away, I —"

The line went dead.

———

When she entered his office the next day she closed the door quietly behind her and leaned back against it. She was wearing a conservative dark blue linen jacket and skirt, with a filmy light blue silk blouse. Her legs were bare. She waited for him to come to her. He ached to hold her, and when he took her in his arms he was consumed with incredible joy. Her fragrance filled his head with the need to possess her.

"Margaux, I —"

"Shush." She took his hand and placed it first on her heart so he could feel its racing beat and then guided it down below her belly.

"Oh God," he moaned. She locked the door and opened herself to him.

———

It was just past ten o'clock when he arrived home. He went straight to the kitchen.

Helen was waiting up for him. She caught her breath when she heard the ice cubes dropping into the glass. Please, God, not tonight, she thought. Getting up, she walked cautiously into the kitchen. Frank had already filled his glass to the brim with scotch.

"Can I make you something to eat?"

"No, I had dinner with a client. Is Jen still up?"

"She's spending the night at Suzy's. Which reminds me. Suzy has invited her to go with her and her parents to their cabin in Maine the last week in July. They'd leave on Thursday, the 24th, and come back a week or so later. I told her I'd check with you."

"Sure, why not?" Frank carried his drink into the living room and turned on the TV.

"I was wondering if maybe you and I could visit my parents for a few days while she's gone. I haven't seen them in over a year, and Dad will be seventy on the 30th."

"I can't get away, but you should go. Stay a month, if you like."

"Oh no, I'd want to be back for Jen, but I'll call them tonight. It's only 7:30 there."

The next morning Helen went to the pastry shop around the corner and picked up freshly baked danish. When she returned to the apartment, Frank was drinking his coffee and reading the *Wall Street Journal*. Neither of them spoke as she went into the kitchen to prepare breakfast. She heard the TV blaring in Jennifer's room. After setting the table, pouring the juice, cutting the fruit, and putting the cereal, milk, and pastries out on the table, she called, "Okay, everyone, soup's on."

Frank moved to the table still reading his paper, without saying a word. He held out his cup and Helen fetched the pot and refilled his coffee. Jennifer wandered into the room carrying a hairbrush. Still in her pajamas, she sat down at the table and automatically held the brush up in the air for her mother to use in brushing and braiding her long blonde hair.

"Well, it's all set," Helen said. "Jen leaves on Friday, the 25th, and I'll fly out that night from LaGuardia at six o'clock. I've arranged to have the master bedroom repainted while I'm away, Frank. I hope you don't mind sleeping in the guest room for a few days."

"I don't care," Frank said, knowing that while Helen was gone, he'd be sleeping with Margaux.

CHAPTER NINETEEN

Helen finished packing and waited for Frank to come home and take her to the airport. When he showed up, she could tell he'd been drinking. He became increasingly angry and frustrated by the bumper-to-bumper gridlock approaching the 59th Street Bridge, but when they finally got off the bridge, the jam-up broke free. "We'll make it," Frank said, weaving in and out of traffic, accelerating and braking, constantly switching lanes to gain a car length or two.

When they arrived at the American Airlines terminal, she grabbed her bag and jumped out of the car. They didn't kiss goodbye.

———

As soon as he returned home, he went directly to the bar and made himself a double scotch. He sat down on the couch and when he reached for the television remote control unit, the phone rang.

"Hello," he answered.

"Darling—"

"Where are you?"

" I'm sorry, honey, I —"

"Where the hell have you been?"

"I got tied up in traffic but I'll be over by 9:30 at the latest, I promise."

"I'll leave the door unlocked for you."

"Yes, love."

He hung up the phone, took off his shirt and trousers, and stumbled toward the bedroom.

CHAPTER TWENTY

Detective Pat Turner had been attempting to arrange a meeting with Margaux for a period of several weeks, without success. She thought Margaux was stonewalling her. Pat needed to complete her interview with Margaux before the briefing Lieutenant Garvey had scheduled for the end of the week. Finally they found a mutually agreeable time to meet at Margaux's home, and Pat invited Ken to come along.

When they entered Margaux's apartment, Pat and Ken were awestruck by its magnificence. Although Margaux was wearing blue jeans and an oversized University of Chicago sweatshirt, Ken decided she was the most spectacularly beautiful woman he'd ever seen. Pat, too, was startled by the beauty of the woman, her tangled mass of black curls, penetrating dark eyes and ivory complexion, her engaging smile and husky voice. Even the way she moved her hands exuded sensuality.

When everyone was settled and coffee had been provided, Margaux said, "Now, how can I help you?"

She directed her question to Ken, but Pat answered, "I'm Sergeant Pat Turner, the chief investigator in the Dunn case. Mr. Wolcott is my associate."

"I'm sorry, Sergeant. I'm ashamed to admit that I just assumed...I hate it when that happens to me," Margaux said.

Pat smiled. "It's no big deal." She opened her notebook.

After twenty minutes of routine questioning relating to Margaux's background, the other attorneys and staff members at the Dunn office, and the nature of Frank's law practice, Pat asked, "Is it fair to say that a time came when you began to enjoy a personal as well as a professional relationship with Mr. Dunn?"

"I suppose that depends on what you mean by personal, and what you mean by relationship."

"Let me put it this way. Were you and Mr. Dunn...intimate friends?"

Margaux opened the cigarette box on the coffee table and took out a cigarette. Tapping it on the back of her hand, she lit it, inhaled deeply and, tilting her head back slightly, blew a thin stream of smoke into the air. Then she turned her head slowly and looked Pat straight in the eye. "I considered myself to be one of Mr. Dunn's closest friends."

"How close?"

Ken felt a trickle of perspiration slide down from his armpit. He leaned forward in his chair almost imperceptibly as Margaux started to speak. She hesitated, shifted her gaze to Ken and said softly, "Very close." She smiled as if she were sharing a special secret with him.

"Mr. Dunn's death must have been very painful for you," Pat said.

"That's true." Margaux's smile vanished.

Pat glanced at her notebook. The words, *confirm phone conversation shortly before victim's death*, were underlined. She took a sip of coffee and then asked casually, "I wonder if you could tell us, when was the last time you spoke with Mr. Dunn prior to his death?"

"Let me think." Margaux closed her eyes. "It's been a while now, and I really haven't thought about that. I know we worked together on the Worthington case on the Friday morning before his death."

"Did you have a chance to speak with Mr. Dunn on the telephone after Friday morning?" Pat observed a slight twitch of Margaux's left eye as she appeared to ponder the question.

"Yes, I spoke with him on the phone that evening. I agreed to stop over to his apartment."

"Did you know that his wife had left town to visit her parents in Dallas?"

"Yes, I knew that."

"How would you characterize your relationship with Mr. Dunn's wife?"

"Cordial, friendly, I would say."

"Wasn't that a little awkward?"

"For whom?" Margaux replied. Ken swallowed a chuckle.

"Well...I guess that's not germane here."

"I agree," Margaux quickly responded.

They sat in awkward silence for a few moments as Pat flipped through her notebook.

Ken glanced at Margaux, who appeared at ease and unconcerned about the direction Pat's questions were taking. She smiled at him shyly, crossed her legs, and leaned forward slightly causing her oversized sweatshirt to slide off her shoulder. A vision of the swell of her breast beneath his own fingertips flashed disturbingly through Ken's mind, and he flushed when she caught him staring at the provocative patch of bare skin. Margaux's covey of gold bracelets jangled like a wind chime as she raised her arm, slipping the bulky shirt back into place.

The sound startled Pat, who looked up from her book. "Did you go to Mr. Dunn's apartment that night?"

"I did, but when I got there, no one answered the door." Margaux hesitated and then asked, "Just for the record, Sergeant, since you haven't advised me of my constitutional rights, may I assume I'm not an object of your investigation?"

"That's a delicate issue, Ms. McBride. At this point I would have to say that everyone who knew Frank Dunn is an object of our investigation, but to avoid any misunderstanding, perhaps I should ..." Pat withdrew a printed card from her briefcase and started to read the Miranda warning aloud.

Margaux interrupted "You don't have to continue. I'm familiar with Miranda, Sergeant. I just wanted to know where I stand, that's all. I realize that anything I say may be used against me." She glanced over at Ken. "However, I am perfectly willing to continue our discussion provided that you give me a copy of your report of this interview so that if I disagree with your interpretation of whatever I've said, I'll have an opportunity to note my objection while our conversation is fresh in all our minds."

Pat nodded. "I can do better than that. I'll give you a copy of the tape."

Pat opened her briefcase and removed a tape recorder.

"Okay, from the top. Frank and I were lovers. I went to his apartment on the night he died. How's that? Can you tell me, please, how much longer you think this will continue? I have a date in an hour, and I'm sure my dinner companion would be disappointed if I showed up in this outfit." Ken thought that he wouldn't care what she was wearing if she were going to dinner with him.

"We're almost finished here, but I hope you'll give us a chance to chat with you again as our investigation progresses," Pat said.

"No problem."

"Had you made arrangements to meet with Mr. Dunn the

night he was killed?" The words of the taped conversation between Dunn and Margaux were ringing in Pat's ears.

"Sort of." Margaux lit another cigarette. "It had been a very tough week. Once I got home from the office, I really didn't want to go back out again, but I'd promised Frank I'd come by. So I showered and changed and took a cab over to his place."

"About what time did you get to Mr. Dunn's apartment?"

"I'm not sure, but I'd say it was somewhere around ten o'clock." Margaux got up from the couch and opened the drapes that spanned the floor-to-ceiling window wall. The lights had come on and the view of the city was breathtaking.

Ken was having difficulty concentrating on Margaux as a murder suspect. It wasn't only the husky timbre of her voice, it was everything about her – the tilt of her head as she pondered each question, her habit of constantly pushing up the sleeves of her sweatshirt, the delicacy of the line of her throat, the jumble of curls that occasionally fell over her eye, and the way she nudged them back into place with her fingertips. When she turned away from the window to face them again, she looked directly at Ken and smiled, as if she knew exactly what he'd been thinking.

"I don't believe the doorman knew me. I'd only visited Frank and Helen a few times at their apartment. I told him I was expected, and he called up to Frank's apartment, but there wasn't any answer. He walked me over to the elevator and activated it so I could access Frank's penthouse, and I went up in the elevator alone. I rang the bell and waited, but there was no answer. I know I rang the bell several more times and then put my ear to the door."

Pat wondered if the partial fingerprint on the doorbell was Margaux's.

Margaux closed her eyes, seemingly to concentrate on what she was saying. Choosing each word carefully, she said, "I thought I heard the television, so I knocked on the door loudly, but there was still no response. I rattled the doorknob. The door was locked. I rang the bell a final time and then returned to the lobby. It was a lovely evening, so I decided to walk home. On the way, I stopped at a little restaurant that I'd never noticed before. I had a drink and ate dinner alone there. I am sure the waiter will remember me because I forgot my credit card, and I literally counted out the change I had in my purse to pay for the meal," she laughed.

"Is it possible that you arrived at Mr. Dunn's apartment before ten o'clock?"

"I don't think so, but I suppose it's possible."

Pat closed her notebook and stared directly at Margaux, who had settled back down on the couch across from her. "Ms. McBride, isn't it true you went to Mr. Dunn's apartment to do what lovers do? When you got there, you found that he was drunk, you got into an argument, he became abusive and you..."

Margaux recognized that an interviewing process, designed to obtain information, had just turned into an interrogation in which Pat was seeking incriminating admissions. She stood up quickly, her eyes flashing. "That's enough, Sergeant Turner, this meeting is over!"

Pat picked up the tape recorder, dropped it in her briefcase, and snapped the locks on the case.

"I want a copy of that tape," Margaux said.

"I'll send you one, as I promised. We'll be in touch." Pat stood up and headed to the door.

Ken followed her out of the apartment and they rode down in the elevator in silence. They didn't speak until they were back in Pat's car headed to the station house.

"What do you think?" Ken asked.

"Do I think she is guilty, or do I think we have proof beyond a reasonable doubt that she killed Frank Dunn?"

"Jesus, it's hard for me to think of her allowing herself to be identified by the doorman, shooting her lover in the head five times, and then walking to the restaurant around the corner and having a quiet little dinner all by herself."

"Tell me, Ken, do you think that woman is capable of murder?"

"I don't know, Sarge. I mean it's possible, I suppose. But how does she fit the MOM profile – means, opportunity, and motive?"

———

Three days later Pat received an anonymous letter with words cut from several different magazines and newspapers.

SUGGEST you check

CAR L   STA SSI

Bayonne   regard ing

Frank Dunn   murder

She summoned Ken to her office.

"Make a copy of this and then take it down to forensics. Follow up on it and keep me posted."

"What the hell is it?"

"Probably a kook, but we've solved more than one crime with notes just like this. It's anonymous. It says Carl Stassi killed Frank Dunn. Could be someone with a grudge. Could be for no reason at all, or could be for real. In any event, we can't ignore it."

"Who the devil is Carl Stassi?" Ken asked

"It's your job to find out, kiddo."

———

By the next morning, they had a fix on Carl Stassi.

"So what have you got for me?" Pat asked when Ken slumped down in a chair in her tiny office.

"I was tempted to tell you that with my brilliance and my super sleuthing skills I tracked down Mr. Stassi and that in my considered opinion he's the S.O.B. who killed Frank Dunn. However, since you have insisted that I never attempt to bullshit you, on pain of immediate discharge from the force, I will modify my report slightly." Ken glanced at Pat to see how she was receiving his comic routine. He was encouraged by a slight, guarded smile. "As it turns out, tracking down Mr. Stassi was a piece of cake. He's a scumbag operating across the river in our sister state, more particularly in Bayonne, the jewel of New Jersey."

"Ken, I really don't want to spoil your fun, but I have half a dozen people waiting for me to call them back, I'm preparing my report for Garvey on the Dunn case, it's 2:30 and I'm starving to death. So please move along."

"But did you know that the Honorable Mr. Stassi did time for assault with a deadly weapon and is presently out on parole? And did you know that he's reputed to be a lieutenant in the Romano Family? And did you happen to remember that your good friend Margaux McBride, alias Maggie Doyle, was born and brought up in Bayonne, and according to the local chief of police, McBride hung around with Stassi when she was a teenager, and —"

"Hold it right there, buster. Are you telling me there is a connection between Black Beauty and this Bayonne piece of garbage?"

"I do believe I've gained the attention of my esteemed —"

"Is McBride involved somehow with this sleaze?"

"It appears that way, Sergeant."

CHAPTER TWENTY-ONE

After Frank's death, Jack Whiting became the senior partner in the Dunn Law firm and quickly discovered how important Margaux was to its ongoing success. Having worked exclusively for and with Frank, she had intimate knowledge of all of his pending matters, and she had ingratiated herself with all his clients to the extent that he feared that if she left the firm, those clients might switch their business to whatever law firm she joined. The anticipated loss of annual gross income from these clients, if Margaux left amounted to several million dollars. Margaux told him she was prepared to offer herself and her client base to the highest bidder, provided it included a partnership interest. Although she never had any intention of joining his office, Margaux used Louis Cardamone as the bait to motivate Jack Whiting to give her a draw of two hundred thousand dollars per year and to change the name of the partnership to Dunn, Whiting, and McBride. The new partnership agreement was consummated three weeks after Frank's death.

When Margaux returned home from the office on the day the new brass letters changing the name of the law firm were installed on the solid mahogany office doors, she went straight to the bar to prepare a celebratory drink. She threw a handful of ice cubes into the shaker, added the vodka and a whisper of vermouth. She poured the contents into a martini glass, popped one cocktail onion into her mouth and two into the drink. She turned on the news and gaped at the screen when the commentator announced that Katrina Shauffler, the founder of the Irving Shauffler School, had died.

She gulped down the remains of the martini, and went back to the kitchen to mix another.

On her arrival at the office on Monday morning there was a message for her to call Mrs. Sarah Nusbaum, Katrina Shauffler's younger sister.

"Mrs. Nusbaum, I was just about to call you. I'm so sorry. Katrina and I had become very close friends. I'll miss her dearly."

"Yes, Katrina was very fond of you. So now we must talk about the estate business. What am I supposed to do?"

"I will prepare the petition for you to sign in order to probate Katrina's will and have you appointed as executor."

"Then I shall wait to hear from you, Miss McBride."

Margaux sat back in her chair and gazed out over the city. It was a bright, clear day in Manhattan.

For over fifty years, Alma Haverstock had been the manager of the Dunn law office. She realized she had no place to go and nothing to do after Frank's father died. Michael Dunn and the law office had consumed her life.

Shortly before Frank was murdered, when she was seventy-eight-years old, she learned that a malignant and inoperable lung tumor had metastasized to her brain. She resigned from the firm, cleaned out her desk that harbored a thousand secret joys and tragedies, and placed a sign on it that said, *Gone Fishing.*

Within hours of Alma's departure from the law office, Margaux had accessed the draft copies of Mrs. Shauffler's will stored in Alma's computer, and had deleted all traces of them. She fed all of the paper copies on file into the shredder. When the task was completed, the only document remaining was the will Mrs. Shauffler had signed giving Margaux life use of her twenty-five million dollar trust fund.

Two weeks later, as Alma was leaving her doctor's office following her regular chemotherapy treatment, her purse slipped out of her hand. When she bent over to retrieve it, the blood coursing through her brain burst through the wall of her left cerebral artery.

CHAPTER TWENTY-TWO

Sarah Nusbaum sat alone at the large, exquisite, mahogany table in the conference room waiting for Jack Whiting, the new senior partner of Dunn, Whiting, and McBride. Margaux had arranged the meeting and requested that Jack supervise the reading of the will.

After introductions, Jack Whiting said, "May I offer you some tea, Mrs. Nusbaum?"

She nodded affirmatively.

Once tea was poured he said, "Let me do the honors," and picked up the large, thick white envelope labeled Last Will and Testament of Katrina Shauffler. The envelope was sealed with a dollop of bright red wax. Jack Whiting took a moment to explain to those present that it was Michael Dunn's custom to give his special clients a signet ring, and then he showed the imprint of Mrs. Shauffler's ring in the wax.

Carefully slitting open the envelope he removed the will. A single red ribbon was laced through each of its fifty-six pages. The ends of the ribbon were tied and they too were sealed with red wax. Mrs. Shauffler's signet ring was imprinted clearly in that wax as well.

"My goodness," Jack said as he lifted the weighty document. He took a moment to glance briefly at the first few pages. "Let me first just read to you the specific bequests." There were over two pages of gifts to distant relatives, friends, and tradespeople, and then there was a gift of Mrs. Shauffler's brownstone residence to Sarah Nusbaum, with the funds necessary to maintain it and support Sarah during her lifetime.

Jack Whiting glanced over at Sarah, who sat stoically. "The next pages are what we lawyers call boilerplate, describing the duties and obligations of the trustee, and then there are the gifts to the charities." Jack began to recite the archaic language of the will.

"'I hereby give, devise and bequeath all the rest, residue, and remainder of my property in trust for the benefit of the following named charitable organizations: New York Symphony, 10 percent; New York Hospital, 10 percent; Columbia University, 10 percent; Irving Shauffler School, 70 percent.'

"So that's the sum and substance of it." He was about to put down the will when his eye caught the phrase, "subject to." He read the next few sentences to himself and then looked over at Margaux, who sat quietly. She seemed detached from what was taking place, immersed in private thoughts.

"Mrs. Nusbaum, I thought I'd read to you all the pertinent provisions of the will, but I've just now seen a condition of the trust which is…" Jack Whiting faltered as he searched for words to describe the impact of what he'd just read. "I must read to you the exact words.

"'The trust created herein is subject to a life use of the income of said trust, which I hereby grant unto my attorney and friend, Frank Dunn. In the event that Frank Dunn shall die before me, I give the income from said trust to Margaux McBride during her natural life.'"

Margaux exclaimed, "Oh my God!"

Sarah Nusbaum glanced at Margaux. "What does that mean, Mr. Whiting?"

Jack coughed nervously and reread the terms of the will to himself before he laid down the document, took out his handkerchief, and cleaned his glasses. Putting his glasses back on, he picked up the will, read the clause a final time to himself, and then turned to Sarah Nusbaum.

"The meaning is clear and unequivocal. It is the sequence of events that have occurred since Mrs. Shauffler signed the will that may be disquieting. The bottom line here is that during her lifetime, Margaux is entitled to all of the income from the trust. When Margaux dies, the principal of the trust will be divided equally between the four charitable organizations I identified earlier."

"That was not Katrina's wish," Sarah hissed. "Sequence of events, what do you mean by that?"

"I mean Frank's untimely death." Jack Whiting turned to Margaux. "Were you aware of this provision in the will, Margaux?"

"Absolutely not about the gift to me."

"But you brought the will to our home, and I heard you tell Katrina you had personally prepared it. I heard that with my own ears!"

"That's true, Mrs. Nusbaum. I did prepare the draft will, but I never knew what was in the final document, which Mr. Dunn prepared, until this very moment." Margaux hesitated. "As you know, Mrs. Nusbaum, Katrina was very fond of Frank, and during the time that I worked with her we became close friends, as well. I mean, she gave me this ring, which you must remember, Mrs. Nusbaum. I wear it every day and treasure it. But I had no idea that —"

Jack Whiting interrupted her. "What you're saying here, Margaux, is that you participated in the preparation of the first drafts of the will but that you had no knowledge of the provisions of the will which Mrs. Shauffler actually signed, the one that I've just read to you?"

"That's right, Jack. I had no idea that Katrina intended to make Frank or me a beneficiary of her estate. In retrospect, of course, I can understand why she didn't discuss it with me, but —"

"I can assure you, Miss McBride, Katrina never intended to make you a beneficiary of her will."

"To be fair, Mrs. Nusbaum," Jack Whiting interjected, "none of us will ever really know what your sister intended. Perhaps Mrs. Shauffler just didn't wish to discuss this with you."

"That's not possible," Sarah Nusbaum spit out the words. "We were sisters. We were as close as any two human beings can ever be. We had no secrets, we shared with each other absolutely everything about our lives. So I tell you there is something wrong here. There is something very wrong." Her wrinkled hands began to tremble. "Aren't there supposed to be witnesses to the will?"

"Oh, indeed. Every will must have at least two witnesses. Here, beneath Mrs. Shauffler's signature, you see the signatures of two witnesses: Alma Haverstock and Frank's secretary, Miss Green."

"Then what about the witnesses?" Sarah asked.

"Alma Haverstock has been with this law firm for over fifty years, and I am sure she would have been able to shed some light on the matter. In fact, she actually typed this will," Jack Whiting said, looking at the outside envelope. "Look here in the lower left hand corner of the envelope. You see the initials 'AH'."

"Well then, we must talk to this Mrs. Haverstock right away."

"Unfortunately, Alma has had some kind of a stroke and is hospitalized."

"How about the secretary, Miss Green?"

"I'm sure she will be helpful and will be able to fill us in on the details, but she is on vacation, and isn't due back until the week after next."

"Mr. Whiting, as I understand it, Katrina appointed Mr. Dunn and me co-executors of her will, isn't that true? So I am now the only executor of this will, aren't I?" Sarah asked.

"Yes, that's right."

"Then please give me the will, Mr. Whiting. I believe I will leave."

"Under the circumstances, I don't think I can do that, Mrs. Nusbaum. There are too many unanswered questions here."

"You have no right to keep it!"

"Well, as attorneys for the estate we — "

"Who says you are the attorneys for the estate? Who hired you? Doesn't the executor hire the attorneys for the estate?"

"Yes, of course, that's true. I just assumed that — "

"Don't assume anything, Mr. Whiting. Ordinarily, I would have engaged the services of your firm, but not now. You may send your bill for this conference, but consider your services terminated as of this moment. Now, may I have the will, please?" Sarah Nusbaum reached for the document.

Jack Whiting slid it away from her. "Just a minute, Mrs. Nusbaum. You have every right to hire whichever law firm you wish to represent the estate, but Mrs. Shauffler put this will into our hands for safekeeping, and I intend to abide by that until I'm directed by a court to deliver it to the appropriate party." Jack saw a million dollar fee slipping through his fingers and made a final effort to placate Mrs. Nusbaum. "Why don't we all sleep on this and meet again tomorrow morning, when we've had a chance to think things through and determine how we should proceed? I'll have photocopies made for all of you and then return the will to our safe. I suggest we adjourn this meeting until ten o'clock tomorrow morning."

As the elevator doors closed behind her, Sarah whispered to herself, "I will not let her get away with it. I will not let that whore get your money, Katrina."

When she reached home her old heart was still pumping in overdrive. She must hire another lawyer right away. But who? She didn't know any lawyers outside the Dunn firm. She made a strong cup of tea and settled into her favorite overstuffed chair. Sipping her drink she thought about the many times she and Katrina had sat here in this room, sharing tea and talking over events of the day. Suddenly she remembered Katrina's telling her, in just such a moment, about her friend on the board of directors of the Shauffler School. He was a professor and a lawyer, too.

By mid-afternoon, Sarah had found Professor Lucas Alexander.

CHAPTER TWENTY-THREE

When Lucas Alexander agreed to join the faculty at Columbia Law School, he welcomed the challenge of teaching. But he sorely missed the exhilaration of victory and the agony of defeat he'd experienced for so many years as a courtroom warrior. He also detested his eight o'clock classes.

It had been a long and wearying day when his secretary announced the arrival of his 4:00 PM. appointment. Luke came from behind his desk and ushered Sarah Nusbaum into his office.

"I am Katrina Shauffler's sister."

"Yes, I know. I was so sorry to learn of her passing. She was a lovely woman and I was very fond of her. How can I help you, Mrs. Nusbaum?"

Sarah explained that she was the executor of her sister's estate and that it was being handled by the law firm of Dunn & Dunn. "I need a lawyer. I must have the best there is. Can you help me, Mr. Alexander? Would you be my lawyer?"

Professor Alexander leaned back in his chair and said, "You flatter me, Mrs. Nusbaum, but I'm not practicing law anymore. I've exchanged the courtroom for the classroom."

"I'm sure that since you teach young people how to become lawyers, you can tell me what I must do to make sure the Shauffler School gets the gift my sister wanted it to have. It is worth a great deal of money."

When Sarah had finished telling him the story, she reached in her purse and placed the Xerox copy of the Shauffler will on his desk.

"So help me God, sir, Katrina would never, never have given all that money to either Frank Dunn or that woman. Never!"

Luke Alexander picked up the document and began to read it. When he reached the part of the will relating to the trust and the gift to the school, he read and reread the words. He glanced at the last few pages of the document and placed it gently back on his desk.

"What is the estimated value of the trust, Mrs. Nusbaum?"

"Twenty-five million dollars, maybe more."

Alexander sucked in his breath and scribbled some numbers on a notepad. "Can you imagine," he sighed, "what $17.5 million could do for the Irving Schauffler school? Let me take a look at something. I must say, this whole thing doesn't smell very good to me." He got up from behind his desk and walked to the wall of books at the far end of his office. He pulled a volume down from the shelf, returned to his desk, and leafed slowly through the book. Finally he looked up and said, "The law is just as I remembered it. Nothing has changed. But we must be very careful that we don't throw the baby out with the bathwater."

"The baby with the bathwater?"

"We don't want to declare the whole will void, we just want to cancel the gift to Ms. McBride."

"Then what must we do now?"

"I don't know at this point, Mrs. Nusbaum. When's this meeting with the lawyers at the Dunn firm supposed to take place?"

"Ten o'clock tomorrow morning."

"I will be there with you." He held up his hand as Sarah started to thank him. "I'm not telling you I'll take this case. I'm only telling you that I'll be there tomorrow morning to protect the interests of the school, which happily seem to coincide with your own wishes."

"Do you know where the Dunn law office is?"

"No, but I'll find it. Dunn & Dunn, you say?" Luke opened the phone book on his desk. "On Madison Avenue?"

"That's it. They're both dead, you know."

"I read about Frank Dunn's murder. I don't think they've found the person who did it yet, have they?"

"I know who did it," Sarah said, sitting straight in her chair.
"You what?"

"I think that lawyer Margaux McBride killed him so that she could get all the money. One thing I know for certain is that Katrina never intended to give her money to either one of those two conniving lawyers."

"Well, I guess we should solve one problem at a time," Alexander said. "But I promise I'll be with you tomorrow morning."

———

When Sarah left his office he went to his computer and dialed up Westlaw, intent on finding a case that would allow the court to void the gift to Margaux but keep all the other provisions of the will intact. Immersed in the effort, he became oblivious to everything else around him. Food, drink, and sleep became necessary evils to be tolerated only when his body screamed for attention. By midnight his library table was strewn with copies of the cases he'd read in his search. "It has to be here somewhere," he said aloud. Certainly in recorded judicial history, Ms. McBride can't be the first lawyer to attempt to become a beneficiary of a will, unbeknownst to the benefactor.

By one o'clock in the morning he'd researched cases back to 1920 without success. Weary, despondent, and barely able to keep his eyes open, he was about to admit defeat for the night when his eye caught a footnote from a decision by the surrogate of Kings County. The case was entitled Matter of the Petition of Thomas McGuire to Prove the Last Will and Testament of Christopher Morrissey, Deceased. When Luke finished reading the complete case, his fatigue had disappeared and his mind was as crisp and clear as the decision.

———

At 9:15 on the following morning Sarah received a call from Luke Alexander's secretary telling her that Professor Alexander had postponed the meeting with Jack Whiting and Margaux McBride until 3:00 in the afternoon.

Jack Whiting and Margaux were already seated at the conference table in the law office when the receptionist ushered Sarah and Alexander into the room. Alexander took a seat next to Sarah, opposite Whiting and Margaux. Opening his briefcase he placed a large stack of documents on the table.

"I assume you understand what the situation is here, but just in case you don't, let me describe the problem as I see it," Whiting said.

"No need to do that. I've been briefed pretty well by Mrs. Nusbaum. The issues are clear to me, and I guess we can dispense with the amenities." Luke met each of their eyes. "I don't think we have a problem here at all. First, let me give you a copy of Judge Casey's order regarding possession of Mrs. Shauffler's will." Alexander slid a document across the polished mahogany tabletop to Jack Whiting. "It's pretty simple, Jack, the judge has directed you to deliver the will 'forthwith' to his office, where it will be held pending a hearing on our claim that Frank Dunn and Ms. McBride defrauded Mrs. Shauffler and the charities she designated as beneficiaries in her will."

"Now, just a minute, Alexander —"

"I don't have a problem with that, Jack," Margaux said casually.

"Then I guess the whole problem is solved. Mrs. Nusbaum gets appointed executor, McBride forfeits her life use of the income from the trust, and the Shauffler School and the other charities get their gifts now!"

"No," Margaux said quickly, looking straight at Lucas. "I don't see it quite that way. You have absolutely no proof of fraud. But I'm perfectly willing to discuss how our differences might be resolved."

Sarah looked nervously at Alexander who was listening carefully to what Margaux was saying.

"But Margaux," Whiting interjected, "they're claiming —"

"No, wait, Jack," Alexander interrupted. "I understand perfectly well what our young colleague is saying. She's saying there's enough to go around for all of us, as long as no one gets greedy. She's saying that if she only received, say, half of the income in a settlement agreement with the executor, maybe she'd be satisfied. Have I read your position accurately, Ms. McBride?"

Whiting stared at one and then the other of them, his mouth open.

"You've stated my position eloquently, Mr. Alexander."

"Thank you, Ms. McBride," Alexander said. "And now let me tell you something, young lady. Our position is that you are not entitled to one penny of the Shauffler estate, and unless you're prepared to concede that, you're in for one hell of a legal battle. Is my position clear to you, Ms. McBride?"

Only Alexander noticed the slight twitch in Margaux's left eye as she said, "Absolutely, Mr. Alexander." She went on. "But you see, I don't have to prove anything. The will speaks for itself. Katrina's gift to me is clear and unequivocal. I only want to make certain that her wishes will be carried out."

"Katrina never intended to give you anything. You are a liar and...and..."

"Now, now, Mrs. Nusbaum," Luke said, touching her arm. "Why don't you folks let Ms. McBride and me have a little chat alone to clarify the issues here?"

"I'll die before she gets a cent of Katrina's money. I will spend whatever it takes to make certain that...that..."

"Give me a chance to talk with Ms. McBride, please, Mrs. Nusbaum." Alexander stood and eased Sarah out of her chair.

"Well, you certainly don't need me here." Jack Whiting quickly gathered up his papers. "I think I'll just take that will down to Judge Casey's office. No doubt that's the best place for it."

When everyone had left except Alexander and Margaux, he took off his jacket, put it on the back of his chair and loosened his tie.

"We have some nasty business to talk about," he said, "so we might as well get on with it. I know you aren't serious about running the risk of being indicted for forgery, grand larceny, and fraud for a few pieces of silver, Ms. McBride."

"Number one, I sure am, and number two, it's not a few pieces of silver, as you well know."

"I'll grant you that four or five hundred thousand dollars a year income isn't so easy to give up, but —"

"Try a minimum of two million per year."

"Okay, so two million. It's only money. But disbarment and jail time aren't a piece of cake. It's true that you're an extremely attractive woman, and smart, too. That's obvious. But juries don't like lawyers very much, and they sure don't like lawyers stealing money from schools for disadvantaged kids."

"C'mon, Lucas, your summation is premature. We both know we're just talking bucks here. I can be reasonable, but you must know that I'm not going to walk away from this empty handed. I didn't create the problem except to the extent that I befriended a lonely old woman and she expressed her appreciation in a most generous manner. No one could have anticipated Frank's untimely death. Do we deal or don't we deal?"

"Let me tell you something, counselor. I've made my share of compromises in my life. We all have. Otherwise nothing would ever get done in this world, we'd all just stand up there and get bloodied. But every once in a while a case comes along that doesn't lend itself to compromise."

"You could engineer it. We both know that. If you say it's the fair and right thing to do, everyone will fall in line, including Judge Casey."

"If that's true, it's because they know how highly I value integrity. But the fact is, this whole thing stinks to high heaven. Frank Dunn did a dirty deed, with or without your knowledge, and old Luke ain't about to get his hands dirty for the first time in his career."

"Remember, Lucas, this is all or nothing."

"For you maybe, but not for us, counselor. We both know you're not going to risk your career and jail time over this."

"Come off it, Lucas. You can't prove fraud. Frank Dunn is dead and Mrs. Haverstock might as well be. She's indispensable to your case and she's totally out of it. You're not claiming that the will wasn't signed by Mrs. Shauffler, are you?"

"Ms. McBride, I'll tell you what I'm claiming when I feel like it. One thing's for certain. I'll do everything possible to keep you from stealing money from our school."

"Did I say your school shouldn't have any money? Did you hear me say that? I want your school to have some money. I just don't want Margaux to have no money. Mrs. Shauffler thought of me like the daughter she never had. What's wrong with that?"

"What's wrong with it is that I don't believe it."

"Well, I'm sorry about that, Lucas. You know, I could take a different position here."

"How's that?"

"Suppose I agree to give half of what I receive to your school each year. Just think what you could do with a million dollars annually for as long as I live. I have a life expectancy of about fifty more years, I believe. That's fifty million dollars for your school. You can't lose, Lucas."

"Except it would be dishonest. A minor matter as you perceive it, I guess, but I view things a bit differently. Why can't I convince you to do this one magnificent thing in your life…to give up the battle and derive satisfaction from the tremendous good that will come from it?"

"Forget it."

He smiled, slowly collected his papers, and stuffed them into his briefcase. Slipping into his coat, he headed for the door. "Call me when you want to talk again."

Lucas Alexander's initial promise, that he would not become involved in the controversy beyond discussing the case with Margaux and Whiting, was about to be broken.

"I just can't let that bitch get away with it," he mumbled to himself as the elevator doors closed behind him.

CHAPTER TWENTY-FOUR

Alma Haverstock lay immobile in her hospital bed, where she'd remained in a coma for more than a week. In earlier times she would have died, but modern medical techniques had kept her alive until she'd regained consciousness, only to discover that although she was able to see and hear and think, she could not speak a word or move a muscle. She had no sense of time, except that a few brilliantly colored leaves drifted by her hospital room window from time to time and informed her that it was fall, probably October.

Her one recurring thought was rage at her physician for allowing her to survive for no purpose.

She passed each day revisiting the significant moments of her life. There were numerous visions of growing up in Brooklyn, of her job interview with Michael Dunn when she graduated from Kathryn Gibbs Secretarial School, including the memory of having worn white gloves and a summer straw hat as prescribed by the Kathryn Gibbs manual. She thought about a long life of sharing Michael's love of the practice of the law, and of caring about his clients as deeply as he did. Fifty years of memories of dear Michael, who had become her best friend in her real life and her lover only in her dreams.

When she closed her eyes she could picture him as they'd grown old together. He wasn't a large, muscular man like Frank, but he was always well-groomed, and with his soft brown eyes and ready smile he made it easy for his clients to confide in him, to leave his office confident that he truly cared about them and would be there when they needed him. She teased him a bit as his hairline receded and his waistline expanded, but there never was another man to take Michael's place in her life.

But memories didn't constitute a life, and each night as she closed her eyes to sleep, she was both hopeful and fearful that she would not awaken in the morning.

One morning a nurse escorted a man into her hospital room. She heard the nurse say, "She may be able to hear us when we speak, but she's had a stroke, you know, and I'm afraid her mind is a blank."

Alma couldn't imagine who the man was. He was tall and lean. His nose looked a little crooked, as if it had been broken and not set properly, but it didn't distract from his strong chiseled features. In fact, in a way, it enhanced his attractiveness. In the dim hospital room she couldn't tell the color of his eyes, but she assumed they were dark because his skin was the color of dark mahogany, maybe Italian, or Greek. She decided he looked a little like Abraham Lincoln without the beard.

"Mrs. Haverstock, my name is Lucas Alexander. I'm an attorney representing Sarah Nusbaum, Katrina Shauffler's sister.

"One of the nurses told me that she believes you may be able to hear what is being said to you, but no one knows for sure."

In her head she screamed, *Yes, yes, I hear you, I understand you. Keep talking to me!*

Alexander looked straight into her eyes but could fathom nothing. Then he moved to the left and her eyes followed him. He moved to the right; again her eyes followed him. He sat down in the chair beside her bed trying to think of some way to determine whether she understood anything, or if she was out of it altogether. She continued to stare at him, but otherwise, it was like being in a room with a corpse. He stared back, hoping to see some change in expression, but there was none, except that she would blink her eyes from time to time.

"Mrs. Haverstock." He leaned closer to her. "If you can hear what I am saying, blink your eyes twice." Mrs. Haverstock blinked twice. "My God, yes. Now two blinks will mean yes and three blinks will mean no." He thought for a few moments and then said, "Is Mickey Mouse president of the United States?"

Mrs. Haverstock blinked three times.

"Is the moon made of blue cheese?" Again she blinked rapidly three times.

"Is your name Alma Haverstock?" She blinked twice.

Luke stood up grinning. "Right on! Now listen to me, please, Mrs. Haverstock. You worked for the Dunn law office, right?"

She blinked twice.

"Do you remember Katrina Shauffler?" She blinked twice.

"I must be absolutely certain that you understand the import of my questions and that your answers are carefully considered and, above all, truthful. Okay?" Alma blinked twice.

"Were you involved with the preparation of Mrs. Shauffler's will?" Luke held his breath as he awaited her answer.

Alma blinked twice, concentrating on every word he said. That was easy to do because he had the voice and the demeanor of a trial lawyer. Finally someone was talking to her about something more interesting than her bodily functions.

"First I must tell you what has happened and why I'm here. Did you know that Mrs. Shauffler died recently?" She blinked twice.

"In the briefest of terms, Mrs. Haverstock, the problem Mrs. Nusbaum and I have is that, when Mrs. Shauffler signed her will, it contained a clause that Sarah Nusbaum says doesn't belong there." Luke spoke slowly, choosing each word. "The will grants a life use of the income from the Shauffler trust to Margaux McBride. Mrs. Haverstock, do you believe Mrs. Shauffler intended to do that?"

She blinked three times and then she blinked three times again and then blinked three times again and again.

"Okay, Mrs. Haverstock. I understand. I understand." Luke squeezed her immobilized hand. "The question is, how did it happen? Who changed the will?"

Mrs. Haverstock stared at him.

"Forgive me. Obviously you can't answer a question stated that way. Let's see. Did you type the Shauffler will in its entirety?" She blinked twice. "Were you a witness to the signing of the will by Mrs. Shauffler?" She blinked twice. "The problem is that, as you know, the pages of the will were laced together with a red ribbon and sealed with red wax with Mrs. Shauffler's signet ring imprint in the wax. So the change must have been made sometime after you typed it but before it was signed."

Luke stopped and stared out the window a moment, thinking. "Did you give the will to Frank Dunn after you prepared it?"

Alma blinked twice and then three times and then two times and then three times. "You're saying yes and no, am I right?" She blinked twice.

Luke glanced at his watch and sighed heavily. "I must go now, Mrs. Haverstock. I have to teach a class in thirty minutes, and there's nothing those lazy youngsters would like better than to escape the quiz I warned them about. But I'll be back as soon as I can, and by God, somehow we are going to find a way for you to tell your whole story."

He stood up. "In the meantime, I want you to try and remember everything you can about Katrina Shauffler. What were the circumstances of your first meeting with her? Who was present? What was said? Had the Dunn office represented her on legal matters other than the preparation of her will? Everything you can think of that may help us find the truth in this matter. I have a feeling you'll be our key witness to make certain Ms. McBride doesn't get a dime of Mrs. Shauffler's money. And next time I'll come better prepared to ask the right questions." He bent down and kissed her cheek, then turned and left the room.

Alma didn't want him to leave. She was afraid he might not come back and she'd have no way to contact him. Before he had come to her room, all she'd been able to think about was her impending death. Now, maybe she had a reason to live a little longer.

Alma had never trusted that McBride girl. She'd had Frank twisted around her little finger. If Michael had been alive, he'd have put her in her place, but there'd been nothing Alma could do about it. She'd just figured that Frank would have to learn from his own mistakes.

So this Mr. Alexander wanted her to remember everything she could about Katrina Shauffler. He probably didn't realize that she and Katrina went back almost fifty years. Alma had met Katrina shortly after she'd gone to work for Michael, when he'd had that little walk-up office in Brooklyn.

My Lord, she thought; that had to be 1955.

———

Irving and Katrina Shauffler were waiting for Michael Dunn when Alma arrived at his office at 7:55.

"Good morning," she said. "Are you waiting for Mr. Dunn?"

"Yes, ma'am," Irving said. "But we don't have an appointment."

"No matter, I happen to know that he's free until ten o'clock and I'm sure he'll be here on the dot of eight." She unlocked the office door and motioned for the Shaufflers to enter. "I'm Alma Haverstock, Mr. Dunn's secretary. Please come in and have a seat."

When Michael Dunn arrived he invited the Shaufflers into his office.

"How may I help you folks?"

"We have a case to discuss with you of great importance to us, Mr. Dunn. We hope you can help us. We're very ignorant of the law."

"Why don't you just tell me the problem and then perhaps we can find a way to solve it. Alma, bring in your book and take notes so I get it straight."

Irving proceeded to tell Michael Dunn his story. He'd given his friend Mr. Goldfarb nine thousand dollars to buy his house, but that night someone had broken in and stolen Irving's money before Goldfarb had given the Shaufflers the deed to his house.

"We don't know what to do," Irving Shauffler said. "It took us five years to earn the money and now it's gone, and the Goldfarbs can't afford to give us a deed if they don't get the money."

"The fact of the matter is," Michael said, "the verbal agreement you and Mr. Goldfarb thought you'd made to buy his house is unenforceable."

"But they agreed to sell us the house for nine thousand dollars and we paid Mr. Goldfarb the money."

"It's my opinion, Mr. Shauffler, that you cannot force Mr. Goldfarb to sell you the house, because the agreement was not in writing, as the law requires for every agreement to buy real estate. So, while you can't force Mr. Goldfarb to give you the deed to the house, he is obligated to pay you back the nine thousand you gave him."

"But he can't, because the money was stolen," Irving repeated.

"Along with their life's savings, Katrina added. "They don't have a penny."

"I understand, of course, but he has the house doesn't he?"

"Yes, but —"

"So if he can't give you back the money, the honorable thing would be for him to follow through and give you the house."

"But we couldn't ask them to do that," Katrina said. "Simon and Myra are our friends, and it's not their fault that the money's gone. And…," Katrina was fighting to hold back the tears, "it's so unfair to everyone."

"Well now, Mrs. Shauffler," Michael said, leaning forward in his chair. "You asked me for my legal opinion. You didn't ask me for my advice, or whether it was fair."

"What should we do, Mr. Dunn?" Irving asked.

"The way I see it, you were both wrong in this situation. It was foolish of you to give Mr. Goldfarb the money without even getting a receipt to show what it was for. And it was even more foolish to give it to him in cash at night, when he wouldn't be able to put it in the bank until the next day."

"But I thought —"

"Yes, I know. You thought the money would be safe with Mr. Goldfarb. I'm sure you didn't wonder about where he could safely put it the night you gave it to him, did you?"

"Of course not, I thought…well, as a matter of fact, I guess I didn't think."

"I agree, Mr. Shauffler. On the other hand, Mr. Goldfarb was equally foolish in accepting money when he didn't have a safe place for it. I mean, how do you know that the money was really stolen? Maybe Mr. Goldfarb is playing a trick on you, or maybe it was Mrs. Goldfarb who stole the money and she has it hidden somewhere."

"How can you say such a terrible thing?" Katrina snapped.

"Don't be upset with me, Mrs. Shauffler. I'm just trying to explain why the law is the way it is, why the agreement should have been in writing, and why you shouldn't have been walking around with nine thousand dollars in cash instead of a bank check."

"It's not what we've done that's important, it's what we must do now that we are concerned about," Irving said.

"Quite right you are, Mr. Shauffler. Now that I have told you what your legal rights are, I feel comfortable telling you what I would do if I were you."

"Please tell us," Katrina said.

"Since I believe you were both wrong, I think you should bear the unhappy consequences equally. I suggest that you make an agreement in writing with the Goldfarbs to buy the house for forty-five hundred dollars, one-half the price you agreed upon. Then you could give them a mortgage for that amount payable over ten years with interest at three percent, which is exactly half of the normal rate."

"Yes," Katrina said immediately, "that is the right thing to do. Don't you agree, Irving?"

"Absolutely," he said, just as promptly.

Dance of the Mantis

The Goldfarbs and the Shaufflers lived side by side and remained best friends until the Shaufflers sold the house in 1952 for twenty-five thousand dollars and gave the Goldfarbs a bonus check for an extra forty-five hundred dollars when they paid off the balance of the mortgage. Michael Dunn, Esq. handled the transaction.

Although Alma could not move her lips, she smiled in her mind as she remembered that first meeting with Katrina, and thought about the letter the Shauffler's had eventually brought in to show Michael and herself, the letter Irving received from a company offering to buy his patent. Alma remembered the details of that meeting as if it were yesterday, even though she couldn't remember what she'd done yesterday.

Michael had moved his offices to Manhattan at about that time, so it had to have been in the sixties.

———

"It's a letter, Mr. Dunn, Miss Alma," Irving said, rummaging through his briefcase. "I have an invention, and this company would like to buy it. They've offered me a lot of money, as you will see in the letter. I was going to accept it, but Katrina…," he hesitated and smiled at his wife with great pride, "Katrina told me I must show the letter to you first, Mr. Dunn, and ask your advice." Irving offered the letter to Michael and sat quietly, staring intently at him while he read it

"Fifty thousand dollars! What did you invent, a substitute for gasoline?"

"No, no, nothing so important, but I think maybe it could help our country. I've always felt bad that I couldn't be more help in the war against Hitler. The Nazis cut off my right leg in a concentration camp," he said, tapping the steel prosthesis with his knuckles. "We are American citizens now, you know."

"I do know that. So tell me about your invention."

"Yah, you see, I am a lens maker, and one night I was working in my laboratory trying to create a chemical film that would protect our most sensitive lenses from being scratched. I knew that when you fuse quartz and sand it becomes a silica glass that's used to manufacture electrical insulators. I thought that perhaps a colloidal dispersion of silica in water might be a good coating agent. I applied this material to the lens of a camera sitting on the desk in my office, and was about to leave for the night when I glanced out my window and saw that a fire had broken out in a building several blocks away.

I picked up the camera, loaded it with film, leaned out the window, and snapped several pictures. Then I sort of forgot about it. But when the pictures were developed, I found that my photos of the fire had produced a series of bizarre color images in bright reds and yellows fading into blues and greens.

At first, they made no sense to me at all, but as I studied them more closely, I realized the red images were not limited to the area where the fire was raging. There was also a series of red splotches running horizontally along the street. With further study and experimentation, I discovered that the photos taken through my specially treated lens were recording heat intensity. The little splotches of red that were interspersed horizontally at random had been created by heat emanating from the automobile engines in the cars being driven on the street.

I immediately realized that I'd stumbled upon an essential element in the process of infrared instrumentation called thermal imagery. That process has been known for many years, but my discovery cuts the cost by 1000 percent."

"Mr. Shauffler, if what you're telling me is true, the fifty thousand dollar offer for your patent is just for openers."

"I don't understand, Mr. Dunn. What is this 'openers' thing?" Katrina asked.

"Sorry, Mrs. Shauffler, it's a term we men use when we play poker. Tell me, would you be willing to pay me twenty percent of whatever I could get for you over what has already been offered?"

Irving looked to Katrina for counsel. "What do I have to lose, Mr. Dunn?"

"Nothing, Irving, nothing at all, but if I'm right, we could all gain."

It took Michael Dunn six months to negotiate an agreement with TBX Technologies Ltd., but when the deal was done Irving Shauffler deposited over one million dollars into a trust fund for his wife Katrina. Irving was in his fifties when he died of a heart attack in 1972. He left his entire estate in trust for his wife Katrina, designating Michael Dunn as trustee. By the time of Michael Dunn's death in 2002, the value of the Shauffler trust, under Michael's stewardship, had increased to over twenty-five million dollars.

Alma had met with Katrina once a month for thirty years to discuss the administration of the Shauffler trust. Katrina and Irving had bought and renovated an abandoned school near Columbia University, and founded the Shauffler School for disadvantaged preteens. They'd donated the facility to the university and endowed the cost of its operation until sufficient state and federal grants were in place to carry it on.

There was absolutely no way Katrina would have changed her mind about supporting the school, as she had directed in the will Alma had typed, giving 70 percent of the trust to the school in Irving's name.

If only I could speak, I would tell the court a thing or two about Margaux McBride.

———

As soon as he returned to his office, Alexander called his old friend Ellis Fretwell, professor emeritus at NYU. After an extended conversation in which Luke outlined all the facts he'd gathered and the difficulty of communicating with Mrs. Haverstock, he asked the professor if it was possible to construct a machine that could somehow transmit Mrs. Haverstock's blinking eyes into a more sophisticated means of communication than just answering yes or no to questions asked of her.

"Give me some time to research the problem, Luke. In the back of my mind I remember reading about a machine that does exactly what you're looking for, but it's bound to cost a lot of money."

"Money we've got, Ellis, but we don't have much time."

The next day Ellis Fretwell told Alexander that he'd located the machine. It was called the Eyegaze Computer System, and it was made by L. C. Technologies of Fairfax, Virginia.

"It can help you beyond your wildest dreams, Luke. This machine will enable your lady to type with her eyes!"

"You've got to be kidding me, Ellis. How does it work?"

Fretwell explained that Mrs. Haverstock would just have to look at an alphabet projected on a miniature television screen built into the inside of a special helmet similar to what astronauts wear. Focusing her eyes on a letter would be tantamount to pressing a key on the keyboard of a computer. She'd be able to type as fast as she could change her gaze from one letter to the next.

"Damn it, professor, you're a genius! Call the company and have them ship that machine up here immediately."

"Consider it done," the professor replied.

———

Luke and Professor Fretwell waited anxiously as the orderlies wheeled Mrs. Haverstock into the hospital conference room. Luke walked over and took her hand in his, a large grin on his face.

"Mrs. Haverstock, we're about to do something pretty exciting. My friend Professor Fretwell, here, has discovered some equipment that will enable you to answer our questions. And you'll be able to talk to us, as well."

Ellis Fretwell meticulously described to her how the equipment worked. He gently placed the helmet on her head, and then asked the question, "Do you understand how this crazy piece of machinery works?"

A multiple-choice menu appeared on the screen inside her helmet. It contained the words *yes, no, maybe,* and *I don't know.* She focused her eyes on the box that contained the word *yes* and the word *yes* appeared on the transmitting monitor screen.

"Hooray!" Luke exclaimed. "Okay, Mrs. H., now here we go. We're going to switch the monitor to the typewriter program so that you can focus on individual letters and write a sentence." In a few seconds, an alphabet was displayed on the screen inside her helmet. Luke and Ellis Fretwell held their breath as they waited for letters to appear on the display screen, which she could observe inside the helmet and they could observe in the equipment located outside the helmet. In a moment, Mrs. Halverstock's first message arrived on their display screen.

She had written with her eyes "I - L O V E - Y O U."

"We've got a winner, professor!" Luke exclaimed, grabbing his friend by the arm. He turned back to Alma, embraced her gently, and kissed her on the cheek. "Mrs. H., we're going to make you a star. Tomorrow we're going to put this on film so there can be no misunderstanding as to how all this has come about."

CHAPTER TWENTY-FIVE

Luke Alexander sat across from Pat Turner. He appeared to her to be in his late forties, but she couldn't be certain. She guessed him to be over six feet tall, and she'd noticed an almost imperceptible limp when he entered her office.

"Thanks for giving me a few moments of your busy day, Sergeant. I know only too well how hard you guys work."

"And still you lawyers beat us up."

"No, no, I've never beaten up on a detective in my life. A few prosecutors, perhaps, but never a detective."

"If you say so. What can I do for you?"

"Have you ever heard of Katrina Shauffler?" Luke asked.

"Doesn't ring a bell. Should it?"

"All right, how about Margaux McBride?"

"Now you've got my attention. You're talking about the lawyer, right?"

"That's the one."

"Why are you interested in her?" Pat leaned back in her chair.

"I've got myself involved in a case where she's playing an important role and I want to make sure I don't misjudge her. It occurred to me that her name might have come up during the investigation of the Dunn murder, and I understand that's your baby, so here I am. What can you tell me?"

"Not much."

"How much?"

"Who's Katrina Shauffler?"

"Okay." Luke laughed. He liked this young lady's style. And she was damned attractive, too. He glanced at her fingers and was pleased to see no rings.

"I'll show you everything I've got, and you can show me everything you've got. Deal?"

"You mean like playing doctor?"

"Not nearly so much fun, but maybe we could talk about that over a drink some time."

Pat turned crimson and immediately got up and stepped over to the file cabinet, turning her back on him to prevent his seeing her burning cheeks. She fussed in the file drawer long enough to regain her composure, retrieved her folder on McBride, and returned to her desk.

"What is it exactly that you want to know?" she asked, thinking that his nose was a bit larger than necessary and a little out of kilter, and his hairline had started to recede, but that it was rather an appealing face, friendly and masculine.

"To begin with, I want to know what the relationship was between McBride and Frank Dunn."

"They were lovers."

"I figured as much. All the signs and symptoms were there. Is she a suspect in the Dunn case?"

"I...I can't tell you that."

"Of course you can't. But if she wasn't a suspect, you could have told me, right?"

"You tricked me. But that's okay. I'm learning. Now it's my turn. What's your interest in this business? How does McBride figure in with this client of yours? Schaefer, is it?"

"Shauffler." Luke told her he believed there was some dirty business between McBride and Frank Dunn. When Dunn was killed, it put McBride in line to inherit two-million a year for life. He thought a colossal fraud had been perpetrated against Mrs. Shauffler's estate.

"Are you telling me that McBride might have been motivated to eliminate Dunn in order to receive a really, really big bunch of money?"

"By motivated, you mean like...say...have a motive to kill Mr. Dunn?"

"You got it."

"I must say the thought has crossed my mind, Sergeant."

"I've got a lot of questions that need answering, Mr. Alexander."

"So do I, Sergeant. So do I."

"I've also got an appointment out of the office in a few minutes, but it seems to me it might serve both our interests if we could meet again soon."

"How about having a drink together after work and preparing an agenda for such a meeting?"

"My father told me never to mix business and pleasure, especially where alcohol is involved. Maybe some other time, after we've finished our business with McBride."

"How about I pick you up here Friday night at seven for a couple of drinks and dinner?"

"I guess you didn't get my message, counselor."

"I got the message all right, but it doesn't make any sense unless —"

"No, I'm not married, I'm just not into…"

"Me either, so why don't we say 7:15, one drink and dinner?"

"Seven-thirty, one drink. That way, if it doesn't go well, either of us can back out gracefully. Besides, I can't stay late. I'm on duty at eight Saturday morning."

"Why don't we just play it by ear?"

The phone rang on Pat's desk. She swiveled her chair around to answer it. When she finished the call and turned back, Lucas was gone.

CHAPTER TWENTY-SIX

On Friday morning, when Pat checked her appointment book, she noted that she'd made a date with Lucas Alexander for that evening. She thought she'd probably enjoy the drink and, indeed, if all went happily, she was prepared to hang in for dinner as well. But she wasn't in the mood for the intimacy most men seemed to think was their due, once they'd paid for a dinner.

She put Luke out of her mind until Ken knocked on her door late in the afternoon with some new information on the Dunn murder weapon.

"I located the shop owner who sold the pistol to Frank Dunn."

Pat immediately put down her pen and straightened up in the chair.

"I told him we were trying to figure out whether Shadrack's pistol was the one he sold to Frank Dunn, even though the registration number was filed off."

"And?"

"He remembered Dunn as an arrogant guy. When the shop owner took the pistol into the back of his shop to wrap it up in a box, he accidentally dropped the gun on the concrete floor, which left a ding in the handle. Ordinarily he would have replaced the gun with one that was undamaged, but he didn't like Dunn so he just wrapped it up and gave it to him. The same ding is in Shadrack's pistol, so Dunn was the owner of the pistol we took from Shadrack. So the bullets that killed Dunn came from the pistol that was originally purchased by Dunn himself. I made an appointment for you to see the fellow who owns the gun shop tonight around 7:30."

Pat leaned back in her chair. She started to tell him that she had a commitment and that talking to the shop owner could wait until tomorrow. But she was Ken's mentor, and she would not allow him to believe that she placed pleasure before business. She sighed and returned to writing in her notebook. "Good job, kiddo," she said. "Give me the fellow's number. I'll take care of it. Now, go to work on the connection between Dunn and Shadrack."

When Ken left the office, Pat cursed her luck and called Luke.

"Mr. Alexander? Sergeant Turner here."

"Hi. I was thinking good thoughts about you at the very moment this phone rang."

"I'm going to have to cancel our date tonight. I've got to work. Maybe we can do it another time. I'm really sorry. I was looking forward to it."

"Oh no! I had the restaurant owner hire a twenty-piece band to play all your favorite songs. The limousine is scheduled to pick us up at 7:30, and I bought a double orchid corsage, which is sitting in my refrigerator as we speak —"

"I can tell the difference between blarney and bushwhack, you know."

"Okay, I confess to just a slight exaggeration. It's a single rose, not two orchids. How about tomorrow night instead? I'll cancel my date with Julia Roberts."

"I'm sorry, Mr. Alexander, you can never make a date with a lady for a Saturday night less than one week in advance. Check it out in *Elle* magazine. However, to make up for canceling out on you tonight, I'd be delighted to have dinner with you next Saturday night, if you wish, and in that way you can keep your date with Julia. But don't you dare give her my rose."

CHAPTER TWENTY-SEVEN

Lt. Bill Garvey was scheduled to retire after forty years of service. He'd been directed to make a recommendation for his replacement. There were four candidates, all technically qualified by education and experience, who he felt could assume leadership of the homicide division. Three of them were men with whom he'd worked for many years, and one of those, Sgt. Jack Donlon, had actually saved his life twenty years earlier. However, the quality of Sgt. Pat Turner's work was outstanding. Among other things, she'd solved seven murder cases that had been sitting in cold storage, classified as unsolved.

Her personnel file lay open on his desk, and her record was flawless. There was no doubt that she was the best qualified candidate. But why did she have to be a woman, goddamn it? How could he face Jack Donlon if he recommended her? How could he tell Donlon he'd chosen a goddamned one hundred twenty-pound girl fifteen years his junior to be his supervisor? Fuck it! He couldn't do it and that was that. Garvey closed the file and shoved it in his desk drawer just as the phone rang. It was Pat Turner, as if it were willed.

"I got a message to call you, sir."

"Tell me, Sergeant, are you going to be ready to conference the Dunn case by tomorrow morning?" He'd never failed to call her Sergeant since the day she'd pointed out that he called all the other detectives by their rank, and she didn't understand why he kept calling her Pat. She'd told him that her rank meant as much to her as it did to them.

"I'm going to do my best, sir." As soon as Pat replaced the receiver, her phone rang.

"Patricia?"

"Lucas? I can't talk now."

"Wait! What about our date for tomorrow night?"

"After my meeting with Lieutenant Garvey on the Dunn case tomorrow morning, I may be comatose."

"Why don't you tell me about it? Maybe I can help."

"You know I can't do that, Lucas. Until there is an indictment, everything is confidential."

"Will there be an indictment?"

"Well, I guess I can tell you that we're very close, but that's all I can say. Now I've got to go, honest."

"Wait a minute. What about tomorrow night?"

"Call me at home tonight. 685-3342. Bye."

———

The babble of animated conversation among the men and women assembled around the table, all of whom had been working on the Dunn case, stopped immediately when Bill Garvey entered the room. He glanced at the clock on the wall and opened the meeting. The exhibits were laid out on the top of the table, and a number of large photos were set up on several easels standing around the room. Garvey nodded to Pat to proceed.

"From early on in the investigation, there've been three suspects we've taken seriously," Pat began. "Joey Pesci, Shadrack, and Margaux McBride. Actually, we recently received an anonymous letter suggesting we should take a look at a guy from Bayonne by the name of Carl Stassi. We haven't had time to really check him out yet, except that we found he's done time for assault and is presently out on parole. Okay, let me take you through them all, one at a time.

"We got onto this kid Pesci because his prints were found in Dunn's apartment. It turns out that Pesci is a teen-age punk who was recently released from Elmira Correctional, where he did a short stretch for car theft. We got a search warrant and found Frank Dunn's gold lighter and his wife's keys sitting on top of Pesci's dresser. It's possible he may have been burglarizing the Dunn apartment when Frank got home after taking his wife to the airport. We thought he could have been hiding in Dunn's bedroom when Frank flipped on the lights and discovered him there. We figured he could have panicked and shot Dunn. However, a couple of days ago I got a call from the Assistant DA He says Pesci's assigned counsel claims Pesci has solid witnesses to prove he was nowhere near the place when Frank was taken down. Of course, the solid witnesses will probably turn out be Pesci's mother and his girlfriend, who'll claim they were playing a quiet game of Parcheesi with him when it all happened. I'm planning to hold him in detention for violation of probation until we complete our investigation. But I think a more plausible story is emerging here."

"What's that?" Garvey asked.

"Well, sir, the serial numbers on the murder weapon that was found in Shadrack's possession were filed off and, ordinarily, there would be no way to identify it. However, we now have convincing evidence that Shadrack's pistol was originally purchased by Frank Dunn, but the problem is we don't know how the pistol got from Dunn to Shadrack, or why."

"I don't much care about the why. It would be a nice solution all the way around if Shadrack's the culprit. It solves the problem without the expense of a trial."

"I agree it could wrap it up neatly. There's no doubt that the bullets that killed Dunn were fired from the pistol they found on Shadrack when they hauled him off to the morgue. And certainly with his criminal record, a murder committed during the course of a burglary is plausible. But let me tell you about the third suspect, Margaux McBride." Pat took a deep breath. "Here's our scenario. McBride has acknowledged that she and Dunn were lovers and that she went to his apartment within the very hour that he was shot."

"What does McBride claim she was doing there?" Garvey asked.

"I want you to listen to this." Pat pushed her tape player into the center of the table. "This is a conversation between Dunn and McBride, recorded on Dunn's answering machine at 8:35, an hour before his death."

"Hello."

"Darling —"

"Where are you?"

" I'm sorry, honey, I —"

"Where the hell have you been?"

"I got tied up in traffic but I'll be over by 9:30 at the latest, I promise."

"I'll leave the door unlocked for you."

"Yes, love."

The room was totally silent as the people sitting around the table digested the significance of the taped conversation.

"Up until last week, the only thing I came up with on motive was a possible lover's quarrel mixed with alcohol that got out of hand, and I still think that's possible. But a few days ago I learned that as a result of Dunn's death, McBride is entitled to collect a couple million bucks a year for life."

Garvey leaned forward. "Insurance?"

"No. The substance of it is that a lady by the name of Shauffler made a will giving Frank Dunn the income from a twenty-five million dollar trust upon her death, but stating that if Frank Dunn died before Mrs. Shauffler, the income would go to McBride. Dunn was murdered shortly before Mrs. Shauffler died, which made McBride the beneficiary of several million dollars a year during the balance of her life.

"Also, the doorman in the Dunn apartment house remembers letting McBride into the building on the night Frank was murdered. So we have opportunity and a big bundle of motivation, but we're having trouble trying to figure out the means. We haven't figured out how the murder weapon got from Dunn to McBride to Shadrack."

"Anything else?" Garvey asked.

"I guess not, except maybe McBride hired Pesci or Shadrack, or maybe even this guy Stassi we just heard about, to eliminate Dunn so she'd receive the Shauffler money. Incidentally, both Stassi and McBride come from Bayonne."

Garvey was tired of it all. It was messy. The DA was pressing him. He wanted the problem to go away. "I've heard all I need," he said. "I don't really care how or why Shadrack ended up with the weapon. In my opinion, the case against McBride can go to the District Attorney. Let him decide whether there's enough evidence to indict her."

"I want to agree, sir, but I'm not really comfortable turning this over to the DA quite yet. The entire case against McBride is based on circumstantial evidence, and as you know, the law says that the facts proved must exclude to a moral certainty every reasonable inference of innocence. I don't see how we can say that yet. We need more proof. We need to put the murder weapon in McBride's hand or in the hand of someone she hired."

"You're an investigator, not a defense lawyer, Sergeant. I said give it to the DA." Garvey stood up and left the room, signaling an end to the conference.

CHAPTER TWENTY-EIGHT

Pat glanced at her watch as she locked up her office to head home. "Damn!" she cursed under her breath. Luke was scheduled to pick her up in an hour for their first date. She was tired, and angered by Garvey's intractability. The thought of having to race home and make the switch from a tough cop to a charming dinner companion magnified her frustration. She was sorely tempted to call Luke and cancel their date, but having already done that once, she decided to press on and hope for the best.

She'd just turned off the blow dryer when the doorbell rang on the very dot of 7:30. When she opened the door, Luke stood tall with a foolish grin. He ceremoniously presented her with a single yellow rose.

"I've been a little worried about my choice of a flower," he said. "Somehow I knew I shouldn't give you a red rose on our first date, so I thought a yellow rose would be okay. But then I couldn't remember what, if anything, a yellow rose stood for, and the kid at the florist shop had no idea what I was talking about. So, anyway, here it is."

The emotional trauma of her work day faded away and on the spot, Staff Sergeant Pat Turner morphed into Miss Patricia Turner, a sparkling Irish colleen.

"Thank you, kind sir," she said, curtsying. "Please come in while I put on the finishing touches. I'm sure you won't believe this, but a yellow rose happens to be my honest-to-goodness favorite flower."

"Then, if I've chosen the right restaurant, we'll be off to a good start."

"Where are we going?" Pat asked, after she'd placed the rose in a bud vase and displayed it prominently on her coffee table.

"To a place I think you'll like. It's called Ouest and my secretary's son Tommy is the owner."

When they arrived and entered the tiny elegant dining room, the place was packed. The mâitre d' appeared out of thin air and offered his hand to Luke. "Good evening, Mr. Alexander, your table is ready. Right this way, sir."

When they were settled comfortably, Pat glanced around the room and said, "How about filling me in on this secretary who controls your social life?"

"She doesn't control it, she just exercises a significant influence. Let's see, what can I tell you? To begin with, her name is Aurora Valenti."

"Sounds like the title of an Italian love song."

"That's nice. I'll tell her you said so. She's very bright, has a great sense of humor, is conscientious, tremendously loyal to her friends —"

"That's enough. I hope she's happily married. Otherwise I don't see how I can compete with her."

"Happily? Who knows? What transpires behind the closed doors of matrimony usually remains there until the divorce. I've come to the conclusion that the phrase 'happily married' is a contradiction in terms."

"I take it from that cynical remark that you've been married. Past tense, I hope." Pat's heart skipped a beat while she waited for his answer to that question, which she realized she should have asked long before she accepted his invitation to dinner.

"My status as a husband is history. I've tasted the joys and sorrows of matrimony, and after two unsuccessful attempts, have concluded that marriage is an institution that has passed its prime. The gatherers no longer need the hunters."

As Pat was trying to decide whether or not Luke was being serious, the waiter appeared. "Would you like to order cocktails first, Mr. Alexander?"

"What's your pleasure, Pat?"

"I'd love a Gray Goose vodka martini, with an olive."

"Sounds perfect. Make it two," Lucas said. "By the way, Pat, when we get to know each other better, please remind me to tell you what Dorothy Parker said about martinis."

"Why must I wait?"

"You'll understand why when I tell you."

"I can't imagine what Dorothy Parker could have said that would offend my senses," she shrugged.

They both began to study their menus.

"Since you've been here many times, Lucas, would you make a recommendation?"

"I have two favorites. Rack of lamb, black on the outside and red on the inside, or Tommy's sautéd baby bay scallops with a scrumptious sauce."

"Why don't we get one of each and share?"

"Perfect. Hey, do we have chemistry here or what?"

"I'm not going to answer that until I know more about your unsuccessful forays into the wilderness of matrimony."

"I guess that's fair, under the circumstances."

Luke leaned back in his chair, started to speak, hesitated, and then, looking directly at Pat, he continued.

"I spent some heavy-duty time in Nam. When I got out, I went back to college and got married in my junior year. We were both too young. We had a child but no money. It was just a big mistake, nobody's fault. And I guess I can't really say it was a mistake because my daughter has turned out spectacularly well, despite her parents' inability to get along. We did stick it out for almost ten years. Soon after the divorce, she remarried, and I guess her marriage is okay. We never talk about it." Luke sighed. "My other marriage failed because my second wife was too young. I had passion and love mixed up. She was a barely legal, nubile, scatterbrained kid with a body that drove me crazy. I should have known better, but it was my whatziz and not my brain that proposed marriage. Who was it that said you can't live on sex alone? Marie Antoinette, maybe?"

"Naw. She said, 'Give me libido or give me death'," Pat deadpanned.

"I'm not even going to try and top that," he laughed.

They chatted aimlessly over their cocktails. The prospect of a new friendship was apparent and exhilarating for both of them.

Lucas was considering another drink when the sommelier arrived. "Compliments of the chef," he said as he ceremoniously opened the bottle and poured a small quantity of the amber wine into Luke's glass.

"I'm sure it's perfect, but I love the ritual." Luke sniffed the fragrance of the wine as he lifted the glass to his lips. "*C'est merveilleux, monsieur.*" When the waiter finished filling their glasses, Luke said,

"This is a Vouvray from a vineyard in France called Chateau de Mon Contour. I visited it many years ago, and this has remained my favorite white wine ever since. I hope you like it."

"Suppose I'd preferred a red wine?" Pat teased

"Then that's what you shall have! Sir —" Luke called out.

"No, no! I was only teasing. I can't drink a whole bottle of wine. The white is fine."

"It's not a problem at all. I shall drink all of the white and half of the red as well," Luke said affably.

"I'm beginning to feel some sympathy for wives one and two."

"And so you should. As they say, I am a fun place to visit, but you wouldn't want to live here."

"I believe I'll withhold judgment about where I want to live until after dinner."

Luke laughed out loud and touched his glass to Pat's. "You are a sparkling jewel."

"How do I love thee, let me count the jewels?"

"How in the name of whatever did the City of New York manage to entice such an attractive woman to work for the homicide division of its police department?"

"They hired me for my brain, and you will do well to remember that, if you want me to hang around for dessert."

"Scout's honor, I won't invite you home tonight to look at my etchings."

Pat gave a short laugh. "Before I taste this wine, I think you better tell me what Dorothy Parker said about martinis."

"Since you insist, and you've only had one, I think it is safe to tell you now.

> *I love to drink martinis,*
> *two at the very most*
> *three I'm under the table*
> *four I'm under my host.*

Pat laughed, put down her wine glass and said, "May I exchange my glass of wine for another martini?"

"You keep this up, and I may have to revise my philosophy of marriage."

"You mustn't do that until I've heard all of it, for goodness' sake. So tell me your philosophy of marriage."

"Well, it all started with Teddy Quinn. He was one of my first clients and he wanted a divorce. Back then, the only grounds for divorce in New York State was adultery, and it was my custom to make sure my client's determination to seek a divorce wasn't a spur of the moment decision. So I asked Teddy if he'd thought the matter over carefully. He said he hadn't thought about anything else for a number of days. I told him that really wasn't a very long time in the scheme of things, and he replied he thought it was, given the fact that he'd only been married one week.

"It seems the taste of the groom's ceremonial kiss was still upon his bride's lips when the bride joined the best man in a duplicitous carnal adventure in the guest bedroom of the bride's home where the wedding reception was taking place.

"So that story plus my two failed marriages have formed my current opinion."

"Which is?"

"That the marriage vow, 'til death do us part', must have been created by a very old man who needed someone to take care of him in his dotage, or by a young pregnant woman with one child on her hip and one at her breast, who was physically unable to fulfill the responsibilities of motherhood without a hunter at her side."

"Lucas Alexander! You are either pulling my leg or you are a cynic beyond redemption."

"I proudly acknowledge being a sinner beyond redemption."

"I said cynic, not sinner, but in your case it probably doesn't make any difference."

"Now wait just a minute. Do you want total honesty or not?"

"I want a knight in shining armor riding a magnificent white stallion to come by and sweep me up in his arms and carry me off into the sunset —"

"I might be your man, Patricia."

"Don't interrupt, let me finish. Carry me off into the sunset and still be in my bed the next morning and the morning after that *ad infinitum*."

"I knew there was a catch," Luke said. "The question is, what will you settle for?"

"A drink next week, but I'm buying, and I get to choose the place."

"You got yourself a date, Sarge."

———

At six o'clock every morning, regardless of the weather, Pat pulled on her sweats, put the coffee on and headed to the park for a three mile jog. Running allowed her brain to free-fall in whatever direction it chose, and on this Saturday morning, it was vacillating between her apprehension about turning the McBride case over to the district attorney, and the fact that she couldn't get Lucas Alexander out of her mind. He'd called her at home a few nights earlier and they'd talked for almost an hour.

She was being silly, she told herself as she trotted by the Tavern on the Green and entered the underpass. She was a forty-one-year-old woman acting like a teenager with a crush on her chemistry teacher. For years, every man she'd dated had turned out to be either a wimp or a macho jerk. Truthfully, except for her concern that her biological clock was running out of time, she'd been more contented this past year, living alone and concentrating on her career, then she had been babysitting a string of immature egocentric creeps. So what was the big deal with this Alexander guy? She had to wonder.

Her thoughts were interrupted when she came across a man and a woman dressed in identical sweat suits, standing in the middle of the trail screaming at each other. They must be married, she decided, veering around them and settling back into her run. But her thoughts immediately took up where they'd left off.

What was it about Luke that makes him different from the others? He certainly wasn't what she'd call good-looking, but he made her laugh and he seemed gentle. Yes, that was it. He seemed strong and yet gentle at the same time.

Thinking about their next date, she decided to take him to Clancy's Bar, the absolute best Irish pub in Brooklyn. Five would get her ten that at some point during the evening, he'd suggest they go back to his place and look at his etchings, and…

A car's brakes screeched, and a horn blasted.

"Are you crazy or what, lady!" the cabby yelled as he swerved around her.

Was she crazy? Probably. But the real question was, would she want to look at Luke's etchings on a second date? And the bigger question was, who was this guy? Why was she acting like a nut case when she really didn't know a damn thing about him? Who the hell was Lucas Alexander, anyway?

CHAPTER TWENTY-NINE
Vietnam 1968

Luke Alexander was eighteen years old and in his first year of college when he came home on spring break and joined the marines to avoid taking his final exams. Following boot camp, Corporal Alexander was sent straight to Vietnam. He ended up in a holding camp outside Saigon awaiting orders that would assign him to an active marine division. He expected to receive his orders within a few days after his arrival, but for no reason known to him, he and half of his original boot camp platoon were left languishing in Saigon.

While out on a weekend pass he stopped in a nearby village, where he found a small shop selling soft drinks and snacks. The young girl who waited on him was one of the most exotic creatures he'd seen in his young adult life. She told him her name was Binh. He pronounced it Binney.

"No, Bin-eh," she said.

"Binney," he repeated. It made her laugh. After he paid for his soda he stayed and talked to her. He didn't want to leave. It didn't matter that they could hardly communicate with each other; she took his breath away. When he finished his drink, Binh smiled and said, "Come back, please, yes? Happy thank you."

"I will come back, yes, happy thank you."

It would be over a month before Luke and his bunkmate Smellor were sent up to the combat base camp at Khe Sanh. Whenever possible, before they left, Luke sneaked out of camp to spend time with Binh. The first time they took a walk together and he tried to kiss her, she laughed and pushed him away. He thought she was making fun of him. When she realized he was embarrassed, she took his hand and said, "I no mean bad. I laugh because I happy, yes, thank you. If you come back I take you my secret place."

Luke returned, eagerly, the following day. As he approached the tiny shop, Binh was serving drinks to a small group of soldiers seated at the wooden table outside the shop. He slipped behind a tree beside the road, hoping they would leave, but they lingered on, flirting with her. He seethed when they made obscene remarks in front of her and offered to pay her to have sex with them. He felt helpless as he watched from the shadows. Binh reached over the shoulder of one of them to take away his empty glass from the table and the soldier turned and grabbed clumsily at her. When she tried to pull away from him, her blouse ripped exposing her breasts. The soldiers cheered. Binh began to cry and ran into the shop. An old woman came out carrying a heavy cane. She screamed at them in Vietnamese and chased them away. Luke was ashamed. It was not the first time he'd witnessed such an encounter, and in fact, shortly after he arrived in Vietnam, he had willingly participated in a similar scene at a bar in Saigon.

But that was different, wasn't it? he asked himself. The waitress in the bar was different, wasn't she?

———

Binh took Luke's hand and led him along a path that began at the back of her shop near the base of a mountain jutting dark into an overcast sky. They climbed silently along the single-file footpath. A gentle rain seeped through the thick jungle foliage overhead. Binh moved effortlessly from rock to rock, pulling herself up from time to time by grasping a root or a fallen branch along the steep trail. Luke, following close behind, frequently glanced up at Binh, admiring her slim body, which moved as gracefully as a ballerina's up the mountainside. Occasionally she would stop, look back at him, and smile. When Binh climbed up an especially steep part of the trail ahead of him, Lucas saw that she wasn't wearing any underclothing. He was aroused by the sight of the forbidden dark shadows of her womanhood, but frightening thoughts began to swirl through his mind. They'd been climbing for at least a half-hour up a well-worn pathway. Suppose she was just masquerading as a friend to the American troops. Could she be leading him into a trap instead of a hideaway for lovers? He'd been warned that many marines, lured into the bush by beautiful Vietnamese girls, had ended up in the record books as MIA. His heart began to beat faster, but whether that was because of the effort of the climb, the fear of betrayal, or the sight of Binh's bare bottom, he didn't know.

As he considered turning around and racing back down the mountain, Binh stopped, reached down for his hand and pulled him up beside her on a rock ledge with an open view of the valley below. "Look, see," she said.

The rain had stopped and the searing Vietnamese sun had burned through the dark clouds. Luke looked around anxiously. The panorama, with its intense greens and overlapping patches of yellow and purple shadows, was awesome. They were standing beside a narrow waterfall that over the centuries had created a natural pool filled to the brim and overflowing with clear mountain water. The air was heavy with the fragrance of an ancient frangipani tree spreading its branches over one end of the pool where a profusion of blood-red blossoms had fallen.

There were no Vietcong soldiers in sight. Binh screamed with surprise and delight when Luke, laughing with relief, picked her up in his arms and swung her into the air. Then he took off his sweat-drenched shirt, lay down on his belly beside the pool, and drank thirstily. He scooped up handfuls of the cool water and poured it over his head and face.

He turned back to invite Binh to join him. She had disappeared. He instinctively reached for his attack knife.

———

When Luke flopped down on his belly beside the pool to drink, Binh had darted behind a huge rock, removed her sarong, and slipped silently into the pool.

"Binh!" Luke cried out, trying to stifle his fear. He peered into the jungle brush surrounding the pool. He heard the splash of water behind him and swirled around, his attack knife at the ready. Binh was standing in the center of the shallow pool, smiling, her bare breasts only half submerged in the water. The edges of her long ebony hair floated behind her. When Luke spun around to face her and she saw the attack knife in his hand, she screamed. "No, no! Please no hurt me." She turned and tried to run through the water, away from him.

Luke threw away his knife and dived into the pool. When he grabbed her from behind, she beat at him with her tiny fists until he caught her up in his arms and covered her with kisses.

CHAPTER THIRTY

Luke was finally assigned to the Seventh Platoon as a rifleman at the Khe Sanh combat base.

On April 7, 1971, it was still dark when they scrambled into the river craft on the Rao Quan river. There were about forty marines huddled together down below the gunnels. Although it was over seventy degrees in the predawn, he was chilled to the bone with fear. They were part of a team planning to make an assault on Hill 558 in the Khe Sanh Valley, which had been recaptured by the NVA. The sky turned from black to gray as the boat moved swiftly and silently up the river. Luke was unnerved by the mumbled prayers of his buddy Smellor and his comrades, and apprehensive about his recent rejection of the concept of the Holy Ghost. But he decided it was too late to return to the fold.

"Get ready, men, one minute to landing." Instinctively they all looked at their watches: 5:45.

"Thirty seconds."

Luke was not comforted by the high-pitched voice of the young second lieutenant, but he cheered with the rest of the men when the squadron of American jets appeared, flying low overhead.

"Fifteen seconds," the lieutenant screamed above the staccato of machine-gun fire from the fighter planes. The *poompff poompff* of bombs followed the lieutenant's final command.

All the young men were crouched at the ready. The sound of their thumping hearts muffled the *ack-ack* of anti-aircraft fire from the enemy pillbox nestled on the hillside. Luke opened his mouth wide, trying to suck in more air to stifle his terror. The steel bottom of the craft screeched on the rocky shore.

"Let's go!" the lieutenant screamed.

Machine-gun bullets began pinging against the side of the boat, drowning out their war cries as they surged forward, spewing orange dragon breath from the mouths of their flamethrowers, zigzagging, searching for any kind of cover — a rock, a log, a mound of dirt. The relentless sound of gunfire and exploding grenades was like the finale of a Fourth of July fireworks display, except it was for real and it never stopped. Two grenades exploded twenty feet in front of Luke. Shrapnel ricocheted off the top of the dirt barrier that protected him from direct fire. He looked behind and to his left and saw his good friend Shelley Fierstein lying on his stomach, exposed to the line of fire from the pillbox, camouflaged in a hooch two hundred feet up the hill.

He screamed, "Shell, get the fuck over here!" There was too much noise, black smoke, and confusion. A single plane made another run low, strafing the area around the impenetrable pillbox. Luke jumped out, grabbed his buddy by the arm, and dragged him up behind his barrier. Shelley was unconscious, but his fingers still held his rifle in a vice grip. Then Luke saw the hole the size of a dime in Shell's forehead, just above his right eye. The ammunition clip in Shell's rifle was still full. He hadn't fired a single bullet.

"He's fucking dead! You fucking gook bastards!"

The machine-gun fire from the dun-colored pillbox was picking off every man who had not found shelter. Luke was trapped, unable to move in any direction, waiting for a mortar shell to wipe him out. He scrutinized the pillbox, designed to blend into the side of the cliff. Its impenetrable concrete walls with the narrow slit openings allowed the Vietcong machine guns to swivel one-hundred eighty degrees to insure death to anyone foolish enough to come within their range.

The steady machine-gun fire kept the men with the flamethrowers pinned down; the only way to take out one of the miniature fortresses was to make a direct hit with heavy artillery, or drop an aerial bomb. Luke knew that unless one or the other arrived soon, it would only be a matter of time before the three Cong machine-gunners would wipe out his whole platoon. He kept looking back, hoping to see the heavy equipment come ashore, but there was nothing.

The skinny, piss-ant lieutenant suddenly ran like a maniac straight up the hill. Machine-gun fire spit up dirt all around him, but the crazy son of a bitch got close enough to throw a grenade through the porthole of the pillbox. The lieutenant leaped behind a boulder just before the explosion...*Kpow*. Then total silence. Within five seconds, from the time the pin on the grenade was pulled, the pillbox became a concrete tomb.

The lieutenant and two of his men advanced cautiously to converge on the pillbox. One of them lobbed another grenade through the porthole and then they smashed in the door. Blood was splattered all over the walls. One surviving gunner raised his arms in surrender and three marine rifles immediately fired simultaneously. The gunner's head burst open like an overripe melon, and he slid down into the tangled mass of torn flesh.

Nineteen marines were dead or dying. Five were seriously injured. Twenty-one survived, unscathed.

———

The second wave of assault troops was landing behind them. There was isolated rifle fire from the new arrivals, mostly aimed at threatening shadows. The young lieutenant led the surviving marines up to the top of the ridge and through a coffee plantation. As the small group moved cautiously along the ridge, an NVA sniper hit them. The lieutenant was the first to go down. Everyone scrambled for cover after the first shots, but the sergeant got it as well, which left Luke in command of the team. The sniper was hidden in the thick foliage at the top of a group of tall trees. Except for the continuing battle sounds below them, there was total silence. No one moved. Luke unhooked two grenades from his belt, pulled both pins at once and heaved them blindly up into the trees. *Whoomph whoomph*. There was no return fire.

He scanned the tops of all the trees and saw blood dripping down from leaf to leaf like a decorative water fountain flowing in slow motion. Within seconds a body fell from the upper branches of one of the trees. For several minutes, Luke stared at it as it lay face down in the mud, then walked cautiously over, his rifle trained at the head of the fallen body. He could see that the sniper was still alive, but he couldn't tell whether the man was faking unconsciousness.

A decision had to be made, immediately. His men were all watching him. He was their leader. He could make the man a prisoner or he could kill him. Luke fired two rounds from his rifle into the back of the sniper's head. The force of the bullets kicked his head around so that he was staring at Luke open-eyed. He looked to be in his late twenties. Luke picked up the sniper's rifle and strapped it over his shoulder. A swabbie would pay at least two hundred bucks for it. Navy guys would buy anything to prove they'd been close to the action.

Kneeling down beside the dead body, eager to see what other souvenirs he might find, Luke ripped open his tunic. There was a miniature Vietnamese flag tied around his gut, worth at least seventy-five bucks, and a blood-soaked leather wallet stashed in an inside pocket. Behind a celluloid window on the inside of the wallet was a portrait of the dead soldier with a young woman and two small children. On the dead man's hand Luke spied a gold ring carved with dragons. The ring would be worth a fortune. He tried to yank it off the man's finger, but it wouldn't come. "Jesus Christ." He hacked the finger off with his attack knife and stuffed the ring into his pocket.

Standing up, he gave a hand signal for his men to move out. He didn't dare look back at them because he was trying to swallow his nausea, and he could feel the tears begin to sting his eyes. "Fucking gooks," he said aloud, as he lead his men safely back down the hill.

But just as they headed back to the base camp, an undetected sniper opened fire, and Luke caught a bullet that shattered his knee. The injury was so severe he was immediately ordered back to the States for special medical treatment to try and save his leg.

Aboard the ship on the way back to the states, Luke sold the rifle for one hundred fifty bucks to a cook in the officers' quarters, and the gold ring and the miniature flag for six hundred dollars to a sailor. By the time the ship pulled into Norfolk Harbor, Luke had lost all the money playing poker.

He spent six weeks in the Norfolk Naval Hospital, where they saved the leg, and after six months of physical therapy, he received a medical discharge and went back to college.

He was deeply agitated about the anti-war protesters on campus. As far as he was concerned, they were traitors and should be arrested as enemies of America. He was called on to speak at rallies organized by political groups that promulgated the idea that the protesters were either naive, or Communist sympathizers supporting the Vietcong who were killing young Americans by the thousands. He found he could easily exaggerate his limp so that when he was escorted to the rostrum to speak, everyone would recognize that he was an honest-to-God veteran who'd paid the price to keep America free from the threat of Communism.

And then he met Sylvia. She sat across from him in his political science class and was a last-semester senior. Luke thought she was the smartest, prettiest, sexiest female he'd ever encountered. But though she socialized with many young men at the university, she always had an excuse why she wasn't available to go with Luke to a movie, or to anything else he suggested. She smiled and apologized, but she never said yes. He became obsessed with her.

He looked forward to the class session devoted to a review of the Vietnam War, which was still going on. He spent extra hours preparing his paper, certain that, since they all knew he was a Nam vet, he'd be called on to present his paper to the class. He was. The other students applauded when he was finished. And then Sylvia was called on to present the opposing view. Luke couldn't believe the things she was saying. How could anyone as bright as she was believe that Commie crap? When she completed her presentation, he was amazed that his classmates gave her a standing ovation.

Later he obtained a copy of her paper, hoping to prove to her, point by point, how wrong she was.

PROTEST By Sylvia Rogers

What are we fighting for in Vietnam? Should young American men and women die to protect and support a corrupt fascist dictator in South Vietnam? Should American blood be spilled so that the puppet Ngo Ding Diem, a Vietnamese who had been living in the United States, could be placed in power in South Vietnam by the CIA? What was the Tonkin Gulf resolution supposed to accomplish? How are our interests being served by destroying Vietnam? What did the Vietnamese do to us that justifies the wholesale slaughter of innocent civilians caused by our indiscriminate mass bombing of Hanoi?

These are just a few of the questions that we must answer before we can begin to understand the political forces at play in the Vietnam War. Of course we are proud of our fighting men in Vietnam, but is the cause a just one? We rightfully take great pride in the American democratic process, and well we should. But do we have the right to force our political ideals on a nation that chooses a different political philosophy? Is that the way democracy is supposed to work?

Did you know that when the French, after fifteen years of fighting the North Vietnamese, finally pulled out in 1954, and elections to unify the country were scheduled to be held in South Vietnam, the U.S. stepped in and put Diem in power, and NO ELECTIONS WERE HELD? Our own President Eisenhower claimed that if elections had been held as planned, Ho Chi Minh would probably have won the election with 80 percent of the vote. I don't claim to have all the answers, but I don't want to see another American soldier die while we are trying to figure it all out. We must bring our troops home NOW!

He'd never really paid serious attention to what the protesters were saying until he studied Sylvia's paper. He didn't even know what the Gulf of Tonkin resolution was. By the end of the week, he was deeply depressed. He asked himself, Could she be right? Is it possible that Shelley Fierstein and all those other guys died in Vietnam for nothing? Dead for nothing? A political mistake, for chrissake? And what about my fucking shattered knee. For nothing? Goddamn it to hell!

Eventually Luke wrote Sylvia a note during class and handed it to her as the class ended.

> Sylvia,
> I want to talk to you about the war.
> Can we get together over a beer?
>
> > Luke

The next morning, he found a card in his letterbox at the dorm. Picasso's dove was etched on the cover of the card. Inside, Sylvia had written:

> PEACE
> I would love to join you for a beer, but I don't think we should debate the war. Let's just talk about you and me.
>
> > Sylvia

Within three months, they were engaged. Sylvia was finishing her last year in college as part of a five-year program to receive a bachelor of science degree as well as a nursing degree. While Luke was in Vietnam, she'd been working as an operating room nurse at New York Hospital. They were both more mature than most of their classmates, and could talk to each other on a different level. Although they occasionally enjoyed participating in weekend parties, they were more excited by quiet evenings together, talking about their good fortune to live and work in America at a time when bigotry and prejudice were being challenged; when separate but allegedly equal educational facilities were unacceptable; when women were demanding that they be treated as equals in the workplace; when the social fabric of American communities that tolerated white chauvinism and de facto discrimination against ethnic minorities was being challenged at all levels. They were thrilled by John and Jackie Kennedy's Camelot and were prepared to battle under the banner of not asking what America could do for them but, indeed, how they could best serve America and win the war against poverty. They were young idealists with little knowledge of the real world, but certain that their desire to heal the sick, feed the poor, and fulfill the dreams of Martin Luther King were achievable objectives.

Two weeks before the wedding date, which they'd scheduled to follow immediately after Sylvia's graduation, Luke received a letter that had been forwarded to him from the U.S. Marine Corps. It had been posted in Vietnam several months earlier.

```
CPL LUKE
I DON'T KNOW YOU GET LETTER ME
YOU HAVE ONE YEAR OLD SON
HE NAME LUKEH
LIFE HERE NO GOOD
YOU HELP ME MAYBE
YES THANK YOU HAVE A HAPPY
                    BINH
```

Luke reread the words several times before putting the note in the envelope with his Marine Corps discharge paper. For the next few days, he thought about what he must do. He was only in his junior year at college and planned to go to law school. He received his tuition and a small monthly stipend under the G.I. bill. Sylvia had already obtained a job at the college, and Luke was working part-time as a runner for a local attorney. Between his full-time construction job during summer vacation and school loans, they figured they'd eke through law school. But there was no room in their budget to care for a Vietnamese baby. Luke wanted to do the right thing, but how could he be certain he was really the father of the child? It could be some other guy's who'd made out with her before or after he had. She didn't even tell him when the kid was born, so how could he figure the odds of his paternity? How could he ever get the money to go to Vietnam and try to find out the truth? And if he admitted to being the father, would he be stuck supporting the child all his life? What if the kid had medical problems? And what would happen if Binh got sick and couldn't take care of the child? Or suppose she died? And suppose the whole thing was a fraud or a scam. Maybe later, after he finished law school, he could check it out.

During his second year in law school, while Luke was a full-time law student and working eight hours a day in a law office, Sylvia gave birth to a daughter. Without Sylvia's income, and with the added expense of the baby, they were living below the poverty level. Luke never heard from Binh again, but he was unable to put her completely out of his mind. He was tormented by his memory of Binh as a beautiful girl; by the thought of his unseen son; by nightmares in which he could clearly see them both without shelter, living hungry and begging in the streets of Saigon, Binh selling her body to feed his son.

CHAPTER THIRTY-ONE
April, 1991

Luke Alexander stared at the headline, WAR, and felt his gut clench. Here we go again, he thought as he ambled into the kitchen and filled a rocks glass with ice and gin. He wanted to chill out and watch a movie on television. He didn't want to think about the Gulf War. The phone rang. He ignored it because he wasn't expecting any good news, but after the eighth ring, he couldn't stand it any longer.

"This is Billy Jefferson of the Seventh Platoon, Third Marine Division. I'd like to speak with Corporal Alexander."

"Is this Picklehead from Biloxi, Mississippi?"

"You got that right, Corporal."

"I don't believe it! I haven't heard from you in twenty years!"

"That's the whole idea, man! This Gulf War has got some of us who survived the Battle of the Ridge thinkin' about things, and we decided we's gonna meet in the capital of this great old U. S. of A. and celebrate bein' alive. And you is coming 'cause you's our leader, even though you is a dumb-ass Yankee. I'll call you later and give you all the details when we git it figured out. And that's an order, Corporal. Platoon dismissed."

The phone line went dead. Luke finished his drink in one swallow and went back to the kitchen to pour another. He smiled as he remembered the first time he'd spoken to Picklehead Jefferson in boot camp at Parris Island. Luke had been tacking up an 8" x 10" photo of his girlfriend on the inside cover of his locker box. She'd posed in a skimpy bikini, sitting on the hood of his 1966 Mustang convertible. He caught Jefferson leering at the picture and said to him, "So what do you think?" Picklehead crouched down on his haunches and scrutinized the picture for several minutes. Finally he stood up, and in a deep southern drawl replied, "Sure is a good-lookin' automobile."

―――

Luke got word that the twentieth reunion of the men who'd fought in Battle of the Ridge would occur on April 7, 1991. They were to meet at the Vietnam Memorial wall.

―――

As Luke walked beside the long reflecting pool that separated the tributes to Washington and Lincoln, he was surrounded by the bright greens of spring in the capitol, the delicate cherry blossoms contrasting with fiery red tulips and vibrant yellow jonquils. He contemplated compatible and incompatible contrasts in color, and in life. He thought about the times in history when contrast grew into confrontation and ultimately to war. When he reached the Lincoln Memorial, he mounted the broad marble staircase and stood quietly before the massive statue of his hero, Abraham Lincoln. He was deeply moved with love and respect for the man's courage, integrity, and compassion. It was Lincoln who'd stood tall at the close of the Civil War, refusing to surrender to the popular demand that Jefferson Davis and General Robert E. Lee be hanged in retribution.

He read the inscription carved above the statue: "In this temple, as in the hearts of the people, for whom he saved the Union, the memory of Abraham Lincoln is enshrined forever."

He thought about that long ago time, about a nation as divided as it was during the war in Vietnam. He thought about war and death and justice, and the part he'd played in America's only military defeat, as he walked slowly toward the massive long black marble wall memorializing the 58,196 Americans who'd lost their lives in Vietnam in a futile effort to impose American-style democracy on that tiny beleaguered country. When he scanned the wall, he realized that among all those who'd lost their lives on the Ridge, the only name he could recall was Shelley Fierstein's. He found Shelley's name and slowly traced the sculpted letters with his fingertips. He was ashamed that he couldn't remember the faces of any others of his fallen comrades, yet the blood-soaked portrait of the enemy soldier he'd killed, the man with the picture of his wife and children in his tunic, was engraved as deeply in his mind as these names were chiseled in stone before him. He leaned his forehead against that ominous black marble wall and he cried for Shelley and he cried for that Vietcong sniper and his wife and children and he cried for Binh and the son he'd never acknowledged, and he cried for himself.

In the days that followed his return home he became obsessed with a renewed search for meaning in his life. He was forty-one years old. He'd spent almost fifteen years working to master his craft and to be accepted by his colleagues as a skilled trial attorney.

But what exactly did that mean, in the scheme of life? Was it enough to devote a lifetime to playing a small part in the judicial process, to the ever-challenging search for truth? Was it enough if every once in awhile he got a chance to make a positive difference in someone's life? Maybe it was, he thought. But to be honest with himself, in reality he was just a hick criminal lawyer with two failed marriages, a legitimate child he saw only every other weekend, and an illegitimate twenty-two-year-old son he'd never seen. He'd already lived more than two-thirds of his life, and his closest companion was his damned cat.

——

For a week he wallowed in self-pity and then, by chance or fate or the hand of God, he received a telephone call from Professor Cook. Luke had been one of Bertram Cook's prize students in his criminal law course at Columbia University Law School. They'd maintained a friendship over the years, and met for dinner at least once a year.

"Luke, it's Bert Cook. How are you doing?"

"Funny you should ask. I've been down in the dumps for the past week and hearing from you is the best thing that could have happened to me today."

"Nothing serious, I hope. Lose a big case, did you?"

"No, no, nothing as simple as that. I'm just having a little midlife crisis, you might say. Somebody told me they call it man-a-pause."

"Been there and done that. Actually I'd be quite happy if I were young enough to do it again. But perhaps I called at the right time."

"You aren't going to cancel our dinner date for next month, I hope."

"Absolutely not. In fact, if this conversation goes well, I was hoping we might move the date up to next week. Luke, I'm facing mandatory retirement this year, and the school is searching for my replacement. I wanted to recommend you for the position, but I wouldn't dare do so without talking to you first and getting your permission."

"Good Lord, Bert. Are you serious? What the devil do I know about teaching law?"

"A lot more than these academic types they keep hiring here. The way I see it, nobody gets hurt if they want to hire legal scholars to teach wills and trusts and real property because if they screw up, it's only money. But with criminal law, we're talking about justice and freedom and keeping the prosecutors on the straight and narrow, and sometimes even saving a man's life."

"You know, Bert, I'd swear those are the same words I heard you say to us twenty-five years ago in your class."

"You're probably right, and they're as true now as they were then. Are you interested?"

"Well, I'm flattered, of course, but like I said, I don't know a damn thing about teaching, and —"

"You will when I get through with you. You can have my course notes, which I've fine-tuned over the past fifty years. And besides, it's your experience these kids are interested in. They want to know how the system works down in the trenches, not what they learn in law review articles. If you're prepared to take a cut in pay in return for an exciting new intellectual challenge and the satisfaction that comes with knowing that what you do can make a real difference in the thousands of lives your students will touch in the course of their professional careers. I guarantee you'll never regret it. Ever!"

There was total silence for a moment and then Luke said, "When shall we meet?"

CHAPTER THIRTY-TWO

"You invited me for a drink, so where are we going?" Luke asked as Pat slipped into the passenger seat of his classic Jaguar XKE. The black leather upholstery was as soft as a pair of French kid gloves. There was a warm green glow from the dashboard lights. Jazz was playing on the stereo.

"It's in Sheepshead Bay, and it's called Clancy's. Where else would a young, innocent, red-headed colleen go in the big city without a chaperone?"

When they entered the place, the bar was three deep with the owners of the dozen or so pickups parked helter-skelter out front. Shania Twain was oozing out of the jukebox like fresh maple syrup. A big friendly Irish setter named Dublin paced back and forth behind the bar with Clancy, a giant of a man with a massive head and beard of tight red curls.

They spotted a small booth at the end of the bar with an unobstructed view of the dozen backsides hunched around the bar. As Luke started to squeeze into the booth, Pat said, "If you really want something to drink, don't bother sitting down. There aren't any waitresses here. Clancy runs the whole show."

Luke started toward the bar, but Pat tugged at his jacket. "Also, please don't order a martini or a whiskey sour or something dumb like that. He'll never forget or forgive you. The choice is, you take your liquor neat or you order a beer. I'll take an Amstel light myself."

Luke returned in a few minutes carrying two bottles of beer and a jigger of whiskey full to the brim.

He held the shot glass up in salute, threw it down in one motion, took a swallow of beer, and settled back in the booth with a wide grin. Pat felt a shiver of pleasure surge through her body.

"Have you any idea how long it's been since I've had a boilermaker in a bar like this?" he shouted above the noise of the crowd as the Yankees' batter smashed a double, driving in a run.

She realized that by bringing him to this workingman's bar, she was emphasizing the difference between their social circles. But as soon as he sat down in the booth he removed his jacket and tie and rolled up his sleeves. He was perfectly at ease and clearly enjoying himself. He told her about his life growing up in Glenwood, a university town in upstate New York, which led to their sharing anecdotes from their high school years. He had played varsity soccer, basketball, and track, and when she told him she was captain of her tennis team in high school, he slapped the flat of his hand on the table.

"Tennis!" he shouted. "That's the passion of my life. With this bum knee I don't play as well as I used to, but… We must play immediately, I mean like tomorrow or the day after. I can't believe it. Captain of your tennis team! That calls for another drink." He was up and out of the booth like a shot before she could protest. When he returned, he was carrying a bottle of champagne, in a mop bucket filled with ice, and two clean beer glasses.

"However did you manage that?" Pat asked, in amazement.

"Just lucked out, I guess. The truth is, it was left over from last year's World Series celebration. It ain't Dom Perignon, you know, but under the circumstances, it's a hell of a lot better." She'd never heard him use the word *ain't* before.

"Did you know Clancy plays tennis? I made a date for us to play doubles with him and his wife Chip next Wednesday night. We're going to play at that club that's on your right when you exit from the Queen's Midtown Tunnel."

"I don't believe it!"

"What's that?" Luke cocked his head, looking perplexed. He'd clearly disturbed her.

"First you manage to wheedle a bottle of champagne out of Clancy, when I've never seen him serve anything like that in this bar, ever. Second, I've been coming here for years and I never knew he was married or played tennis, and third, how could you make a date for us to play tennis without even asking me first?"

"I don't understand. Don't you want to play?"

"Of course I do, but…but I expect to be asked, not told."

"Oh, right. Cool. How would you like to play tennis with Clancy and Chip next Wednesday night?"

"I guess I'll have to think about it."

"You're kidding, right?"

"How do you know he's really married?"

"What's that got to do with it?"

"And how do you know his wife, what's her name, Chip, has agreed to play?"

"Well, of course I don't, and I would guess he doesn't either, I just assumed —"

"And that's the problem. You guys just assume that whatever you want to do is the way it has to be."

"Now I understand. It's a woman thing. You want to talk about it, right? "

"What's wrong with that?"

"Nothing! It's just not…hey, you're right. I'll tell Clancy, maybe we can make it some other time."

"No, no, no. You still don't get it. I want to play with you on Wednesday, but I don't —"

"Great. I'll go tell Clancy." Luke slid out of the booth before she could object.

"Damn!" she cursed when he was out of earshot.

When the bar started thinning out around seven o'clock, Luke said, "Now we're going to go get something to eat at this little seafood restaurant I know. It's not far from here. The guy serves the best clam chowder in the universe."

"Is that an invitation or an order?"

"Excuse me?"

"Never mind, it's too complicated."

When the meal was over she said, "That happens to be the best clam chowder I've ever had in my life. But why couldn't you have asked me if…" Pat hesitated. Maybe she was letting her feminism get in the way, here. "Never mind. I guess I'm ready for you to tell me everything about your life – besides your sordid views on marriage."

"Everything? I'm sure you don't want to know everything, but I'm willing to give you the highlights."

"I don't want the expurgated version where you leave out the juicy parts. I'm a big girl, you know. The fact is, Mr. Alexander, it's the dark side of you that I am most interested in right now."

"But if I shed light on my dark side, the intrigue will be gone and then you'll become bored with me. I don't want to lose you."

"You're so full of blarney, Luke. We've been on only two dates. We haven't even…," She hesitated, feeling her cheeks flush, "watched a movie together or walked in the park or shared *The New York Times* over brunch at my favorite Sunday restaurant. The fact is, we don't know each other at all. How can you say you don't want to lose me?" Pat knew the relationship was heating up and, while that excited her it also left her feeling deeply vulnerable. Luke seemed to embody all the traits that she sought in a mate, except that he was a bit macho, too assured and domineering. She was used to giving orders as well as taking them. But what was she looking for, anyway? A male friend? A lover? A husband? If she wasn't even sure what she was seeking, how could she —

"I don't want to lose you because I think you're lovely to look at, you're bright and funny and…the chemistry is right." He placed his hand over hers on the tabletop.

His touch excited her. She wanted to say, You don't happen to have any etchings at your place, do you? But instead she said, "Well, I won't trust the chemistry until I know every detail about your life, good, bad, or otherwise. The stakes are too high here."

"You're right, this is a high-stakes adventure. Higher for me than for you perhaps, because I've been involved in a number of relationships and two failed marriages, as I told you. Emotionally, I can't afford another mistake. And it's true that we don't know much about each other, but both my head and my heart are telling me to take a chance here."

"Then spill it all, now, while I'm still in possession of my faculties and not allowing my imagination to run wild." She squeezed his hand, her eyes pleading for the truth and her mind fearing what that might disclose.

Luke reached over, lifted the wine bottle from the ice bucket and filled their glasses. Then he leaned back and said, "Okay, the down-and-dirty truth is that aside from the scores of people who have shaped my life, such as a mother who abandoned me when I was a baby and a father who, when faced with the choice of keeping me or his paramour, chose the paramour, other experiences have had a most profound effect on my life too. But I don't think there's time enough tonight to share those stories with you."

Pat glanced at her watch. "Oh my God! Do you know what time it is? Let's go, counselor. It's been absolutely delicious, both the meal and the company, and as much as I'd like to stay with you until dawn, learning everything about your dark past, this sergeant has to be on duty at 7:30 AM I have an unhappy date with the district attorney tomorrow morning at nine o'clock."

"Just one more reason to loathe and despise the DA," Luke said, shrugging his shoulders. "But I'll only leave now if you promise to join me at my cottage out on the island some weekend to go sailing and listen to all the gory details of my life."

"I don't know how to sail."

"You will, I promise."

"I suppose you could talk me into it. I have the second weekend of every month off."

Luke pulled his appointment book out of his pocket and exclaimed, "But that was last weekend. That means you won't have another weekend off until three weeks from now!"

"You got it. But I'm not made of paper mâché, you know. I won't disintegrate in the rain between now and then."

"You're right, of course, but...okay, how about sailing lessons the second weekend in October?"

"You got yourself a date, Counselor."

"So what are we going to do with ourselves between now and then? Besides tennis on Wednesday, I mean. I'm not planning to go into hibernation," Luke quipped.

"We're in the Big Apple, sir. There's Joe Papp's Theater in the Park, the Circle Line Cruise around Manhattan, Saturday Night Jazz at Lincoln Center, Nathan's hot dogs at Coney Island. There's an off-Broadway revival of *Man of La Mancha*, one of my favorite shows, there's —"

"I get it, I get it."

———

The next morning, Pat received a special delivery package. It was an exquisite, hand-tooled leather appointment book in which Lucas's name was printed on every Wednesday and Saturday night from September through December. Gold stars were pasted in the second weekend of October and big question marks were written on Thanksgiving, Christmas, and New Year's Day.

CHAPTER THIRTY-THREE

Pat had interviewed both Helen and Jennifer shortly after each returned to New York. Pat confirmed that the keys found in Joey Pesci's apartment belonged to Helen, who said that when she realized they were missing, she assumed she'd misplaced them and that they would eventually show up. But they hadn't.

Jennifer, apparently, had been reading every article about the case, including the speculation that whenever a murder is committed in a bedroom, there is probably a love triangle involved somehow. She had become totally focused on the investigation, especially after rumors of Frank's affairs filtered down to her through classmates, who were overhearing conversations between their parents. She asked Pat to share as much information as she could with her, so on one occasion Pat offered to show her the lab where the forensic work was performed and allowed her to look through the high-powered microscope at some random specimen slides. Pat was taken aback when Jennifer asked to see the bullets that had killed her father. She said that wasn't possible, and the girl seemed to drop the subject.

Instead, she asked, "How come they don't have a man in charge of my dad's case?"

"Because they thought I was the best person to do the job, and I agree with them," Pat said.

"As soon as you find out who did it, I'm going to kill him." Jennifer studied the ballistics chart tacked up on the wall.

Pat was shocked by the girl's remark and was uncertain how to respond. "Let's go back to my office and talk about it," she said, putting her arm around Jennifer's shoulder and leading her out of the lab. Neither of them spoke as they walked down the long corridor and took the elevator up two flights to Pat's office. Pat closed the door and settled in behind her old wooden desk. The child walked around the tiny office, studying the diplomas and awards displayed on the wall. Pat waited patiently for Jennifer to settle down. When she finally slid into the chair opposite Pat's desk, she looked directly at Pat for the first time.

"Shall we talk about it, Jennifer?"

"Okay."

"No one has the right to take the law into their own hands, Jen. I know exactly how you feel, but —"

"You can't know how I feel. That's impossible."

"Oh, but I do. When I was just a few years older than you, my father was killed senselessly too. I know all about your pain… and your hate."

"I don't believe you."

Pat opened her desk drawer and slid the framed citation across the desk.

Sgt. Patrick Turner, killed in the line of duty…

"I'm sorry but it's not the same. My dad loved me more than anybody. It's not fair!" Jennifer began to cry.

"No, it's not fair. But we'll find the person who killed your father and he'll be punished. That's why we have laws and courts and judges, to make certain justice gets done," Pat said. "Let me take you home to your mom. She's hurting too, you know."

After dropping Jennifer off, Pat returned to her office to finish up paperwork, and it was after nine o'clock by the time she arrived home. The phone was ringing as she opened the door. She was hoping it might be Luke, but it was Jennifer.

"I've been thinking about what you asked me, like about strangers that came to our apartment, like salesmen, or repair guys. Would that also be like a pizza delivery guy?"

"Sure, I guess it could be. What do you remember?"

"Well, there was this guy who delivered a pizza for mom and me one night. I mean he was friendly, but he was also sort of weird, if you know what I mean."

"Not exactly, Jen. In what way was he weird? Was it something he said, or something he did?"

"I don't know, he just acted sort of, you know, sort of goofy."

"Do you remember if that was when your mom ordered a pizza from the Neapolitan Pizza place?"

"Yeah, that's where we always get our pizzas. It's on East 69th."

"Do you remember what the guy looked like?" The image of Joey Pesci flashed through her mind.

"Sort of, but not really. He was taller than me, but I'm only 5' 4". He had a moustache and I think he was Hispanic, but I'm not sure."

"How old would you say he was?"

"Maybe like eighteen or ninteen."

"Would you remember him if you saw him again?"

"Oh, yeah, I'm sure I'd remember him."

"The young man I'm thinking of isn't so tall and he's Italian, not Hispanic, but he does have a moustache," Pat said.

"I'm not exactly sure about the Hispanic thing, and maybe he wasn't so tall, but I know he had a moustache."

First thing the next morning, Pat told Ken to contact Detective Dick Gonzalez. "Give him the dope on Pesci and send him up to the Neapolitan Pizza Parlor on East 69th. Tell him to find out if Pesci ever worked for them and if he ever made a delivery to the Dunn apartment."

———

Detective Richard Gonzalez was a solid veteran of the New York City Police Department. His promotions had come slowly but steadily, and he could be counted on to do the job right. When he entered the Neapolitan Pizza Parlor that evening, there was only one person behind the counter, and he appeared to be the manager, cook, order-taker, and cashier. Gonzalez had to hang around for about twenty minutes before he got a chance to talk to him.

When that time came, Gonzalez pulled out his wallet and displayed his badge. "Sorry to bother you, sir. I'm Detective Richard Gonzalez, New York City Police Department. Is it possible you might remember who delivered a pizza from your place to an apartment on FDR Drive some time before July 27, say maybe within a week or so of that date?"

"Yeah, sure," the man grunted, his voice as surly as his face. "It's right on the tip of my tongue. I've only delivered about fifteen hundred pizzas in the last ten days."

"I was hoping you might remember. It was delivered to a family by the name of Dunn. A penthouse on FDR Drive."

"The Dunns? Yeah, I remember! I'm looking for that kid, too. You know him?"

"Not really, I —"

"That's good 'cause if you was a friend of his, I'd throw yer ass outta here."

"As a matter of fact, I —"

"The kid ripped me off, but the fuckin' cops say they can't do nothin'. The fuckin' cops are as bad as the rest of them."

"Do you know his name?"

"Naw, he come in lookin' for work and my delivery kid had just quit on me. I was busier than hell and like a jerk I took a chance on him without checkin' him out. He made a couple deliveries and run off with the money. I never saw him again. So what's the deal? What do you want him for?" Gollardo asked. "I hope it's something real bad so's they'll cut off his balls. I bust my ass in here twelve to fourteen hours a day, seven days a week, so maybe I clear two hundred bucks a day, and that little pisspot steals half of it. The first night he's working here, his last delivery had a hundred dollar ticket. The little bastard never come back with the money, and besides, when I cashed out that night, I was over two hundred short. I know it was him that stole it, but I can't prove nothing except for the hundred bucks, and the cops say it ain't worth bothering with. You know, they're too busy giving out parking tickets to my customers."

"Yeah, I know what you mean. It don't seem right."

"That's what the other cop said, but nothing happens."

"I promise I'll look into it. Sometimes we just ain't got time, you know."

"I know, I know."

Gollardo went to take care of a customer and then sidled back to where Gonzalez was waiting at the end of the counter. He wiped off the counter and lit up a cigarette.

"So what do you want to know?" he asked, inhaling deeply and then letting the smoke drift out the corner of his mouth.

———

When Jennifer got home from school the next day there was a message on the answering machine to call Pat as soon as she could.

"Can you come to my office when you get out of school tomorrow, say at four o'clock?"

"Sure," Jennifer said; "what's up?"

"I'm going to have you look at some men in a line-up. We'll see how good your memory is."

"A lineup, a real lineup, like on television? Jeez, will the pizza guy be in it?"

"That's what we're going to find out, right? But you must promise me that if you aren't certain, you won't guess. Understand?"

"Yeah, but it's kind of scary. Will the guy be able to see me?"

"No, you and your mom will be in a room with one-way glass. I'll see you both tomorrow."

———

Joey Pesci's bravado had diminished while he sat in the Manhattan detention center. Petty larceny and car theft were Joey's specialty, though he'd dreamed of more ambitious adventures, like burglarizing the Dunn apartment. But being a suspect in a murder case and facing a possible life sentence was a whole different ballgame. "I didn't do nothing," he kept saying to himself and to anybody else who would listen to him.

Pat ushered Helen and Jennifer into the tiny viewing room from which they could see the men in the lineup, but couldn't be seen themselves. Pat glanced briefly at Pesci and then waited to see Jennifer and Helen's reactions, if they recognized him. But they had no reactions, and when it was over they both confirmed that Pesci was not the person who'd delivered the pizza.

So, Pat asked herself, if Pesci didn't deliver the pizza, who did? And if it wasn't Pesci, when and how did his fingerprints get on the foyer table? If he didn't burglarize the apartment how did he get the keys and the cigarette lighter? How could she prove that the burglary occurred the night Dunn was killed?

But if Pesci did kill him, how did Shadrack end up with the murder weapon?

CHAPTER THIRTY-FOUR

The hearing before Surrogate Court Judge Casey, with respect to the validity of the gift to Margaux McBride in Katrina Shauffler's will, began in the second week of September 2003. Its purpose was to determine whether the gift to Margaux was the product of a fraud perpetrated upon Mrs. Shauffler by Frank and Margaux.

Several different law firms, representing the different charities, were present, and Luke was designated lead counsel. Margaux had engaged the services of Barney Rifkin, an attorney with many years' experience as a successful trial lawyer.

The attorneys all rose as Judge Casey entered the court to begin the proceeding.

"Good morning, gentlemen. My court is rarely honored with so many distinguished members of our bar. If you will each stand and identify yourself, indicating the client you represent, I'll try to keep a scorecard of who's who in this controversy."

After the identification of the lawyers, Judge Casey said, "I see that you represent the petitioner in this matter, Lucas, so I guess you're up first."

"Thank you, sir." Luke stepped up to the lectern and gave the judge an overview of the facts. He indicated that the Shauffler Trust Fund had an estimated value of twenty-five million dollars and was earning about two million dollars a year.

"The issue in this case is fraud. The will states that the corpus of the trust fund is to be divided among four charities. However, it also provides that the income from the trust is to be paid first to Frank Dunn, Mrs. Shauffler's attorney, or in the event that he died before her, which he did, the income is to be paid to his associate Margaux McBride. This means the gifts to the charities would be postponed forty years or more until the death of Margaux McBride.

"It is our claim that the gift to Ms. McBride is the result of a fraud practiced upon Mrs. Shauffler, that it was never her intention to reward her attorneys by a gift that amounts to over two million dollars a year during the lifetime of Ms. McBride." Luke noticed that the judge's eyebrows shifted slightly upward when he understood what was at stake.

"Anything else, Lucas?" the judge asked.

"No, sir. Primarily we propose to introduce evidence to prove that Mrs. Shauffler never intended to make a gift to Ms. McBride."

"I think I've got a handle on your side of this case, Lucas. Now, Barney, what have you got to say about all of this?"

Barney Rifkin eased his tall, lanky frame out of his chair. and said, "I suppose, Judge, it comes as no surprise to you that we have a totally different view of the facts, and I would appreciate a chance to tell you our side of the story."

"I expected you might, Barney."

Barney Rifkin placed his carefully penned notes on top of the lectern. He removed his glasses, fogged them with his breath, wiped them slowly with a crisp white handkerchief, and put them gently back on.

"Judge," Barney drawled, "on one side of this case we have my client, a distinguished member of the New York Bar, and on the other side, we've got a lot of dead people. Lucas here is going to try and convince Your Honor as to what all these dead people said and did on the day the will was signed, though I can't quite figure out how he's planning to do that.

"We're going to prove what occurred over the course of many months as my client and Mrs. Shauffler worked together preparing Mrs. Shauffler's will. We will prove that Mrs. Shauffler always wanted a child, but the good Lord didn't see fit to grant her that wish. And then one day, in the twilight of her life, she met Margaux, who had been abandoned by her father when she was born, and orphaned at a very young age. Margaux never dreamed that one day she'd meet and be succored by a woman whose need for a child's love was as deep as her own craving for a mother. They considered their meeting to be a miracle. Many hours were shared between them exchanging their most intimate thoughts and aspirations. One day Katrina gave Margaux a valuable antique gold dinner ring and told her it had been her mother's — so she was giving it to Margaux as if Margaux were her own daughter.

"Then a time came when she told Margaux that since Frank Dunn was going to be the executor of her will, she had a few minor details she wished to discuss with him. And indeed, the evidence will disclose that she did meet with Frank Dunn on the day before she signed her will. Unfortunately, neither of them can appear before Your Honor to testify as to what they said to each other, but obviously, the will, which Frank Dunn prepared and Your Honor has before him, is the product of that conversation."

Oh my God, such lies! Sarah Nusbaum was seated in the first row of spectators.

"The fact is, Judge, we all know how meticulous Mike Dunn was when it came to the preparation of his client's wills, and his son Frank followed in his footsteps in that regard. Now when you fold the will back together, you'll see how those red ribbons are laced through each page and then sealed with red wax and stamped with Mrs. Shauffler's signet ring to make absolutely certain that no one could tamper with it."

The judge followed the attorney's instructions and folded the will back together. "Yes, I see that, Barney."

"So what we have here, Judge, is a case in which a lonely and loving old woman wanted to share her wealth, first with her sister Sarah Nusbaum, then with Frank Dunn, who had been like a son to her, and then with her new-found daughter, Margaux McBride. Apparently the petitioners are not satisfied with the gift of twenty-five million dollars upon Margaux's death. They want it all now!" Barney removed his glasses slowly and looked up at the judge. "I'm certain that when you've heard both sides of this case, you'll find that the ends of justice will be served by allowing the wishes of Katrina Shauffler to be carried out exactly as she directed. Thank you, Your Honor." Barney picked up his notes and lumbered back to the counsel table.

"All right, gentlemen, I think I have a pretty good grasp of the disputed facts, but I need a little time to study the pleadings and the legal issues. That will also give you a chance to organize your witnesses, Lucas." Judge Casey stood up. The court clerk banged the gavel and intoned, "Court is adjourned until 2:00 PM"

Sarah and Luke went to lunch at a restaurant just around the corner from the courthouse. After they'd ordered Sarah said, "How could that lawyer say such things? They're all lies. He didn't say one thing that was true. Lies, lies, lies."

"You mustn't get upset, Mrs. Nusbaum. The judge doesn't pay much attention to what the lawyers argue; he's only interested in the evidence and the law. Incidentally, since the will has now been approved, all of Katrina's gifts to you are protected."

"Oh, Mr. Alexander, it's not me I'm thinking about. It's Katrina. She was so happy and proud to be able to make those gifts in memory of Irving. When I hear that woman's lies, I get so angry I could…" She didn't finish her sentence.

CHAPTER THIRTY-FIVE

"Hear ye, hear ye, this court is now open and ready for business with the Honorable John Casey presiding, all rise."

Judge Casey entered the court, slid into the antique leather chair and said, "All right, Lucas, you may call your first witness."

Luke turned and motioned to a gentlemen seated in the back of the courtroom, who immediately came forward. The clerk intoned, "Raise your right hand, please. Do you swear or affirm to tell the truth, the whole truth, and nothing but the truth?"

"I do."

The clerk held open the gate to allow the witness to take the stand. Luke picked up a sheaf of papers from the counsel table and addressed the man. "What is your name and occupation, sir?"

"Dr. Adam Sindelar. I am a physician with a specialty in internal medicine."

"Are you acquainted with Mrs. Alma Haverstock?"

"Yes, sir. She's a patient of mine at New York Hospital."

"What is her present medical condition?"

"Mrs. Haverstock suffered a cerebral hemorrhage. She's totally paralyzed as a result of a blockage of the blood supply to the brain. The full extent of her brain damage has been extremely difficult to ascertain because she's unable to speak, and since she is totally paralyzed, she cannot write. It's very difficult to communicate with her."

"Now, doctor, please tell us how you are able to ask questions of Mrs. Haverstock."

Dr. Sindelar described in detail how Mrs. Haverstock could answer questions by blinking her eyes, and that it was his professional opinion that she was capable of cognitive thinking.

"No further questions."

Judge Casey turned to Barney. "Any cross examination, Barney?"

"Just a few questions, Judge," Barney said, as he eased himself up and over to the lectern.

"Doctor, my name is Barney Rifkin, and I'm the attorney for the young lady over there at the counsel table." Barney pointed to Margaux. "If you don't understand any question I ask, just tell me and I'll rephrase it so you do. Okay?"

"I'll do my best."

"I'm sure you will, doctor, because, of course, you haven't taken sides in this case, have you?"

"No, sir. In fact, I'm not even sure what the controversy is."

"I assume you did have a chance to talk to Mr. Alexander before you came here to testify, right?"

"Yes, I did."

"And, of course, you're being paid to testify, right?"

"No, I'm not being paid to testify. I'm being paid for the time I've spent reviewing the medical records and rendering medical opinions. Besides, I had to cancel a number of patients in order to come here today."

"Sure, I understand. You fellows have to make a living too, right?" Barney smiled in a disarming fashion.

"Yes, that's true." Dr. Sindelar returned his conspiratorial smile.

"Doctor, have you ever asked Mrs. Haverstock any questions concerning any subject other than the state of her health? For example, have you ever asked her any questions about her work?"

"Let me think, counselor…" Dr. Sindelar hesitated thoughtfully for a few moments. "Yes, as a matter of fact, I remember a few days ago, I recall asking if she were retired and her answer was 'yes and no'."

"Well, which was it?"

"I understood her to mean that she wasn't completely retired or that she was still involved in her work somehow. It's hard to explain, but when you are trying to communicate with her, there are many things you take into consideration. The expression in her eyes, for example."

"Are you telling us, doctor, that you can tell what she's thinking by the expression in her eyes?" Barney demanded scornfully.

"Well, no, I guess I am not saying that."

"Did you ever ask her whether or not she believes in God? That's a question that only calls for a yes or no answer."

"No, I did not. I didn't have any reason to ask her such a question."

"So, for example, you didn't ask her 'Do you swear to tell the truth...so help you God?'"

"No, counselor, I didn't ask her that."

"Then tell me, doctor, when you asked her a question, how could you tell whether or not she was telling you the truth?"

"There was absolutely no reason why she should lie!"

"Then tell me, please, sir, suppose there was a reason for her to lie. How would you know if she were telling the truth?"

"Frankly, I never thought about it."

"Well, doctor, I'm now asking you to think about it."

"I really don't know how to answer your question."

"All right, let me put it this way. Do you think that anyone has ever lied to you?"

"You mean ever? Of course."

"How could you tell?"

"I believe there are many ways you can tell when someone's lying. Maybe they act nervous or perhaps they don't look you in the eye or they blush or − I don't know. But you can get a pretty good idea of it by the way a person acts."

"Suppose they can't act?"

"What do you mean?"

"Suppose they physically can't react...like Mrs. Haverstock. She can look you in the eye, but she can't move a muscle. She has absolutely no facial expressions. So tell me, Doctor, how can you tell when Mrs. Haverstock tells a lie?"

"I guess you really can't."

"Thank you, doctor." Barney smiled and returned to his seat at the counsel table.

"Mr. Alexander, do you have any further questions?"

"Perhaps just one, Judge." Luke returned to the podium.

"Doctor, during the time you spent with Mrs. Haverstock, did she ever answer a question untruthfully?" Barney started to object, but before he had a chance, Dr. Sindelar replied, "As Mr. Rifkin brought out, how could I tell?"

"No further questions," Luke mumbled, glancing over at Barney who smiled and winked at him. "Petitioner calls her next witness." Luke was disgusted with himself for having asked one question too many.

"What is your name and occupation, please?"

"Jason Whitman. I'm head of forensics for the New York City Police Department."

"Mr. Whitman, will you describe for us the tests you performed at my request?"

"I examined the last will and testament of Katrina Shauffler and made a comparison between page fifty-four and the rest of the pages of the will."

"Please examine the will and tell us whether you're certain that the document you're holding in your hand right now is the same will you examined in the office of the surrogate."

The witness quickly riffled the pages of the will and answered, "Yes, it is."

"How can you tell?"

"I put a pinhole in the corner of each page I examined."

"Let me see that will, please," Judge Casey said. He peered at the lower left hand corner of several pages of the will. He smiled but made no comment and returned the will to the witness.

"Please describe for the court your findings with regard to the differences, if any, between page fifty-four and the rest of the pages of the Shauffler will."

"First, the location. The juxtaposition of the holes at the top of each page of the will forms a discernible pattern. Page fifty-four doesn't fit the pattern."

Judge Casey leaned down towards the witness and asked, "What do you mean by that?"

Jason reached over and picked up the will and held it up for the judge to see as he continued his testimony. "The purpose of these two holes in the top of each page is to allow the ribbon to be laced through the pages, thus preventing tampering of any sort. In this case, these holes were made by this simple mechanical device I found in Mrs. Haverstock's cubicle at the Dunn law office." He picked up the device and held it up along side the will. "You put the paper in here and pull down the handle and two holes are punched in the top of the paper." The witness slipped several pieces of blank paper in the device and pulled down the handle. "I measured the location of all the holes in the pages of the will and I found that the

Dance of the Mantis   **175**

holes in page fifty-four are different from those in the other pages of the will, all of which follow a pattern. It is therefore my opinion that the holes in page fifty-four were made either before or after all of the other pages were punched."

Judge Casey settled back in his chair thoughtfully and made a note on his pad. Luke considered that a good sign. He continued with his questioning.

"What other observations did you make?"

"The most significant finding I made was that page fifty-four came from a different ream of paper. The knives that cut copy paper in a mill each have their own characteristics, as unique as a fingerprint. If a single sheet of paper from one ream is inserted into the center of a different ream, we're able to identify that single page by observing the end cut pattern of the ream. May I have the photos, Mr. Alexander?"

"Exhibits seven through ninteen, Your Honor," Luke said after showing them to Barney. The witness selected two photographs and turned back to the judge.

"These two exhibits pretty much tell the whole story, Your Honor." The witness held them up for the judge to see, and Barney approached the bench so he could follow the testimony.

"This first photo is a ten-plus enlargement of the end cut of all fifty-six pages of the Shauffler will. As anyone can tell, page fifty-four disrupts the unique pattern demonstrated by the other fifty-five pages. See, here it sticks out like a sore thumb. It is therefore my opinion that page fifty-four was printed before or after the other pages in the will."

"Anything else?" Luke asked.

"Yes, sir. The format of page fifty-four is different from the rest of the pages. Someone adjusted the computer to allow additional words to fit on page fifty-four. You can't tell that at first glance, but I measured the margins of these pages and there are eighty-four spaces per line on page fifty-four, whereas there are only seventy-eight spaces per line on all the other pages."

"You may examine," Luke said, as he resumed his seat at the counsel table.

Barney eased up to the lectern and began his cross-examination. "First of all, Mr. Whitman, I assume you'll agree with me that the printer connected to the computer does not have an endless supply of paper, isn't that so?"

"Of course."

"So that if the operator were printing the Shauffler will and the printer ran out of paper at page fifty-three, the operator would have to insert another batch of paper, isn't that right?"

"Yes, sir."

"Under those circumstances, wouldn't you agree that there could have been two different kinds of paper which were used when the Shauffler will was printed?"

"Of course, but if that were the case, you'd expect to find the last three pages of the will to all be the same, and they're not."

Barney ignored the answer and continued his questioning.

"Mr. Whitman, you don't claim to know who, in fact, typed up the Shauffler will, do you?"

"No, sir, I have no idea."

"All you're telling us is that in your opinion, page fifty-four was typed up on a piece of paper that came from a different ream of paper than the others. Isn't that true?"

"Yes, sir, that's true."

"And you certainly don't know which lawyer asked which secretary to type which pages, am I right?"

"You're right, sir."

"And indeed, correcting a mistake in the middle of a multi-paged document happens all the time, doesn't it?"

"I suppose so."

"No further cross-examination." Barney sighed audibly and sat down.

"Give the court your full name, please," Luke asked.

"Ellis Fretwell."

"And the nature of your profession?"

"I'm an electronics engineer, but I've spent a lot of time teaching, mostly at NYU. I'm what they call a professor emeritus. It means they give me some modest retirement benefits and a desk in a corner."

"Now, Professor, are you familiar with any type of electronic equipment that will allow Alma Haverstock to testify in this case?" Luke asked.

"Yes, sir. The Eyegaze Communications System, known as ECS, empowers people to communicate with the world using only the movement of their eyes. Simply by looking at control keys displayed on a screen for approximately a second allows users to perform a broad variety of functions which would certainly include the ability to testify here in court.

"Could you describe how that system works, Professor?"

"To operate the Eyegaze system, the Eyegaze camera is focused on one eye. The camera continually observes the user's eye, and specialized image processing software in the system determines where the user is looking on the screen. The system enables the user to control entire on-screen computer keyboards. I have a photograph here which depicts the flat-paneled display screen, with the camera attached at the lower portion of the screen, and the processor."

Lucas took the photograph from Professor Fretwell and handed it to the clerk to be marked as an exhibit.

"I also have a photo here that describes how the equipment is attached to a wheelchair to be used by the operator."

When the exhibits were accepted in evidence, Lucas said, "Your Honor, I believe these photographs will help the court through this process. I offer them in evidence."

"I will receive them, Mr. Alexander, on the basis that anything that will help this feeble old brain of mine is always welcome."

Luke tacked the photographs up on the exhibit board.

"Any objections, Mr. Rifkin?" Judge Casey asked.

Barney walked casually over to the exhibit easel and studied the drawing carefully. "Not now, Judge, but I'm going to have a bagful of objections if Luke attempts to offer that contraption in evidence," Barney said solemnly.

Luke continued with his questions to Ellis Fretwell. "Tell us, please, whether in your opinion, a person such as Mrs. Haverstock can communicate her thoughts to us solely with her eyes, by means of this computer system?" Luke asked.

Barney was immediately on his feet, "Objection, Your Honor."

"I'll hear you, Mr. Rifkin," the judge replied.

"Judge, Lucas is attempting to make a circus out of this court with all this electronic gadgetry."

"Objection denied. You may proceed, Professor Fretwell." the judge said calmly.

"The equipment you see here not only has the ability to allow Mrs. Haverstock to respond to simple questions with a *yes* or *no* answer, but it enables her to communicate words to express her thoughts."

Barney was on his feet again. "Objection, Your Honor! There is no proof that Mrs. Haverstock has any thoughts to express."

"Objection overruled. And the next time you have an objection, Mr. Rifkin, it had better have the power of the United States Supreme Court behind it. Now, let's get on with it."

"I have the right to protect the record of this proceeding in case of an appeal," Barney whined.

"You do, absolutely, Mr. Rifkin, but not now! Proceed, Professor."

"There are three monitors here, Judge, which look like TV screens," Professor Fretwell explained.

"I'm with you so far." The judge leaned forward on the bench.

"All right, sir, now let's suppose you wish to ask the question, 'What is your name?' The computer works in the same way as your ordinary word processor, except for one significant difference. When you press the letter *a* with your finger on a keyboard, it magically appears both on the screen above your keyboard and also somewhere in the innards of the computer, so that when you later activate the printer, it prints the letter *a* on a piece of paper. Now, this piece of equipment here enables the operator to focus her eyes on certain preselected words and phrases such as *yes, no, I don't know*, and *I don't recall*.

"But it also permits the operator to put letters together to make words and sentences. Here's how that works. When the alphabet is displayed on the monitor, the operator selects the letter *a*, for example, by looking at the letter *a* on the monitor. When she does that, the lens of the camera, which is focused on her eyes, transmits that information to the computer, which causes the letter *a* to appear on the display screen and on the printer mechanism. The operator then focuses her eyes on the next letters, and the process is repeated until she has selected each of the letters in each word she wishes to write. See how that works, Your Honor?"

"Absolutely," the judge said, "though I may need a few more instructions later on. I certainly expect to operate this machine myself. If I can figure it out, anybody can. So where do we go from here, Mr. Alexander?"

"I have no further questions at this time, Your Honor."

After an hour of cross-examination, Barney was unsuccessful in challenging Professor Fretwell's testimony.

The courtroom was hushed as Alma Haverstock was wheeled in and placed in front of the Eyeglaze Computer System. Luke addressed Judge Casey. "May I proceed, sir?"

Barney jumped up and said, "I object to Mr. Alexander making a mockery of the judicial process."

"Mr. Rifkin, I not only overrule your objection, I applaud what seems to be happening here. The search for truth takes many forms, even a novel one like this. I shall carefully weigh the testimony offered to determine what, if any, weight should be given to it. But under no circumstances will I deny this witness the opportunity to give testimony, no matter how tortured the process may be." He then turned to Luke, saying, "You may proceed."

Luke stood beside Alma Haverstock who was seated in a special wheelchair.

Luke then turned to the clerk. "Mr. Robins, will you please swear in the witness?"

"Do you swear or affirm to tell the truth, the whole truth, and nothing but the truth?"

The word *yes* appeared on the monitor.

Luke picked up his notes and began the questioning.

"Is your name Alma Haverstock?"

Yes.

"Were you employed by the office of Dunn and Dunn?"

Yes.

"Does that office practice medicine?"

No.

"Is it a law office?"

Yes.

"Did you work for the Dunn law office for more than thirty-five years?"

Yes.

"For most of those years, were you Michael Dunn's executive secretary and office manager?"

Yes.

"Do you recall the events surrounding the preparation of Mrs. Shauffler's last will and testament?"

Yes.

Barney Rifkin stood up. "Your Honor, I'm sure the court appreciates that the questions Mr. Alexander has been asking are all objectionable in that they are leading questions. However, I felt that in view of Your Honor's earlier comments, the court would not look kindly on any objection I might make. But we are now entering a very sensitive part of the witness's testimony and to properly represent my client and protect this record, I must advise the court that I intend to object to any further questions which are designed to lead the witness."

"I appreciate your position, Mr. Rifkin," the judge replied. "Please phrase your questions with care, Mr. Alexander."

"Now, Mrs. Haverstock, did you type up the will that Mrs. Shauffler signed?"

Yes flashed on the monitor screen.

Luke turned the pages of Mrs. Shauffler's will to page fifty-four and held it in front of Mrs. Haverstock. "Please read page fifty-four to yourself, Mrs. Haverstock." There was total silence for a few minutes and then Luke asked, "Did you type page fifty-four of this will as you see it here in court today?"

No, no, no.

Luke flipped a switch on the device and immediately a large alphabet appeared on the monitor screen. "Now listen carefully, Mrs. Haverstock. When you finished typing Mrs. Shauffler's will, what did you do with it?"

Slowly the letters appeared on the display screen, *Gave to Frank Dunn.*

"No further questions," Luke said.

The judge turned to Barney. "Mr. Rifkin, do you choose to cross-examine the witness?"

"Yes, Your Honor, I'm going to try to do that." Barney walked slowly over and stood in front of Mrs. Haverstock.

"Mrs. Haverstock, I have just a few questions for you. After you gave the will to Frank Dunn, did you ever see it again before Mrs. Shauffler signed it?"

No.

Barney was about to ask another question, thought better of it, and instead asked Judge Casey if he could have a few moments to confer with his client.

"As a matter of fact, gentlemen, I think this would be a good time to take a short recess."

Barney and Margaux were huddled in a corner of the hallway outside the courtroom. Margaux looked very concerned as she said, "Barney, I think it's a mistake to cross-examine the old lady any further. The point's been made that Frank was the last person to have the will before it was signed. That doesn't hurt me. Mrs. Haverstock is obviously lucid, and the more questions you ask her, the more believable she becomes."

"I think you're wrong, Margaux. There's no way Mrs. Haverstock can hurt us now."

"Famous last words. I can tell you one thing for certain. Judge Casey is hanging on every word she says. Who wouldn't? It's like her words are coming directly from the Virgin Mary. I'm telling you to go back into court and tell Judge Casey you don't have any further questions for Mrs. Haverstock."

"But — "

"No buts, Barney. I pay you, I call the shots."

"Okay, baby, it's your funeral."

"Maybe so, but I'm not going to hand them the shovel to dig the grave."

When court reconvened, Barney stood up and advised Judge Casey that he had no further questions for the witness.

Barney then introduced an array of witnesses, beginning with the law office receptionist, who testified that Mrs. Shauffler spent an hour with Frank in his office the day before the will was signed, and that Mrs. Haverstock didn't work that day. Barney then called Betsy Green, Frank Dunn's secretary. She told the judge that on many occasions, Frank typed things up on his computer in the evening after she'd left the office for the day and that it was not unusual for her to find something he'd typed waiting on her desk the next morning. She testified further that she had not typed page fifty-four of the will and that Frank Dunn brought the will with him to the conference room where the signing ceremony took place.

By the end of the first day of testimony offered by Barney, Luke began to worry. Barney was making a pretty strong case that Frank was the one who had typed up the controversial page fifty-four. He knew he had to discredit Margaux on cross-examination when she took the stand. He also knew Barney would put her on as his last witness, in order to give her testimony maximum impact.

———

When court convened the following afternoon, Luke's team was weary but confident that they could destroy Margaux's case on cross-examination.

Judge Casey entered the courtroom, arranged his papers and addressed the attorneys. "Good afternoon, gentlemen. Ready to proceed, Barney?"

Barney Rifkin stood up slowly. "Your Honor, I don't have any further witnesses."

"All right, Mr. Rifkin. Then we will proceed with the testimony of Ms. McBride. Please take the stand and be sworn in, Ms. McBride."

"Actually, Your Honor, Ms. McBride has elected not to testify. We rest our case."

Judge Casey started to say something and then changed his mind. He turned to Luke, "Do you have any rebuttal testimony, Mr. Alexander?"

Luke felt a leaden weight in the pit of his stomach. If Margaux didn't take the stand, obviously she couldn't be cross-examined. He was caught totally off guard.

"May I have a few moments to consult with the attorneys who represent the co-petitioners?" Luke said, stalling for time.

"Of course."

The other lawyers gathered around Luke, who said, "We've been fucked, gentlemen."

"That old fox has stuck it up our ass, Luke," one of the other attorneys whispered.

"It wasn't the old fox, it was the young vixen. That maneuver has Margaux McBride written all over it," Luke hissed.

"So what do you suggest?"

"I'm not sure," Luke replied, "but I've got an idea."

"Your Honor, I expect my rebuttal witness will take most of a day. May we adjourn now and resume on Monday morning?"

"I have to object to that, Judge," Barney said. "Lucas is stalling. I don't believe he has a rebuttal witness and I want to move this case along."

"Well, now, Barney, I've never heard you object to going home early on a Friday afternoon, and frankly I've never opposed the idea myself. But if you insist, I guess you are entitled."

Luke stood up and addressed the bench. "I call Margaux McBride to the stand."

Barney was on his feet immediately. "Now wait a minute, Lucas, you can't do that!" He turned to the bench. "Judge, he can't do that, it's ridiculous! Whoever heard of a person being called as a witness to testify against their own case?" Barney stammered.

"I'll admit it's a bit unusual, but this isn't a criminal case, Mr. Rifkin. I don't know of any law that says he can't do it. Unless you're claiming that your client wishes to assert her Fifth Amendment rights against self-incrimination for a possible crime she may have committed."

"Well, no, she doesn't intend to do that, it's just that, I... she," Barney sputtered.

"All right, Ms. McBride, I guess we're going to hear what you've got to say after all," Judge Casey said.

Barney held up his hand. "Excuse me, Judge. I think you were right about adjourning this case until Monday."

Now it was Luke who was on his feet immediately. "I object, Your Honor. I want to examine Ms. McBride right now, not after Barney has the weekend to rehearse her."

"Just a minute here —" Barney countered.

"Gentlemen," Judge Casey interrupted, rapping his gavel. "That's enough! We're adjourned until 9:30 Monday morning." The judge slipped off the bench and disappeared, leaving the lawyers glaring at each other.

———

When court reconvened on Monday, the clerk advised the lawyers that Judge Casey wished to see all of them in his chambers.

When they'd all filed into his office Judge Casey said, "I have a matter of concern to discuss with you, gentlemen." There was total silence as the judge fastidiously rearranged some papers on his desk. "I've received a call from the district attorney's office advising me that on Friday, the grand jury handed down an indictment for the murder of Frank Dunn. A warrant has been issued for Margaux McBride's arrest, charging her with his murder." Judge Casey hesitated. The lawyers were stunned, silent. He continued. "The police are on their way over here now to execute the warrant. Judge Hamilton will be handling the preliminary arraignment. Now, with regard to our matter here, I suggest you rest your case, Lucas. I don't need Ms. McBride's testimony. Is the evidence closed, gentlemen?"

Luke glanced over at Barney. His face was ashen. "Yes, sir, "they both replied quickly.

"All right, then I'll give you my decision now." The judge turned to Barney. "I'm satisfied, Barney, that Katrina Shauffler never intended to give either Frank Dunn or Margaux McBride a penny. I'm going to give your client the benefit of the doubt and assume that it was Frank Dunn alone who engineered the alteration of the will. But I can tell you, I think this whole thing stinks to high heaven. No wonder the public believes that most lawyers are crooks."

CHAPTER THIRTY-SIX

When Barney brought Margaux into the attorney's room, she said, "What's this all about? Has Alexander agreed to settle? I can be reasonable."

"Sit down, please, Margaux. I've got bad news."

"Don't tell me His Honor has decided the case against me?"

"That too, but…Jesus, Margaux, Casey tells me they've indicted you for Frank Dunn's murder and the police are on their way over here right now."

"Those fucking bastards! It was that bitch cop, Turner! I should have known better than to talk to her. But they don't have shit proof. I never even saw Frank the night he was shot, and I was pissed at him because I thought he'd passed out drunk and couldn't answer the door."

"I don't know what you're talking about, Margaux, but I've got to take you downstairs to Judge Hamilton's court. Casey says they've agreed not to arrest you if I bring you down voluntarily."

"Those rotten, rat-fink, pisspot cops! I'll beat this, Barney, and I'll sue their asses good and I'll —"

"Calm down, Margaux. This is awful, I know, but you've got to cool it here. You can bet the press will be there, and I don't want you to show up ranting and raving like a wild woman."

When they reached Judge Hamilton's court, three floors below, a battery of reporters and photographers were milling around, waiting for Margaux to appear. As soon as she was recognized, flashbulbs began to pop like Roman candles. Barney protected her as best he could, but they had to fight their way through the throng of newspaper people to enter the courtroom.

Assistant DA Robin McCray was waiting for them. She gave a copy of the indictment to both Barney and Margaux while they waited for the judge to appear.

Barney approached McCray and said, "I suppose you know Ms. McBride is an attorney. What are your thoughts on bail here?"

The assistant DA shrugged her shoulders. "Murder is murder."

Barney was unwilling to let the subject drop. "I'm sure you're not forgetting that Ms. McBride is presumed to be innocent."

McCray looked up sharply at Barney. "Mr. Rifkin, I'm the prosecuting attorney. I suggest you save your arguments for the judge."

With that, she turned her back on Barney and began sorting through the papers in her briefcase.

Barney returned to his seat beside Margaux, who leaned close to him. "I couldn't hear what she said," she whispered.

"She's unwilling to discuss bail. She ain't what you'd call a wilting petunia."

"What does that mean?"

"It means that she appears to be a real b — "

"All rise," the court attendant announced, as Judge Hamilton entered the courtroom.

After the indictment had been read and the matter of bail was argued, the judge stated, "I'm setting bail in this matter at one hundred thousand dollars. I will allow the defendant to be released in your custody, Mr. Rifkin, for a period of one week, to enable her to raise bail. We will take the defendant's plea at that time. All preliminary motions are to be made by defense counsel no later than October 31. If there are no questions, the case is adjourned until next week."

Without waiting for a response, Judge Hamilton left the courtroom. The assistant district attorney advised the bailiff to clear the courtroom except for Barney and Margaux. When the courtroom was quieted once again, the prosecuting attorney reminded Barney that it would be necessary for Margaux to be taken into custody for fingerprinting and mug shots. Several policemen then escorted Margaux through the throng of reporters to the precinct offices, where she was held in a detention facility with ninteen other women who'd been arrested during the previous few hours.

The reporters were waiting for her again as she emerged from the police building. Several of them followed her cab. When she arrived at her apartment, she slipped out of the cab quickly and told the doorman she would take no calls and receive no visitors. Once inside, she locked and bolted her door, poured herself a drink, and sat down in her twenty-five-hundred-dollar Italian leather chair. She rifled through the pages of the telephone book until she found Lucas's number and dialed

"I'm sorry I can't come to the phone right now, but if —"

"Damn!" she cursed, slamming down the phone.

CHAPTER THIRTY-SEVEN

As weeks had passed and the pace quickened, Pat had studiously avoided any situation in which bedding down was inevitable. Although her body was screaming for sex, her mind took charge. "I don't want to screw this one up," she said aloud, smiling at her choice of words. On their first two dates, Luke had been aggressive enough, at least verbally, but then he too had eased off with the innuendoes and had begun to accept the fact that this liaison was not to be taken lightly. He was letting her set the pace. There had been a few moments when one more kiss would have toppled the cherry tree, but lust had succumbed to reason, and their hot but chaste affair continued.

On a Friday afternoon she sat in her office thinking about the weekend adventure ahead of her. They were going to spend Saturday and Sunday at Luke's summer cottage at Montauk Point on the south shore of Long Island. He'd spoken of it often and they'd compared notes: Pat extolling the virtues of the mountains and the lake where she had her tiny cabin, and Luke affectionately describing his cottage beside the sea. They hadn't discussed their sleeping arrangements for Saturday night, but she knew there was no way she could get through the weekend without unbridled passion. Nor did she wish to.

Her first serious love affair had begun shortly after her sixteenth birthday and had consumed all of one glorious summer, when she and her boyfriend were junior counselors at adjoining camps in Maine. It had ended in sweet sorrow and tears when she returned to school in Brooklyn and he went back home to Michigan to begin his freshman year at Michigan State.

As a college student she fell in and out of love more than once, and after her father's death, she'd gone steady with a graduate student at NYU for almost a year before they decided their aspirations were incompatible.

Her search for a mate ended when she met Vic Moretti. Although their relationship was platonic, it was the most rewarding friendship she'd ever experienced, and she'd been quite prepared to spend her life with a kind man who adored her. She was devastated by Vic's tragic death and decided to put the romantic part of her life on hold.

But she'd been alone longer than she'd intended to be by the time Luke appeared on the scene. She suspected that her lengthy abstinence from the dating game had left her overripe, because whatever it was with Lucas, he had an overwhelming impact on her. Her first thoughts were of him when she awakened in the morning, and throughout the day she would remember with delight bits and pieces of their time together, like the evening they'd strolled along the boardwalk at Coney Island. Luke had looked up at the Ferris wheel and said to her, "A Ferris wheel's sort of like a love affair, isn't it. It's a thing of wonder with its tantalizing lights and its offer of a journey to the stars, promising that when the ride's over the lovers will come back down safely to earth. But if we step too closely," he grinned at her "we see the peeling paint, and the rusted struts, the missing light bulbs. We can hear the gears grinding and we can smell the hot engine —"

"No, Luke," she'd protested, laughing. "Don't tell me about that! I don't want to come back down to earth! I love it up here in the clouds." She threw her arms around him and kissed him soundly, to the applause of those passing by.

As she started to pack her overnight bag, trying to decide what she should bring along for the weekend, she recognized that she was in a precarious emotional state. In fact, her intellect was screaming in protest but she was like a feather in a hurricane. "I don't want it to end, ever," she said aloud, trying to think of a reason to call Luke, just for the joy of hearing his voice.

———

Luke was ten years older than Pat and had tasted a hundred tongues, yet he too was powerless to think rationally about the direction their affair was taking them. He was wary because of his two failed marriages and he kept reminding himself that he was not a twenty-two-year-old, in love for the first time. He'd been through that wonderful, crazy passion business before, but he was old enough, and wise enough, to know that this intensity of passion would begin to diminish one day. He also knew he should stop trying to analyze it, and just enjoy the miracle of it.

He was reminded of a poem he'd written in the midst of such passion while courting his second wife, Vera. He'd just turned forty and she was ninteen. Luke went through old files and pulled the poem out. He felt as if he were holding an ancient treasure. Vera had laughed when she'd read it, but now, as he stared at the tattered copy of the poem, he was startled by the truth buried in his words.

> A woman/child, impetuous, wild,
> unburdened by the chains of wisdom,
> touches his weathered soul
> with the fragrance of her youth.
>
> She speaks of love without shadows, without pain,
> a magical, lyrical, miracle thing
> where reason is lost in the crevices of passion.

After the divorce, he'd studiously avoided any woman who even remotely expressed a desire for a permanent relationship. His life had fallen into a very comfortable pattern of friendships with successful professional women who put their careers above all else, yet still enjoyed intimate male companionship without a need for commitment. In his wildest imaginings, he'd never thought he could fall in love with a forty-one-year-old cop. He laughed out loud at the irony of it. But there was one serious problem that he kept pushing to the back of his mind. Pat wanted to have a child. He already had one child he'd neglected, and a twenty-three-year-old son he'd never seen. Besides, if he had a child with Pat, he'd be over seventy years old when he…or she…graduated from high school.

At the very moment of that distasteful thought, the phone rang.

"What clothes am I supposed to pack for this nefarious adventure at Camelot? "

"I don't know, jeans, a couple of T-shirts and maybe something fancy if we decide to go out to dinner."

"You're a big help, Luke."

"Would you believe I was just thinking about you…about us?"

"That's nice. As a matter of fact you crossed my mind a bit ago. I'll tell you about it tomorrow. So what time are you planning to pick me up in the morning?"

"Eight o'clock sharp."

"Aye, aye, sir. Bye."

"Hey, wait a minute," Luke said, but she'd already hung up.

"She's crazy," he chuckled.

———

It was a spectacular end-of-summer day as they joined the exodus from the city. By the time they arrived at Luke's cottage, snuggled down unpretentiously among the dunes on Long Island's southeast shore, the deep blue cloudless sky was ablaze with a big fat October sun.

After lunch, a cool pungent sea breeze picked up, and Luke suggested they go sailing. Although Pat was a fine swimmer and loved the water, she knew little about the art of sailing and was pleased to discover that Luke was an expert at it. Under his patient tutelage, she learned quickly and immediately became enamored of the sport. She was exhilarated by the beauty of the sleek, smooth hull slicing silently through the water while warm salt spray splashed over them as they came about. It was thrilling to balance high on the gunnel as Luke skillfully pointed the bow of the craft close to the wind, causing it to heel within a razor's edge of capsizing. It was like being on the downhill rush of a roller coaster, when you scream with a mixture of fear and delight.

After they returned to the dock, hauled down the sails, and stowed the gear, they trudged up through the dunes with Luke's arm around her shoulder, singing a sea chantey he insisted she learn, about Minnie the mermaid who lost her morals down among the corals. All afternoon, Pat's body had been responding to his in a way she'd never experienced, and now, as they climbed toward the house, swaying together like two drunken sailors, she knew that a new chapter in her life was about to unfold. She'd become aroused on the boat when she studied his strong athletic body. He had the legs of a long-distance runner, flat stomach, and sinewy arms. She couldn't help occasionally glancing at the front of his tight, faded cutoffs, and she'd been filled with wonder at what would be happening before the day was done.

When they reached the cottage, Luke suggested she settle in one of the lounge chairs on the deck while he made her a "Mamba," the special drink he'd discovered in the Caribbean. When he brought the fancy, frosted concoction to her, he leaned over and kissed her tenderly. The smell of the sea and his sweat-stained body made her ache with desire to be held by him. He settled back in the dilapidated beach chair, smiled thoughtfully at her and said, "Is this the right time for me to describe my dark side to you?"

"Honestly?"

"Of course I want your honest answer."

"Then my answer is no, not now. When I finish this drink, I want to take a shower and change, and then, perhaps, I'll be ready," she said. "Is that okay?"

"Sure. Just take a right at the top of the stairs. I put your bag in the bedroom. There are plenty of towels and whatever else you might need in the bathroom. But you only have half an hour because you must be back down in time for the sunset. It's going to be a beauty, I can tell."

"Wouldn't miss it for the world."

The spacious black marbled tile bathroom offered twin sculptured sinks, full-length gold-framed mirrors, a polished natural-stone Jacuzzi, stained-glass skylights, an Oriental rug, and a life-size replica of Michelangelo's *David*. Everything fought with everything else for attention in the bizarre, fascinating combination of color, line, and texture. As she began to dry her hair, there was a tapping on the bathroom door, "Pat?"

"Yes?"

"May I come in?"

Pat started to say, "Just give me a few minutes," but instead she said, "If you like."

As he entered the steamy room, her back was to him. She removed her towel and casually made a turban out of it. "Sweet Jesus," he moaned when she turned around to him. He picked her nude body up in his arms and carried her into the master bedroom with its floor-to-ceiling open windows facing the sea and the pounding surf below.

She never wanted to hear about his dark side, Pat decided then and there.

CHAPTER THIRTY-EIGHT

Luke had initially refused to talk to Margaux when she called him after her arraignment in Judge Hamilton's court. After she persistently phoned him every day for over a week, he finally agreed to listen to what she had to say.

"Please, Lucas, whatever differences we may have had with regard to the Shauffler matter, that was just business. I'm now talking about my life," she pleaded.

"Margaux, there's no way I can —"

"Before you say no, at least give me a chance to see you."

"There are ten million reasons I can't get involved in this thing. Conflict of interest and —"

"Lucas, I just want to talk to you. I need help, Lucas. Please."

"Look, Margaux, you know I…oh hell, when do you want to come in?"

"I know it's a terrible imposition, but could you please come here, instead?"

"No way. If you want to come to my office, I guess I'm willing to listen, but that's all, Margaux, I'm just going to listen."

"When do you want me?"

Luke looked at his watch. It was four o'clock. He had a dinner date with Pat at seven.

"If you can get here by five, I can see you for an hour."

"I'll be there." She hung up before he had a chance to change his mind.

Luke cursed himself for giving in to her.

She arrived at ten minutes past six.

When she was seated across from his desk, Luke thought to himself that although there had been no shortage of beautiful women to pass through his life, Margaux topped them all.

"First of all, Lucas, thank you for seeing me. I'm sorry I'm late. Getting a cab at five o'clock in Manhattan is impossible."

"I don't have much time, Margaux," he said. "Although our paths haven't had too many pleasant crossings, I'm really sorry about your situation if you're innocent, as you claim. I've been through this with more than a few clients, and I know how bad it is."

"I want you to know I'm not looking for sympathy. It's your brain and your experience I need..." Luke started to interrupt but Margaux put up her hand. "No, wait, please, let me finish. I know you're retired from the trial bar and that if it hadn't been for your involvement in the Shauffler School, you wouldn't have taken the case, but I beg you to hear me out."

Luke shrugged and leaned back in his chair.

"To begin with, I am absolutely and completely innocent. I did not kill Frank Dunn. Whatever else you may think of me, I hope by the end of this conversation you'll be convinced that I'm telling you the truth."

"Margaux, I don't think you should even be talking to me. Since I'm not your attorney, whatever you say to me is not privileged. I'm sure Barney wouldn't approve of this meeting, if he knew about it."

"I've only hired Barney in a preliminary way. I wanted to talk to you first. I don't know what the district attorney thinks he has against me, but I want the best lawyer I can get."

"Barney's a first-class lawyer, Margaux."

"But he's not the best, Lucas. You're the best, and I want you. I need you. "

"Margaux, I don't mean to sound like a broken record, but I —"

"All I'm asking is that you give me an opportunity to prove my innocence, and I don't mean like self-defense or temporary insanity. I mean, innocence, pure, absolute, total. I'm telling you, Lucas, they have the wrong person. I did not kill Frank Dunn."

"Do you know who did?"

"Unfortunately, I don't have a clue, but please let me tell you what I do know."

194   *Wally Wiggins*

"Okay, I'll listen, but not as your lawyer." Luke leaned back in his chair and closed his eyes.

"Let's put aside the fact I don't know who my father is, and my mother didn't know either because she was drunk out of her mind at a fraternity party when I was conceived. She was what you college guys called a "townie." She'd accept any invitation to any party where there was free booze and pot, and I understand that she loved sex. She didn't sell her body, she eagerly gave it away. I guess nothing changed much until she died when I was two years old. They sent me to live with my grandmother in Newfield."

"Newfield? Newfield, New York?"

"I thought that might wake you up. When I searched you on the Internet, I saw that you'd practiced in Glenwood. I went to high school in Glenwood."

"That's amazing. How old are you?"

"A gentleman never asks a lady her age, you know, but I guess you're entitled, under the circumstances. I'm thirty-one."

Just a baby, Luke laughed to himself. "So what happened after high school?"

"When I was a senior, I got the brilliant idea that I should stop giving my sex away and start to barter it for the things I wanted in life. I rarely had to ask for money or anything else, for that matter. I always relied upon the generosity of my suitors, so to speak. In my young mind, I felt that made a significant difference and elevated me above the level of a prostitute. On the other hand, if a lover didn't express his appreciation with more than words after our first mating, I bit off his head and spit him out, like a praying mantis."

Again Luke laughed. "The predilection of the female mantis was part of my sex education in high school. I think it was responsible for my remaining a virgin until I was seventeen years old."

"Such a pity."

Luke felt himself coming under the spell of her sensuality, and knew he should change the subject, but…

"You better get yourself a drink because this is going to take a little while," Margaux purred.

He never touched alcohol during working hours. He automatically looked at his watch and saw that it was 6:35. "Jesus," he cursed as he grabbed his cell phone and walked away, out of earshot. Pat's line was busy. He waited a minute or so to try it again, but it was still busy. He intended to call again in ten minutes.

Oh well, he decided. He was just listening, not really working, and it was after five o'clock. In for a penny, in for a pound. "Want one?" he asked as he poured himself a drink.

"No thanks, I only drink in social situations."

"Okay, make it fast. I'm already late for an appointment. What's next in the McBride saga?" Luke reseated himself, took a swallow, and put his drink down on top of the green blotter on his desk.

Margaux hesitated, concerned by what she was about to say. Lucas assumed she couldn't make up her mind about whether or not to tell him the truth.

"Do you remember a client of yours by the name of Bronski?" she asked.

"Bronski? It rings a bell. What kind of a case was it?"

"It was a criminal case. It was many years ago."

"I have trouble recalling what I did a month ago, for God's sake. What was it about?"

"It was an assault case."

"I've only handled a hundred assault cases in my career, you know – wait a minute! Bronski. John Bronski. Sure I remember that case."

———

After Lucas Alexander received his law degree at Columbia University, he went to work for a well-respected criminal lawyer in Glenwood, a small town with a big university in upstate New York. After losing his first few cases, he had a string of victories, and word got out on the street that Luke Alexander was a fighter.

He'd been practicing law for a dozen years when he agreed to defend John Bronski, who was charged with assault.

Bronski was slumped in his chair beside Luke at the counsel table on September 12, 1988, when the court clerk recited the ancient dirge.

"Hear ye, this court is now in session, Honorable Robert Stevens presiding. All rise." Judge Stevens greeted the jurors and instructed the district attorney to proceed with his first witness.

The DA called the alleged victim to the stand.

She was 5'9", one hundred twenty pounds, had black hair and an alabaster complexion. Her makeup made her look as old as her fake ID, stating her birth date as June 23, 1966, claimed. Her rightful birth year was 1972.

"Raise your right hand, please. Do you swear or affirm to tell the whole truth, and nothing but the truth?"

"I do."

"You may be seated."

After she took her place in the witness chair, the district attorney began his questioning.

"Where do you live?"

"In Newfield."

"Are you living with your parents?"

"I don't have any parents. I live with my grandmother."

"How long have you lived there?"

"All my life."

"How old are you?"

"Sixteen."

"Are you still in school?"

"I'm a sophomore in high school. "

The DA retrieved his yellow legal pad from the counsel table, studied it for a few moments and resumed his questioning.

"Now, tell me, did a time come a few months ago," he glanced down again to his notes, "June 21, to be precise, when you went to the Blue Dragon Club?"

"Yes."

"What time did you arrive there?"

"Around midnight."

"Were you alone?"

"Yeah, me and my girlfriend had a fight when we were at the Sportsbar, so I took off for the Dragon on my own."

"Was the defendant, Mr. Bronski, there when you arrived?"

"He was leaning against his car, parked in front of the club."

"Did you have a conversation with him at that time?"

"Not really, I never saw him before."

"I mean, did you say anything to him?"

"Yeah. I said, 'Nice car.'"

"You said, 'Nice car,' and what did he say?"

"He said, 'I just bought it today,' and then he asks me if I want to take a ride around the block. He said I'd be his first passenger. He tells me the club was dead…just a couple old guys drinking at the bar. So I said okay, why not, and he says he'll get us some drinks to take along. I told him to get me a Bacardi Coke. When he came back, he had the drinks in coffee containers. He handed me my drink and goes, 'One for my baby and one more for the road,' like he was a crooner, you know. I could tell he was a little high, but I figured he was harmless."

"What happened next?" the district attorney asked, sidling closer to the witness.

"We take off, and he heads out on Route 34. We was drivin' awhile and then he turns into the Old Quarry Road and parks the car, so we're lookin' down over the harbor. We sat there listening to his tape deck. It was a Bruce Springsteen album. When we finished the drinks, he throws the cups out the window and puts on another tape. Patsy Cline singin' *Crazy for Lovin' You*. He smiles at me and I figure he's okay and I smile back at him. We don't say anything to each other. We're just sittin' there listening to the music and he's keeping time by beating his hand on the steering wheel. He stares out the windshield as if he's thinking about something important."

"Tell us what happened next. And please speak slowly and tell us everything you can remember in as much detail as possible."

She hesitated, turned to face the jury, and took a deep breath.

"Nothing happened for a while. I mean he wasn't saying anything, and it was sort of weird, and I was getting a little nervous because the place was deserted. It was really dark and sort of creepy, and I began to wonder if I'd made a bad mistake in going with him. But then he looks at me and smiles and leans over and kisses me, gentle-like. I let him do it because it wasn't like serious, but then he puts his hand inside my blouse…and I push him away and I says, 'Hey mister, it's past my bedtime, we better head back.' But then he puts his arm around my shoulders and slips his other hand down between my legs, and it hurts and I scream at him. I was scared. I try to jump out of the car but I can't find the door handle, and by that time he's trying to climb over onto my side, but there's bucket seats and the stick shift is in the way, so he grabs me by the hair and that's when I scratched his face and jumped out of the car."

She started to sob, quietly. But she didn't lower her eyes. She sat in the chair, staring straight ahead, the tears sliding down her cheeks. She sniffled and wiped her eyes with the back of her hand. The district attorney took her a glass of water.

"We'll take a brief recess here," the judge said solemnly.

Bronski leaned over toward Luke and hissed, "She's lying, Mr. Alexander. That little fuckin' whore-bitch is lying. I never did them things like she's saying. She's the one who started everything."

The district attorney's next witnesses were a young couple

who had come to park at the harbor overlook around one o'clock in the morning. They related that Maggie had come stumbling into the beam of their headlights from the wooded area beside the road. She was crying, her face was scratched, and her clothes were disheveled. They took her to the emergency room at the hospital, and the police were called.

Copies of the photos taken by the police in the emergency room were introduced into evidence showing that Maggie's face was scratched, her right eye was swollen, and she had a small cut on the back of her head.

The district attorney's last witness was an investigator from the state police. He testified that within twenty-four hours, they had a match between Bronski and the secondhand Pontiac Firebird he'd bought that day. They obtained a search warrant for the car, where they found the Patsy Cline tape still in the tape deck. They also discovered several black hairs on the passenger's seat. They sent all of these items, along with a dried blood sample they took from the doorframe, to the New York State Police forensic laboratory. Each exhibit confirmed conclusively that Maggie had been in Bronski's car.

"After giving him a Miranda warning, did you interview the defendant, Sergeant?" the district attorney demanded.

"Yes, sir."

"When was that?"

The sergeant consulted his notes and replied, "At eighteen hundred six hours on the evening of June 25, 1988."

"What did he tell you?"

"Well, at first he denied everything, but then I showed him the statement we got from the bartender at the Blue Dragon Club that said Bronski had bought a scotch and a Bacardi Coke from him around midnight. And after I showed him the proof we had of the victim's and his fingerprints on the cups we found in the parking lot at the overlook, and after I told him about the hairs we found on the seat of his car, and after I showed him the plaster model of the tire print we picked up in the mud at the lookout, which perfectly matched his rear tire, well, then he admitted that maybe he had picked her up and taken her to the lookout."

"Your witness, Mr. Alexander," the district attorney said, nodding to Luke.

"No questions."

It was early afternoon on the third day of the trial when

Bronski finally got his chance to take the stand. "When did you first see that young lady?" Luke asked, pointing to the girl seated beside the DA.

"It was when I come out of the club. We got to talking and she was going on about how beautiful my car was, and I felt good about that, you know, so I asked her if she'd like to have a ride. Then she goes, 'Okay, if you give me a lift home and buy me a drink.' I figured I might have something going with her, you know what I mean, so I says, 'Sure, why not.' So, I went back in the Dragon and bought us some drinks and then I headed out to the address she give me.

"We hadn't gone very far when she hands me a lit cigarette and sticks her tongue in my ear. Then she laughs and lays back in the seat and puts her feet up on the dash. I remember that for sure because I really didn't want her to do that with my new car, and I was going to say something, you know what I mean, but when I glanced over at her I seen that her skirt had slid up around her belly and she wasn't wearing anything underneath. So when we come to that straightaway out by Henderson's garage along the harbor road, I stepped heavy on the gas. It was like we was flying."

"So what happened next?"

"She was squealing and laughing, and then she goes, 'Hey, what do you say we take a breather down at the lookout on Old Quarry Road?' Them's her exact words, 'Let's take a breather,' and I says 'Sure,' 'cause I figured she was horny and wanted to get laid and I was hot and what the hell, you know? But when I pulls in and parks there, she goes, 'I can make you feel real good, honey, but I need a little moolah, right?'

"'Ain't got none of that stuff,' I says, laughing. She goes, 'I know better'n that, 'cause I felt a big wad of it in your pocket.' And I says, 'That was just big old me you was feelin'.' And we was laughin' together and all and having a good time, and then she reaches in my pocket and pulls out all my money. It was my whole week's pay, at least twelve twenty dollar bills, and she stuffs them all down her shirt. I was still laughing, you know, and I says, 'Okay, kid, gimme back my dough.' And then when I reached down inside her shirt to get my money back, she screams and scratches my face bad, you can still see the scar." Bronski turned again to face the jury and ran his fingertip along the red welt that started just below his temple and ran down to the corner of his mouth.

"Then what did you do?"

"To be honest, sir, I took a swing at her. When she was scrambling to get out of the car I caught her shoulder and I think maybe she hit her head on the doorframe. But then she was gone, I mean she took right off into them woods that run down into the park by the lake, and I never seen her again until I seen her here in court."

"What about the money?"

"She ran off with all my money. I had over two hundred bucks on me, like I said, and she grabbed it all. I run after her and I could hear her crashing through the woods, but it was real dark and I was worried about leavin' my car, you know, so I quit chasin' her and drove home."

Luke walked back to the counsel table, shuffled his papers around and then returned to stand squarely in front of Bronski. He leaned down and stared straight into Bronski's eyes. He spoke slowly and deliberately.

"At any time, from the moment you picked her up until the moment you drove home, did you ever strike that young woman intending to cause her serious harm?"

"I swear to God, Mr. Alexander, I never meant to hurt her. I was pissed when she stole my money. It was my whole week's pay and I was dead broke 'cause I'd put every dime I owned into my new car."

"At any time from the moment you picked her up until the time you left her, did you ever intend to have intercourse with her?"

He hesitated. "You mean, like, did I ever intend to have sex with her?"

"That's exactly what I mean, John."

"Well yeah, I did. I mean she was comin' onto me like you wouldn't believe. But I never did things like she said I did. I didn't know she was a hooker. I thought we was just two people wanting to do the same thing, if you see what I mean. It was only when she stole my money that I messed her up a little, but it had nothin' to do with sex."

"What about these pictures?" Luke handed him the photos of Maggie's bruised face that had been taken by the police at the hospital.

"Look, I admit when I pushed her, she could've hit the back of her head on the doorframe. I admit that. But them marks on her face, I had nothin' to do with them. She must've run into some branches or somethin' in the dark when I was trying to catch her to get my money back. I swear I never did that to her."

"If you were so upset about the money, why didn't you go to the police and report her?"

Bronski looked at Luke as if it were the dumbest question he ever heard. "I was embarrassed, man. The kid had suckered me. So what are the cops going to do? You think if they picked her up she's gonna admit stealin' my money? So it's her word against mine. I ain't got no proof. So I figure I should just take the hit and forget it."

When Bronski got off the stand and came back to the counsel table, he asked Luke, "Did I do all right?"

Luke didn't answer him. Bronski pressed. "You don't figure the jury will believe that little Mick-whore, do you? I mean, what do you think, Mr. Alexander?"

Luke just shrugged his shoulders, but when he returned to his office and grabbed a cold drink out of the tiny fridge in the snack closet, he repeated Bronski's question to himself. "What do you think, Mr. Alexander?"

———

Judge Stevens glanced up at the antique clock on the courtroom wall.

"Ladies and gentlemen, we will now hear from each of the attorneys. This will be their final address to you. We call it their summations. Mr. Alexander?" He nodded for Luke to begin his summation.

At first Luke spoke very slowly, reminding the jurors of the promise they'd each made to him when they were selected to serve: that they would not convict Bronski unless they were satisfied beyond a reasonable doubt that he was guilty as charged.

"The key words here are *as charged*, ladies and gentlemen. Guilty as charged. So now let us examine that charge, you and I. Not as you sit here in this massive, intimidating room, but as we might if we were sitting together around a kitchen table, discussing the case and trying to decide how the ends of justice could best be served." Lucas took a step closer to the jury box.

"I say to you that no man has the right to strike a woman except in self-defense to save his own life. If you find that John Bronski struck Maggie Doyle because she wouldn't return his money, he must be punished. The sample of Miss Doyle's blood offered in evidence convinces me beyond a reasonable doubt that, one way or the other, John Bronski assaulted Maggie Doyle, and as far as I am concerned…" he hesitated, "he is guilty of assault beyond a reasonable doubt."

There were gasps in the courtroom. When the spectators quieted down, Luke picked up a large law book from the counsel table and carried it back to the jury box.

"Now let me tell you why it would be a travesty of justice to find this young man guilty of the charge against him. The law says that if you find that John Bronski intended to cause that young lady serious injury when he parked his car at the overlook, he is guilty and can be sentenced to seven years in jail. But if John didn't mean to seriously hurt her, he is not guilty of the felony. He'd be guilty only of a violation that carries a penalty of no more than fifteen days in jail. Members of the jury, find John Bronski guilty of the crime that fits the wrongdoing. Let the judge punish him accordingly, and let us all get on with our lives. Thank you."

It was five hours before the rap on the jury room door signaled the end of the jury's deliberations. Luke was back in his office when the court clerk called him with the familiar words, "The jury's got a verdict."

Luke replaced the receiver and sat motionless in his big green leather chair. He reached over and picked up the thick brown file envelope labeled *People v. John Bronski* and walked out of the office. It seemed to him that the distance between his office and the courthouse next door had lengthened over the years, giving him a bit more time to agonize over the verdict, know the loneliness of the walk, and feel the churning in his gut.

As soon as Luke entered the courtroom, the judge ordered the jury to be brought in. Luke tried to read the verdict on the jurors' faces as they climbed into the box, but there was no sign. There rarely was.

"Ladies and gentlemen, have you reached a verdict?" the judge asked. The number one juror rose and said, "We have, Your Honor."

Luke heard Bronski whispering a prayer. *Too late for that, John,* Luke thought to himself.

"What is your verdict?"

The foreman started to speak, but nerves blocked his speech. Finally he blurted, "We find the defendant guilty of the smaller assault that Mr. Alexander talked about. The fifteen-days-in-prison one."

"Yes, Mr. Foreman, I understand the verdict very well. Will the defendant please rise?"

Bronski stood up slowly. The scar on his cheek was clearly visible.

"I sentence you to the fifteen days you have already served in jail, Mr. Bronski. This court is adjourned."

———

"I remember that case very well, Margaux. I hated Bronski. I was convinced that he'd lied to me, but I was wrong. So how did you know about that case? Did you know Bronski?"

"Yeah. I knew him and the girl he assaulted, too. Why do you say you were wrong about thinking he was guilty?"

"Because after the trial I was talking to a merchant in town who told me that the girl, I can't recall her name, bought a motorcycle jacket from his shop a few days after Bronski was arrested. It cost a couple of hundred dollars and she paid for it with twenty-dollar bills. I'm sure she paid for it with Bronski's money. Damn, what the devil was that kid's name? "

"Maggie Doyle."

"Maggie Doyle! That's right. How the hell do you know her?"

"What did you think of her?"

"Like I said, I originally thought Bronski was lying to me, but later I decided the girl was the liar and a thief as well. So how did you know her?"

"It's a long story for another time. Right now I want to tell you why you must represent me. At the time I came to New York to interview for my job with Dunn and Dunn, I hated all men. Every man I'd ever met tried to take advantage of me. And then I met Frank and he never once let me down, except by getting himself killed. I know now that the whole Shauffler fiasco was Frank's way of trying to protect me if something were to happen to him, but I swear to you, Lucas, I knew nothing about the changes Frank made in Katrina's will. If I'd been successful in that case, I'd have made certain that your school received every penny it was entitled to."

Luke had gotten carried away telling his Bronski story and by the time Margaux began to describe her interview with Sergeant Turner, it was after nine o'clock. When she mentioned Pat's name, he looked at his watch.

"Oh God," he cursed. "Excuse me." He picked up his cell

phone again and went into his library. Pat didn't answer her phone. When he returned to his office, he said, "To tell you the truth, Margaux, I think you're an unscrupulous con artist and I wish you'd chosen to be an actress instead of a lawyer. But I can't see you pumping five slugs into Dunn." Margaux sat stoically and focused her eyes on the light bulb behind Luke's head, forcing herself not to blink until her eyes burned and the tears began to run down her cheeks. Luke studied her face in the long silence.

"I can't stand to see a woman cry," he finally said, handing her a Kleenex. "I don't always do my best legal thinking after two drinks, and I can't be your attorney of record, but maybe I'll be able to help a little."

Margaux stepped close to him. The mixture of Chanel and woman-sweat filled his nostrils. Her breast brushed against his arm as she reached up and caressed his face with her fingertips. He knew he should push her away. But he didn't.

CHAPTER THIRTY-NINE

Luke called Pat several times the following day. Each time, he left a message asking her to return his call, but by late afternoon, she still hadn't done so. Finally he reached her on her cell phone. She answered on the first ring.

"Pat. I've been trying to get you all day. I'm sorry about last night. I tried to call you several times, but you didn't answer. I left messages for you to call me."

"I did. You weren't home. Where were you? You were supposed to pick me up at seven o'clock."

"I know, I was at my office. I got caught up in a serious case, and…I'm really sorry."

"Me, too."

"I couldn't help it, honest."

"So?"

"So, let's have dinner together tonight. I want to discuss this case with you. I'll pick you up at your apartment at seven sharp."

"You don't deserve me, Luke, damn it. I'm too good for you."

"I know. I'm going to hang up now before you change your mind." The line went dead.

It's really not fair, Pat thought. The son of a bitch stands me up, and all it takes to shake my withers is the sound of his voice.

———

"Nice to have you with us again, Mr. Alexander. It's been too long."

"You're right, Tomas. Meet my special friend, Ms. Turner. I think you'll be seeing quite a bit of her from now on."

The handsome maître d' bowed and took Pat's hand gently in both of his. "It's a pleasure, Miss Turner. Mr. Alexander is one of our favorite customers. Welcome to Sandman's."

They followed Tomas to a secluded corner table. The restaurant was located in the basement of a brownstone mansion. The original brick-and-mortar walls, polished mahogany banquets, subdued lighting, and crisp white tablecloths guaranteed that the portions would be small and the prices high.

Throughout the meal Luke was solicitous, thoughtful, amusing – all the things that had made it so easy for Pat to fall in love with him. She allowed him to order for her, and, indeed, the fettuccini Alfredo was superb. She glanced at the wine menu as he gave their order: it was vintage French, one hundred thirty dollars for the bottle. By the time the coffee arrived, she was comforted by the food, the wine, and the warmth of Luke's company.

"So tell me, Counselor, what's this case that was so important you couldn't find time to call me until after nine o'clock?"

"It was just a stupid mistake, and I really don't want to talk about it." Luke lifted her fingers to his lips.

Pat pulled her hand back, sensing danger. "It's okay, Luke, I'm a big girl. So where were you?"

"I was at the office. It was just business. I was with a client."

"Who?"

Luke hesitated, toyed with the idea of lying to her, thought better of it and said, "Margaux McBride."

Pat sat silently for a moment, then picked up her purse and started to slide out of the booth.

Luke jumped up to block her exit. "Pat, please —"

"You're a real shit, Alexander," she hissed, as she tried to push past him.

They struggled momentarily. "Let go of me, you're hurting my arm!"

Luke released his grip and Pat ran out of the restaurant. He threw some bills down on the table and tried to follow her, but by the time he got to the sidewalk, she was out of sight.

———

He called her every day, but she wouldn't accept any of his calls. He wrote to her explaining that he didn't intend to represent

Margaux, that she'd hired Barney to defend her and that he, Luke, had only agreed to act as a consultant and help them with strategy and research. It was true that he'd become convinced she was innocent of the charges against her, but he swore that his relationship with Margaux was strictly professional. He concluded the letter by saying, "I miss you very much. Please do not allow a misunderstanding to destroy our friendship which has become such an important part of my life."

Pat was disturbed by Luke's letter for a number of reasons. First of all, she missed him, but he'd cheated on her. She knew it in her bones. Call it mental telepathy, call it woman's intuition, call it her powers of perception as a police officer when a suspect wasn't leveling with her. Call it whatever you want, Pat was certain that Luke had slept with Margaux and she was deeply hurt and angry. And what made it worse was that she herself had never felt satisfied there was enough evidence to convict McBride. Lt. Garvey had forced her to turn the case over to the district attorney despite her doubts. She recognized that being unable to prove Margaux guilty beyond a reasonable doubt didn't mean Margaux was innocent, but it was difficult to separate the two concepts. Pat wondered if she would be as angry with Luke if Margaux were an unattractive, middle-aged lady.

She couldn't decide if she should answer his letter. She wanted to tell him she missed him too; she wanted to tell him she loved him and that that was why the incident was so painful. But she knew she couldn't do that.

So she didn't do anything.

———

The judge ordered the district attorney to meet with Barney and give him all the information he was entitled to under the criminal procedure law. Barney called Luke to ask if he could handle the matter, because Barney was going to be in Boston on the date the judge had set for the discovery conference.

The assistant DA had asked Pat to bring her file to the meeting. When she arrived in the conference room, Luke was the only one there. His eyes came alive when he saw her. "Hello, Pat," he said softly.

"Lucas. Where's Mr. Rifkin?"

"He's in Boston and couldn't make the meeting. He asked me to fill in. I was told that you'd gone away somewhere."

"I guess you could say that. On the other hand..." She left the unfinished sentence suspended in the air and turned away from him. She couldn't believe the effect on her of just seeing him. The assistant DA arrived, breaking the silence that neither of them was able to deal with.

"I'm Robin McCray, the ADA handling the McBride case at the moment. Where's Mr. Rifkin?"

"He couldn't make the meeting and asked me to fill in for him. I'm Lucas Alexander." Luke glanced over at Pat. Her face remained impassive, a touch of sadness darkening the corners of her eyes.

"So, Mr. Alexander, what can we do to make your job easier?" the ADA said.

"Admit you've indicted the wrong person, I suppose."

"'I'm afraid that's not in the cards, but I've been advised to give you everything we've got."

"Everything?"

"Everything you're entitled to."

It was almost 7:30 in the evening by the time an agreement was reached. Luke had obtained a copy of the tape that contained Frank Dunn's last telephone conversation with Margaux shortly before his death, a detailed report and analysis of all the fingerprints taken in the Dunn apartment during the first hours of the investigation, the ballistics report, and photos of the crime scene.

At the end of the meeting, he began packing all those documents into his briefcase. The ADA departed, leaving him alone once again with Pat. As she was gathering up the materials that were to remain within the exclusive possession of the DA, Luke put his hand lightly on her shoulder and said softly, "I wonder if I could have a few moments with my friend Pat?"

Pat turned and looked directly at him, intending to cut him down. But somehow, before she knew what was happening, she was in his arms, responding fiercely to his kisses. They stumbled over to the dilapidated couch at the end of the conference room. Interspersed between their muffled cries of joy and pleasure, Luke repeated the words he'd withheld from any woman for over ten years.

"I love you. Jesus, God, I love you, Pat."

When the passion subsided, Pat said, "Screw Margaux McBride."

"Is that an order?" Luke asked.

"That's not funny, damn you, Alexander."

CHAPTER FORTY

Pat sat down at her desk and checked her phone messages. As she glanced at them quickly, the name Sy Sherman caught her eye. Recalling that he was the superintendent of the Dunn apartment house, she returned his call immediately.

"It's about Mr. Hill," Mr. Sherman said, when Pat got him on the line. "He lives in the apartment above the Dunns. I wasn't sure whether I told you about him."

Pat opened her notebook. "No, I can't say that you did."

"It was the bullet, don't you know?"

Pat came to attention immediately. "What bullet?"

"The one that missed Mr. Dunn."

"I don't get you." Pat turned on the tape recorder.

"You see, that young fella what come to see me and took my statement told me that you all thought the gun had only five bullets in it because that's all you found in Mr. Dunn's body, may he rest in peace, but there was a sixth bullet 'cause I found it."

"Where?"

"In the chase way."

"Suppose I come over and you can show it to me."

"Sure, why not?"

When Pat arrived at the old man's apartment, he brought her into the kitchen and dumped the contents of a mason jar out carefully on the table. He picked up the spent bullet from among the flotsam of odd screws and bolts, and handed it over to her. She held it cautiously between her fingertips.

"Where did you say you found this?"

"Well, now, ma'am, it was like a mystery story, how it all happened, but it turned out to be Mr. Hill's television, don't you know. He didn't tell me about it until he come back from vacation. 'Course he's a bit hard of hearing, you know. He told me he couldn't get his TV to work, but when he plugged it in another outlet, it worked fine."

"And the bullet?"

"Something was shorting out the line that fed power to the outlet that his TV was plugged into."

"The bullet!"

"You got it, young lady. This here little chunk of lead." He picked up the spent bullet and rolled it around in the palm of his hand. "It was lodged tight as you please right in that power cable there in the chase way between the Dunn apartment and Mr. Hill's apartment. You see, when that fella shot at Mr. Dunn, this here bullet missed him and went right into that power line where it sat until I found it."

"I don't understand how we could have missed the bullet hole in the wall," Pat said, shaking her head.

"Because this here bullet went right through one of them holes in the cold air return duct and smack into the cable. That's when the TV conked out."

Pat could feel her pulse quicken. "Did he tell you what time this happened to him?"

"No, I can't say as how he did."

"I'll need to borrow this little fellow for a bit," she said, taking the bullet and dropping into a plastic envelope. "What is the number of Mr. Hill's apartment? I'll have to ask him a few questions."

"He don't live here no more."

"Where does he live now?" Pat asked anxiously.

"He and his missus are moving to Seattle. They left yesterday."

"Shit!"

"Excuse me, ma'am?"

"Sorry, Mr. Sherman. Could you give me his address in Seattle?"

"Sure can, but he's staying with his daughter until tomorrow, out on the Island in Sea Cliff. I've got her address, if you'd like it."

Pat knocked on the front door of a lovely old home overlooking Roslyn Harbor in the tiny village of Sea Cliff on the north shore of Long Island. A young woman answered the door.

"Ma'am, I'm Sergeant Turner with the New York City Police Department. I understand Mr. Hill is staying here with you for a bit. I wonder if I might speak with him a few moments."

"There's no trouble, is there?" the woman asked anxiously.

"Oh no, it's just that Mr. Hill has some information that may be helpful to us."

"Sure, please come in."

Mr. Hill was a tall, no-nonsense gentleman in his mid-seventies.

Pat explained the situation and the mission that had brought her.

"I remember the incident well because I was upset when the TV conked out. I left town early the next morning, so I didn't learn about Frank Dunn's death until I read of it in the newspaper when I returned."

"It's the time that your television went off that is very important to me, sir. If you could remember what you were watching when it went off, we might be able to put it in a particular time frame."

The elderly gentleman closed his eyes for a bit and finally said, "I'd say within ten minutes after nine o'clock – soon after the eight o'clock news hour ended."

Pat instantly recalled the time – 9:06 – that was recorded on the telephone tape, marking the moment Dunn had hung up the phone after talking to Margaux.

"Mr. Hill, the person charged with killing Mr. Dunn was talking to him on the telephone until 9:06. Could you be mistaken about the time your television cut out?"

"I assure you, young lady, I know what happened, and I will swear to it. Maybe it is you who is mistaken," he snapped.

"The problem is, nobody can be in two places at the same time."

"That's usually the case, but these days you never know."

———

Pat returned to her office after interviewing Mr. Hill and removed the tape from the evidence locker. She listened to it again intently. Each time, as soon as Frank hung up the phone, she pushed the rewind button and played the tape over again. The final time

through, she just let it run. And that's when she heard it: Click…
Click.

What the devil was that? she asked herself of the second click. My God! It was the sound of someone hanging up an extension phone.

Someone had been in the apartment listening to the conversation between Dunn and McBride.

———

Pat was waiting outside Lieutenant Garvey's office when he arrived the following morning.

"Come in, Sergeant. What can I do for you?"

Pat closed the office door and slid into the chair across from him. "It's a pretty serious problem, Chief. I'm afraid we may have indicted the wrong person in the Dunn case."

"Haven't we been through this already, Sergeant?" I'm aware of your concerns, but I've made a decision and that's the end of it. Let a jury decide this matter. That's what juries are for."

"But, sir, I have some new information that's very disturbing to me."

Pat described what she'd learned from Sy Sherman, the superintendent of the Dunn apartment house, Hill's statement concerning his TV failure, and finally the second click on the phone tape. When she finished, Garvey said, "I don't see that what you just told me means anything."

"It wouldn't have been possible for McBride to be talking on the phone with Dunn at 9:06 and fire a pistol at him at 9:10."

"C'mon, Sergeant, you're getting carried away here."

"How can you say that, sir?"

"I can say it based on being in this job for longer than you've lived, Sergeant. What do you want me to do, go to the DA and tell him that I've got a rookie female detective who has a cockamamie theory that ignores the fact that McBride stood to inherit two million a year for life upon Dunn's death, that she was in his apartment at about the time he was murdered, and that she lied about speaking to Dunn on the phone shortly before his death? I tell that to the DA, and he'll send me to the nearest psychiatric ward."

Pat tried to calm herself with a deep breath. "Although it's true that I'm a female detective, I don't see what that has to do with anything, and I'm not a rookie, and —"

"I'm sorry about the female rookie remark, you're right about that, but —"

"And I'm right that when McBride and Dunn were talking on the phone, someone else had to have been in Dunn's apartment listening to the conversation on the extension phone. Because when you study the tape, you can hear the click when they hang up after Dunn did."

"The click, the click. Come off it, Sergeant. You're claiming McBride couldn't have called Dunn from her apartment, and then been able to get over to his place within five minutes in order to wipe him out. Am I right? So suppose she didn't call him from her apartment. Suppose she called him from the pay phone on the corner next to Dunn's place? Or have you ever heard of a cell phone? She could've called him while she was standing outside the door to his apartment, for God's sake. Or suppose there was someone listening on an extension in McBride's apartment who hung up the phone after she did? Look Pat, you're trying to explain away all of the solid evidence with a far-out theory, based on the time that an old guy claims his TV went on the blink. Let's get back to the real world here. Maybe that night the old man fell asleep watching TV, or the time clock on the recording device was wrong, or who knows what. It's ridiculous. Do you know what would happen if the DA dismissed the indictment now?"

Pat shook her head negatively, biting her lip, trying to keep her emotions under control.

"I'll tell you what would happen. Your fancy lady lawyer would sue the City of New York for false arrest and malicious prosecution. Do you have any idea how much that case would cost the city? She'd claim her brilliant legal career was destroyed by the carelessness of the NYPD, and she would win, goddamn it! But if the jury buys your argument, so be it. It will cost the city nothing. It's no skin off our ass one way or the other. Now, I suggest you take your clicks and the bullet that came out of the chase way and your old man Hill and you bury them all in the bottom of your file, which you then staple shut and mark *case closed*. Is that clear?"

Pat stood up defiantly. "You're telling me to withhold evidence that could raise a doubt about the defendant's guilt. That's wrong!"

"Don't tell me what's right and wrong! I'll tell you what's wrong. Letting a murderess go free, that's what's wrong."

Pat picked up her file and marched out of the office.

If I resign or get fired the bastard wins, she thought. When she got back to her office she picked up the telephone and dialed.

A sleepy male voice answered, "Hello."

"Luke, we gotta talk. When can I see you?"

"Jesus, you're pregnant," Luke said, wide awake.

"No, this is strictly business."

"In that case, I'm available anytime."

"I'm coming right over, put the coffee on." Pat hung up the phone, grabbed her coat and left the office. When Luke opened the door to his apartment, he was wearing his Golden Gloves bathrobe and carrying an oversized mug of steaming coffee. He was barefoot and unshaven, and his hair was still wet from the shower.

"Come in, come in. God, you look good early in the morning."

"You're looking pretty sexy yourself, counselor," she said, giving the belt of his bathrobe a tug.

He bent down and kissed her, being careful not to spill the coffee as he pulled her close to him. She pushed him away.

"Hey, what's the matter?"

Pat walked past him into the kitchen and poured herself a cup of coffee. He followed her.

"I don't get it. You wake me up in the middle of the night, tell me you have some urgent business that you have to talk to me about, come waltzing into my apartment looking like Miss America, and then cast me aside like yesterday's newspaper. I mean, what goes here?"

"It's 8:30 in the morning, and I'm on duty."

"What's time got to do with it?" he asked. "Do you want me to jump your bones or not?"

"Of course I do, but not now."

Pat kept her back turned to him. If she looked at him one more time, even for just a moment, they'd end up spending the morning in bed. She poured in the milk and sugar, stirred the brew, and then turned to face him. He had discarded his robe and stood stark naked in the center of the kitchen, munching on a giant donut and wearing another. Pat burst out laughing. "What am I supposed to do? Play ring toss?" The donut Luke was wearing slipped to the floor. He looked down and said, "Now see what you've done. He's gone back to sleep. I might as well join him." He turned and started to leave the kitchen.

"Wait, Luke, I think I can wake him up," she said in her early morning husky voice.

Later, when they returned to the kitchen, Luke said, "Now that you have paid your dues, what is this urgent business all about?"

"I have a very tough problem."

"Lay it on me," he said, turning the wooden chair around backwards and pulling it up to the table.

"It's the Dunn case, and it involves Lieutenant Garvey and the bitch."

"Hold it. I assume you're talking about McBride and we agreed we weren't ever going to discuss that case. It can only open old wounds."

"I know. You're right. But my career may be on the line."

"In that case, I guess we don't have a choice."

"The difficulty is, I hate the idea of sharing information with you that will help that bimbo and might also get me fired. On the other hand, it's a violation of the law if we don't tell Mr. Rifkin what we know."

"Let's slow down here. Yes, if you have evidence that proves McBride is innocent, you must disclose it to the DA and he must give it to Barney."

"Garvey has instructed me to bury it before it gets to the DA."

"That sounds like dirty business. Why'd he do that?"

"He says it's because what I've uncovered is theory, not fact, and therefore doesn't need to be given to the DA."

"If he's right, I agree with him. A prosecutor isn't required to give defense counsel theories that might exonerate the defendant."

"But that's not the case. I've uncovered facts that I believe might cast doubt on her guilt. The problem is, I still think she probably killed Frank Dunn."

Luke sat thoughtfully for a few moments and then got up and poured himself his third cup of coffee of the day.

"I believe I know what you should do, but you aren't going to like it, so I think I'll keep it to myself."

"Oh no you don't. First you deflower me between your second and third cups of coffee, and then you tell me that although you know what I should do, you're going to keep it to yourself."

"Okay, here's what I think. Going over Garvey's head is too risky for you. And withholding evidence in a murder case is unconscionable."

"So what do I do?"

"Find the real killer."

CHAPTER FORTY-ONE

Helen Dunn had finished hosing down the runs at the back of the kennel and was walking toward the reception area when she saw him. He sensed her approach and turned toward her.

"Helen."

She stood still, trying to calm her excitement. It had been many months since she'd last seen him. At their last meeting, he'd told her he was going to Kuwait to work on a large construction project. Being the CEO of his own small engineering company, it wasn't uncommon for him to leave the country.

"Chet, it's nice to see you again. And Regina, you're looking as beautiful as ever." The dog nuzzled Helen and responded with a yelp of recognition.

"I just came in on British Airways from London. I'm spending the night here in New York and then I'm off to Chicago in the morning. Regina suggested we stop and say hello on our way into the city. She thought she might like to spend the night with you, if you had room."

"She must know by now that she's always welcome here."

"Wonderful. I hope things have gone well for you while I've been gone. How's the family?" Chet asked, casually.

My God, Helen thought. He doesn't know about Frank's death.

"My husband Frank was...was...died last year," she said.

"Oh no." Chet put his arm around her shoulder. "I'm truly sorry, Helen. He was so young. What happened?"

"I'm afraid I'm not up to telling the whole story right now, Chet. Perhaps another time."

Chet's shock at learning of Frank's death was soon replaced by a feeling of hopefulness. He felt somewhat ashamed of himself, but couldn't stop from taking her hand and saying, "Could we pick up where we left off?"

"I think I would like that very much."

———

When Chet returned from Chicago he let Helen set the pace. He could see that she was distraught by Frank's death and her difficult relationship with Jennifer, and that she needed his patience and understanding. One evening he took her to see an off-Broadway revival of *West Side Story*, and after the show he suggested they go dancing at a little jazz club, a favorite of his. She said she'd promised Jen she'd be home no later than ten o'clock, and invited him to come home with her for coffee, instead.

Once there, Helen checked on Jen and found her sound asleep in her room. She and Chet settled down comfortably in the living room and began to discuss the show. They talked about the clash of cultures at the heart of Leonard Bernstein's musical, and how such ethnic and religious differences were still tearing the world apart. Chet described his adventures in North Africa. He talked about the problems he encountered there because the Arab world was totally alien to him and his American mentality. "It is not a place for a modern woman to live, or in my opinion, for any woman to live," he said. "Wives are physically abused for no discernible reason except perhaps that they inadvertently displeased their husbands. I'm very happy to have that experience behind me and I do not plan to return there in the foreseeable future."

The words tumbled unexpectedly from her mouth. "I'm not a stranger to physical abuse." She started to cry.

Chet came and sat beside her, putting his arm around her while she buried her face in his shoulder. "I don't know what to do," she sobbed. "Jennifer sees my affection for you as a betrayal of her father. Her increasing hostility towards me is tearing me apart. The situation is impossible."

"Nothing is impossible, Helen. We'll just take it one day at a time."

"We can't." She cried harder. "I'm not what I appear to be. I'm an emotional cripple. If you knew everything about me you'd run away as fast as you could. If I can't live with myself, how can anyone else?"

"You're talking in riddles, Helen. We just need to work through whatever is troubling you. I can help. I know I can."

"It's too late for that."

"All I ask is that you let me help carry the burden. I'm not leaving until we talk the whole thing out."

It was after four o'clock in the morning before Chet finally went home.

———

Pat sat in her office watching the clock and waiting for Luke to call. He'd started calling her every day at precisely four o'clock. At one minute to four the phone rang. She picked it up on the first ring.

"Hi, big fella!"

"This is Jen."

"Oh, Jen," she laughed, "I was expecting another call."

"I have to see you right away. I have something very important to tell you about who killed my father. I can't talk about it over the phone."

"I assume you've read that Margaux McBride has been charged and will be going to trial soon."

"That's why I have to talk to you right away. Margaux didn't do it, somebody else did, and I know who it is," she whispered.

"Come right over to my office, I'll be waiting." Pat glanced at her calendar. It was filled until an hour before she was scheduled to meet Luke for dinner, but she didn't dare assume that Jen was just a kid with a lot of imagination. Somehow or other, she'd fit her in.

When Luke finally got through to her she asked if they could make dinner at nine o'clock instead of eight.

"Don't see why not."

"How come you're always so easy to get along with? When is the other shoe going to drop?"

"Just before we climb into bed… which reminds me…"

"Never mind. Tell me later. I'll see you at the Ibex at nine o'clock."

It was after seven before Pat was able to see Jen, who had waited patiently for more than two hours.

"Okay, Jen, tell me what this is all about."

"Last night the creep took my mom out to the theater. I fell asleep before she came home."

"The creep?"

"Chet Bartlett. He's been dating my mom since my father died, and he's a creep."

"Is he really strange, or is it that you just don't like the idea of your mom dating?"

"He's a creep, big time. Hey look. I'm almost fourteen, and it's not like I don't know what's going on between them. I woke up in the middle of the night and I heard them talking in the living room. Apparently they didn't hear me get up to go to the bathroom, because they just kept talking real soft-like. But I could hear everything they said. The creep goes, 'Look, Helen, he was a monster. The guy who did it deserves a medal.'" Jennifer's lower lip began to tremble. "My father wasn't a monster, Pat. He was wonderful and he loved me more than anybody, and it was that miserable creep who killed my father. He sort of confessed the whole thing, I swear. And my mom knew the creep before Daddy was killed, 'cause I heard them talking about the first time they met at the kennel, like maybe years before, so that proves the creep wanted to get my dad out of the way so he could mess with my mom. He's just a rotten, stinking son of a bitch, creep, bastard," she cried.

Thoughts were racing through Pat's mind. Was this a distraught child's fantasy, or could it be true? Was this a love triangle murder?

———

Pat called Helen at home and asked if Jen could spend the night with her. She explained as best she could without revealing the true cause of Jen's distress why it seemed like a good idea, saying that Jen was upset and didn't want to come home right away. Helen asked to speak to Jen, who confirmed her wish to spend the night with Pat. Helen gave her permission.

Pat cancelled her date with Luke and after several more hours of talking with Jen about her mother and Chet, she decided she should go to Dallas and interview Jennifer's grandfather as soon as possible.

CHAPTER FORTY-TWO

The phone ringing in Luke's dream turned out to be real.

"Luke, it's Pat."

He glanced at the illuminated digital clock. "Jesus, Pat, it's 2:15 in the morning. I was sound asleep."

"That's funny," Pat giggled. "My watch says it's just after midnight. I figured you'd still be awake watching the late show and thinking about me."

"The reason for this call better be good, after standing me up last night."

"It is. But of course, if you'd rather have me call in the morning, you know —"

"Okay, out with it. Where are you?"

"I'm in Greenville, Texas."

"What the hell are you doing there at two o'clock in the morning?"

"You told me to find the killer, so I did."

"In Greenville, Texas? Spit it out, Turner."

"Greenville is a little town just outside Dallas. I've spent the last four hours with Helen Dunn's parents, who live here. It turns out that on the night Dunn was killed, Helen Dunn missed the plane that was supposed to bring her here to visit her parents. She didn't arrive here until one o'clock in the morning, Dallas time."

"So?"

"So the good Lady Dunn's airtight alibi isn't so airtight anymore. She lied to us about her departure time from LaGuardia.

I'm going to find out where she was between seven, when she arrived at the airport, and eleven when she left LaGuardia.

Something else. It turns out that a guy named Bartlett, Chester Bartlett, and Lady Dunn were probably having an affair at the time Dunn was killed. And finally, Dunn was a wife beater, especially when he was drunk. I don't just mean an occasional black eye, I'm talking serious stuff. Broken nose, concussion. Once he hit her so hard she suffered a detached retina. After I got the parents started, they related one horror story after another about Frank Dunn and their daughter. Helen kept it from them for years, but when she ended up in the hospital for a week with the detached retina, she broke down and told her mother everything."

Luke carried the portable phone into the kitchen and put the coffee on. "Is it possible she was the one on the phone when Margaux called Lover Boy? You know the click-click routine?"

"That's what I'm thinking. I don't exactly know where this Bartlett fits into the picture, but for sure Lady Dunn is a big fat liar. Hey, look, I'm booked on a flight that should get me back to New York this afternoon. How about dinner in some dark, romantic restaurant?"

"How about I fix dinner at my place and turn out the lights, instead?"

"You're on, counselor. By the way, I don't remember hearing you say you love me yet."

"It goes without saying. You know I don't function too well in the middle of the night."

"I can personally attest to the fact that you function very well in the middle of the night. And incidentally, it doesn't go without saying, so say it!"

"I love you, babe, a lot."

"That'll do nicely. Bye."

When Pat got back to her office, there were a dozen messages waiting for her, one of which particularly caught her eye: "Call Helen Dunn, ASAP." The call had come in the previous morning as she was on her way to Dallas. Pat immediately dialed the number.

"Sergeant Turner, I need to talk to you as soon as possible. Could you come to my home?"

"I'll come right over."

CHAPTER FORTY-THREE

When Pat arrived at the Dunn apartment, Helen led the way into the living room. Chet Bartlett was there. A copy of the *Post* was on the coffee table. The headlines screamed *BLACK BEAUTY INDICTED...Victim's Lover Accused*. A photograph of Margaux McBride, her voluptuous body spilling out of a bikini, was splashed across the front page.

After being introduced to Chet, Pat sat in a chair opposite the couch where Helen and he were seated. There was an awkward silence while Pat waited patiently for one of them to open the conversation. Finally Helen said, "I have something I must tell you about my husband's death."

"Before you say anything, Mrs. Dunn, I think I better give you what is called a Miranda warning." Pat removed a small card from her briefcase and read the warning. When she finished, she added, "The most important part of that right now might be that you have the right to speak with an attorney before you say anything."

"I don't want an attorney," Helen said, barely above a whisper.

"I don't agree with that, "Chet said, "but Helen insists on doing this her way."

"All right. I'd like to record our conversation. Do you have any objection?"

Helen shook her head no and Pat placed the tape recorder on the coffee table.

Helen began. "As soon as I learned that Margaux had been indicted for Frank's murder, I knew I could no longer remain silent. I hate her, but she didn't kill Frank." Helen hesitated, covered her face with her hands, and said, "I killed him." She started to cry softly. "It's all so awful," she whispered. Chet gave her his handkerchief and put his arm around her shoulder. Pat waited patiently and sympathetically until Helen was able to continue.

"Frank was obsessed with her," Helen began. "He used to get up at two o'clock in the morning and sneak out to the telephone to call her. He didn't realize I knew he did that, and I kept hoping it would pass like his other affairs had, but it didn't. It just seemed to intensify, and so did his abusive behavior toward me. Then one day, he urged me to visit my parents in Dallas. I thought he was being considerate, but I realized later that he just wanted me gone so he could be with her. He was such a bastard.

"When Frank came to pick me up and take me to the airport, I knew he'd been drinking. It was late and traffic was terrible. I was worried that we wouldn't make it to the airport on time, but I didn't dare say anything to Frank, not in his awful mood. But I was right. When we finally got there, I jumped out of the car and ran into the terminal building, but by the time I got to the departure gate, it was closed. They told me I could either take an 11:00 PM flight to Dallas with a two-hour layover in Raleigh-Durham, or I could leave at 8:00 AM the next morning. My parents are elderly and live in Greenville, fifty miles north of the airport. I didn't want to keep them up until all hours of the night, so I decided to go home, get a good night's sleep, and take off early in the morning. I called my parents and told them what had happened, and that I wouldn't be getting in until about ten the following morning.

"I arrived back at the apartment house around seven thirty. The doorman had apparently gone off for a cigarette. In any event, he wasn't at the door, and no one else was at home. I let myself into the lobby with my own key."

"But we have a written statement from the doorman in which he emphatically claims he never left the entrance that night," Pat interrupted. "I think his name is Julien."

"Yes, it would have been Julien. He's a delightful young man, but you can't believe a word he says about not leaving his station. The doormen aren't allowed to smoke on the job, and Julien's a heavy smoker. He'd been warned several times not to sneak off to smoke, and if he'd told the truth about where he was, I'm sure he would have been fired. He has a lovely wife and three beautiful children, and no one has the heart to see him fired. In any event, I swear to you that when I came back home, he wasn't there. I let myself in with my own key and came directly up here to our apartment." Helen heaved a deep sigh.

"Do you want to take a break?" Pat asked.

"No, no, I have to keep going," Helen said. "I mixed myself a drink and decided to take a hot bath and go to bed early because I had to be up by 5:30 in the morning. The drink and the hot bath combined eased me into a deep sleep shortly after I got into bed." She hesitated momentarily, unable to continue. She started to shiver.

"I was awakened by the phone ringing. It must have rung a couple of times before I picked it up. I was about to say hello when I heard the voices of Frank and Margaux. Apparently I hadn't even heard Frank come home, and there I was, listening to his and Margaux's plans to have sex in my house...in my bed! Oh God!" Pat sat silently until Helen regained her composure. When she started to speak again, her eyes were glazed and Pat had to lean forward to hear what she was saying.

"When they finished their conversation, I could scarcely breathe. All I could think of was that I wanted to die, that I didn't want to live and face the aftermath of this obscenity. Jennifer would have her father to herself, and it was obvious that at that time in her life she didn't need or want me. So I hung up the phone, opened the drawer of the nightstand, and took out the pistol Frank had bought a few months earlier, when there'd been several burglaries in our apartment house. I lost all sense of reality. It felt like I was watching a film in slow motion. I turned the pistol over in my hand, one way and then the other. I hesitated, trying to decide whether to point it at my temple or my heart. Just as I raised the gun, Frank opened the bedroom door, and when he saw me he screamed at me. Then he raised his fist and lurched at me. I must have blacked out because the next thing I remember is that the gun was still in my hand and Frank was on the floor beside the bed. I watched blood bubble out of a wound in the left side of his neck. I saw a bullet hole just above his left eye and more blood oozing from there. His eyes were open... staring...I knelt down beside him and put my ear against his bare chest. There was no heartbeat. There was no pulse. He was dead.

"I couldn't understand why I was so calm. The bodice of my nightgown was saturated with blood. Blood was everywhere. I was careful not to step in it and leave any footprints. For some reason I've never understood, I picked up the brass casings, wrapped them in toilet paper and flushed them down the john. I dressed quickly, and threw my blood-soaked nightgown in my suitcase, which was already packed.

"I started pulling dresser drawers out and emptying them on the floor. I went into the living room and pulled Frank's wallet from his trousers on the couch. I took out all the money he had and wiped the wallet clean with his shirt and then went back into the bedroom to pick up the pistol. Then I raced down to the garage, jumped in my car, and headed back to the airport to try and catch the eleven o'clock flight. As I drove over the 59th Street Bridge, I slowed down and threw the pistol out the window. I arrived at the departure gate a few minutes before the plane left.

"I've agonized over and over about not calling an ambulance, not calling the police. The thing that drove every other rational thought from my mind was that Jennifer loved her father very much and I knew. I absolutely knew that she would never forgive me for causing Frank's death, even though I didn't mean to do it."

Helen began to sob again. She whimpered and rocked back and forth. Pat was having difficulty controlling her own emotions. She turned off the tape recorder. Chet picked up the empty water glass, and took it into the kitchen to refill it. Almost a half hour passed before Helen was able to continue.

"I still don't know how I'm going to face Jennifer with the truth."

In a moment Pat said, "There might be something I can do to help. Can I borrow a telephone and speak in private somewhere?"

"Use the phone in the bedroom. You go right through there."

Pat went in and closed the door. She was standing in the bedroom where Frank Dunn had been killed. Her mind played out the scene of Helen sitting up in bed and firing at Frank as he lunged toward her. She felt a shiver of anxiety as she picked up the phone and held it to her ear, exactly as Helen had done when she overheard the conversation between Frank and Margaux.

Pat called Luke.

"Hey, you better not be calling to cancel our dinner date."

"I'm at Helen Dunn's apartment. She has just confessed to killing her husband."

"Congratulations!"

"I can't say I feel great about it. The problem is, she really needs a lawyer. Will you help her. Please?"

"Well, she certainly needs representation, but —"

"Here, let me have her talk to you." Before he could protest, Pat carried the portable phone to the living room, and telling Helen who was on the line, she handed her the phone.

"Why don't you come to my office, Mrs. Dunn? Sergeant Turner will tell you how to get here."

"Yes, all right, I'll be there as soon as I can."

"I'll see you shortly then. Let me speak with Sergeant Turner again, please."

Helen handed the phone back to Pat.

"I'm willing to talk to this woman, but you do understand that there's no possible way I can teach law and handle a murder case at the same time. Incidentally, how come you're not worried about a conflict of interest here, like you were when I was trying to help Margaux?"

"Go to hell, Alexander," she whispered, and hung up.

CHAPTER FORTY-FOUR

Chet advised Helen not to meet with Luke. He said it didn't make any sense for her to hire the lawyer the police had recommended, but Helen was adamant. She trusted Pat totally, she said, adding that if she didn't feel comfortable with Lucas Alexander, she'd take Chet's advice.

When Helen finished telling Luke her story in his office, she asked in a barely audible voice, "What will they do to me, Mr. Alexander?"

Luke looked at the distraught woman seated across the desk from him and said, "First of all, Mrs. Dunn, if everything you've told me is true, I think you might be able to convince a jury that you did not intentionally kill your husband, or that you were acting under extreme emotional distress, or that you shot him in self-defense. Any of those situations would reduce the crime from murder to manslaughter."

"I just can't understand why I did such a terrible thing."

"That's exactly your defense, Mrs. Dunn. It's the *why* that sometimes makes the difference between innocence and guilt. Your best defense is probably self-defense. Incidentally, how tall was he, how much did he weigh?"

"Almost six-two and about two-hundred twenty-five pounds."

"And you?"

"Five-feet four and one hundred twenty pounds."

"So you see, there's no way you could have defended yourself against him without a weapon, and as you say, he had a long history of assaulting you. The threat of harm was real...that's your defense. But it has some serious problems, I'm afraid."

"What do you mean?"

"In order to avail yourself of that defense you must prove you only used that degree of force necessary to defend yourself. Otherwise, you become the aggressor. The problem here is that while you can probably justify the use of a gun in view of his size and his having severely injured you with his fists in the past, you have to deal with the fact that you fired six shots at him. Without further explanation, a jury could find that in firing more than one shot, you were not just defending yourself, but rather, you were intending to mortally wound your husband."

"But that's not true, Mr. Alexander. I don't know anything about guns. I don't even remember firing the gun at all."

"I believe you, really I do, but in order to properly defend you, your attorney must address the weaknesses of your case as well as its strengths, and I must point out that the weapon you fired was not an automatic. In order to have fired the six shots, you had to actually pull the trigger six times. The prosecutor can argue that even assuming you initially only intended to defend yourself, you had time between firing the first and the last bullet to form the necessary intent to commit the crime. In other words, in the fraction of a second between the time you fired the first and the second bullet, you had time to *premeditate* killing your husband."

"Oh God, is that what you believe? Does that mean you won't defend me?"

Luke hesitated before answering her. He was in a quandary. The adrenaline had started to kick in. The fact was that, although he enjoyed teaching very much, he missed working in the courtroom. It wasn't just the excitement and the exhilaration of winning, although he readily admitted that victory was heady stuff, it was also the fact that as a teacher you could only talk about justice; in the courtroom you had an opportunity to help create justice.

He looked hard at Helen. There was no doubt that she needed an experienced criminal lawyer. He wanted to help her, but with his responsibilities at the university he couldn't see how it could be done. If he agreed to represent Helen, from the time of her arraignment until many months later when the jury reached its verdict, he would be preparing her defense almost every waking moment of his life. He'd be spending enormous amounts of money for expert witnesses, forensic tests, graphic exhibits, private investigators, and whatever else might help convince the jury that she hadn't intended to kill her husband. He knew very well that defending a murder case for a client whom he believed to be innocent was the most challenging, emotionally exhausting, and professionally rewarding experience a trial lawyer can experience.

After an exhausting silence, Luke finally said, "No, Mrs. Dunn, I don't think you intended to kill your husband, but I can't represent you."

"Please Mr. Alexander, I…" Helen turned away, unable to continue.

———

Before Helen left his office, Luke promised to find an experienced lawyer to defend her, but he agonized over his decision. Truth be told, he didn't think anyone he knew could defend her better than he could. He was not so arrogant as to believe that among the twenty-five thousand attorneys practicing in the metropolitan area there wasn't one who couldn't do a better job of it. But who would put his heart as well as his mind to the task as thoroughly as he would? Would anyone else devote almost every moment of his life for the next three months to studying the thousands of documents the district attorney would be ordered to turn over to defense counsel? There'd be pages and pages of interrogation transcripts, fingerprint reports, DNA reports, autopsy reports, crime scene investigation reports, crime scene photographs. Every single document would have to be scrutinized to avoid overlooking a single word, concept, error, clue, or discrepancy in the statements of the prospective witnesses for the prosecution.

And the law? What about the law? Who else would research the myriad of legal issues he could anticipate being raised during trial? Who else would personally handle the multitude of pretrial motions that would be argued? He had no secretary. He had no legal staff, he had no investigative staff. He would have to resign his teaching position at the University. It was crazy to consider defending her. It was fucking impossible.

He got up and slid back the wall panel that concealed his refreshment bar. Throwing a handful of ice into a rocks glass, he opened the bottle of Gray Goose vodka, filled the glass halfway and then poured in some grapefruit juice. He slumped back down in his chair, took a hefty slug of his drink and stared out the window at the people going in and out of the bar across the street until he fell asleep.

When he awakened the lights from the bar had been turned off. It took him a few minutes to become oriented, and then he checked his rolodex and dialed a number. It rang and rang but no one picked up. Not even the answering machine. As he was about to hang up, a sleepy, unfriendly voice said, "Hello. It better be important."

Luke glanced at the clock on the wall and winced. It was 4:20 in the morning.

"What are your plans for the next six months?" he demanded of the man he considered to be the best private investigator in the city.

"Are you drunk?" Charlie Utah replied.

CHAPTER FORTY-FIVE

Luke arranged for Helen to be arrested, booked, and released on one hundred thousand dollars bail. Judge Hamilton had retained jurisdiction of the case and agreed to conduct the arraignment at an unannounced time, to avoid the media circus. The fact that the victim's exotic lover, Black Beauty, had been exonerated and his wife had been indicted was a uniquely newsworthy event. Photos of Margaux and Helen side by side on the front pages of the tabloids carried such headlines as, *Wife Takes Black Beauty Off the Hook* and *Wife Done Dunn*. After the arraignment, Luke handed assistant DA Sandy Livingston written notice that he intended to introduce psychiatric testimony in defending Helen.

The next day he got a call from the district attorney's office. "Mr. Alexander? Sandy Livingston. I've read the notice you gave me yesterday, that you intend to introduce psychiatric testimony, and of course I expect you will put in a defense of severe emotional distress in order to reduce it from murder to manslaughter. I just wanted to tell you that we can save you a lot of money for psychiatrists and save us both a lot of time. We're willing to take a plea to manslaughter one."

"I appreciate that offer, Ms. Livingston, but the fact is, I think we've got a chance of getting an acquittal here."

"She shot at her husband with six bullets at close range. It doesn't sound to me like she was playing patty-cake. You're not claiming she was crazy, are you?"

"Not a bit. Fact is, she's a lovely, bright, articulate woman."

"That may be true, and the DA might even consider man-slaughter second because of her good character and the victim's involvement with that McBride woman. I recognize there are some extenuating circumstances here, but there is no way she's going to walk."

"But I think —"

"Look, sir, I'll open my file to you. I mean the judge is going to order me to do it anyway. If you've got something I don't know about, just tell me and we'll try to work it out."

"I'm claiming self-defense."

"What? The deceased was unarmed and the defendant made Swiss cheese out of him."

"I'll also be claiming the defense of Battered Woman Syndrome, and I was certain that with your considerable experience in that field, you'd be sympathetic to the defendant and agree to dismiss this case."

"Sympathy has nothing to do with it. She took her husband's life. You know very well that if the DA agreed to dismiss a murder case because a husband may have pushed his wife around a little, we'd have to open the door to the state prison and let half the women out."

"Might not be a bad idea. The world is changing, Ms. Livingston. The Neanderthal man has finally become an endangered species, thank God."

"I agree with you on that, and between you and me, I wish we could do better. But there's no way I can offer less than manslaughter two."

"Then I guess we'll take our chances," Luke said, with more bravado than he felt.

CHAPTER FORTY-SIX

It was one of those cold, blustery mid-March days in Manhattan. Luke put his arm protectively around Helen as they climbed the steps to the courthouse. He could feel her frail body trembling as he pushed their way through the crowd of reporters blocking the entranceway. The small courtroom was filled to capacity, mostly with media people and the usual coterie of court watchers who found the drama of real life more interesting than the soaps.

At precisely 9:30 Judge Hamilton entered the courtroom and took her seat on the bench. She looked over the jury of eight women and four men that it had taken three days to select. She opened the proceedings.

"Good morning, ladies and gentlemen. First I want to explain to you a little bit about what you can expect today. This morning, the attorneys are going to describe what they intend to prove during the course of this trial. Listen carefully to what they have to say, but understand that whatever they tell you is not evidence. This matter is of great importance to both the People and the defendant, and I therefore expect you to give it your thoughtful attention right from the beginning so that you'll be able to render a verdict that will do justice." The judge then turned to the assistant district attorney and said, "Ms. Livingston, you may proceed."

In the 1950s, one out of every twenty law school graduates was female. By the 90s, four out of ten law school graduates were women who went on to become active in all phases of the practice of law. Sandy Livingston was one of the most accomplished members of the district attorney's staff. Although she handled all of the major sex crimes, this would be her first murder case, and she was uneasy about the case. Most of the assault cases she'd prosecuted involved female victims who'd been physically abused by their mates, and her personal sympathies leaned in favor of the victim. Technically she was well qualified to prosecute Helen Dunn, but emotionally, the case was very troublesome to her. She picked up her yellow pad and took a few steps to position herself in front of the jury.

"Ladies and gentlemen of the jury, this is a homicide case and I bear the responsibility of representing the People of the State of New York. The charge against Helen Dunn is that on the night of July 25, 2003, she intentionally fired five .38 caliber bullets into the head and body of her husband, Frank Dunn, at close range, thereby causing his death. In most murder cases, there are many issues of fact in dispute. In this case, the defendant has admitted that she killed her husband, but she claims that she was justified in taking his life because he had physically abused her at some time in the past. But from our perspective, there is but a single issue in this case, and that is whether or not the defendant was acting under the influence of extreme emotional distress at the time she killed her husband, which would reduce the charge from murder to manslaughter. That will, of course, be a matter for you to judge. The defendant claims that she had no motive to kill her husband. However, the People will prove that at the time she shot and killed her husband, not only was she the sole beneficiary of a one million dollar life insurance policy on her husband's life, but she was also pursuing a romantic affair with a recently divorced man, Mr. Chester Bartlett, who is sitting in this courtroom." Sandy turned and pointed to Chet. "Right there in the front row wearing the brown suit and yellow tie." Ms. Livingston paused to allow the jury to absorb her accusation, and then continued.

"And finally, we will prove that the defendant had become insanely jealous of an associate in her husband's law office named Margaux McBride, and had allowed Ms. McBride to be falsely accused of the murder of her husband. We will also prove that the defendant did not come forward and acknowledge that it was she, and not Ms. McBride, who had put an end to her husband's life until after Detective Patricia Turner confronted her with conclusive proof that she had killed her husband."

Helen covered her face with her hands and began to weep

softly. Her shoulders shook with the effort of trying to control herself. The jury stared at her impassively. Luke poured a glass of water and offered it to her. The ADA waited patiently until she was satisfied that she once again had the full attention of the jurors.

"Your task will not be an easy one, but you must fairly and objectively weigh the proof in this case and not be swayed by sympathy. After you've heard all of the evidence, I am certain that you will find the defendant guilty as charged."

Luke was impressed by the skill his young adversary had demonstrated. She'd made a short and effective address. Clearly the DA had chosen wisely when he assigned Sandy Livingston to prosecute Helen Dunn.

Judge Hamilton turned to Luke and said, "Mr. Alexander."

Luke glanced a final time at Charlie Utah's biographical report on each of the jurors, took his glasses off, and ambled slowly up to the jury box. He turned towards Judge Hamilton and said, "May it please the court," then turned back to the jurors, who looked, as they always did, stern and serious. He briefly looked them over, trying to decide which was his favorite. He'd learned that if he felt good about a juror, in most cases he or she felt good about him. It wasn't an infallible rule, but it had served him well over the years.

"Ladies and gentlemen of the jury," he began, looking directly at the teacher he'd selected as his favorite juror, "I've had the privilege of addressing a few juries in my life, and by this time, the butterflies in my stomach shouldn't be there. But they are, because of the awesome responsibility I bear in this case. The destiny of Helen Dunn rests in your hands, and it is my job to produce the evidence that will enable you to find Helen Dunn not guilty, because justice commands such a verdict. I'm going to begin that task by talking to you a little bit about the three cornerstones of criminal justice. The first one is the presumption of innocence. I'm sure you all remember that from your high school civics class and you've probably heard it a few hundred times on television. But this may be the first time you've had an opportunity to really understand its meaning and how it works in our system of justice. The law demands that as we begin this trial, and continuing up until the moment you give your verdict, you must presume that Helen Dunn is innocent.

"The second cornerstone is called the burden of proof. It is the prosecutor who carries that burden. It is the prosecutor who must bring into this courtroom credible evidence to support the charges against Helen, and it is how you treat that evidence that constitutes the third and final cornerstone of justice, embodied in the words, 'beyond a reasonable doubt.' In summary, you the jury must presume that Helen Dunn is innocent, and require the prosecutor to overcome that presumption of innocence, by bearing the burden of proving her guilt beyond a reasonable doubt.

"This very able young prosecutor has suggested to you, in a most eloquent opening address, that this case is just a matter of deciding whether or not Helen Dunn intended to kill her husband with malice aforethought, or whether she caused his death while under the influence of severe emotional distress. But I now tell you, ladies and gentlemen of the jury, that there is a third course which you may follow in your pursuit of justice. I promise that I will produce evidence here that Frank Dunn, by his physical, mental, and emotional abuse of his wife, set into motion certain psychological forces in Helen Dunn's mind which were beyond her ability to control. These forces created by Frank Dunn were so powerful and pervasive that they led inexorably to his death.

"Frank Dunn was an abusive man, a man without decency, a man without honor, a man who was guided solely by his wish to fulfill his carnal desires, regardless of the price his infidelities exacted from his wife and thirteen-year-old daughter. Ladies and gentlemen, during this trial you will bear witness to tragedy, but you have the power and the opportunity to prevent an even greater tragedy. When you've heard both sides of this sordid affair, you'll find that the only thing Helen Dunn is guilty of is devoting her life to a man who lied to her, made a mockery of his marriage vows, a man who physically abused her with sufficient force to fracture the bones in her body, caused her to suffer a brain concussion and to lose 50 percent of the sight in her right eye, at the very same time that he was helping his mistress live like royalty in a Park Avenue penthouse.

"I am convinced beyond all shadow of doubt that when the evidence is closed, and Judge Hamilton delivers this case into your hands for deliberation, you will unanimously agree that it is Frank Dunn who is the wrongdoer and that it is Helen Dunn who is the victim in this case.

"The symbol of justice, that stately woman you see sculpted in bronze above the door of this chamber, blindfolded, proudly holding the balanced scales of justice aloft in her hand, cries out for a verdict of not guilty. When you have heard all of the evidence in this case, I'm confident that you will set Helen Dunn free so that she may pick up the pieces of her shattered life."

Luke walked slowly back to the counsel table, fearful that he had said too little or too much. As always, he was immersed in self-doubt about his ability to convince the jury that there are exceptions to the seventh commandment: Thou shalt not kill.

CHAPTER FORTY-SEVEN

During the first day of trial, the prosecution introduced a parade of witnesses testifying to the measurements of the bedroom, location of the body, and the cause of death. Luke did not cross-examine a single witness until the testimony of the medical examiner was introduced.

"Dr. Sinclair, my name is Lucas Alexander. I represent Helen Dunn, the defendant in this case. I have a few questions which I hope you can answer for me." Luke picked up his yellow pad with his scribbled notes and stood in front of the witness. "Did it appear from your examination of the body, Doctor, that the bullets were fired from close range?"

"Oh yes, it is my opinion that the weapon was less than a foot away from the victim when it was fired."

"Why don't you explain for us how you could tell that the pistol was fired at close range?" Luke asked, as if he and the witness were old friends.

"There were flash-burn marks surrounding the bullet holes in the body." Luke nodded thoughtfully and made a note on his yellow pad to indicate to the jury that this was a fact worth remembering.

"And from your examination of the body, Doctor, were you able to ascertain the trajectory of the bullets?"

"Yes, we could follow the path of each bullet from the time it entered the body."

"And, Doctor, did you learn from your investigation of this

matter that another bullet that was fired at the same time was later retrieved from the chase-way just above the bedroom ceiling?"

"Yes, I saw that report."

"And can you tell me, Doctor, whether or not your finding with regard to the trajectory of the bullets which struck Frank Dunn was compatible with the trajectory of the bullet which was found in the chase-way."

"It was."

"Now, Doctor, I'd like you to assume, if you would, that Helen Dunn was seated in her bed when she fired the pistol which caused her husband's death. Can you tell me, given those circumstances, where you believe Frank Dunn was positioned at the moment those bullets entered his body?"

"As I said, he was very close to the weapon, and since the trajectory of the bullets was in an upward direction, that would obviously put him in a position above his wife."

Luke walked back to the counsel table and removed a large computer generated drawing that he asked the court reporter to mark as an exhibit. He set it up on an easel in front of the witness.

"Dr. Sinclair, this is a drawing of the Dunn master bedroom including the precise location of the bed and the metal grating in the chase way. I want you to assume that everything in this drawing is precisely to scale, including the bed and this white cutout of Mrs. Dunn. I've got some sticky stuff on the back of the cutout which will allow us to place it in any position on the bed that we wish." Luke placed Helen's silhouette cutout on the board and made the adjustments to conform to the previous testimony.

"All right, Doctor, I have now placed Mrs. Dunn's silhouette on the bed with the right arm holding a revolver extended upward in such a way that it matches the trajectory of a bullet entering the chase-way. Can you see that all right?"

"Yes, I can."

"Now, sir, I have here a silhouette proportioned precisely to the measurements of Frank Dunn's body as you indicated in your autopsy report. You remember, I'm sure, Doctor, that Mr. Dunn was a very large man weighing about two hundred twenty-five pounds, and I wonder if you would step down from the witness box and place his silhouette on the drawing in the position you believe Frank Dunn was in at the time the bullets entered his body."

Dr. Sinclair carefully examined the silhouette, which was solid black and designed to allow the arms and legs to be moved into different positions.

"First of all, Mr. Alexander, I can tell you that Mr. Dunn's right arm was raised at the time he was shot."

Luke was delighted. He'd thought he would have to prove that fact by his own expert witness. Coming from the prosecution's witness on cross-examination, the information became much more effective.

"How could you tell that, Doctor?" Luke asked innocently.

"We determined that fact by closely examining the relationship between the bullet hole in the surface of the skin covering the decedent's left rib cage, and its path through the subcutaneous tissue and the musculature of Mr. Dunn's body. When your arms are at your side, the relationship between the skin and the soft tissue beneath it is different from when your arms are in a raised position." Dr. Sinclair demonstrated by raising and lowering his arms. "In order to line up the trajectory of the bullets with the position of the figure in the drawing as you've indicated, it's my opinion that immediately prior to the pistol being fired, Mr. Dunn would have been in a position something like this."

Luke grinned inwardly when Dr. Sinclair placed the black silhouette of Frank Dunn with his right arm raised menacingly in a position hovering over the white cutout of Helen's body.

"I offer defendant's Exhibit 1 marked for identification in evidence, Your Honor."

"Any objections, Counselor?" Judge Hamilton said, turning to the prosecutor.

Luke had caught the prosecutor off guard. Her own witness had now placed Frank Dunn's six-foot, two-hundred-twenty-pound body in such a way on the diagram that it appeared as if Frank was leaping upon the one-hundred-twenty-pound body of Helen Dunn. The prosecutor started to object and quickly realized that her objection would undoubtedly be overruled, which would give even greater weight to the exhibit. She replied casually, "No objection."

"Defendant's Exhibit 1 received in evidence," Judge Hamilton said. "Anything further, Mr. Alexander?"

"Nothing more at this time, Your Honor."

When Pat Turner was called to testify on behalf of the prosecution, she remained totally professional, impassive and unemotional, and stared straight ahead during her testimony. Upon completion of her direct examination, the prosecutor introduced the audiocassette in which Helen had admitted killing her husband.

Dance of the Mantis   **241**

Before Luke agreed to take the case, he'd told Helen Dunn he had grave misgivings about doing so for a number of reasons, one of which was that he knew the district attorney would have to call Pat Turner as a witness for the prosecution and that Luke would be required to cross-examine her. He had no difficulty assuring Helen that he would use every skill at his disposal to discredit any testimony that was harmful to Helen, but knowing Pat as he did, he was certain she would give as much as she got. He was also deeply concerned about the perception of impropriety arising from the fact that he'd assisted Barney Rifkin in defending Margaux McBride between the time she was indicted up to the time the charges against her were dropped, when Helen acknowledged that she had killed her husband.

At the time, Helen had easily dispelled any concerns he had on either count, but now he was no longer dealing with the hypothetical. Now he was facing the reality of cross-examining the woman he loved, who had just given testimony that could send his client to jail for twenty-five years to life. She was the prosecution's key witness, because without Helen's admission, the district attorney had only circumstantial evidence to tie Helen to the crime. If Helen Dunn had exercised her Fifth Amendment right to remain silent, there wouldn't have been a shred of hard evidence implicating her in the murder of her husband.

Luke stood up slowly, checked his notes one final time, and walked over to the witness box.

"Sergeant Turner, I'm Lucas Alexander. I represent Mrs. Dunn in this matter, and I have a few questions for you."

"I know who you are, Mr. Alexander," Pat said solemnly.

"Sergeant, when you were answering the prosecutor's questions, I noticed that you made reference from time to time to a notebook. May I see that please?"

Pat looked over at the prosecutor who nodded affirmatively, indicating that Luke had the right to examine her notes. She handed the book to him. Luke leafed through it, searching for the information he was certain he'd find. In turning its pages, he was startled to see, in the corner of one of the pages, a little drawing of a heart with the initials "PT" and "LA" entwined inside. When he looked at Pat, she avoided his gaze.

"Now," he said, "calling your attention to page thirty-seven of your notebook here, it appears that you visited with Mr. and Mrs. Ransom, the parents of Helen Dunn, who live in Greenville, near

Dallas. Is that right?" Luke handed the notebook back to her. Pat glanced at the page that he'd indicated, noticed her heart-shaped doodle, and turned crimson.

"Yes."

"Can you tell me when you visited Helen's parents, please?"

Pat glanced at the notebook and said, "November 23, 2003."

"Now please, Sergeant, can you show me in your notebook what notes you made concerning your conversations with her parents?"

"Actually, all of these pages here are devoted to that interview," she said, indicating about a dozen pages in her book.

Luke once again glanced through the notebook and said, "Isn't it true, Sergeant, as your notebook indicates, that most of the discussion you had with Mr. and Mrs. Ransom concerned the physical abuse that Helen Dunn suffered at the hands of Frank Dunn, beginning on their honeymoon and continuing until the time of his death?"

"Yes, that's true."

"And was that abuse of such severity that it required Helen Dunn to be hospitalized on a number of occasions?"

"That's what they told me."

"Well, Sergeant, you verified those facts by checking the hospital records yourself, isn't that true?"

"Yes, that's true."

"And as it says on page forty-two of your notebook, if I can read your handwriting here," Luke lifted the book up close to his eyes and squinted, "'On one occasion, her husband struck her with such force as to detach the retina in her eye, and her vision has been severely impaired ever since.'"

"Yes, that was confirmed."

"And when you returned from Texas and interviewed Helen Dunn, at her invitation, you learned, did you not, that in addition to the instances which her parents had described to you, there were a multitude of other occasions when she was physically abused, escalating in severity as the years passed. Isn't that true?"

"It's true that that's what she told me, yes."

"Do you have any reason to believe she wasn't telling you the truth?"

"No, not at all."

"Now, Sergeant, prior to the time you were assigned to the homicide division, did you ever have occasion to investigate crimes committed against women by their spouses?"

"I spent two years working almost exclusively with battered women, if that's what you mean."

"Yes, that's exactly what I mean, and I guess that you and the prosecutor here, Ms. Livingston, probably worked on a number of those cases together, did you not?"

"That's true."

"All right now, Sergeant, tell me, have you ever heard the phrase 'learned helplessness'?"

"I know what it means, counselor."

"Would you be kind enough to share your understanding of its meaning with us, Sergeant?"

"It's one of the elements of Battered Woman Syndrome."

"So you know about Battered Woman Syndrome?"

"Yes, I do. I'm not an expert, but I'm familiar with it."

"And you saw it firsthand when you dealt with scores of women who'd been abused for years and years, isn't that true?"

"Yes."

"And you saw patterns of similarity in most of those battered women cases, didn't you?"

"I did."

"Then tell me, Sergeant, prior to the time you arrested Mrs. Dunn, charging her with murdering her husband, did you take into consideration that she had been the victim of his physical, mental, and sexual abuse for many, many years?"

Pat looked Luke straight in the eye and replied, "Mr. Alexander, I'm an investigator. The defendant admitted to me that she had fired five bullets into her husband's head and body causing his death. It's my job to present the facts to the district attorney's office. I didn't write the law. It was not my decision whether this case should be taken to the grand jury. It was the grand jury that handed down the indictment charging Mrs. Dunn with murder, and it will be this jury, and not me, who will decide if she is innocent or guilty."

Lucas admired the cogency of her response, but as Helen's attorney, he was disturbed that it brought to the jury's attention that there were a number of people beside the prosecutor who had considered the evidence and decided that Helen should be charged with murder. He felt compelled to pursue the matter, though he knew he was moving into a dangerous area of inquiry.

"But if you personally were given the opportunity to make any one of those decisions, Mrs. Dunn wouldn't be in this courtroom right now, would she?"

The prosecutor was on her feet in a flash, "Objection."

Judge Hamilton's immediate response was, "Sustained."

Luke quickly changed the direction of his questioning.

"It's true, is it not, Sergeant Turner, that Mrs. Dunn made an appointment with you and told you what happened on the night Frank Dunn died before you or anyone else advised her that she was under investigation?"

"That's true."

"Were you in the courtroom when the prosecutor made her opening remarks to the jury in this case?"

"No, I wasn't."

"Would it surprise you to learn that in her opening address the prosecutor told this jury that…" Luke stepped over to the counsel table and picked up a sheet of paper, then turned back to Pat. "Let me read to you exactly what the prosecutor said at that time." Luke proceeded to recite solemnly from the typewritten transcript: "'We will also prove that the defendant did not come forward and acknowledge that it was she and not Ms. McBride who had put an end to her husband's life until after Detective Patricia Turner confronted her with conclusive proof that she had killed her husband.'" Luke paused to allow the jury to fully understand the direction of his question and then continued, "Now that's not true, is it, Sergeant?"

Pat glanced over at the prosecutor who avoided her gaze. She hesitated, looked back at Luke, lowered her eyes, and said softly, "No, that's not true."

"No further questions, thank you, Sergeant." Luke turned and walked back to the counsel table, thankful that the ordeal was over. He wasn't sure whether he'd won or lost in the exchange, but his respect as well as his affection for Pat Turner was certainly not diminished.

CHAPTER FORTY-EIGHT

The prosecutor had Helen's statement marked as an exhibit. She turned to the judge and said, "I offer the defendant's confession into evidence."

Luke was on his feet immediately. "Objection, Your Honor."

"On what grounds, Mr. Alexander?"

"Mrs. Dunn's statement is not a confession of anything. It is a recitation of facts. She has never confessed to committing the crime charged against her."

"Your point is well taken, Counselor." The judge turned to the jury. "The defendant's statement is received in evidence, but it shall not be characterized as a confession."

"With the court's permission, I wish to play the tape to the jury at this time," the prosecutor said.

"You have that right, Counselor. Proceed."

"Ladies and gentlemen of the jury, People's Exhibit 27 is a tape recording of a statement given by the defendant to Sergeant Turner on August 19, 2003, in which she acknowledges firing five .38 caliber bullets into the head and body of her husband, causing his death." The prosecutor turned on the machine, and Helen's voice filled the silent chamber. It was the first time the jury had had an opportunity to relate directly with Helen, and they each leaned forward to listen carefully to her words. The tape concluded with the words, "Just as I raised the gun, Frank opened the bedroom door, and when he saw me he screamed at me. Then he raised his fist and lurched at me. I must have blacked out because the next thing I remember is that the gun was still in my hand and Frank was on the floor beside the bed. I watched blood bubble out of a wound in the left side of his neck. I saw a bullet hole just above his left eye and more blood oozing from there. His eyes were open…staring . . . I knelt down beside him and put my ear against his bare chest. There was no heartbeat. There was no pulse. He was dead."

The prosecutor turned off the tape player. The words, *he was dead* echoed in the ominously silent courtroom."

"The People rest."

As Helen listened intently to the recording, all of her energies focused on the recording, a startling memory flashed through her mind. *As I raised the gun.* Her words on the tape suddenly came back to her with force, and just as clearly, Frank's last words came screaming into her consciousness: *No, you stupid bitch!*

Frank had opened the bedroom door. She'd screamed. He'd yelled at her, " No, you stupid bitch!"

Helen could hardly breathe as she now remembered exactly what had happened just before she pulled the trigger. *I hesitated…trying to decide whether to point it at my temple or my heart.* Oh my God. Had Frank been trying to stop her from blowing out *his* brains – or *hers*?

Had he tried to save his life, or hers?

———

Luke's first witnesses were Helen's parents, who testified about the abuse they'd observed. But on cross-examination the ADA elicited from them that they hadn't actually observed Frank physically abusing Helen. They only saw the bruises afterward and Helen told them that Frank had caused the injuries. The ADA asked that the testimony be stricken from the record. The judge agreed it was hearsay and advised the jury to disregard it, but, studying their faces, Luke sensed the jury didn't pay much attention to the hearsay rule because they were satisfied that Helen and her parents were telling the truth.

During their testimony, several jurors glanced furtively over at Helen. She sat staring trancelike into space. Her clothing hung loosely on her body, giving testament to the physical price the trial was demanding of her.

But behind her ashen mask, a battle was raging in Helen's mind. A lifetime of integrity was at war with her primeval struggle to survive. Conflicting words and phrases kept racing through her mind.

Was she guilty of murder? Who would care for Jennifer if she went to jail? Were her parents too old to raise her? Would Kate be willing to take Jennifer in? Had Frank really been trying to save her life? How could she be certain? Nobody but she knew what had really happened. Did she have to tell Mr. Alexander? How old would she be when she got out of jail? Would they put her in jail for life? Oh God, oh God.

———

After introducing medical and hospital records confirming the dates and seriousness of the injuries Frank had inflicted upon Helen, Lucas put Helen's friend Kate Connors on the stand. She testified with respect to Helen's humiliation in trying to explain away her facial and body bruises.

Next Luke called Dr. Eloise Kirkpatrick, a forensic psycholo-gist known throughout the country as an expert on the subject of Battered Woman Syndrome, its history, applicability, and consequences. Dr. Kirkpatrick had examined Helen extensively over a period of three days at her office and laboratory in Boston.

"Dr. Kirkpatrick, would you tell the jury what your professional specialty is?"

"I have spent most of my career studying violence against women and children, specifically the area of battered women and sexually abused women and children."

"Have you written books on the subject?"

"In 1978 I wrote a book entitled *Women and Violence* and in 1991 I wrote *Who's Guilty?* and three years ago my latest book, *Male/Female, a Tragedy*, was recently published."

"Based on your research, did you determine that there are seven predominant factors with respect to women who have been abused?"

"Yes. First we find that there is almost always a cycle of violence that escalates over time. That is to say, the violence becomes more frequent and more serious.

"The second factor to be considered in a case of this kind is 'marital rape.' Sometimes the sex becomes very rough, especially if the husband is having difficulty maintaining an erection or achieving orgasm. The wife is abused by being forced to participate in sex over an extended period of time by a man who doesn't know or care if his wife is being hurt."

"Did all the victims with whom you spoke in your clinic recognize that what was happening to them was a rape?" Luke asked.

"Some women did, most did not. Even today, most women do not."

"Why is that?"

"Most married women believe that marriage constitutes automatic consent for sex. The wife is supposed to pleasure her husband sexually on demand. Also, if a woman has some sexual desires and wants the man sexually, but he later gets rough or it turns unpleasant and she wants to stop it, she doesn't think she has the right to say no at any point.

"The third element is what we call the power and control variable, the need for the man to be in control of the woman's time. He considers her his property. What's his is his and what's hers is his. He believes he has the absolute right to intrude on her life whenever and however he wishes.

"Next is the jealously factor. In psychological terms, we call it a reaction formation. The man blames the woman for his own extramarital affairs, and this was particularly compelling in Mrs. Dunn's case.

"The fifth variable is the repeated threat to kill. This increases over time in most battering relationships.

"The sixth factor is what we call psychological torture. Waking the woman in the middle of the night, not letting her go to sleep, long, loud harangues, continually correcting her when he believes she has done something wrong or not to his liking. This is generally carried out in a one-sided conversation in which he does all the talking.

"And finally, there's the problem of alcohol and drug abuse, which has played such a significant part in the case to be decided here."

"Doctor, at my request, did you undertake an examination and evaluation of Helen Dunn?"

"Yes, I did."

"What did you do?"

"After the clinical interview, I asked Mrs. Dunn to complete a Battered Woman Syndrome questionnaire which I created many years ago. It contains the same questions I've asked over six hundred women who have also killed in self-defense. I then compared the results of Mrs. Dunn's tests with the standardized norms."

"And do you have an opinion, based upon a reasonable degree of psychological certainty, as to whether or not Helen Dunn was suffering from Battered Woman's Syndrome at the time of her husband's death?"

"Yes, Mr. Alexander, in my opinion, the evidence is clear and unequivocal. Helen Dunn was compelled to act as she did as a consequence of years of physical, mental, and sexual abuse. She was terrified that she was about to be seriously injured or killed. Within the space of microseconds, her desire to survive overcame her wish to die by her own hand. She was obeying the most primitive instinct in humans, the will to live."

Luke spoke barely above a whisper. "No further questions." Then he returned to the counsel table with Dr. Kirkpatrick's final words, *the will to live*, reverberating in the somber chamber.

Judge Hamilton nodded toward the assistant district attorney, "Do you wish to cross-examine?"

"Yes, Your Honor, I have a few questions."

The prosecutor gathered up the extensive notes she'd taken throughout Dr. Kirkpatrick's testimony and slowly approached the witness. Some of the jurors leaned forward imperceptibly in anticipation of the confrontation between the key witness for the defense and the assistant district attorney. It was clear in everyone's mind that unless Dr. Kirkpatrick's testimony could be shaken, she had carried the day for the defendant. Given the power of Dr. Kirkpatrick's opinion, a jury would have great difficulty in convicting Helen Dunn of murder.

"Dr. Kirkpatrick, I take it this is not the first case in which you've testified as an expert."

"That's true."

"Could you tell us how many times you've testified on behalf of a female defendant charged with assault or homicide?"

"Many, unfortunately," Dr. Kirkpatrick said.

"How many?" Ms. Livingston pressed.

"I can't give you a precise number, Counselor. Perhaps two hundred or more over a ten-year period."

"Is it fair to say that most of your testimony has been given during the past five years?"

"I'd say that's probably true," Dr. Kirkpatrick answered warily.

"In fact, during the past two years, you've testified in over sixty cases, haven't you?"

"I haven't actually counted the number of times, but that sounds about right."

"In fact, you've spent more days in court than you have in your office, isn't that true?"

Dr. Kirkpatrick leaned forward in the witness chair and replied slowly and precisely. "It is true that I have been willing to help innocent women throughout the country whenever they have needed me."

Bravo! Luke said to himself.

"I move the witness's answer be stricken from the record as not responsive, Your Honor."

"Yes, please disregard the witness's answer, ladies and gentlemen," Judge Hamilton said.

"And you charge a fee every time you testify, don't you, Doctor?"

"Yes, I charge a fee. I don't always collect it, but I charge it."

"I assume you know that the defendant is the beneficiary of a one million dollar life insurance policy, so you don't have any concern about being paid in this case, unless, of course, she's convicted, in which event she'll receive no insurance money. And incidentally, Doctor, what is your fee for testifying in this case?"

"I wouldn't call it a fee for testifying, Counselor. I'm a professional. I charge a fee for performing professional services. Included in those services is testifying with regard to my opinion when that is called for."

"How much, Doctor?"

"Twenty-five thousand dollars plus expenses."

Most of the jurors sucked in their breath.

"You travel first class, of course, Doctor."

"I work while I'm flying."

"Otherwise you wouldn't have time to testify almost once a week for the past two years, isn't that right, Doctor?"

Dr. Kirkpatrick did not bother to reply. Luke was feeling uncomfortable. Ms. Livingston returned to the counsel table, shuffled through her notes, and resumed her attack.

"Now, tell us please, Doctor, did you discuss with Mrs. Dunn the events which immediately followed the moment she shot and killed her husband?"

"I'm not sure I understand your question."

"I want to know whether or not Mrs. Dunn told you that after firing five bullets into her husband's body, she gathered up her bloody nightclothes, packed them away and later destroyed them, wrapped the bullet casings in toilet tissue and flushed them down the toilet, and then ransacked the dresser and the desk to make it appear as if the apartment had been burglarized and that someone else had killed her husband?"

"Yes, Mrs. Dunn told me that. It was not surprising. In fact, in many cases involving battered women, there is an attempt to cover up their actions. They're convinced that no one will understand what prompted them to act as they did. They try to avoid the reality of the situation and sometimes even convince themselves that someone else has actually committed the act. I would say it is typical. Normal."

"It's normal to try and deceive the police?"

"You don't understand, Ms. Livingston. These women don't perceive the situation in those terms. Most of the time, they're not even able to acknowledge to themselves what they've done. Since their actions are totally out of character, they can't believe they've committed a violent act. They try to erase it from their minds by creating a different scenario, an explanation for the act which excludes them as a perpetrator."

"You mean they try to avoid the consequences of their actions by making it look as if someone else did the killing."

"I would say that is natural."

"Is it natural to allow an innocent person to be arrested and put in jail for a crime the defendant committed?"

"Well, I don't mean that, what I mean is — "

"Was it natural for the defendant to leave her husband bleeding to death, after pumping five .38 caliber bullets into his head, and make no attempt to obtain medical assistance to save his life, then gather up the brass bullet casings, pack up her bloody nightgown, and fly off to Dallas on a pleasure trip? Do you claim that's natural?"

"Objection, Your Honor, this isn't cross-examination. The prosecutor is giving her summation, she's —" Luke sputtered.

"I have the right to ask this witness — " the ADA said, her eyes blazing.

Judge Hamilton slammed down her gavel, "That's enough, counselors."

Helen began to sob uncontrollably. "I can't go on with this! Mr. Alexander, please, please!"

Judge Hamilton, perceiving the situation, said, "Let's take a short break here. We'll recess for fifteen minutes. Court's adjourned."

Luke had not been prepared for the power of Ms. Livingston's cross-examination and its emotional impact on the jury. He escorted Dr. Kirkpatrick to a secluded corner of the courtroom.

"She's very good, Mr. Alexander. As you know, I'm not a novice in this business, but I'd say she's one of the best," Dr. Kirkpatrick said admiringly.

"True, but this case is a long way from over. If Livingston is smart, she'll terminate her cross-examination right now. We just have to make certain that you have a chance to explain that Helen's subsequent actions had no bearing on her state of mind when she pulled the trigger."

"Have faith, Mr. Alexander," Dr. Kirkpatrick said, putting her hand gently on his arm.

Luke went back to see how Helen was doing. She looked up tearfully when he entered the attorney's room. "I'm so sorry, Mr. Alexander, I just couldn't help it. Everything that young woman was saying is true. I should have called an ambulance, I should have called the police, I should have stayed with Frank even though I knew he was dead."

Luke reached out and took her hand. "Look, Helen, we've come a long way together. You did what you did, nothing has changed."

"I don't know how I can go back in there."

"It's almost over. Just a few more hours."

There was a knock on the door from the bailiff. "The judge is ready to reconvene," he announced.

"You may continue with your cross-examination, Ms. Livingston," Judge Hamilton said.

"No further questions," the ADA replied.

The judge turned to Luke. "How many more witnesses do you have, Mr. Alexander?"

"Just Mrs. Dunn, Your Honor."

"Then this seems like a good time to adjourn until tomorrow morning," Judge Hamilton said.

The courtroom emptied quickly, leaving only Helen and Luke, who was gathering up his papers and stuffing them into his briefcase.

"There's something I have to talk to you about," Helen said.

Luke glanced at his watch. "Sure, but I'm going to see you

in my office in a bit to go over your testimony. It's not by accident that I've arranged our witnesses in such a way that you'll be on the stand first thing in the morning, while the jurors' minds are fresh and they've had a chance to think about what Dr. Kirkpatrick has told them this afternoon."

"But that's what I want to talk about."

Luke loosened his tie and slumped down in his chair. He was emotionally drained and was looking forward to a little time alone in his den with a drink in hand before beginning the task of preparing Helen for the rigors of Sandy Livingston's cross-examination. "Okay, you have my undivided attention, Helen."

She hesitated and then said, "I've decided not to testify."

"You've decided what?"

"I'm not going to testify. I've thought it through very carefully, and I am aware of the consequences, but I'm not going to do it."

Luke looked at her sharply, distastefully. "What brought this about, for God's sake, Helen? If the jury doesn't hear you say in your own words that you never intended to kill your husband, your chances of getting an acquittal are damned slim."

He was trying not to let his anger and frustration show, but it had been a long day, he was exhausted, and he didn't want to have to deal with the problem Helen was presenting to him. The law was clear that the defendant in a criminal case had the absolute right to decide whether or not to testify. It was also clear that jurors didn't like the idea of defendants exercising their Fifth Amendment right not to testify.

"It's crazy, Helen. This jury wants to hear you tell them loud and clear that you're innocent. I can feel they're with us, but if you don't testify, they're going to think you have something to hide."

Helen looked directly at Luke. "Maybe I do."

"What the devil do you mean? "

"It's something that was blocked out of my mind until I heard the tape of the statement I gave to Pat Turner... I... I —"

"Wait a minute, Helen." Luke immediately understood what was happening. It was not the first time a client had suddenly remembered a critical fact in the middle of a trial. Ethically, he was on very dangerous ground. Things had to be handled with great care.

"Let's not discuss it now. We'll talk about it this evening. It's been a long day for both of us. I'll see you in my office at 7:30 this evening."

"I may have lost my courage by that time. I — "

"That's the whole idea. Maybe it's something you need to think through very carefully."

"But it's all I've been thinking about for the past two days, I —"

Before she could finish her sentence, Luke took her arm and escorted her out of the courthouse. After they'd plowed through the reporters, he put her in a cab and said, "I'll see you later at my office."

———

Luke was in turmoil as he waited for Helen to arrive back at his office. In order to properly advise her, it was imperative that he know the whole truth. But the fear consuming him was that although she might be concerned about some inconsequential fact that was meaningless to her defense, it could just as easily be something that would guarantee her conviction. How could he continue to proclaim her innocence to the jury in his summation if he learned for a certainty she was guilty?

The word *certainty* jolted loose the memory of a conversation he'd once had with his neighbor, Emily Martin, early in his career. He'd been at a cocktail party, where he'd been telling her the story of his first criminal case.

"My poor client was sentenced to a year in jail because of my inexperience," he said.

"Did you think he was innocent?" Emily asked.

"It doesn't matter what I thought. It was my responsibility to defend him, not to judge him."

"That's such a cop-out, Luke! Could you defend a man you thought was guilty of killing someone — like his wife, for example?"

"That's not a simple question," he said. "It's a matter of how he killed her and what he was thinking at the very moment before he killed her."

"Stop dancing around and answer my question! No wonder they call you lawyers slippery. Just tell me, if your client actually told you he'd intentionally killed his wife and he was glad he did it, what would you do?"

"Well," Luke answered, "up until 1974, in a first-degree murder case, a plea of not guilty would have been automatically entered by the court. But the law never stands still, and since that time…"

Emily didn't let him finish his sentence. "I'm not asking for a lecture on the history of the law. Can't you ever give a direct answer, Luke?"

"I'm trying, but it's not easy," he'd said. "First it must be determined whether he acted under the influence of extreme emotional disturbance for which there was a reasonable explanation or excuse, the reasonableness of which — "

"Oh, forget it, Luke. I'm going to get another drink."

Now, sitting alone in his empty office, he asked himself the same question his friend Emily had put to him. If Helen told him she'd intended to kill her husband, then what would he do? If he made a mistake, Helen could be sentenced from twenty-five years to life in state prison.

CHAPTER FORTY-NINE

Luke was keenly aware of the media and the spectators packed into the courtroom. When Helen took the stand it would be everyone's first opportunity to evaluate her. He knew that the demeanor of the accused on the stand was always a critical factor. The manner in which the defendant testified could be as important as what he had to say. Everyone knew it shouldn't be that way because such impressions could impact heavily against defendants whose ethnic and social backgrounds were alien to the jurors who judged them. But in this case, Luke was certain that Helen would make a favorable impression. They would want to believe her because she was one of them.

She wore a gray wool skirt and dark blue jacket. She sat erect at the counsel table. Her face was pale. She appeared distraught. Luke was speaking quietly to her when the court crier announced the opening of the court and the judge took the bench.

"Bring the jury in," she said. When the jurors were settled, she addressed Luke. "All right, Mr. Alexander, you may proceed."

Luke leaned close to Helen. "You're sure?" he whispered. She nodded. He rose slowly, almost painfully, "The defense rests, Your Honor."

Judge Hamilton was startled. She looked over at Sandy Livingston. "Do you have any rebuttal testimony, Ms. Livingston?"

"Well, I didn't expect. No, Your Honor, the People rest also."

"Are you prepared to sum up, Mr. Alexander?" Judge Hamilton asked.

"I am, Your Honor."

"Very well. Ladies and gentlemen, we will now hear from Mr. Alexander on behalf of the defendant. Remember, what the attorneys say during their summations is not evidence. But you must listen to their words with care because they'll be summarizing the evidence as they believe it to be, and their comments may be helpful to you in your analysis of the testimony that has been presented during the course of the trial. Mr. Alexander, you may proceed."

"Thank you, Your Honor." Luke gathered up his notes, placed them carefully on the podium and looked solemnly at the jury.

"Members of the jury," he began, "my responsibilities in this case are almost over, but your sacred duty is about to begin. Never before, and in all probability never again during your lives will you bear the burden of deciding whether someone shall live or die. The prosecutor may tell you that she doesn't seek the death penalty in this case, but the reality is that if you find Helen Dunn guilty of murder, her life will be over. Of course, this case must be decided on the evidence, and I'm confident you will do that. So let me share with you my thoughts about what the prosecution has charged, and what she has proven.

"The single most important word in the indictment against Helen Dunn is intent. Helen has been accused of intentionally taking the life of her husband, the father of her child. The assistant district attorney will ask you to find as a fact beyond reasonable doubt that Helen Dunn consciously, and with malice aforethought, sent five bullets into the body of the man she continued to love, despite the physical and emotional abuse she'd suffered at his hands from the day of their marriage."

Helen closed her eyes as Luke walked the jury through the evidence, piece by piece. Instead of using the simple tape recorder which the prosecutor had used to play the recording of Frank Dunn's last telephone conversation with Margaux, Luke had set up a sophisticated sound system, so sensitive that the courtroom could actually hear the sound of Frank's and Margaux's breathing.

"Now, ladies and gentlemen," he said, "I'm going to ask you to close your eyes and listen to this recording as if you were overhearing the conversation between Frank Dunn and his lover Margaux McBride, just as Helen Dunn heard it on that terrible night." All of the jurors, except one of the males, closed their eyes obediently as Luke pushed the play button. Frank and Margaux's voices filled the courtroom. Luke smiled as he noticed that Judge Hamilton had bowed her head and closed her eyes.

"Hello."

"Darling —"

"Where are you?"

" I'm sorry, honey, I —"

"Where the hell have you been?"

"I got tied up in traffic, but I'll be over by 9:30 at the latest, I promise."

"I'll leave the door unlocked for you."

"Yes, love."

———

When the conversation ended, the sounds of the three telephone disconnects were like thunderclaps in the hushed courtroom. Luke turned off the machine and picked up Helen's statement. He began to read it aloud to the jury:

"When they finished their conversation, I could scarcely breathe. I was unwilling to live and face the aftermath of this obscenity. I hung up the phone, opened the drawer of the nightstand, and took out the pistol Frank had bought a few months earlier because there'd been several burglaries in our apartment house. I lost all sense of reality. It felt like I was watching a film in slow motion. I turned the pistol over in my hand, one way and then the other. I hesitated…trying to decide whether to point it at my temple or my heart. As I raised the gun, Frank opened the door. I screamed. He yelled at me. Then he raised his fist and lurched at me."

Luke walked slowly back to the counsel table and carefully placed the transcript of Helen's statement there as if it were a sacred testament. He returned to face the jurors. Helen felt a chill surge through her body as Luke picked up the silhouette drawing of Frank hurtling himself at her, arm raised above his head, prepared to strike her full force. He placed the exhibit on an easel directly in front of the jury box and stood silently beside it. Every juror strained forward to examine the exquisitely created image. Frank's large black silhouette was in stark contrast to the frailty of Helen's slim, pale body. It was a compelling indictment of Frank Dunn, the wife beater; a two-hundred-twenty-pound man with his fist upraised to punish his wife for spoiling a tryst with his lover.

The silence in the courtroom was suffocating. The jurors waited patiently for Luke to resume his summation.

"From the time of recorded history, women have been considered chattel. They were possessions that could be bartered or purchased. Let me read to you the Tenth Commandment that concerns itself with property rights." Luke stepped over to the counsel table and picked up a well-worn copy of the Bible. He handled it reverently in such a way that every juror would understand that it was *his* well-worn Bible. He put on his glasses carefully and opened to a place marked with a red ribbon. Then he looked up at the jurors as he recited the commandment by heart.

"Thou shalt not covet thy neighbor's house. Thou shalt not covet thy neighbor's wife, nor his ox nor his ass nor any thing that is thy neighbor's."

Luke closed the Bible gently but continued to hold it in his hand. "In many parts of the world, the insidious literal translation of the tenth commandment and its counterpart in the Koran, in which women are treated as chattel, continues to be sanctioned by law. But here in the United States we have come to our senses and decreed that a man has no right to thrash his wife as he does his oxen. A man has no right in this country to impose his will upon a woman by the use of brute force. Many women are trapped into accepting their husbands' physical and sexual abuse because of their need to hold a family together, by their inability to care for their children adequately without support from the fathers of their children, so they suffer abuse year after year after year, and then sometimes, as Dr. Kirkpatrick has explained to us, the mental burden becomes too great and the woman breaks emotionally. The years of anger, frustration, and resentment finally explode into a single uncontrolled act of retribution."

Luke hesitated and returned to the counsel table, gently laying down his Bible and picking up a textbook. "Ladies and gentlemen of the jury," he said as he leafed through the book, "you may remember I asked Sergeant Turner if she was aware of the phrase 'learned helplessness,' and she indicated that it had something to do with Battered Woman Syndrome. It's not a phrase that's used in common parlance, certainly, but it is a very important element in understanding the meaning of Battered Woman Syndrome."

He found what he was looking for and continued. "It's a fascinating aspect of what sometimes motivates wives to act in a way that is totally uncharacteristic of their normal demeanor. There's a psychologist by the name of Seligman who conducted an experiment with dogs. He constructed a double cage with a doorway between. Sometimes the door between the cages was open and sometimes it was closed. He would then shock the dog with an electric prod intermittently with no discernible regularity.

260   *Wally Wiggins*

In the beginning of the experiment, the dog would race away into the other cage if the door were open, but Seligman would pursue him there and prod him further with the electric prod. After a while, even though the connecting door to the adjoining cage was open, the dog would remain cowering in the corner of his cage. The experiment stands for what has come to be known as learned helplessness. The animals learned that there was no exit. They would ultimately accept the fact that they were in a helpless situation from which they could not extricate themselves, except by eliminating the cause of the pain. It's the same with women who have been abused over a period of years. The abuse is arbitrary, undeserved, and unpredictable. The woman who pulled the trigger killing Frank Dunn was not his wife Helen. The force that pulled that trigger was created by years of physical, sexual, and emotional abuse that took absolute and total control of Helen's mind and body when Frank Dunn lunged at her like a battering ram.

"The tragedy of it, ladies and gentlemen," he said, barely above a whisper, "the terrible tragedy of it all. And now the prosecutor wants to compound this…this abomination," he spit out the word, "by putting the victim in jail for a minimum of —"

"Objection!" the ADA practically screamed. "Counsel has no right to —"

"Sustained!"

"But, Your Honor, we're talking mandatory —"

"That's enough, Mr. Alexander!" Judge Hamilton hissed, slamming her gavel on the bench. "The jury will be excused for a short recess. I'll see the attorneys in chambers."

Judge Hamilton sat stonefaced behind her desk in her private office. When the attorneys were seated, she stared straight at Luke. "You'd better have a good excuse, Mr. Alexander. Whatever possessed you to blatantly violate the rules of this court? You have absolutely no right to comment on sentencing to the jury. That is my province, mine and mine alone, and you damn well know it. You aren't a novice at this business."

Luke stared back at the judge and then spoke very softly. "The rule is archaic. The jury has the right to know that if they find Helen Dunn guilty of murder in the second degree, Your Honor has no discretion as to sentencing. She will get long-term jail time."

Judge Hamilton started to reply, and then hesitated. She shared Luke's view that, indeed, mandatory sentencing was a stupid law. If the jury found Helen Dunn guilty, the court would be required to sentence her to a minimum of fifteen years to life in prison, regardless of the circumstances of the case or the character of the defendant. Her only discretion would be whether the minimum confinement should be fifteen or twenty-five years.

"I'm going to let you off the hook this one time, Mr. Alexander. But I give you fair warning here and now that if you ever try that stunt again in my courtroom, you'll be spending time in jail with your client, and I ain't kidding, mister. Do you understand me?" She didn't wait for an answer. "Now let's get on with it," she said forcefully.

When the jury returned, totally perplexed by what the fuss was all about, Luke continued his summation. But the fevered pitch had passed. It was a time for gentleness; a time for reflection.

"Ladies and gentlemen, the prosecution asks you to find, beyond a reasonable doubt, that within a few horrifying seconds, as she prepared to take her own life, Helen devised a plan to kill her husband. But the evidence clearly demonstrates that Frank Dunn was the aggressor, and Helen was and still is the victim in this case.

"I suggest that never again in your lives will you hold the destiny of a total stranger in your hands. In a few months, this experience will begin to fade from your memory, but Helen Dunn and her young daughter must live with your decision for the rest of their lives. I beseech you to look into your hearts and say, 'Enough!' Justice demands that this tragedy come to an end. Your verdict of not guilty will allow Helen Dunn's broken mind and abused body to heal so that she can struggle to build a future for herself and her thirteen-year-old child.

"I have nothing more," Luke said. He turned away and walked slowly back to the counsel table.

CHAPTER FIFTY

The prosecutor reminded the jury that they had promised to decide the case on the facts and not upon sympathy. "And the facts are that Helen Dunn fired five bullets into the head and body of her husband," she said. She reminded them that all they had was the defendant's word that Frank Dunn had lunged at her in a threatening manner. "And even if he had, can it possibly justify taking his life?" she demanded. "Do we really know what happened in those few moments before the defendant shot and killed her husband in cold blood? We aren't concerned here with wild dogs in a cage, we're talking about a man who had as much right to life as the defendant did. I would not, for a single moment, attempt to justify Frank Dunn's physical abuse of the defendant, I have spent most of my professional career putting such men in jail, but we don't execute them!"

Luke began to squirm. This young prosecutor was good. She was hitting him over and over in the one spot where he was vulnerable. He wanted to stand up and object somehow, to stop the barrage of logical argument, but he couldn't. It was Sandy Livingstone's turn to convince the jury that this was not a frivolous charge.

"We aren't talking about self-defense, ladies and gentlemen of the jury. We're talking murder. We don't claim that the defendant plotted and planned to kill her husband. That's not the issue here. The defendant has admitted she pulled the trigger that sent five red hot bullets into the neck and the forehead and the eye and the jaw and the heart of her husband."

She held up the exhibit introduced by the coroner that graphically displayed the location of each bullet hole in Frank's head and body, and then she held up the enlarged photograph of Frank taken in the morgue, showing the flesh torn from the bones of his face.

"We claim and we have proved beyond a reasonable doubt that when the defendant pulled the trigger on this single-shot revolver – it's not automatic, mind you," the prosecutor reached over and held up the menacing weapon – "when she pulled the trigger of this weapon," she held the revolver and pointed it high above the jurors heads, "when she pulled this trigger, once… POW… twice… POW… and again… POW… and again… POW… and again and again… POW… POW… six times, she knew, ladies and gentlemen, she knew that every time she pulled that trigger she was firing a bullet into the face and the body and the heart of her husband and that doing so would kill him. And that, ladies and gentlemen of the jury, is murder. Helen Dunn is guilty of murder as charged!"

———

The summations were completed. The judge charged the jury as to the rules of law that applied to the case. "Although the jurors are the sole arbiters of the facts," she said, "in every criminal matter, whenever the defendant demands a jury trial, the jury must follow the rules of law given to them by the court. In the case against Helen Dunn, the question of intent is a critical one.

"The mere fact that the defendant fired a gun and thereby killed her husband does not alone suffice to establish her guilty of murder," she said. "The offense, as here charged, is an intent crime, and the law requires that it be proved beyond a reasonable doubt that the defendant acted intentionally. Before you can convict this defendant of murder, you must conclude, after considering all the evidence, that it was her conscious objective to cause her husband's death."

So far, so good, Luke assured himself.

The judge continued. "Intent is a mental operation, which can usually be proven by the facts and circumstances leading up to, surrounding, and following the events in question." Luke winced when he thought about Helen's failure to call an ambulance or the police, her actions in ransacking the living room to give the impression that a robbery had taken place, and her immediate flight to Dallas.

264   *Wally Wiggins*

"Contrary to what you may have heard in your favorite television program, premeditation is not a prerequisite in determining intent. Intent may be formed in a brief instant before the commission of the act. You may, but are not required to, presume that a person intends the natural consequences of his act." Luke tried desperately not to show his disappointment in Judge Hamilton's hard line, but then she added, "However, this permissible inference in no way whatsoever shifts the burden of proof beyond a reasonable doubt from the shoulders of the prosecution."

Luke felt his hopes rising and falling with every word the judge spoke.

"The defendant has raised several defenses in this case. These come under the heading of justification. And they include self-defense." Luke applauded inwardly. "However, the law permits the use of deadly force only when the actor, in this case the defendant Helen Dunn, reasonably believed that her husband was about to use deadly force against her.

"On the other hand," she went on, "even if the defendant here was mistaken in her belief as to her husband's intentions, the defense is valid if her belief was a reasonable one, given all of the circumstances."

Judge Hamilton paused, rearranged her notes, poured herself a glass of water, took a sip, and looked intently at the jury. "Now, we come to a unique and important aspect of this case. Counsel and the expert witness for the defense, Dr. Kirkpatrick, have referred to it as the Battered Woman Syndrome, and it has been accepted as a legitimate defense in the New York courts for ten years or more.

I kiss you, Judge, Luke thought.

"However, you must listen carefully to my instructions regarding it. The Battered Woman Syndrome is a multistage form of marital disease. In stage one, there is verbal and perhaps minor physical abuse. Stage two involves an escalation of physical abuse in degree and quantity. Stage three occurs when the physical abuse gets out of control.

"The crucial issue for you to decide is this: What was the defendant's state of mind at the time she acted to blunt her husband's aggression? If you find that, in fact, he was the aggressor and that the defendant subjectively believed she was in a life-threatening situation, you may, but you are not required to, accept that defense.

"I must also advise you that the fact that the defendant did not testify in her own behalf is not a factor from which any inference unfavorable to the defendant may be drawn. And finally, you must never consider or speculate concerning matters relating to the consequences of your verdict."

When Judge Hamilton completed her charge to the jury and retired to her chambers, her confidential clerk asked her, "What do you think, Judge?"

"I'm troubled by one question," the judge replied. "Why did the defendant fire *six* bullets?"

CHAPTER FIFTY-ONE

As soon as the jurors filed out of the courtroom, Helen tugged at Luke's jacket.

"You said that if I decided not to testify, I couldn't talk with you until after you'd delivered your summation. That was our bargain, right?" Luke looked at her tortured expression. The realization that within hours she could be put in jail for life was taking its toll.

"I know how difficult this is for you, Helen," he said. "I wish there were more I could do to help, but I'm afraid that now it's in the lap of the gods."

"I think it will help me a great deal if you let me share my memory with you."

"The trial's over. you need to put it all behind you."

"Mr. Alexander, when I first talked to Pat about what happened, and then when I told you the whole story, all I could remember was trying to decide how to kill myself a few moments before Frank lunged at me. I couldn't remember anything else. I had blocked the horror of the following few seconds out of my mind. But when I heard the tape of my statement, and then again when you read it to the jury during your summation, the scene came back to me as clearly as if it had happened just a few moments before." Helen hesitated, covering her face with her hands momentarily.

"I'd decided to point the gun at my temple and was about to pull the trigger when Frank lunged at me and struck my arm. I still had the gun in my hand. He hovered over me. I saw his bloodshot eyes filled with hate, sneering at me, and I smelled the stink of the whiskey. He shouted, 'No, you stupid bitch!' Then I must have pulled the trigger again and again until there were no more bullets left." Helen's shoulders sagged. She stared at the floor. "When I fired those shots, I must have wanted him dead."

She knew Luke was staring at her, but she could not look at him. She took a Kleenex from her pocket and wiped her red eyes.

CHAPTER FIFTY-TWO

The jury room was a windowless drab space containing a large wooden table scarred by scores of cigarette burns from the days when smoking was allowed there. Wooden captain's chairs, a blackboard, and a water cooler completed the furnishings.

The jurors entered the now-familiar room with a bit of apprehension. It was clear from the beginning that an early unanimous vote was unlikely. Although one might have expected the women to be on one side of the issue and the men on the other, such was not the case. Each juror brought to the jury room his own collection of experiences that touched on the issues in the trial. The tone of the deliberations was established in an early exchange between Jack Duquesne, an aggressive young male truck driver, who was prepared to immediately vote for conviction to avoid any possibility that he might miss the Monday night football game at Rosie's Bar, and an elderly preschool teacher.

"Look at it this way," Duquesne said, "if she was innocent, she would've took the stand and said so. It's clear as a bell. She hated her old man for messin' around with that McBride lady lawyer, and then, of course, there's the little matter of the million bucks in life insurance she's gonna collect if she walks outta here scot-free."

Jean O'Shaunessy, a Montessori schoolteacher, replied, "First of all, the judge told us she had the absolute right not to take the stand. There could be many reasons she didn't testify that have nothing to do with guilt or innocence. She looks half dead as it is, just sitting at that table. I can imagine how terrible it would be for her if she had to go through it all again on the stand. In any event, Mr. Duquesne, I think I should tell you that I'll sit here until hell freezes over before I vote guilty."

"And there's no way in hell you're going to convince me she didn't intend to kill the guy," Duquesne said.

Near the end of the first day of deliberations they took their first secret vote. The forewoman announced the count. "Two guilty, one not guilty, nine undecided."

At that moment the court attendant knocked on the door and announced that the judge wanted to talk with them. When they returned to the jury box, Judge Hamilton said, "Ladies and gentlemen, it would help us in planning for your comfort if you could give us some idea how your deliberations are proceeding. Ms. Wallace, I understand that you are the foreperson of the jury. How are you coming along?"

Sorrel Wallace stood up and said, "My own view is that we are not likely to reach a verdict tonight, Your Honor."

Judge Hamilton noticed that a number of jurors nodded their approval of Ms. Wallace's remarks. "Well then, I think we'll just go ahead and plan on your spending the night at the expense of the county."

Jack Duquesne groaned audibly as the judge continued to speak to the jury. "Arrangements will be made so that you can contact your families, but as I have cautioned you earlier, you must not discuss this case with anyone other than your fellow jurors."

At eleven o'clock on the following morning, the jurors voted again: four guilty, three not guilty, and five undecided. By 4:30 in the afternoon, it was seven guilty and five not guilty.

"Now we're getting somewhere," Duquesne exclaimed when the votes were tallied. "Let's button it up. If we're going to do this democratic, like it should be, it's majority rule, right?"

"Wrong!" Jean O'Shaunessy said. "If you think you're going to bully me into changing my vote, you've got another think coming."

"Okay, Mrs. Bleeding Heart," Duquesne jeered.

"You're right, Duquesne. And I recognize a bleeding rear end when I see one," O'Shaunessy quipped.

"Hey, no lousy Mick is going to call me a — "

Sorrel Wallace stood up and rapped on the table. "I think it's time we abandon this secret ballot idea and all of us put our cards on the table."

By the time the attendant rapped on the door to announce

that it was time to go to dinner, each member of the jury had openly stated his vote and given his reasons for it. The tally was still seven in favor of a guilty verdict and five in favor of a not-guilty verdict.

"Geez, we're going to be here a month," one of the jurors grumbled.

"But we can't send an innocent woman to prison in order to avoid a few days of discomfort," another said.

Duquesne jumped up. "Prison's got nothing to do with it, Kensington. The judge said we were not to get involved with that. How do you know what the judge might do with her? For all we know, she'll slap her wrist and give her six months' probation. That's what they do with most of the murderers in this city anyway. How about it, Miss Kincaid?" Duquesne asked, turning to one of the older women. "Want to join us and make it eight to four?"

Before she had a chance to reply, Jean O'Shaunessy said, "I've struggled for two days with what I'm going to tell you. I didn't think it would be necessary because I was certain we'd all see this case the same way. Obviously I was wrong, because there are now seven of you who are prepared to render a guilty verdict. I don't know what the consequences of what I'm about to say may be, but I must tell you all that I will never, never vote guilty in this case. There is no argument any of you can give that will persuade me to change my vote. So it's not fair to the rest of you who wish to continue to deliberate the issues, hoping we might find a unanimous verdict when, in fact, nothing you can say will change my mind."

Duquesne jumped up. "See, that's what's wrong with this system. She's admitting she won't listen to reason."

"I'm willing to listen to reason, but you're right, Mr. Duquesne. You aren't going to change your mind, and I'm not going to change mine, and we are both wrong in that regard. Except I've walked in Helen Dunn's footsteps, and you don't have a clue as to what that's like. So I suggest that unless there's a chance of turning this vote around, we might as well report to the judge that we're deadlocked." Jean O'Shaunessy folded her arms across her ample chest and stared defiantly at Duquesne.

After a few moments of silence, Joe Baron, a pipe fitter, spoke up. "I want to get this thing over with and go on with my life just like everybody else. But frankly, I switched my vote from not guilty to guilty because it looked like that was the way things were going, and after three days of this I just wanted it to end. But now I've changed my mind again. It just hit me that sometimes you have to stand and fight. I'm ready to stand and fight."

Within an hour three more jurors had switched their vote from guilty to not guilty, and by four o'clock, Duquesne was the lone holdout. Finally, a few minutes before they were to be locked up again for the night, Duquesne grabbed his last ballot back, marked it *not guilty*, and threw it in the center of the table. "Assholes," he mumbled.

At 5:07, the court clerk entered a verdict of not guilty into the record of the case of the People Against Helen Dunn.

CHAPTER FIFTY-THREE

A few months after the Dunn case was over and Luke had settled comfortably back into teaching full-time, he received a letter from Sarah Nusbaum. He opened the letter and read:

Dear Mr. Alexander: I tried to reach you by phone several times without success, so I thought I would sit down and write you a letter. I want you to know that I am very grateful to you for everything you did to prevent that McBride woman from getting away with Katrina's trust fund. I still think she knew all about it, and now I've come across a few things in Katrina's trust fund records that don't look right to me. Please call me.
Your friend, Sarah Nusbaum.

Luke called and gave her the name of Charlie Utah.

———

After his initial meeting with Sarah, Charlie Utah reviewed the list of assets of the Shauffler trust in great detail and concluded that Sarah Nusbaum's suspicions were unconfirmed, with the exception of one high-yield investment he had not been able to track down.

Utah was in the process of finalizing his report when his mail arrived. The letter he'd addressed to International Properties, Ltd. was returned to him with the notation Addressee Unknown. Wanting to confirm its address, he checked through the records until he found the prospectus for International Properties, Ltd. in the material Mrs. Nusbaum had given him. The address was the same as what he'd put on his letter. There was no telephone number listed in the prospectus.

He called information, but no such company was listed in the Bermuda directory. Then he called a number of Bermuda governmental agencies and was advised that they were not at liberty to disclose the information he requested. He called more than a dozen investment-banking firms in the United States which specialized in foreign investments. None of them had ever heard of International Properties, Ltd.

Charlie Utah searched through the Shauffler trust estate records for additional information concerning this enigmatic Bermuda corporation, but found nothing but the prospectus, the entry in the receivable journal indicating the timely receipt of the quarterly dividends, and two canceled checks, each in the amount of one hundred thousand dollars, drawn against the Shauffler trust account and made payable to International Properties, Ltd. Frank Dunn had signed the checks as trustee and they were both endorsed by the president of the corporation, but the signature was totally illegible.

Charlie immediately made arrangements to travel to Bermuda. Upon his return three days later he went to visit Mrs. Nusbaum.

"So what have you found out for me?" Sarah demanded.

"I think Mr. Frank Dunn was either an absolute idiot or a crook," he said.

"That does not surprise me. So tell me."

"I found that while Frank Dunn was acting as trustee of the Shauffler trust, he paid two hundred thousand dollars for some preferred stock in a company called International Properties, Ltd. At first it looked very good because the trust was receiving twelve percent quarterly dividends, but after Dunn was murdered, there were no more dividends paid. I tried to find an address for the company, but there was none. The stock of the company isn't listed with any exchange, and it's not sold over the counter. Nobody knows anything about it.

"So I flew to Bermuda and discovered that International Properties, Ltd. was indeed registered there. I talked to the lawyer who registered the corporation, but he wouldn't tell me anything about his client. He said it was confidential information and, of course, he's right about that, but that didn't stop me," Utah said, smiling.

"So what did you do?"

"I went to the immigration services and got the names of all of the people who flew from New York to Bermuda during the week before the corporation was registered, and from Bermuda to New York during the week after it was registered. What do you think I found, Mrs. Nusbaum?"

"I think you are a very big tease, Mr. Utah. So why don't you tell me what you found?"

"I found the name of a lady...Margaux McBride," he said triumphantly. "I've got her coming and going."

"The whore!" Sarah hissed.

"Yes, Mrs. Nusbaum, I think you're right. I think Frank Dunn and Margaux McBride worked together somehow to cheat the trust, but I don't know what to do next, except go to the police."

"That's exactly what you must do."

———

The phone rang as Pat was about to leave her office. She started for the door without answering it but was unable to ignore it. She picked up the receiver.

"Sergeant Turner?"

"Yes, Ken, what is it? I was on my way home."

"Sorry, but I just finished interviewing a private investigator by the name of Charlie Utah. I'd like to bring him up to your office."

"It better be important."

"Yeah, well, does the name McBride sound familiar? Looks like she's been a bad girl again."

"Your girlfriend, Black Beauty?"

"The very same."

"So what did she do this time?"

"I'm not sure, but it looks like she might have been mixed up in stealing about two hundred thousand dollars from the Shauffler estate."

"Send him up. I'll see him." Pat hung up the phone, took off her coat, and sat back down at her desk.

———

It took almost a year to bring Margaux to trial for stealing from the Shauffler trust. Her attorney, Barney Rifkin, had used his vast experience as a criminal lawyer to delay the case, hoping that the DA would tire of the effort, or that Margaux would be willing to cop a plea. Because of the problems of piercing the protective wall of the Bermuda offshore banking laws, the DA considered allowing the case to languish and die, but Sarah Nusbaum was relentless in badgering his office about it. She begged, pleaded, cajoled, and threatened. He finally concluded that Sarah Nusbaum would never give up, and he assigned the case to a young ADA to get it over with, one way or the other.

"What do you think, Barney?" Margaux whispered at the end of the case as the jury retired to the jury room to begin their deliberations.

"I don't know," he replied, frowning. "If they believe it was all Frank's idea and you were an innocent party, they have to let you off. I mean the evidence against you is almost all circumstantial, except for that guy from the print shop who recognized you as the person who had the phony prospectus printed up. He really hurt us. Why didn't you tell me about him?"

"I honestly forgot." Margaux glanced back to the front row of spectator seats where Sarah Nusbaum sat watching impassively. "I don't know where they found the brochure. It was probably that old bitch Nusbaum. Frank must have foolishly given one to Mrs. Shauffler."

Margaux had testified that she knew nothing about Frank's purchase of two hundred thousand dollars worth of the Bermuda company stock and that she was just a young lawyer in Dunn's law office, following his instructions, when she created the corporation. But Barney had been unable to shake the printer's claim that it was Margaux who'd brought him the material for the prospectus and described exactly how she wished to have it printed. The man thought it was strange that despite the expensive color separations and artwork, she only wanted a few copies printed.

"We can probably still get them to accept a plea to grand larceny third degree. There's a big difference in the sentence, you know," Barney said, still hoping to convince Margaux to plead guilty to a lesser charge.

"No way, Barney. If I'm convicted of a felony, I'll be disbarred. I'm not worried about jail time, there's no way in hell they'd ever put me away, but a felony conviction will end my legal career."

"It's your decision," Barney said, shrugging his shoulders.

It took the jury six hours to return a verdict of guilty to the charge of grand larceny in the second degree.

Margaux was stunned. She felt she'd given the best performance of her life and had maintained eye contact with all the male
jurors throughout the trial. How could she have misjudged them?
She'd practically invited them to sleep with her. What had gone
wrong?

"Sentencing will be scheduled when the presentence
investigation is completed," Judge Masson said solemnly.

Margaux knew they'd put her on probation, which would
be a nuisance because she'd have to report to her probation officer
at least once a week for up to five years. She had decided to go into
the real estate business, and by the time of the sentencing she had
already slept her way into the largest real estate brokerage company
in Manhattan.

She chose a very simple black dress for her appearance at the
sentencing. Margaux's beauty and previous publicity surrounding
her indictment for the murder of Frank Dunn had made her a
media celebrity. The noisy courtroom immediately settled down as
Judge Masson was announced. After the final pleas were offered by
Barney and the prosecutor, Margaux was given the opportunity to
speak on her own behalf.

"Your Honor." Margaux spoke so softly, the judge had to
lean forward to hear her. "If I am guilty, as the jury has determined,
it can only be guilty of loving Frank Dunn so completely that I
became blind to his greed. I realize now that all during the time
he professed to love me, he was just using me in order to steal from
the Shauffler estate. It's only now that I can see how he lied to me.
I trusted him, just like Mrs. Shauffler did, but as you've seen, he
violated that trust again and again. When I entered the Dunn law
firm, I was fresh out of law school, totally innocent of the ways of
men like Frank Dunn."

Margaux hesitated momentarily, then she raised her head
high as the tears began to slide down her cheeks.

"If I had known the terrible things Frank was doing, I could
have stopped him, I'm certain of it. But I thought he could do no
wrong, Your Honor, I was so deeply in love with him. He was my
best friend, he was my god! Katrina and I were both victims of
his treachery, and now I alone am asked to pay the penalty for his
breach of trust. I know I must accept that, but I beg the court to give
me the opportunity to repay Frank's debt to society. I promise the
court and the memory of Katrina Shauffler, the only real mother I
ever had, that I'll make truth and decency the cornerstones of each
new day of my life."

As Margaux sat down slowly, her eyes continued to plead for forgiveness.

The spectators, except for Sarah Nusbaum, were mesmerized by Margaux's eloquence. The courtroom was hushed as Judge Masson leaned forward and spoke directly to Margaux.

"Ms. McBride, as you know, I've had the benefit of a comprehensive presentence investigation report which describes how you grew up with no father and little supervision. Your excellent performance in high school and college enabled you to graduate from the University of Maryland after the tragic death of your husband, and then graduate from Blackstone Law School. I've read the letters submitted to me by your teachers and others, all attesting to your intelligence, industriousness, and good character, and, of course, I've heard Mr. Rifkin's very moving plea on your behalf. Finally, I have listened to your own words, which describe so eloquently the dilemma you faced as a young professional woman who fell in love with her mentor." Judge Masson settled back in her ornately carved chair and took a sip of water. Margaux looked up at her with reverence as the judge picked up her notes and once again leaned forward to look directly at Margaux.

"I must tell you, Ms. McBride, that I have agonized over this decision. It became painfully clear to me, as the evidence was disclosed during the trial, that a terrible crime had been committed against Mrs. Shauffler and her estate by someone. The jury found you guilty of the charges against you. I'm unable to say they were mistaken in their judgment, for if it had been my decision to make, I would have found you guilty as well. However, today, we are only concerned with what punishment, if any, you should receive for your participation in the scheme that defrauded the Shauffler trust of two hundred thousand dollars."

Margaux nodded her head, wiping away the last of her tears with the back of her hand. Judge Masson hesitated again, looked away from her notes and stared out the window a few moments. The wail of a police siren dominated the room.

"As a first offender of a nonviolent crime, of course, probation and restitution are the most appropriate penalties, and I came to court today prepared to give you the benefit of the doubt. However, after listening to the words I know you chose with great care, Ms. McBride, I believe you are a consummate liar and an absolute disgrace to the legal profession. Breach of trust, Ms. McBride. It's abundantly clear to me that you participated in a breach of trust, the enormity of which boggles my mind. Perhaps if in your final plea to me you'd said 'I'm sorry…I'm sorry, Mrs. Shauffler, I'm sorry, Mrs. Nusbaum, I'm sorry, fellow members of the judiciary for disgracing the honorable profession of the law'. But instead, you brazenly denied culpability as the tears rolled down your cheeks. I'm ashamed that you are a lawyer and I am especially ashamed that you are a woman.

"It is the decision of this court that the defendant, Margaux McBride, be sentenced to one to three years in state prison and that she pay restitution to the estate of Katrina Shauffler in the amount of two hundred thousand dollars with interest at the legal rate of 9 percent from the time of the theft. Bail is hereby revoked. Remand the prisoner to county jail. Court is adjourned."

"Jesus," Barney choked.

Margaux gripped the counsel table with both hands, knuckles white, the blood drained from her face.

The reporters scurried out of the courtroom like ants converging on a handful of breadcrumbs. In a few moments, the room had emptied except for Sarah Nusbaum, who sat quietly in the seat she had occupied all through the trial. She stared at the gold-leaf inscription carved upon the wall behind the judge's chair: *In God We Trust*, it said.

"Yes, that's true," she whispered aloud, "but sometimes —"

She left the rest of her thought hanging in the air like a torn cobweb.

CHAPTER FIFTY-FOUR

In late spring, Luke and Pat drove to Pat's cabin in New Hampshire to spend a week together and talk about whether they wanted to marry and have a child. They'd been living together since shortly after his success in obtaining an acquittal for Helen Dunn, who had since remarried. Jennifer, he'd heard, unhappy with "the creep," was temporarily living with Kate Connors.

Luke had been putting off telling Pat about his Vietnamese son and the fact that he'd killed an injured, defenseless Vietcong soldier to prove he was tough and to pick up some souvenirs. It was time, past time, to tell Pat all of it, and he would do so here, in the mountains of New Hampshire. He dreaded it. He'd never forgiven himself for these things. Why should she?

When he finally blurted out both stories, Pat sat quite still for a few moments, digesting what he'd told her. He couldn't believe it when she said, "It's not too late, Luke. By now you probably have a grandchild we could help."

The next morning, Pat awoke a little before dawn. She and Luke were cuddled as tightly as newborn kittens; she could feel his breath steady on the back of her neck and the warmth of his body the full length of her own. A ceiling fan turned slowly over the bed. She watched its silent vigil, trying to decide whether to go back to sleep or…

Luke stirred and she felt his maleness against her thigh. That does it, she thought, and reached behind her, letting her fingertips drift along his back.

"Good morning, darling," she whispered as she turned and gently kissed each eyelid.

"Jesus, what a way to wake up," he said, taking her into his arms. Lovemaking is a wondrous gift, he thought, and making love when you are in love is the most exquisite of all human pleasures.

"What are you thinking?" she asked shyly.

"That I love you and I want us to make mad passionate love again and again and again."

"Motion granted, Counselor." She slithered down under the sheet.

Luke started to move on her. "No, no, no, Alexander, I'm in charge of this investigation." She pushed him back down on the bed. "Just lie there and relax — well don't relax everything," she grinned. "Tell me, sir, how long have you owned this weapon?"

"About half a century."

"My God, it's an antique!"

"You could say it's been in a few skirmishes."

"I think I'd better make a closer inspection of this blunder-buss," she said, peering at it through an imaginary magnifying glass. "My God, it's huge!"

"Throw away the magnifier, stupid."

Pat tossed away her imaginary prop with a flourish.

"By golly, you're right. It is sort of puny, isn't it?"

"Now just a minute —"

"Well, just how big is this weapon anyway?"

"Actually, I never measured it."

"I'd say it's sort of run of the mill."

"What the hell do you mean 'run of the mill'?"

"Of course, I'm only speaking from my own experiences," Pat quipped.

"I don't want to hear about your experiences."

"I wasn't going to tell you about them, as a matter of fact, because they're none of your business. Hmmm, it seems to be growing right before my eyes. Tell me, what kind of bullets does it shoot?"

"Very powerful ones."

"Do you store the bullets in these two small chambers?" she asked, taking them gently in her hands. Then she knelt over him. "Oh Lordy, Luke."

Later she insisted on washing his hair as they showered, taking delight in lathering him with gobs of shampoo. After they'd rinsed off, they ate wedges of cold watermelon in the shower, letting the sweet juice dribble down their chins as the warm water continued to wash over them.

He rubbed her down and then carried her out on the patio where they lay huddled together, watching the sun rise between the mountain peaks.

The next morning Luke was awakened by the sound of a flock of Canadian geese flying overhead in the early dawn. Pat was curled up in a ball; her red hair, in disarray on the stark white pillow, glistened like burnished copper in the soft morning light. He slipped quietly out of bed, taking care not to disturb her, pulled on his jeans, and tiptoed out of the room. The flagstone kitchen floor was like ice beneath his bare feet as he lit the stove for coffee. He slipped on a heavy woolen shirt, stepped outside, gathered up some wood, and built a new fire in the huge fireplace. In a few minutes, the early-morning chill began to give way. He poured himself a mug of hot coffee and grabbed a pad and a stub of pencil.

There was a heavy dew on the greenery along each side of the path as he walked down to the dock, but the sun was coming up strong. He sat down on the pier and watched a school of pike feeding beneath the deck. Taking out the remains of his pencil he began to write. Every so often he would straighten up, take the mug in both hands, sip the hot sweet coffee, and then return to his writing, adding a word here and there, crossing out whole lines, and starting over. When he was finally satisfied, he recopied his work, folded the paper neatly and stuffed it in his shirt pocket. Returning to the cabin, he opened the door quietly and peeked into the bedroom.

Pat was still sleeping. He went back into the kitchen, squeezed some oranges, scrambled some eggs, and put some bread in the oven to toast. When everything was ready he stepped outside, picked a few spring leaves and placed them on the breakfast tray. As he entered the bedroom Pat immediately awakened and sat up. She pulled the sheet up around her, ran her fingers through her hair, and stretched her arms out to the sunlight, now streaming through the window.

"Good morning, love," Luke said brightly, as he placed the tray on her lap.

"Oh Luke, I can't believe you're real. Are you real?"

"Well, suppose I give you a real good morning kiss. Will that convince you?"